"This is the subaltern life, that of a minority within a minority, revealed as never before."
—**Seamus Deane,** author of *Reading in the Dark*, shortlisted for the Booker Prize

"Bravo! A cracking read that should never end . . ."
—**Brendan O'Carroll,** bestselling author of *The Mammy*

Set in the hills of Northern Ireland in the 1960's and 70's, *A Son Called Gabriel* is a deeply felt and often funny coming-of-age novel that is ultimately unforgettable.

Gabriel Harkin, the eldest of four children in a working-class family, struggles through a loving yet often brutal childhood. It's a turbulent time in Ulster, and in the staunchly Catholic community to which Gabriel belongs, the rigid code for belief and behavior is clear. As Gabriel begins to suspect that he's not like other boys, he tries desperately to lock away his feelings, and his fears. But secrets have a way of being discovered, and Gabriel learns that his might not be the only one in the Harkin family.

A SON CALLED GABRIEL

A Novel

Damian McNicholl

CDS BOOKS • NEW YORK

A short story published in *The Bucks County Writer* magazine formed the basis of an early part of this novel.

Copyright © 2004 Damian McNicholl

For information please address:
CDS Books
425 Madison Avenue
New York, NY 10017

ISBN: 1-59315-231-0

Orders, inquiries, and correspondence should be addressed to:
CDS Books
425 Madison Avenue
New York, NY 10017
(212) 223-2969   FAX (212) 223-1504

Design by Holly Johnson

Printed in the United States of America

10 9 8 7 6 5 4 3 2 1

To Mum, Dad, and Larry

PART ONE

September 1964 — August 1970

CHAPTER ONE

THE CHOICE WAS SCHOOL or the big stick and seemed easy to make. My younger sister Caroline and any boy in the whole of Ireland would choose school, but I knew I was right in refusing to go. I was six, had been going there for almost a year, was tired of being picked on, spat at, and just wanted to leave. I glanced down the road one more time and saw my friend Fergal was now sandwiched between Jennifer and Noel, her twin brother. They stopped and looked back for a moment before disappearing over the brow of the hill.

"I'm definitely not going," I shouted at Mammy.

The idea of staying at home with my sister and James, my four-year-old brother, seemed far more sensible. My mother stood at the front gate with an angry look on her round face and hands pressed against her hips.

"Who do you think you are?" she said. "Get to school this instant or I'll fetch a sally rod and beat the living daylights out of you."

I stared at the birdshite on the tarmac for a few moments before starting toward the house. "It's all right for you to say I must go, but you don't have to deal with Henry Lynch every day. He makes the others gang up on me and you won't listen."

"You must go to school or you'll just be a stupid Harkin."

"I don't care."

She always said my father's family was stupid when she was cross like this.

"Last year, you wanted to go so much, I went and got permission

3

for you to start school very young. I did that for you, Gabriel, and if you don't go now, I'll be a laughingstock."

That part was true. Fergal was over a year older than me and, when he started last year, I'd cried and demanded to go there with him. I'd cried so hard for two days that my mother took me to the primary school and spoke to Mrs. Bradley, the headmistress, who tested my thinking and speech and then said I could start because I was bright and way ahead of my years.

"That was before I knew Henry Lynch would be in my class."

"You must try harder to get him to like you. Talk to him instead of shying away . . . and don't take his name-calling to heart. You must be a man, Gabriel. Nobody likes a boy who's too sensitive."

That wasn't the reason Henry hated me. He hated me because I wasn't interested in playing football with him and the other boys. Where was the fun in chasing a ball around a mucky field? I wondered. I preferred playing stuck-in-the-muck with the senior girls. Even though they were eight, nine, and ten, I was every bit as fast as them. And stuck-in-the-muck wasn't just a girl's game like Henry kept saying. You had to be every bit as fast and skillful as footballers in order to avoid the person playing the jailer, otherwise she tagged and sent a body into the jail corner.

"I'm still not going," I said as I walked toward my mother.

She wagged her finger before she ran to a nearby hedge, tore off a sally rod, and started charging at me.

"I'm not putting up with this nonsense. Your sister's starting after the summer holidays, and I'm *not* going to tolerate you showing her a bad example."

Mammy seized my arm, and I watched the rod with its baby green shoots just like kitten claws rise until it became a thin, dark line against the sky. It fell and rose, fell and rose. Hot stings spread out over my bare legs, one thump hit the exact same spot as the first, and I started to dance about the road. I tasted the salt of my tears as I tried to dig my heels into the tarmac, but she was so much stronger and dragged me down the road.

A car came behind us as we reached the brow of the hill. The driver honked as it passed, I could see its blurry red taillights, and stopped five yards ahead. It was old Mr. O'Kane. Quickly, I wiped my eyes and cleaned my nose on my pullover sleeve as we drew up to the window of the car.

"Howdy, Eileen," he said. "Do you want a lift?"

"This one's decided he doesn't like school and is refusing to go this morning." She laughed. "If I don't teach him who's boss, he'll end up in Borstal."

Borstal was not a place I wanted to go. Declan Keefrey was in Borstal, had been sent there for stealing, but boys didn't get sent there simply for refusing to go to school.

"I was never one for school or the books myself." He winked at me. "Son, you have to go to school to learn, because a body can't get anywhere nowadays without the education behind them." As he smiled, gaps between the tiny purple veins that looked like spider webs on his cheeks seemed to stretch and widen. "I dare say if you're anything like your uncle Brendan, you'll be a smart fella."

Uncle Brendan was a priest in the foreign missions whom I'd never met because he didn't ever come home for a visit. My grandmother wanted him home, but he never came.

"Hop in and I'll take you to school," he said.

I knew I'd have to go now, I couldn't refuse in front of a neighbor, but Mr. O'Kane's car was the joke of Knockburn. It was shaped like an egg at the back, was also the same color as an egg, and had tires almost as narrow as pram wheels. All the boys laughed at it when it passed us by on the road, and now Henry Lynch would see me getting out of it at the school.

"I'll walk, thanks," I said.

"Get in the car at once because you're now late," said Mammy. Her lips stretched horribly thin again.

Ancient and very small, the school had a slate roof and thick walls with three large windows on either side that each had sixteen small glass panes. It stood perched on a height at the end of a long, winding lane and was surrounded by a dry moat ringed with beech trees. Coal black crows nested in their silvery branches, and about twenty rose into the air cawing as we drove along the driveway. Fergal and the others were climbing the height, a short-cut everyone took to reach the school building, and I crouched down in the seat and turned my head away as we passed by so he wouldn't see me. Luckily, Henry wasn't by the main door as Mr. O'Kane pulled up, so I bounded out and disappeared inside.

At my desk, I thought about what my mother had said about trying harder with Henry, but I couldn't think what to do until an idea jumped into my head just before lunch. Every day we ate at our desks under the supervision of Miss Murray, our teacher, and I'd noticed Henry always had the same food to eat. It was always strawberry jam on bright yellow Indian meal scones. He never had ham or a chocolate bar like me, because his father was on the dole and couldn't afford it.

As Henry shared the desk immediately behind me with Simple Brian, a much older boy who was a spastic and blew spit-tle bubbles through his rubbery lips—bubbles that always dribbled down his chin—I turned around, forced a smile and said, "Henry, would you like one of my ham sandwiches?"

Henry had wiry hair that reminded me of the scrubbing pads Mammy used to clean saucepans, and his sneaky eyes stared at me under his lashes. She said he had bad hair, not good hair like mine which was straight and glossy brown. She also said he wasn't good-looking like me, because I had my father's "black Irish" col-oring which looked brown and healthy all year.

"Why would you give me one of your sandwiches, Harkin?" he asked.

I always made sure to meet Henry's stare to show him I wasn't frightened. "I thought you might like to try something different."

"Have you spit on it?"

"I have *not* indeed." His eyes darted to the sandwich I held in my hand. Simple Brian watched, slimy dribbles trailing from his mouth, and I knew I wouldn't eat my chocolate bar, either. "I'll also give you my chocolate today."

"I'll take the chocolate bar, but I won't have the sandwich unless you eat a piece of my Indian scone."

6

Henry's family lived in government housing and I was sure his house wouldn't be clean like mine. I glanced at the horrible-looking yellow scone and saw where the red jam had seeped out and dried around its edges.

"I'm not so very hungry today."

"Is my scone not good enough for you to eat? Is that what this is about?"

"No. I just thought you'd like some ham for a change, that's all."

"Harkin, are you saying my ma can't afford to buy ham?"

Of course they couldn't afford it. I laid my sandwich on the desk before him. "I'll have a tiny, tiny piece, then."

He broke off a huge piece and watched as I took a bite. It was dry as straw, I could swear I'd seen a black hair on it as I'd raised it to my lips, and I wanted to hurl it away. Henry took a bite of the ham sandwich, and we watched each other chew.

"How do you like my ma's scone?"

"Delicious."

"In that case, you can have the rest and I'll take another ham sandwich."

"You're sharing each other's lunches, boys," Miss Murray said. "Look, girls and boys! Look at the example Henry and Gabriel are setting. They're sharing. Sharing is so good to do. Now, who can raise their hand and tell me another person who shared a feast?"

No one raised a hand.

"I'll give you a hint. His name begins with a 'J.'"

Still no one raised a hand.

"Jesus, boys and girls. Remember . . . remember I told you Jesus gave his body to the apostles to eat?" The teacher looked at Henry. "Oh my goodness! Goodness! Henry, quick, quick. Clean Brian's mouth this instant because he's dribbling badly."

Henry hated sitting beside Simple Brian because she always made him wipe his mouth. The corn in the scone felt like cement powder in my mouth and I wanted to vomit.

My plan worked, however, because Henry stopped calling me sissy and getting the others to gang up on me. So long as I gave him a sandwich and half of my chocolate bar every day, he didn't bother me. Then, one afternoon after school a few weeks later, he came up to me, prodded me on the chest, and told me I had to hand over all the chocolate bar or whatever other treat I had for lunch from the next day on. Although it didn't seem right, I did it until I grew angry with myself. I grew angry because, every time I gave up the bar, I was reminded of how I was completely in his power.

"I can't give it to you anymore," I said at the beginning of the second week. My voice shook, and I could hardly look him in the eye.

"I'm going to make it very rough for you again, cunt," he said.

"What you're doing is wrong, Henry."

"Don't tell me what to do, you fucking sissy boy." He prodded my chest with his finger like a jackhammer again. "I'll give you a good thrashing if you don't give me the stuff."

Still, I refused, but he didn't hit me. Instead, the name-calling and spitting returned much worse than before.

After the summer holidays, at least once a week, Henry and some other boys started to come around to where I played with the girls and would cause me trouble. They'd try to trip me up as I ran about releasing girls from jail. They'd call me nasty names that cut my mind to ribbons. I tried to ignore everything, but the words would not be blocked. They'd get inside. They felt like my mother's sharp carving knife slicing into my heart and brain. I'd try to go on with the stuck-in-the-muck game and felt so ashamed in front of the girls. They tried to stop Henry. They often sent him away, but minutes later he and the others would come back, and eventually Jennifer and the others gave up.

I also started getting it bad from Daddy. My friend Fergal and I had had an argument coming from school one afternoon. My father was weeding in the garden and, as we drew up to the gate, he asked Fergal jokingly which one of us was the better footballer. Fergal told him I didn't play because I preferred being with girls. I knew it was only his anger talking, but it set my father off. He demanded I start to play with the boys. To please him, I decided to make an effort. All the boys had a favorite English football team, so I studied the teams and picked one to have ready for the next time I was teased about not having one.

"Hey, Harkin, haven't you picked a soccer team to support yet?" Henry said at lunch a few weeks later, after Miss Murray had disappeared behind the pink curtain. The curtain ran across the width of the room, dividing it into the senior and junior sections, and she always went into the senior section to drink black tea with the headmistress after we'd finished our lunch.

"I quite like Chelsea."

His eyes widened with surprise.

The other boys crowded around now.

"Why?" Henry's sneaky eyes moved slowly from face to face to make sure everyone was listening.

"I like the color of their outfits . . . and Chelsea is a nicer part of England."

"The color of their kit doesn't matter a fuck." Henry stood and smacked the top of my head with his palm.

This was the first time he'd smacked me and I needed to tell him to stop, but couldn't bring myself to say anything. He wasn't fooled by my answer, either. I'd picked Chelsea because I liked the photographs of the players in their blue shorts, not because of their skills.

"Seeing as you have a team now, I think you should play with us today," Henry said, and he looked at the others real sneaky again. "You can't support a team properly until you understand the game."

"Yes, come on, Gabriel," said another boy.

The sun was shining when we got outside and the girls had started their game. My sister Caroline was running about the yard in her purple and white pinafore, a matching ribbon in her long dark hair. The jailer wasn't at all interested in her, though. She was only six, a small fry, too small to play with them. They allowed her only because of me. They should just put her in jail like I was forever telling them, and she'd be happy. Caroline's eyes locked in mine and she waved. The girls' laughter and cries filled the playground, I wanted badly to join in, but Henry had a point that I should give football another try.

"Gabriel, come and free me," Jennifer said. She was Noel's twin, but didn't have yellow-green teeth like him because she brushed hers.

"I'm going to give football another go."

"Ach, why, Gabriel? Don't play with them. I *must* be released."

I turned to Henry. "I'll come and play with you in a minute." Running over to the jailer, I whispered, "Put our Caroline in jail."

"If you promise to release me before anyone else when I'm next in jail," she said.

"I will."

"Even before freckle-faced Jennifer."

"Yes, I'll release you first."

She ran over to my sister and tagged her.

"I'm catched, Gabriel. Look, she catched me," Caroline said, and she ran joyfully into the shady, damp corner that was our jail.

I ran to the other side of the school. Some boys and girls were lining up to slide down the hill to the bottom of the moat. Their trousers and skirts were streaked brown and gray from cinders and ashes dumped there from Mrs. Bradley's fireplace. Henry was picking the sides as I drew up.

"You're on the other team because you're useless," he said.

He was picking for both teams even though he had no right to do so, and they were obeying him. A few minutes later, the game started. Every time the ball rolled in my direction, I prayed it would stop, or someone would reach it before it came to me. Boys swarmed around me, pulled at my sweater, cursed, kicked my shins. Twice, Henry came over and smacked my head in the middle of the tackling.

"Stop hitting me, Henry," I said, after he smacked me much harder a third time. "That's not allowed in the rules."

"How the fuck would you know the rules?"

He hit me again on the side of my face. "Come on, Harkin. Fight me, or are you a yellabelly?"

I just looked at him.

"Let's see you fight him," another boy said.

The game was forgotten as the boys huddled closer. Tears welled in my eyes. I wanted to hit him but knew fighting was wrong. I turned away.

"Le . . . le . . . leave him be, Hen . . . Henry," said stuttering Anthony. "You . . . you . . . you asked him to . . . to play ball and . . . and . . . and he did."

"Shut up, Stuttery-mouth," Henry said.

Fergal watched, but said nothing. He was my friend, my best friend, but he also liked the other boys. I met his eye and he looked quickly at the ground. Henry was king in the playground.

Suddenly, Henry lifted his foot and kicked my arse. He stuck up his fists like Cassius Clay and began to dance around me. It looked silly, but the boys loved it and cheered. Fergal laughed, too. Seeing him laugh gave me a much sharper pain than the one in my arse. Henry's fist hit my nose. I heard the crack inside my head. I put my hand up and felt my nose, and when I brought it down, I saw blood streaked on my bar of fingers. The boys saw my streaky blood and cheered.

"Hit him back, Harkin," one of them cried. "Let's see the thickness of his blood."

Older boys gathered around now. My blood excited them as well. They ordered me to floor Henry. My head was sore, I raised my hands and formed fists, but still I could not hit him.

"Gabriel, kill him," said Noel. "Don't let us down. Don't let a boy from the other side of Knockburn beat the shite out of you."

"I don't want to fight."

"Coward! Coward!" the boys cawed.

"Fighting's for animals. They don't know better." I dropped my fists to my sides and started to leave. Henry pushed me hard in the back and shoved me out of the opening ring.

"Gabriel is a coward. He's a big sissy," the older boys yelled. "Gabriel Harkin's a sissy boy."

I ran back to the girls to get away from their teasing. Caroline was on her hunkers in the jail corner, but I didn't feel like releasing her. Standing near a pile of twigs and split logs alongside the school wall, I waited for Fergal to come and find me. I waited as the coal black crows shrieked above. The boys' yells mixed with the girls' laughter and the crows' shrieks. Still, he didn't come. A hot tear slid down my cheek.

"Oh, stop your damned crying," I said aloud, and gritted my teeth till they began to hurt.

A few minutes later the headmistress came out, rang the brass bell, and I went inside. Another lunchtime was over, but something had changed forever. I didn't want to fight. I really hadn't known I would never fight. The boys knew now, too. Henry knew he could hit me and I would not fight back.

That night, I told my mother I'd been in a fight and walked away.

"That's the proper thing to do. You won the fight because you did the proper thing, Gabriel. You're the winner and a real man as a result."

I did not feel like a real man. Nor did my mother have the power to make me the winner. Only the boys had power like that.

"It's come to fighting now," she said to Daddy later. "Should we speak to Henry's mother or the teacher? Which?"

"Quit your talking. This'll toughen the lad up. He can't run to teachers about things like that, because it'll only make it worse. He's got to learn to hold his own." Father rubbed his large nose for a moment with a finger blackened by the oily grease of the truck he drove. "You've got to stand up for yourself and not let that Henry Lynch push you around. Fight back like a man. Real men stand their ground, Gabriel. They don't run away under any circumstances."

I looked over at my mother, but her eyes were fixed on the TV screen.

CHAPTER TWO

Aₜₜₑᵣ...

A͟F͟T͟E͟R͟ G͟R͟A͟N͟D͟A͟ H͟A͟R͟K͟I͟N͟ D͟I͟E͟D͟ in May there was a huge rumpus because Uncle Brendan didn't come home for the funeral. Granny Harkin was heart-sore for weeks afterward because he hadn't come, which made Auntie Celia even more angry at him, and I overheard my mother say to Daddy he was a priest, should know what was proper, and wasn't he the bad article. When I asked why Uncle Brendan was a 'bad article', she got angry and told me to mind my own business. In the middle of all the tears and anger, Uncle Tommy, another brother of my father, married. Even though Mammy said the neighbors would talk because he was marrying so soon after Granda's funeral, Uncle Tommy decided to go ahead because the priest was booked and good money had been paid for the hotel reception.

After their honeymoon in Wexford, they moved into our house and I couldn't understand why. I just couldn't understand, nor did I like it, because James and I had to leave our bedroom and share with Caroline. When I asked my mother, whose stomach was growing very big, she said they were staying until their new house was built.

"When it's finished, they'll leave and things will get back to normal round here, thank God," she said. "Until then, you'll be extremely nice to your new auntie Bernie."

Friendly for the most part, our home was a one-story bungalow with a tiled roof, three small bedrooms, a living room where we watched TV, and a kitchen with tan-colored tiles, sky blue cupboards and a square table that could open out bigger when needed. One sky blue cupboard was a larder where two plastic buckets stood on a concrete shelf on one side: a faded red one to keep the milk bottles cool, and a blue one for our drinking water. It was my job every Saturday and Sunday to fetch water in the blue bucket from the spring in our fields. We also had a sitting room, the prettiest room in the house. It had shiny white bird ornaments that Uncle Brendan had given my parents as a wedding gift, a round brass mirror above the fireplace, and a dark red sofa and armchairs that felt, but didn't smell, like leather.

"Give your auntie a hug," Daddy said to me as we were all watching TV on their second night in our home.

"I don't want to give her a hug."

I was still cross about her moving in, and what's more I had sneaked into my bedroom that morning and found her sleeping on my side of the bed.

"Luksee, Gabriel, did you hear me?" he said.

Caroline was on my aunt's knee, fingering the white beads Auntie Bernie wore around her neck. They had once belonged to her dead mother, and Auntie Bernie used them to hide a raised brown mole with a hair in its middle that she was always asking Mammy about until she was black in the face. Auntie Bernie always put Caroline and James on her lap. She never asked me to sit there; not that I wanted her to ask me because I was too old and found her perfume fierce bad.

"Gabriel thinks he's too old for hugs, don't you?" Auntie Bernie said. She began to straighten Caroline's hair ribbon.

"When will you be leaving our house, Auntie Bernie?" I said.

Her fingers froze on the ribbon curl.

"That's very rude," my father said. He winked at Uncle Tommy.

"This house is too small, and Mammy said she'll be very happy when your new house is finished and things can get back to normal round here."

Auntie giggled high as she pushed Caroline off her lap.

"I said *no* such thing," said Mammy. "Honestly, the lies children dream up." She looked at me sharply. "Don't tell lies."

"We'll be leaving in a few months," Uncle Tommy said.

He smiled as he played with his dark ginger sideburns that ended near the bottom of his cheeks. Uncle Tommy was forever twisting and playing with them, and Auntie Bernie was forever telling him to stop. I liked his sideburns, and I also liked feeling the hard bump when he bent his arm and told me to feel his muscles. His lower arms had reddish hairs just like the Chelsea players, and they felt silky under my fingers when he grabbed my arms and swung me round and round in the garden until my head spun. I liked him to do that even though I was now over seven years old: my shoes would fly off and the cool air would rush into my striped socks, right between my toes, and when he put me down I'd be drunk with dizziness. That made him laugh, and I'd clown about and pretend to be really drunk until my father would talk to him and he'd forget about me.

Uncle Tommy and Daddy were Granny Harkin's sons. Caroline, James and I were powerful scared of Granny Neeson, our other grandmother, because she never smiled and was so sour-faced. We had to be very quiet when we visited her because she liked neither noise nor children. Her face was almost square, and she had a red sty in the corner of her right eye that I hated to look at yet saw every time she asked a question, because then it was rude not to look at her.

Even my father didn't like visiting Granny Neeson. When we had to visit, he always made excuses he had to go to places with Joe, his best friend, and that always caused enormous arguments. Mammy would shout at him in the scullery, he'd roar back an answer, and then she'd say he didn't want to visit because her family wasn't good enough for the Harkins.

When she got really cross, she screamed. She'd scream Granda Harkin had never liked her, even when he'd come to her cap in hand to ask for the big favor and she'd helped. "Who the hell are the Harkins but a bunch of damned sheep farmers with bad land at the end of the day?" she'd always say during a row. Daddy always told her to shut her mouth because she'd promised never to repeat anything about the big favor, and then he'd grab pots and bang them against the draining board of the sink. Caroline, James, and I hated the banging and we'd gather in a ring in the middle of the scullery. At these times, my father would never pick Caroline up and hug her when she started crying. She was forgotten, and I'd pray for it all to stop, which always worked even though it took a while because my mother would come to me.

"I'm sorry, Gabriel," she'd say. "I don't know what I'm saying when your daddy makes me this mad."

I didn't know what she was talking about, either. I asked about the big favor once, but her voice grew sharp and she warned me not to be nosy because she'd only been getting back at my father, and that my granda had been a holy man, may God have mercy on his soul.

On the other hand, visiting Granny Harkin was much easier because she lived only two miles away and James, Caroline, and I were allowed to go there when we pleased. Her home lay at the end of a long gravel lane winding through purple heather and looked like a shoebox with a thatched roof. Pink, sweet-smelling roses as big as men's fists grew on one side of the front door. Uncle John, my godfather, lived with her because he wasn't married.

Though we didn't like to talk about it too much, Caroline and I agreed Granny Harkin's house wasn't as tidy as Granny Neeson's, because Uncle John's sheepdog had fleas, stank quite a bit, and slept under the kitchen table. Also, her ragged sofa cushions were never straight, the cream range was never shiny, and the top of the walls and white ceiling were black with turf soot. Uncle John didn't do any housework because he was a man, and Auntie Celia, my favorite cousin's mother who had a shop in Duncarlow, was useless and far too grand to come out and help Granny, whose leg was bad.

When I visited alone, I liked to sit at the green Formica table and watch Granny take off her elastic hairnet and undo her bun.

Her hair was long and shiny and looked like Caroline's, except that the ropes were silver not black. Sometimes she allowed me to brush it if I promised not to do it hard.

"Gabriel, you and Caroline are the picture of your uncle Brendan when he was your age," she said as I brushed. "He was the handsomest man in Knockburn, and your granda had to hunt the girls away. When he was a teenager, the girls were forever trying to kiss him."

My grandmother stopped talking and looked out over the fields for so long, her eyes began to water.

"Oh, it's hard, Gabriel. Nobody but your poor old granny knows how hard it is."

"But when you look at me or Caroline, then you can still imagine him, Granny," I said. It was stupid to say that, because I didn't have black wavy hair like Uncle Brendan or Daddy. Mine was dark brown and straight, I had a bull's lick for a fringe, and my eyes were hazel, not gray like my father's. "Even if I don't have the wavy Harkin hair."

"It doesn't have to be wavy to be Harkin hair."

"Mammy says it's too soft and corn-stalk straight to be Harkin—"

"Your mammy's arse and parsley. Jesus, you have the Harkin hair . . . and you and Caroline have Brendan's and your daddy's brains as well. So that mother of yours needn't be going about the country saying that you haven't got Harkin hair."

I always said something like this if we were alone when she talked sadly about Uncle Brendan. It made her stop crying. She'd forget, because her face would redden and tiny balls of spittle would fly from her mouth and spark on the table as she spoke. Granny was very kind and holy, but she liked Caroline and me better than James because he had the square face and shortness of the Neesons. Sometimes, she gave Caroline and me a half-crown apiece, but only gave him a shilling. That made Mammy mad, but my father would only laugh.

"I hope he's happy in Kenya, Gabriel," Granny said, and she

sighed hard. "Ouch! Jesus, Gabriel, don't brush my hair so damned hard or you'll leave me with none."

"Sorry." I brushed in silence because Granny was thinking about Uncle Brendan in Kenya again.

"Yes, he's been away long enough," she said. "He should come home where he belongs because the whole thing's forgotten. He can get a parish here. Sure, they're crying out for priests in Ireland. I don't know why the hell he has to stay in that godforsaken place when there's a lot of souls in need of saving here. Aye, he should just come home to his mammy."

"What's forgotten, Granny?"

She said these things when she talked about Uncle Brendan, but every time I asked about the forgotten thing she wouldn't say what it was. She'd say "all's well" or "my dotage is beginning, Gabriel," and all I could get was Uncle Brendan wouldn't come home and she wanted him home. Not even Cousin Martin could find out what she was talking about if he happened to be around when she said things like that. Once, Granny cried really sorely because it was Uncle Brendan's birthday and she couldn't see him. I'd never seen her crying so hard. As soon as I got home that afternoon, I told Mammy and asked why he didn't come to see Granny and what was the thing that was forgotten. After sitting on an armchair and pulling me in front of her, she made me say word for word what Granny and I had been talking about. "Your grandmother is starting to lose it," she said after I'd finished, "and I want you to promise me you'll ask no more questions about this ever again. If you don't promise, I'm going to stop you going up to see her alone." She also made me cross my heart never to bother Granny with such questions ever again.

"Your godfather's taking my lambs to the market this afternoon," Granny said out of the blue. "Yours will be also be going, so I'm going to give you your fiver today."

Every year she gave me a lamb—this year I'd named it Bonny—and when market time came round she gave me five pounds. Of course I always wanted to take the lamb home and make it my pet, but she'd only allow me to see it a few times throughout the summer. I was never allowed to make it a true pet.

"I'm old now and don't wish my lamb to go to the market this year. I want her to stay, so I won't take the fiver, if you don't mind."

She took the brush from me and laid it on the table. "That's not possible."

Granny made a plait, swirled it into a bun, and put on the hairnet again. It was silly that she brushed her hair only to tie it up the same way again. She hummed as she pushed the sticking-out bits underneath the net. I waited until she'd finished and looked at me again.

"Why not?" I gave her my biggest Harkin smile.

"It'll go to the market and you'll get the money."

"What will it do at the market?"

"It'll be sold and taken to another place."

"Why not let it stay on in Uncle John's fields?"

"*Who's* saying they're your uncle's fields?" My grandmother rose and hobbled toward the door. "Aye, I'm not dead and buried yet." She stopped after she'd opened the door. "I'm just going outside for a minute. Put on the kettle for tea."

I went to the side window and peeped out. The cream-colored paint on the dusty sill was cracked and bulging in the corner where rain had leaked in. Granny stood in the little garden, fumbled underneath her long skirt, then hunkered down in front of the blood-red and green stalks of her rhubarb patch. She always peed there during the daylight, which was a reason I pretended I didn't like rhubarb jam when she wanted to make me a sandwich. As she was pulling up her knickers, I put the dented kettle on the hob and, meeting her at the door, told her I was going up to the mountain to see Uncle John and ran off in case she tried to stop me.

Granda's old carthorse with the star and three white socks was grazing in the meadow, and I stopped to watch him for a moment. "Hello aul Rory," I shouted, but he was deaf. Uncle John didn't put him inside the shafts of the blue and orange cart and let me ride with him like Granda had done. He had bought a tractor with the armfuls of money he'd got in Granda's will so Rory wasn't needed anymore. I thought about Granda for a moment. I thought about him sitting in his favorite chair near the range, watching me watching him from the other chair as he puffed on his pipe. I could see his gray hair, his hazel eyes, the brown spots on his hands, and his curly pipe now lying on top of the window pelmet. His pipe lay dusty and forgotten on top of the pelmet, and his overalls and Sunday suit were on hangers in the storage room. They didn't have his smell anymore. His suit now smelled of dampness, the cloth cold and limp between my fingers.

When I reached "Half-mile Hill," I saw Uncle John near the sheep-dipping pen. A helper, wearing dungarees that were too big because he'd tied a hay bale rope around his waist, was with him. As I drew closer, I could smell the sheep shite. The ewes were running about with bulged and rolling eyes, glistening round marbles dropping from their dirty arses because Uncle John was grabbing their lambs and shoving them into a smaller pen. Uncle John dragged a ewe roughly by its horns up to a pot of bright red paint and then jammed its head between his legs. His fat tummy almost touched the sheep's back as he bent over and grabbed a stick from the paint pot with his crooked fingers broken years ago in a Gaelic football game.

"Where's my lamb, Uncle John?" He continued to form the "J" of his "JH" mark on the sheep's side.

"Over in the other pen."

The sheep bucked, and he cursed and yanked its fleece. I ran over to the smaller pen and, grasping the smooth metal side rails, jumped up on the narrow concrete ledge and looked about for her. Lambs bleated in every corner. Two were scared witless, many had small horns popping from their heads, but all the ones with black-and-white faces looked the same. The helper came over with another, fumbled open the narrow gate to the pen with one hand, and dragged it inside where it skidded on the shite after he freed it.

"Which is my lamb?" I asked.

"What are you talking about?"

"Where is the one my grandmother gave me?" I looked behind to see if Uncle John was still marking the sheep before I turned back to the man again. "There's so many of them. How do they get to the market?"

"We take them in that trailer over there. Do you want to come? We're leaving in an hour or so."

The trailer was small, about twice the size of a horse box, with slatted sides. I couldn't see how all the lambs could fit into such a small space.

"All the lambs fit in there?"

"Aye."

"How long do they stay at the market?"

"Until they're sold and taken to the abattoir."

I loved the sound of that name. "Will the lambs run as free there as on this mountain?"

The man's eyes narrowed, and creases as puffy as the wrinkles on my school shirt formed at their sides. "You're quite the joker."

"What do you mean?"

He laughed.

"What do you mean?"

"Sure you know as well as I do they're shot and then sliced up nice as pie so your mother can buy a nice chop or two for your Sunday dinner."

My legs buckled. I watched Uncle John mark another ewe with the blood-colored paint. Charging from the pens, I hurtled down the hill and over the meadow, not stopping until I'd reached the last gate before my grandmother's house. My chest was tight. I could scarcely breathe. I forced myself to take a gulp of air before climbing the gate. A stitch started up in my side as I ran across the final pasture and forced me to slow down. Auntie Celia's car was parked alongside the rhubarb patch. I wondered if Cousin Martin had come with her, then heard his younger brother, Connor, asking Granny for a glass of orangeade as I opened the door. Even though Martin was nine and Connor only a year older than me, I liked Martin better because we loved to read adventure books and talk about them afterward. Connor didn't like reading, and was also sneaky: if Granny said he couldn't have juice, he'd take it behind her back, anyway.

Martin was in the living room and, while happy to see him, it also made things tricky on account Granny had warned me not to tell my cousins she gave me a lamb every year. I sat on the sofa beside Martin and waited for a chance to speak to her alone. The clock's big black hands jerked and moved, jerked and moved. At last, Connor said we should go to the river and poison the trout with disinfectant.

"What a good idea," I said.

Martin's eyes widened because we hated killing trouts.

"You can go provided you don't go near the deep part," Auntie Celia said. "Go and make your dam. By that time, I'll have measured out the disinfectant, and one of you can come and fetch it."

"Go on to the river and I'll wait for Auntie Celia to measure out the stuff," I said to my cousins as soon as we got outside. "That way, I'll make sure she gives us plenty."

"I'll wait, too," said Martin.

"No. Go and help Connor make the dam."

Martin's very fair skin, usually white as my pillowcase, turned patchy red. It always turned like that when he was either angry or telling lies, the last thing being something Connor was better than Martin at doing because he never looked into your face when he talked, which made it hard to judge if he was telling the truth or not. After turning away sharply, Martin started down the lane, his arms swinging like a soldier on the march and his stumpy legs moving even faster to keep up with them.

"Why are you here, Gabriel?" Auntie Celia said as I came inside.

"I need to ask Granny something."

"Off you go with your cousins."

The skin in the middle part of Auntie Celia's upper lip was cracked and must have been dry all the time because she was forever wetting it with her tongue. Auntie was also thin but had the widest bottom Caroline and I had ever seen, and she wore a gold gate bracelet that looked nothing like a gate. It was also loose and forever moving up and down her wrist because she talked with her hands as well as her mouth.

"It's important I speak to Granny."

Auntie Celia wrinkled her nose as if I'd farted. "Well hurry up and then run and catch up with the boys, because she and I wish to talk."

I went to my grandmother and put my lips to her ears.

"No whispering," said Auntie Celia. "Didn't your mother tell you that's extremely rude?"

"It's only for her ears."

Her tongue paused on her upper lip for a second. "He's very sneaky, isn't he? Wants to keep secrets from his auntie Celia who's so good, she's invited him to stay at her house for part of the summer holiday. I wonder where he gets his sneaky streak. Certainly not from the Harkins, that's for sure."

The big clock hand was on the twelve now.

"I shan't have you staying in my house if you're sneaky. I shan't, because I don't want Martin or Connor learning to keep things from their mother like you country boys do."

"Your aunt's right, Gabriel. You can say what you need to say in front of her."

"So it's okay to say?"

She fixed her hairnet as she nodded.

"Uncle John's taking my lamb to the killing place to be turned into chops and he must be stopped."

Grandmother's hands dropped to her lap like a falling hatchet.

"And what might this be about?" Auntie Celia said. Her smile flew off her face, and she stood up like she'd been whacked across the back of the head. She walked up to the range and rested her wide bottom on the shiny metal bar running across its front. "You gave *him* a lamb. Why did you not give Martin a lamb? They're best friends. Is there a reason *he* gets a lamb that might escape me?" She shifted her arse, the bar turned, and a tea towel with a brown stain fell to the floor. Auntie Celia stared, but didn't pick it up. "Why don't you think to give my son, your grandson I might also add, a wee lamb for the abattoir?"

"I don't want any more fivers if this is what happens to the lambs you give me every year." I tightened my mouth and looked at my grandmother. "Please, please stop Uncle John taking—"

"A *fiver!* You're spoiling this boy rotten. Jesus, a fiver." As Auntie pointed at me, her bracelet slid to where her thumb joined with her hand. "He's special, is that it? Just because he's . . . well . . . just because Harry's children live out here in the country, you tend to them hand and foot and give then fivers. Mine get nothing. Not a single sausage."

"Please save my lamb."

"Not a sausage do my boys get from you from one end of the year to the other."

"The trailer will soon be leaving with my lamb inside."

"They get enough to do them," said Granny. "Sure, you've got a shop that's making you cartloads of money."

"And I work myself to the bone for every penny."

"Granny, I'm begging you not to let my lamb go away."

"Go to your cousins at once," said Auntie Celia.

"Stop being so hard on him, Celia." My grandmother hobbled over to me. "Uncle John will come in for his tea before he leaves for the market. I'll get him to take yours out and put her back in the field."

"And take the whole damned can of disinfectant to Martin," said Auntie Celia.

I raced to my cousins, told them why I'd wanted them to leave for the river, and said I was sorry. Martin forgave me, and all three of us ran back to the house and hid behind the high ditch opposite the rhubarb patch. Uncle John and the helper came, parked the trailer, and went inside for tea. The lambs bleated, though I could see only wool sticking out between the slats. I tried to open the door, but the bolt was too stiff and wouldn't budge. Connor tried, then Martin, who was strong even though he was smaller, but none of us could make it move. In a little while Uncle came out again, and I ordered him to take my lamb out of the trailer.

"She's right in at the back." Uncle didn't even check. "Don't worry. I'll bring her home."

"You're lying, Uncle John. First, you took it from its parents, and now you're taking it away to be killed."

"Stop this silly talk, Gabriel. That wee lamb doesn't know who its parents are."

CHAPTER THREE

M Y MOTHER WAS STILL screaming in the bedroom as Nurse Noonan drove into the driveway. She got out quickly, opened the backdoor of her car, and leaned inside. She took out a chunky black case and ran into the house without closing the door of her car. We'd been told she was delivering our new baby, though I didn't think it could be in Nurse's case. It looked far too small. Twenty minutes later, Auntie Bernie came into the garage where Jennifer had set up a pretend school and told us God had appeared in the bedroom and brought us a sister.

Nuala was trouble from the beginning. She never wanted to sleep, when she did it was only for stretches at a time, and Mammy's heart was broke because she hadn't had a good night's rest for weeks. Everyone was given orders to be very quiet when the baby was asleep. We had to be especially quiet in our bedrooms and, because we had no indoor lavatory, if we needed to do more than a pee, we had to creep down the hall because Nuala heard the smallest noises. Early one morning I woke up needing to go outside. As I passed Uncle Tommy and Auntie Bernie's bedroom, I heard a great deal of noise, which meant Auntie was disobeying orders and would waken the baby.

After I opened their door, I couldn't make heads or tails of what they were talking about because the bedsprings were squeaking every bit as loud as James and I make them squeak. The room was dim, a tiny slice of morning light squeezed past the crack in the curtain, and I could see my top sheet, the one I liked with the pattern of yellow flowers, was dipping on the floor. Uncle Tommy was on top of Auntie Bernie and he was pumping her like a bull and cow I'd once seen in a field, and she had her legs wrapped tightly around his very white backside. She was also talking as if she was out of breath in between whimpering like a puppy badly in need of petting.

"Why are you pumping Auntie Bernie?"

They stopped and turned to look at me. Everything went in slow motion before my eyes as their arms and legs moved and they parted from each other. Uncle Tommy rose and walked down the bed, his long dokey jerking up and down, and I saw Auntie Bernie also had red hair in her private place before she snapped her legs shut. She put her arm over the bed and tried to grab the top sheet, but missed. She tried again, raising her back and turning a bit, and I could see her hanging tummies with brown red knobs. They were exactly like a sow's tummies, only there were two, not twenty.

"You're not supposed to be in here," she said.

The slow motion stopped as soon as Auntie spoke. Uncle Tommy swiped his underpants off the top of the vanity, though he fell against it as he raised one leg and tried to hop into them.

"Nuala will wake up because of this noise."

"That's all right," Uncle Tommy said. "Thank you for reminding us. You may go back to bed now."

I turned to leave but then looked back. "Why were you pumping her like a bull?"

"Don't ask cheeky questions that only concern grown-ups," Auntie Bernie said.

"Why is it cheeky?"

"Your auntie needed to be pumped because she had a puncture." Uncle Tommy smiled at Auntie Bernie, who looked at him crossly.

"Does Daddy fix Mammy's punctures?"

"Yes."

"Who fixes yours?"

Uncle Tommy laughed. "Men don't get punctures."

"Why not?"

"Leave my bedroom this instant," said Auntie Bernie.

"It's *my* bedroom," I said, and left.

Later, I overheard Auntie Bernie talking about me in the kitchen.

"He saw my breasts, but I don't think he saw my pussy . . . and he saw Tommy's thing . . . you know . . . a bit stirred."

Mammy giggled.

"Do you think it could hurt him at his age?" I could tell by her voice that Auntie was worried. "I don't want him to be damaged by what he saw us doing."

"Gabriel's a softie and more sensitive than Caroline or James, but it'll do him no harm. He's not the first youngster to have walked in on a bit of fun and he'll not be the last."

"All the same, I wish I could be sure."

"We'll watch and see what happens."

"I read somewhere that it's good to give a child a wee shock if they witness anything out of the ordinary and appear troubled by it. It's supposed to distract them or something. Do you think we should try it if we think he's troubled?"

"We could."

"Auntie Bernie wants to give me a 'wee shock' to make me forget something I saw," I said to Fergal on the way to school next day.

"That's bad, Gabriel," he said, after I'd told him what I'd seen. "Watch out. My brother caught Daddy doing that to my mother, too. He dragged him out to the byre and thrashed him for watching. He was beaten so hard, the marks turned blue. *That's* the 'wee shock.' "

For the following two days, every time Auntie Bernie came into the living room, I went outside to play or sat as far away from her as I could. I tried not to even speak to her until she'd forget I'd seen the pumping.

"Gabriel, why are you always looking under your eyes at me these days?" she asked when I was in the room with Mammy and her early one evening.

"I didn't know I was looking at you under my eyes."

"Why do you always sit so far away from me?"

They were watching *Crossroads*, their favorite TV program during which we were never allowed to talk, and my mother turned from the screen to look at me. I knew also I couldn't tell a large lie because I was making my First Confession soon.

"I'm not staying out of your way or anything."

"Why would you even say that?" she said.

"No reason." My palms felt sweaty, and I rubbed them against my pant legs.

"Tell the truth, Gabriel," my mother said. "First Confession's coming up, which means you can't tell lies anymore."

"Because I saw you make Uncle Tommy pump you and you're trying to shock me."

She nodded at my mother, and they rose from their chairs together. Mammy switched off the TV, told me that she and Auntie were going to the generator shed, and I was to knock on its door in exactly one minute. After counting to sixty, I went out and Mammy opened the door. Above the generator, light streamed though tiny holes in the zinc roof that Daddy had been asked to fix but hadn't. The stink of diesel mixed with Auntie Bernie's fierce bad perfume, and I could see a black oily stain on the concrete bed upon which the generator sat. My mother stepped out into the sunlight as Auntie came to the door opening.

"Put out your hands and close your eyes until I say you can open them," she said. "Don't even peek."

"I don't want to be hit."

"You won't be hit. I have a little present for you, that's all."

"Do as you're told," Mammy said.

I stretched out my hands and felt something light being put into them.

"Okay, you may open them now," Auntie Bernie said.

It was a very long, white-pink thing with an angry face, black eyes, and small brown-red horns like knobs. The face was so angry, I was surprised, until I saw it was just a stupid balloon.

"Aren't those little horns just like the little horns you saw on

Auntie Bernie's chest a few days ago? She was wearing balloons, and Uncle Tommy was pumping them up that morning. Isn't that so, Bernie?"

"Aha."

It wasn't the same, and their 'wee shock' was just a balloon with an angry face. Why were they trying to frighten me with a worm balloon with tiny brown-red horns and saying Auntie was wearing the same? My mother picked up a twig and dug its jagged end into the balloon. It burst into a big piece of wet rubber with the brown-red horns still sticking out.

"Now that you know why Uncle Tommy was helping me in the bedroom, you can forget all about what you saw," said Auntie Bernie. "Let your mind think about First Confession, instead."

"You won't go into her bedroom again, will you?" said Mammy.

"No."

"Do you promise?"

"Yes."

"Give your auntie a kiss to say you're sorry and you may leave."

I was supposed to be sorry. I didn't want to kiss her, yet wouldn't be excused until I did. I went to her and put my drawn-in lips to her cheek, keeping my eyes open and making sure not to breathe in her perfume.

"That's my best nephew," Auntie Bernie said. She swept my bull's lick away from my eyes. "It's all out of your mind now, isn't it?"

"Can I tell what I saw as a sin when the priest hears my confession?"

"You can *not* indeed."

"Say nothing about this to the priest," my mother said.

"But if I do, then I'll really be able to forget because it'll be truly forgiven."

"Jesus, you will not tell such a thing to the priest," said Auntie Bernie. "He won't, will he, Eileen?"

"He won't."

"Will you be telling him what you were doing when you go to confession?"

Auntie looked at my mother. "Yes, that's it exactly. I'll tell him. Now remember Gabriel, if you tell him *my* sin, the priest will know . . . and God will not take away the large stain on your soul. In fact, he will add another larger—"

"Bernie!" said Mammy. "Just tell him you've disobeyed me, Gabriel . . . or tell him you stole a chocolate bar behind my back, if you can't come up with a proper sin by then."

"But I haven't."

"Just tell him anyway, son."

First Holy Communion took place a week after First Confession. The headmistress and Father McAtamney had been giving us catechism classes every lunchtime for months, and we'd been told we'd receive beautiful white prayer books and rosary beads after the Communion Mass. One day before, the priest came to the school and made the catechism class sit in the front three rows while Miss Murray kept Simple Brian and the infants on their best behavior. He sat at her desk, removed a circular, silver box from his pocket, opened it and took out a large wafer and held it up.

"Children, this is a piece of bread which represents the body of Christ. Now, today is just a practice. Our Lord will not be so big tomorrow. I will break pieces of this and, after I say 'Corpus Christi,' you must respond, 'Amen.' " He looked at Henry Lynch. "What will you say?"

"Amen, Father."

"That's correct. Jesus will look after you and guide you after you've received Him. One last thing: you must not chew Our Lord. He must be swallowed whole. Why must He be swallowed whole, Gabriel?"

"Because, Father, our teeth would likely hurt Him."

Father McAtamney smiled. "No, that's wrong."

The boys and girls laughed, and my cheeks grew warm. Henry

had got his question right, I had got mine wrong, and now I mightn't be allowed to receive Our Lord.

"Your Uncle Brendan is a priest, isn't he?" Father asked.

"Yes, Father."

"Ask him next time he's at home and he'll tell you why it's forbidden. Will you remember to ask?"

"I won't be asking, Father."

"Why would that be?"

"I'll not see him. He never wants to come home."

"Oh? Why doesn't he want to come home, do you think?"

"Mammy won't tell me." My face was dead hot now.

"Don't tell fibs, Gabriel," Father McAtamney said. "Fibs are venial sins and stain the soul only a little bit less than mortal ones."

He asked if anyone else had committed any venial or mortal sins since their confession. Everyone shook their heads, just as our teacher had warned us to do, and he then asked the final catechism questions. I got everything right, Fergal did as well, and we would now sit together in the pew nearest the altar rails at the Communion Mass. Henry got two questions wrong, and I was surprised when the priest said he could still make his Communion. He'd got his catechism wrong and he was also in a state of mortal sin because he'd told Fergal he'd stolen a shilling from his Mammy's purse, bought sweets, and not confessed it. God was all knowing, so Fergal and I believed Our Lord would be furious and race up his throat as soon as he received Him at Mass.

At First Communion, Our Lord tasted no different from the practice bread Father had given us at school. Fergal and I watched as Henry knelt at the rails and received. He chewed Him three times and looked at us with his sneaky eyes as he walked by. I expected choking or vomiting to begin, but nothing happened. Henry was in a state of mortal sin, he had chewed Our Lord, and nothing happened. His soul was black with sin, yet Our Lord had stayed inside him, just as if he'd been as spotless as Fergal and me.

After Mass, Father McAtamney came up to Mammy and me as we stood outside the church. He patted my head and told her the strange thing I'd said about Uncle Brendan not wanting to come home.

"Come to think of it," he said, and stopped speaking as he looked into the graveyard for a moment. "Brendan *hasn't* been home for a long while. Is there any word of a visit in the offing?"

"Not in the immediate future, Father, though I'm sure soon. The missions are so very busy, aren't they?" Mammy colored and laughed falsely as she laid her hands on my shoulders. "It's so funny you should bring this up when I was just thinking the same thing a few days ago." Her fingers tightened and dug into my skin as she lied. She dug so hard I almost cried out.

"That is a coincidence, indeed," he said, and looked at her without blinking.

"We can't be selfish." Mammy coughed. "Much as the family wants him home for a visit, mission work comes first, doesn't it?"

"Indeed."

My mother was silent the entire journey home. No sooner had we got into the kitchen than she fetched the wooden spoon and attacked my arse and back. "Don't let me *ever* . . . don't you *ever* . . ." she breathed hard as she whacked, ". . . don't let me ever hear that you've told any news you've heard within these four walls to the priest or anyone . . . and don't make up stories, either. Your uncle Brendan will be home when he can get away from the missions, do you hear?" She stopped hitting me. "If I hear another story like that come from the priest's mouth, it'll be the last story out of yours, because I'll cut your tongue out. Now, *get* to your room this instant."

Instead of collecting money and praise for First Communion from visiting relatives, I found myself alone in my room, punished for lying when it wasn't me who'd lied. I listened to everyone's laughter, grew angry, and decided my mother needed to be punished, too. Taking a pencil, I drew animals, houses, and figures on the wallpaper, but it still wasn't punishment enough because they could be erased. I took my pen and drew ten more, though just below the headboard where she couldn't see them. But *I* knew they were there, and that was enough.

Later, she came and told me I could come out again if I apologized and promised never to tell lies about Uncle Brendan. I said I was sorry without meaning a word, but the matter wasn't forgotten on her part, either. She wouldn't look at me, nor did she even speak to me until Uncle Tommy came home from working on his new house that evening. After giving me ten shillings for being a real Catholic now I'd tasted Our Lord, he told her that Auntie Bernie and he would be moving out because their new furniture had arrived that afternoon. *Then*, Mammy's stony face changed. *Then*, I was the greatest son because I was the first of her children to receive Our Lord and nothing bad would ever happen to me because He was now inside.

CHAPTER FOUR

ON ONE SIDE OF our house was a small garden with a high tree whose rough, reddish trunk was thick and curved up from the bottom like a bow. After Uncle Tommy and Auntie Bernie left, James and I moved back to our bedroom, and I could look out the window again and hear its branches creak as they swayed in the wind. I would watch for ages and wonder how my tree could stay up in the driving winds despite its curvy trunk. Noel, whose two front teeth now shared a brownish spot where they met, had taught me to climb it. The best way was to sprint to it, stick your fingers into its scaled, corky bark as you raced up the trunk, and grab its lowest branch and hoist yourself into it.

Partway up, the tree split into two smaller limbs and it was tight to squeeze past the upper branches because there were so many. Its limbs were bendable at the top, and I would pull them toward me and peer out to see the rusty tin roof of the long outbuilding stretching all the way across the bottom of the garden, and beyond to where sheep and cows grazed in Knockburn fields that were ten shades of green.

One Saturday afternoon, Noel and I were chatting inside my tree, and he asked me to come into the outbuilding with him because he wanted to show me something. On the building's gable overlooking the road was a scarlet mailbox where we put letters and, as we climbed the gate next to it, Mr. Smith, our bald Protestant postman with bandy legs, drew up in his Royal Mail van. We watched as he took letters out of the box and laid them in a wire basket, which he then placed inside the back of the van.

"Noel, do you want to take home your mother's bills and a letter from England?" Mr. Smith asked.

"I'm not going home to the aul doll yet."

Noel always called his mother "the aul doll" behind her back. His father called her that name and Noel liked to talk like him, though my mother said it was naughty and if he were her son, she'd break his back.

After Mr. Smith left, we hopped over the crumbling, whitewashed wall and walked up to the empty pigsties where Mammy had once bred pigs until she grew tired of the work. Noel drew back the bolt of the door that had a broken hinge and holes at the bottom where rats had gnawed at it. Inside, the dim silence smelled of stale hay and dust. The sty was divided into two pens; an old dented trough and a long metal pigging crate with a wide base narrowing like a capital "A" stood in one, and broken hay bales, yellowing newspapers, and a bundle of clothes were in the other. A thick concrete wall separated the pens. Eight feet above was a narrow wooden beam running into the blackness at one end of the loft.

"Jump up on the pillar and walk across the beam," Noel said. "It's in the dark part of the loft."

"But the rats are up there." It was high, I didn't like heights, and I feared I'd slip and fall to the concrete floor.

"Don't be an eejit. Follow me."

Noel jumped up on the beam like a monkey, spread his arms to keep his balance, and ran across. I jumped up on the wall and hoisted myself very slowly on the beam. Where the tin roof met the top of the stone walls, thin wooden planks jutted out at twofoot spaces and were nailed to the underside of the beam. Three planks were broken and dipped like lopsided seesaws toward the floor of the pen housing the pigging crate.

My stomach lurched. "I don't want to go over there, Noel."

"Don't be a coward like you are with Henry Lynch."

I narrowed my eyes but still couldn't see him.

"It's easy. I'll come over again and fetch you." Suddenly, a light shot out from the dark, and Noel walked across holding a torch. "Stretch out your arms and walk fast like this." He spun around and crossed the beam again.

"What do you want to show me? Why don't you bring it over here?"

"It's a big secret. You'll like it. Once I show it to you, it'll become our secret . . . just yours and mine."

Stretching out my hands, not daring to blink or take my eyes off the beam, I started across but felt as if I was losing my balance near the end, so I ran the final five steps. I found Noel sitting inside a nest of hay. It reminded me of the nests Granny Neeson's laying hens had in their coop, only it was much bigger and smelled very musty. A thin line of bright light streamed in from a small hole in the roof where it had rusted away, and I could hear Caroline and James playing in our backyard.

"Is this it? A nest of hay."

"No."

Noel fumbled within the hay on the far side of the nest. Dust rose into the air and I sneezed. A moment later, he brought out something and set it before me.

"What is it?"

"Dirty magazines." Noel laid the torch on the side of the nest so it shone on the magazines, opened one, and pushed it toward me. The light made two fuzzy rings and a white-hot dot on a picture of a woman with black hair lying on a bale of hay. I stared at her for just half a second yet saw everything. I saw every single thing. She was naked. She had the same knobs as Auntie Bernie's, her tongue was pointed and curled up over her upper lip, and her fingers dipped inside her private place.

"Auntie Bernie has hair down there, too."

"That can be called either her fanny or her pussy. And these are her tits." Noel kissed all over the page as he made slurping noises. "You have to do it now."

"I don't want to do that . . . the rats."

"Kiss her tits, *now*."

"No."

"Do it, or I'll push you off the beam when we leave."

As I looked at the picture, my knees and arms began to shake at the thought of crossing the beam again. "I want out of here. You shouldn't have brought me here. I want out."

"Shut up, shut your mouth." Noel leaned over and pressed his moist hands with tiny pieces of hay on them hard against my mouth. He pushed until I could taste his salty skin. "Shut up or I'll hit you something fierce."

I nodded and he took away his hand. Immediately I started wiping my tongue with the sleeve of my sweater.

"Kiss her tits and then we'll go. Gabriel, you must do this to make it our secret."

"If I do, can we go home?"

"Yes."

I took the magazine in my hands. The paper was glossy, and pages were bubbled and stuck together where the magazine had once been wet. It smelled so old and dirty. I closed my eyes and kissed fast.

Noel snatched the magazine away and tucked it back into the side of the nest. "Okay, let's go."

I didn't trust my shaking legs, so I crawled across the beam slowly, mounted the concrete wall, jumped to the floor, and ran into the sunshine again where my eyes hurt sharply at first. At the letterbox, Noel stopped and put his face close to mine, half-closing his eyes the way he always did when he was going to give me a warning.

"Those magazines are our secret. Just yours and mine. If you tell your aul doll about them, I'll have to tell her that you kissed a woman's tits. And don't tell it as a sin at confession either, because Father McAtamney will leap out of his box, grab your hair, and yell at you in front of everybody."

Most nights in bed, I concocted funny stories about our neighbors to entertain James before he went to sleep. Often, Caroline would sneak into our bedroom to listen. To keep them interesting, I watched people, noticing how our Knockburn neighbors talked or the funny ways they moved their heads or hands, so I could put them into the stories. Caroline and James' favorite ones were about Jennifer, but I'd used her so often, it was becoming very difficult to make up new things to say about her. One evening Caroline stopped a new story about someone else five minutes into its telling.

"It's not funny. It's just like one we heard before." She looked at James. "Do you think it's funny?"

He shook his head.

"Tell us one about Jennifer," she said.

James also wanted a Jennifer story, though not another about her stealing from our mother's kitchen cupboards behind her back, or the one where she made us play school and slapped our hands hard for making spelling mistakes. I thought for a minute and began a story about her and me out riding horses in the fields and how she came upon a wallet full of money on the ground and stole fifteen pounds. About halfway through, the police gave chase, Jennifer saw a barn, and we ran inside to hide. The police passed us by and we were safe, but then Jennifer spied a hay bale, lay on it, and asked me to kiss her tits.

"What are tits?" asked James.

"The things Auntie Bernie and Mammy have . . . I'll draw what they look like underneath their bras." I fetched a school exercise book, tore out a page, and drew a woman with long hair lying on a hay bale. Then I drew the tits with their knobs. "Auntie Bernie's hair is ginger down there." I drew squiggly lines between her legs.

"On her bottom?" Caroline asked.

"That's not her bottom. It's called a fanny or a pussy. Take off your pajamas and show James yours."

Caroline didn't want to take off her pajama bottoms, but James kept asking until she did. It looked the same as the hay woman's, except Caroline's was bald like baby Nuala's and looked like the mouth of a mail box. I whispered in James' ear to ask if she would let us touch it. She shook her head when he did and ordered us to take off our pajamas and show her ours. I wouldn't, but James pulled down his pants.

"I think you could put a very tiny envelope inside yours," I said to Caroline.

James giggled.

Caroline shook her head so quickly, her fringe swept to the side. "James and you are made of slugs and snails . . . and your thing's the puppy dog's tail." She stood up and pulled up her pajamas. "I would *never* want a tail."

"Well, you'll get tits and you won't be able to wear an undershirt anymore," I said. "You'll have to wear a bra, *and* your pussy will have ugly hair."

"Don't say *that*."

"You will, because I saw Auntie Bernie's."

Caroline started to cry. James laid his hand on her shoulder, but she shook it off with a jerk.

"I'll go and ask Mammy and that'll sort it out once and for all," James said, and he climbed out of the bed.

I leaped out of bed and slammed the bedroom door shut, almost squashing the tips of my brother's fingers, and winked at him as I told Caroline I was only joking. She peeked through her fingers, and the tears changed to huffy sniffs.

"We mustn't tell Mammy we know words like tits or she'll be very angry. Nor can either of you mention to Noel that I told you these words."

"Why not?" Caroline said.

My sister always asked questions that got to the bottom of things.

"Because they're grown-up words that we're not supposed to know yet."

"I see . . . very good."

Her "I see"s and "very good"s were annoying. She liked to behave like Mammy and act as if the answer to her question was now to her liking and the matter was at an end. I needed to be surer. I went to my mother's bedroom, fetched her Sunday missal, and made them swear upon it in turn that they wouldn't repeat it to anyone, Caroline agreeing only after I promised to tell a story about Jennifer at the seaside.

The seaside was on our minds because it was summer and our parents took us there on Sunday outings. I loved to walk along the high harbor walls and look down at the boats bobbing in the dark green water. Everything was so colorful; the boats were painted brightly, and large white and pale gray seagulls flew squealing above them in the sunny air. Some of the gulls swam like ducks with puffy chests, while others walked on their bright orange legs on the wet rocks covered with slime and rubbery seaweed.

"The people who own those yachts are rotten rich," Daddy said to James and me at the harbor one afternoon. I followed the direction of his pointed finger to a pale blue boat with a silvery sail.

"Yacht" was as lovely a word as the thing itself. I whispered it four times to make sure I'd remember it so I could put Jennifer in one during a bedtime story.

"Can we get a yacht?" I asked.

"Not for a long time. They're very expensive, and I'm not rotten rich."

A large yacht with two rotten rich people on it began to move. It sailed out of the narrow mouth of black rocks and headed toward the blue-gray distance where a ship was crossing. How I wished we could be rotten rich and sail into the misty blue-gray distance.

"We'd best return to the others," said my father.

To get to the beach, we had to cross a wooden bridge with two- or three-inch spaces between the old planks and I could see the water, bobbing rotten wood, and seaweed far below. It didn't have handrails either, and I feared a plank might break and we'd fall into the water. James was not afraid. Slipping his hand from our father's, he skipped into its middle, stooped to his knees, and peered beneath.

"Oh come on, Gabriel. Your brother wasn't scared. James did it no problem, and you're older than him." Daddy looked down at my brother. "You're a brave man, aren't you, James? Brave, just like your daddy."

"That makes me bigger than him," my brother said.

My father liked to compare James and me and say my brother was just like him. He said it because my brother loved football and played with toy lorries. He said it because their favorite color was red, almost the same red as the lorry in which he drove excavators to shows in at work. James always wanted Santa to bring him lorries, while I wanted pencil cases, or cows and horses for my farm-yard set. Being older, I knew Santa didn't exist, and the idea to tell my brother so before I walked across the bridge came into my head, but I didn't.

Caroline, baby Nuala, and my mother were sitting on a red-and-black-checked rug she'd laid out on the soft, warm sand. Most people sat on rugs, though there were also people who'd hired green-and-red-striped deckchairs from a man in a small hut far-ther along the beach. My father put on a pair of maroon swim-ming shorts with a moth hole on the right side and ran toward the sea.

"I want to go in the water today," I said.

"You've got no swimming trunks, so shut up and put on some sun cream," said Mammy. She didn't want us going near water because she feared we'd drown and the lack of swimming trunks was always her handy excuse.

A band of men and women walked slowly up the beach. The men wore navy blue trousers with stripes almost the same color as my father's swimming shorts, and their jackets had small cloth pieces of the same color on their shoulders. A few carried horns and trumpets, and rays of sunshine sometimes caught on the biggest ones and made them flash like cameras. As they drew nearer, an old woman with seagull-white hair in a bun stopped, raised her hand to her eyes, and then pointed to an empty spot about twenty feet from us.

"Who are those people, Mammy?" I said.

She peered at them for a moment. "It's the Salvation Army."

"What do they do?" asked James.

"They're the other sort and they sing," Mammy said in a lower voice before making three tongue clicks of annoyance. "The nerve of them . . . coming to try and convert us on the beach. I don't know why they can't leave people alone." She said this out of the side of her mouth because she didn't want anyone sitting nearby to overhear.

Caroline nudged me in the arm because the old woman was stepping up on a box. After she'd climbed up, she waved a thin rod slowly and the band began to play. Others started singing "The Lord Is My Shepherd," the same hymn we sang at Benediction.

"Why are the Protestants playing a Catholic hymn?" Caroline said.

"Shush. It's a hymn for all denominations."

"I see . . . very good."

"But they change the words a bit, of course," Mammy said.

"Do they change the words of all our hymns when they sing them?" I said.

"I think so, but not the ones about the Blessed Virgin. They never sing hymns about Our Lady because they don't believe in Her."

Her quiet voice was dead silly because no one was listening. A woman lying nearby was reading, her husband was asleep, and their children were building sandcastles.

"Why do they change our hymns?" Caroline said.

"Because *they* think their words are better."

"I see . . . very good."

Protestants are really damned, I thought.

"But they're not, of course," Mammy said.

The singing stopped, and the old woman started preaching.

"Better not to have been born than to sin and close your hearts to Jesus. Yes, I say, better not to have been born than not to be saved." Her voice grew louder, and her arms thrashed about because she was growing excited. "Sinners among you who are sunning yourselves and cavorting on this golden beach, hear my words. I say, listen and repent. Accept Jesus and be saved. Accept Him and be saved because only God's kingdom is golden." The woman went on for what seemed like hours about repenting and getting saved. After she stopped, she looked about for a moment before stepping down off the box, taking out a white hanky and wiping her brow after she'd done so.

"Can we be saved even if we're Catholics, Mammy?" I said.

"*Stop* listening to their gibberish, Gabriel." Mammy looked about quickly as if she'd just remembered we were on the beach. "Those words are not for our ears," she said more gently. "We have a different system for taking care of our souls."

"She's talking about Our Lord too, so why is their system different?"

"It's about how *they* adore Jesus."

"So their Jesus is a different man?"

Mammy smiled widely at the woman who'd been reading and was now watching us closely. After the woman returned to her book, my mother bared her teeth and looked at me hard. "James and Caroline, when your father comes back, I just might ask him to take you for ice cream. I just might do that if you're *all* very quiet."

"But Mammy, is their Jesus a—"

"Shut up, Gabriel," said Caroline.

It was the last week of school, and I was in big trouble with Mrs. Bradley, the headmistress, and it had nothing to do with Protestants or hymns. It had nothing to do with me, either. It was Henry Lynch's fault. I knew it as soon as he'd told the lie.

I'd heard Mrs. Bradley's shrieks from the other side of the pink curtain that ran across the middle of the room and separated the junior and senior classes. A rumpus broke out next as the senior girls began screaming. At first, the headmistress blamed the older boys for putting the mice in her drawer. I heard her shouting at them, but then she ordered Noel and another boy to take down the dividing curtain a few minutes later. As soon as it was down, she asked the juniors to stand up, turn around, and asked us one by one if we'd done the deed. The idea of her hand touching a mouse was very funny until she came to Henry. He blamed me.

"Are you sure it was him?" she said.

"Yes, miss. I saw him go into the senior room with his hands in his pockets this morning. He definitely went in there and I knew he had no business being in your room."

Three more of Henry's friends swore they'd seen me go behind the curtain, too. Henry's older brother, who was sitting in front of Mrs. Bradley's table, raised his hand and said he also remembered seeing me near her desk, but had thought I was on an errand.

"Gabriel Harkin, come and see me this minute." Mrs. Bradley looked at Noel and nodded. "Put the curtain up again . . . but do it so it doesn't sag in the middle quite so much."

"I can't believe you put mice in my drawer to eat the hand of me. You, Gabriel Harkin, you of all people." She leaned toward me until her clear blue eyes were level with mine. "Now confess and I may not punish you as hard as I intend to."

Mrs. Bradley's mouth was small and tight, her face purplish, and little lines were gathered just above her upper lip. She didn't blink, to make sure I was frightened.

"I didn't do it, Miss. I don't know why they're blaming me."

"The words I want to hear are 'I'm sorry.'" She sighed. "Well, they say still waters run deep, and now I know they most certainly do." Her mouth turned down. "You'll be trying to tell me the mice chewed their way inside of their own accord."

The senior girls and boys laughed in the rows of desks stretching across the room. I lifted my head a little and peeked under my eyebrows until I came to Jennifer's freckled face. She was laughing. Mrs. Bradley looked at them before she rose and fetched a stick propped against the fireplace.

"Hold out one hand and then the other."

I did as she asked, and she gave me two slaps on each hand.

"Now say you're sorry and the matter will be closed."

My eyes and hands stung.

"I'm very sorry, Mrs. Bradley."

"And you'll never try to scare a teacher again?"

"No."

She gave me one more slap on each hand before sending me away. Everyone turned to stare as I lifted up the curtain and walked through. Miss Murray looked sad. I wanted to point and shout at Henry. Instead, I sat at my desk and tried to go on as if nothing had happened, but I couldn't concentrate. I turned back to Henry and saw his evil smile. A tear ran down my cheek, so I turned back quickly and wiped it away. Another followed, and I wiped it away, too. Miss Murray didn't ask me a single question; even the multiplication ones the others didn't know. She asked Henry the hard ones, and I put up my hand when he got them wrong. Still, she ignored me. I'd been punished and was now dead to her.

"Was it very sore?" Fergal said at lunchtime.

I'd just finished my sandwiches and found him standing outside the school door when I came out. I was surprised to see him, because I knew he always played with Henry and the others.

"Of course, it was sore."

"That Henry's a bad article. He shouldn't have done that. I feel bad you got punished for something you didn't do."

"Why didn't you stand up and say I didn't do it, then?"

He looked into my eyes before allowing his gaze to drop to the ground, the way he always did when he knew he was wrong.

"Thanks for asking, and now you'd better go before the football teams are picked and Henry starts wondering where you are."

CHAPTER FIVE

S HE FINISHED READING THE blue envelope with the red-, white-, and blue-edged stripes which the postman had asked me to give her when he saw me turning into Granny's lane. Her eyes shone misty when she looked from it to me.

"You're going to meet your uncle Brendan," she said. "He's coming to visit us."

I looked at the sky blue page Granny had laid on the table. I'd seen the backward writing when I held the envelope up to the sun as I walked up the lane, but couldn't understand how the pages of a letter could be inside because it was so thin and light. Grandmother had known though, because she hadn't ripped it open like she normally did envelopes, and instead had pulled back its gummy flap carefully and unfolded it into a one-page letter.

A family get-together took place at her house the following evening. As soon as Auntie Bernie arrived, the stink of Uncle John's dog gave in to her nasty perfume. Uncle John sat in my grandfather's old chair, dressed in a Sunday suit that was becoming too tight because his belly bulged over the narrow trouser belt.

"Children, the grown-ups wish to discuss Uncle Brendan's visit, so you must go outside and play," said Auntie Celia.

She signaled Uncle Frank, her Scottish husband who sometimes wore his kilt to Mass on Sundays, to give up his armchair to her by a number of small, quick waves of her hand. Auntie Celia disliked small chairs on account of her very wide hips. As he rose, Uncle Frank glared at her with the same sunken, black eyes as Connor's, the only difference between them being my uncle looked you in the face when he spoke to you.

"And don't come back for an hour if you know what's good for you," she said while she watched us file out.

"Mammy doesn't really want Uncle Brendan to come home," said Martin before we started our game of piggy-in-the-middle.

"Why not?" asked Caroline. She pushed a rope of hair behind her ear.

"She doesn't like him because he disgraced the family. Mammy says he shouldn't stir the pot and should just stay out among his Africans at the missions. That's all I could get. When I asked some more, she slapped my ear and said I shouldn't be listening to other people's conversations . . . and you know she *always* beats Connor, never me."

After a while, Martin and I got bored with the game and decided to sneak inside, but Uncle John's smelly dog came out from under the table, wagging its tail. Auntie Celia looked over her shoulder and stopped talking. She called Martin over and made him sit at her feet. My grandmother, Auntie Celia, and Mammy had been crying because their eyes were puffy. As I crossed the floor to sit on the sofa beside my mother, Uncle John and Granny watched without giving me a wink or smile.

"Tell everyone what you won in the big GAA raffle last week, Martin," Auntie Celia said, as she ran her fingers through his wavy, dark blond hair that she lightened in the summer with lemon juice. She peered down at Martin with her mouth slightly open, ready to move her lips in time to his words, something she always did when she asked him to tell a bit of news.

Martin had flat feet, was only an inch taller than me, and had white china-colored skin that turned red when he was in the sun. It turned red even when the sun was as weak as the tea Auntie Bernie liked to drink. He was also very careful about his teeth and brushed after every meal, although I didn't think they looked a bit whiter than mine. Behind his back, Connor said his brother was touched in the head, because he'd once caught him brushing after eating an apple. "Anyone with an ounce of sense knows apples are good for you," he'd told me, but I stopped him from saying any more because Martin was like God to me.

"I won a two-foot doll in a scarlet flamenco dress and her eyes open and close when she sleeps," said Martin. "She's very, *very* expensive."

Auntie's cracked lips stilled at the same time Martin stopped talking. She leaned toward my mother slightly. "My Martin's lucky in the raffles, Eileen, eh?"

"It appears so."

I was a little hurt Martin hadn't mentioned the doll to me because I thought we told one another everything.

"What does he want wey a damned doll at his age, Celia?" Uncle Frank said. "Give it tey Harry and Eileen's wee lass."

Martin's lips became a thin line as he looked at his father.

"What good is a prize like that tey a boy?" said Uncle Frank. "You know I'm right. They should have given him its value in money instead."

"Seeing as you're Scottish, it's expected you'd make a remark like that, isn't it, Frank?" said Auntie Celia.

Uncle John and Daddy laughed.

Auntie Celia passed one hand over her long fingers as she said Martin had asked her to keep it for him so he could give it to his future wife one day. "So I've stored it away in the attic, where it'll remain." Without stopping for a breath, she told Uncle John he needed to lose weight fast because his stomach was a disgrace, and a new argument began.

"Big Sunday," the official closing of the summer season, was very hot for a day in September. We arrived at the beach earlier than usual because my father said there would be more people in attendance than usual. He changed quickly into his swimming togs and went to the water. His snow white arms flashed and cut into the water as he swam against glassy waves that lifted him up and down like a floating cork. The water looked so pretty, so inviting, I was determined to get into it, even if my need caused a low-voiced argument between my parents in public. I waited till Daddy came out and, before he dried himself off, asked extremely nicely if he'd teach me to swim because I was old enough, adding it was my last chance this summer.

"You *can't* go in the water because you have no swimming trunks, so that's that," said Mammy, her words coming out faster than a turkey makes a gobble. "Next year, maybe."

"A boy of eight should know how to swim," said my father. "He can wear his underpants."

"He will *not* indeed, Harry." She looked about her. "No swimming trunks means no swimming, simple as that."

Immediately, Daddy seized my hand, and we marched to the man in the green hut who rented the deckchairs to see if he sold cheap swimming trunks. The old man wore a grubby, white handkerchief with four knots on his bald head and had a tattoo of an anchor with a bit of rope on one leathery upper arm. He eyed me up and down a few times before shaking his head.

"I don't sell them, but I have a pair I found the other week on the beach and you're welcome to them. I don't think they'll fit, though."

Even before I saw the mustard-colored trunks, I'd decided they'd fit.

After my mother learned they were secondhand, she took them from me, and her eyes and nose crinkled in strict examination. "They need to be washed because you don't know who was last in them, and that all adds up to no swimming today."

"Nonsense," said my father, "the saltwater will sanitize them."

I slipped into them hurriedly for fear she'd change her mind.

"They're a little big, but they're free, so they'll do," she said.

Caroline said she wanted to swim as well, started to huff, and, as she always did, Mammy gave in and allowed her to wear her stripy pink knickers. James arrived bare-arsed just as we reached the point where the raggedy edge of the foamy water disappears into the sand before it can reverse to the sea again.

My father held me and tried to show me how to float. In all honesty, when he held me in his arms, that was every bit as magical as learning how to do it. He put his hands under my tummy, I was dead surprised it didn't tickle but supposed that was because of the cold water, and held me up and told me to paddle like a dog. The sight of my paddling made him laugh, just like Uncle Tommy had laughed when I used to act drunk after he'd swung me around in the garden. I'd never heard Daddy laugh so loudly about anything I'd ever done. All around me was suddenly beautiful: the sparkling water, the laughing people, Caroline pushing back her glistening hair, James scooping handfuls of water and hurling it at us. Each time my father took away his arms, I'd sink and swallow mouthfuls of the salty water, but he just picked me up and told me to try again. I kept trying, trying, trying.

"Well done, Gabriel," he said, after I swam five feet but had to then stop because my arms and legs were heavy. "I knew you could do it, son."

Even the cold waves gently brushing my sides as they moved toward the shore felt warm as I stood licking the salty water dribbling over my upper lip. Everything inside me glowed hotter than the sun's rays cutting through the water to the golden floor beneath.

"Next year, you'll be able to swim better than me," he said, and the four of us began to horse about and hurl water at one another for a while.

After Daddy had left to go back and change, we played at the water's edge until I got bored and said we should walk up to the curving concrete seawall. The wall was ten feet high and shaped like a cresting wave; its uppermost part cast a band of black shadow on the sand where we sat and dug our feet into the coolness. Farther along the beach, the Protestant Salvation Army band began to play their hymns.

A man in jet-black swimming trunks walked toward us. He stopped beside a woman sitting a few feet in front of me and talked to her as he picked up a towel, rubbed his wet hair a little, and flipped it over his head to dry his back. His body was healthy brown, and water droplets glittered like tiny diamonds on his legs and chest. I couldn't stop looking. I took in every inch of him. His ice-blue eyes looked over the woman's head and caught me watching. He smiled, my heart skipped a beat, and I looked away quickly. I pretended to play with a handful of sand and stole another peek when I thought it might be safe. As my gaze reached his face and our eyes touched once more, my heart skipped another beat. I couldn't understand what was happening.

Taking a pair of underpants and red shorts out of a bag, he placed them on the sand, turned his back on me, and put the wet towel loosely around his waist. I crawled closer and watched as he wriggled out of his swimming trunks. They dropped to his sand-covered feet, he kicked them toward the girl, and began to dry his private parts. After he'd finished, he picked up his underpants, stood on one foot, and put the other through its leg hole. I crawled over, stuck my head beneath the towel, and looked up. I don't know why. I needed to see him there.

"Shoo, you naughty boy," the woman said, in the same kind of voice Auntie Bernie had used when I'd seen her privates.

I pulled my head out fast.

"You shouldn't do such naughty things."

My face felt fierier than the sand underneath my fingertips. Caroline and James watched, still as shop window dummies. The man looked down at me and laughed.

"I'm very sorry I looked at you when you were changing, mister." I lowered my gaze to his legs.

"That's quite all right, young fella."

"Go to your mother at once," the woman said.

The three of us raced like frightened dogs over the sand. Caroline told Mammy what I'd done and I was scolded. That night, my sister sneaked in to hear me tell a bedtime story, but I pretended to be angry and ordered her to leave. My anger was fake, an excuse, because I didn't want to tell a story. I wanted to fall asleep remembering the beautiful man's face, and how the water droplets glittered like diamonds on his healthy brown back and legs.

Auntie Celia placed a large bundle of notes beside the canvas bag full of coins, put on the kettle, and told Martin and me to follow her into the living room where she settled into an armchair. She'd invited my parents to tea and had closed her shop half an hour early without counting the takings or writing out her banking slips.

"You know my feelings about Brendan," she said. "I just don't know how I'll react until I see him in the flesh. But since he's to come, we'll have to wallpaper, paint, and clean Mother's house. People will be visiting him there, and we can't have the neighbors seeing how shabby the place looks in daylight. She's no longer fit to keep the place tidy . . . and that stinky dog of John's will have to be tied to a stake outside, where it belongs anyway." Auntie turned round to Mammy. "I'm sure I can count on you to help with the decorating, and it goes without saying that we'll all chip in and buy the wallpaper and any other bits and bobs."

"Chip in," said Mammy. "John will be getting the house when she dies, so he should pay for the bits and bobs that's needed." Her mouth snapped firmly shut.

"Oh . . . oh, I don't know if our John will be getting the house or all that's in it," said Auntie Celia. "What do you say, Harry?" She leaned forward in her chair. "Sure she hasn't made the will yet. Or has she, and I haven't been made privy . . . just like some other things I haven't been made privy to these last few years?"

"What are you talking about?" my mother asked.

"Well, I didn't want to raise this indelicacy but . . . well, seeing as you've touched on things, there's the giving of a lamb, for starters."

"Jasus, don't you know John will get everything?" said Daddy. "He's the eldest. None of us are interested in farming."

"The lamb-giving has nothing to do with us," said Mammy. "Besides, I don't like to go up to *your* mother's to clean and paper and do things a daughter's supposed to do." There was a short silence. "She treats me enough as an outsider as things stand."

"Hmm," said Auntie Celia. Her tongue flicked up and rested on her upper lip.

"Why the hmming, Celia?" my mother said. "Children, leave the room at once, because the adults need to talk about your uncle Brendan's arrival."

"Well, I certainly can't be expected to do everything given my sentiments about Brendan. And now I learn there's a will. Harry, is there or is there not a will?"

"What are you talking about?" he asked. "Your sentiments, my bloody arse. If anybody's entitled to sentiments, it's me and Eileen, and we don't."

Auntie Celia took a handkerchief from her cardigan sleeve and sniffed as she dabbed each nostril. "Aye, I suppose it'll be sentiments that explains the lamb-giving, then."

"Gabriel! Martin! Everybody, clear this room *now*," Mammy said. "The grown-ups want to discuss the cleaning of your granny's house for Uncle Brendan's arrival."

"But does Granny have a will, Mammy?" said Martin.

"Get out now, you nosy thing," said Auntie Celia.

"Would you like to see the doll?" Martin said to Caroline and me after we went upstairs. "I found it the other day."

"Yes, let's," said Caroline.

The attic was crammed with schoolbooks, old chairs, a huge TV set, and was almost as dusty as Noel's nest in the pigsty. In one corner stood a large wooden horse that Martin and I had played with years ago. He went into the opposite corner, cast off an old towel covering a cardboard box about twice the size of a shoebox, and brought it over. Inside was a doll in a gown that was a foaming sea of frills. After taking it out of the box, Martin began to nurse it as if it were a baby.

"Let me hold it," Caroline said, though he made no move to give it to her.

Caroline watched him rock it for a few moments before giving me a look that said I must tell him to hand it over immediately because she was the girl. In truth, it wasn't right he wouldn't give it to her, but I also couldn't scold him. Martin was just like me: the town boys hated him as Henry hated me. They called him a pansy because he was forever swinging back or fixing his fringe. The difference between us was Martin didn't care what the boys called him. They were dirt in his eyes, although he did warn Connor often that he wasn't to tell them he owned a Spanish doll.

My sister's look turned sour, but still I said nothing. I picked up a bundle of old photographs lying on the seat of a dusty chair. The top ones were brown and white, contained people I didn't know, and there were also black and white ones at the bottom of the pile.

"I asked if I could hold the doll, Martin, and I think you *must* give—"

"This photo's got Auntie Celia in it," I said. She wore a wedding dress and stood with a large crowd of people on the steps of a church. "And here's one of her beside our uncles and aunts. Daddy mustn't have known Mammy when Auntie Celia and Uncle Frank got married because she's not here."

"Let me see that," said Caroline.

"Uncle Brendan's not in priest's clothes, either," she said.

I studied my father and Uncle Brendan's faces and saw they were alike, except Uncle's hair was wavier.

"Mammy doesn't even keep photographs of Uncle Brendan on the walls," said Martin while he put the doll back in its box. "Not even the ones of his ordination that he sent her. Those are stuck in her chest of drawers."

"Why?" I said.

"She doesn't like him and won't tell me why."

Carnival week in Knockburn brought the football season to a close. Football teams from surrounding areas competed during the week to reach the final, which was played early Sunday evening, and a silver cup was presented to the winners following a guest tea and concert that night. Everyone in Knockburn came to the carnival. It was the highlight of the year, a chance for neighbors to chat in a place other than the churchyard after Mass on Sundays.

James went to the carnival because of the football, Caroline because she could walk around the perimeter of the field eating ice cream with friends, and I because of the amusements. There was hoopla, an air gun target practice area, and a set of five swing boats painted in bright pinks and apple-greens with gold trim that stood near a row of hawthorn and tall beech trees overlooking the road.

Jennifer was best to take up in a boat because, though now eleven and bossy, she screamed louder than any of the other girls. She even let go of the rope to grip the metal bars if she was dead frightened. When she closed her eyes and screamed, I'd pull the rope with all my power, pulling until I felt my arse rise off the bench and my body grow weightless as the boat arced and almost passed over the crossbar in a complete circle.

"That's enough, you scamp. Your time's up. Stop pulling and bring that boat down now," the owner called up. "You're scaring the life out of your girlfriend."

I obeyed, and closed my eyes to enjoy the last arcs of the boat.

"I've got one more shilling," I said, when the rocking began to slow to a stop. "Do you want to go one more time?"

She shook her head and started to climb out. "Let's go meet the others at the fire on the other side of the field."

It was at the point where day was under attack by millions of tiny spots of darkness and its silvery light was being squeezed to blackness. Here and there, around the edge of the field, people had lit fires to make smoke and stop the gnats feasting on their blood.

"Over here, Jennifer," said her friend Kathleen as we drew near.

Ten girls and five boys were also there, some of whom I didn't know because they weren't from Knockburn. Kathleen broke away from a boy she'd been standing beside and ran up to us.

"Jennifer, I've got something to tell you," she said. "That tall boy I was standing beside comes from Craigban. He says he's twelve and fancies you something rotten. He asked me to ask you if you'd like to go on a swing boat with him."

The sweetish smell of burning grass was very strong. As Jennifer looked the boy over, her nose crinkled like she'd smelled something dead. "He's skinny, but I'll think about it."

The boy kept grinning, and Jennifer pretended to ignore him as we stood holding our hands out to the fire even though there wasn't any flame. As the players ran up and down the field, their shouts to pass the ball mingled with insults from some of the adult spectators. The boy edged closer and closer until he was at Jennifer's side. Soon their quick glances became smiles, which became low talking and giggles.

A few minutes later, she turned to Kathleen and me. "I'm just taking a quick spin on the boat with Mickey. Now don't go away from here, because I'll definitely be back."

While they ran off in the direction of the swing boats, I saw four figures step from the sideline of the field and walk toward the fire. As they neared, the smoldering grass flared and I spotted the band of nose to stumpy tail dogs running across the chest of one boy's crimson sweater. I knew the sweater. I didn't need to see his face. I wanted to run.

"Where have you been hiding all week?" asked Henry.

"I've been about." I scratched behind my ear to kill a gnat, felt a great surge of warmth in my armpits.

"Midgets eating at you, are they?"

"Hey, Henry, we sure whipped you in the under-twelve game yesterday," said one of the boys I didn't know as he heaped grass on the fire. The others laughed. "We beat you solidly . . . and on your home ground, too."

"You were lucky, that's all," said Henry. He turned his sneaky eyes away from me and took a step toward the boy.

"Luck had nothing to do with it. We won fair and square."

I started to back away, slowly.

"Where do you think you're going?" Henry asked.

"I have to go."

"Let's ask sissy boy here what he thinks. Were they lucky or not?"

Everything was quiet as all eyes fell upon me.

"Well?"

"I didn't see the game." My mouth was dry as fluffy cotton.

"Why didn't you?"

He didn't give my tongue time to free itself from the roof of my mouth and move to form a reply.

"Because you're a pansy, that's why. A pansy who'd rather be on a swing boat."

The others circling the fire laughed.

Henry took the step back to me. "Am I right or wrong?"

I stared at the nose to tail dogs and didn't answer. There were eight dogs in all, all the same size, all with the same heads and tails.

He jabbed my chest with his finger. "I didn't hear you. Are you a sissy or a pansy?"

It was a beautiful sweater. I couldn't decide if the dogs were Labradors; they had the outline of Labradors, but then that breed was honey colored, not black. And they didn't have stumpy tails, or did they?

"Speak up, Harkin."

I met Henry's eyes. I pleaded into his dark pupils now grown large because the flames had gone out again. They had no pity. My gaze fell to the Labradors again. I wished I could say I was a sissy, let him have his laugh, and then it would all be over. But my tongue refused to form the words.

Henry grabbed my shirt. I heard a tear. A button popped and spun to the ground.

"You only have to look at his fucking jeans," he said. "Hey, everybody, look at Harkin's jeans. They're purple, for fuck's sake."

It was true. My jeans were purple. I had made my mother buy them for me as soon as I'd set eyes on them. They had white stitching on the seams and were so different from any jeans I'd ever seen before. I'd begged her to let me have them. Now, I wished she'd have put down her foot and bought me blue ones just like the ones other boys wore.

"Henry, I want to go. I haven't done anything to you."

"Admit you're a sissy as loud as you can so everyone can hear. *Then*, I'll let you go."

I prayed Jennifer was on her way back from the swing boats. "You know, I can't say that."

He threw me on the ground and fell upon me. "Help me take off Harkin's jeans," he said.

I felt every word pass into my body. No one tried to stop him and his friends as they pinned me down. I struggled and jerked to push them off, even tried to scratch their faces like a girl. They seized my arms and pulled down my trousers. Henry gripped the elastic band of my underpants on both sides of my waist and with a sharp tug made me naked. I felt everyone's eyes on my thing, a girl's high-pitched giggle arced across the smoke, and still the boys held my arms fast.

"Admit you're a sissy and I'll give them back to you." Henry rose and stood over me, my bunched jeans in his hands. "Come on, Harkin. It's very easy. Just say, '*I'm* a sissy.'"

Strangers knew every inch of my body. I didn't want them staring at my thing anymore. "Please give me back my jeans because . . . because—"

"What's going on here?" Henry's friends let go of my arms and rose as Jennifer marched up. Instantly, I reached for my underpants and pulled them up.

"Why aren't you and Mickey on the swing boats?" said Kathleen.

"There's was a long line . . . and you, Henry Lynch, give Gabriel back his trousers right now or I'll order the girls to take off yours. *Then*, we'll see how big you act when everybody has a gawk at your smelly little thing." She nodded at Kathleen and the other girls. "Grab him and get his knickers off."

Henry dropped my jeans, and he and his friends fled as some of the girls gave chase into the darkness.

"Thanks, Jennifer," I said, after I'd put on my pants. She'd also seen everything and I couldn't bring myself to look her in the eye.

"You don't have to hang your head like that. I've seen Noel's many times, and yours is certainly no different."

CHAPTER SIX

WE WERE SITTING CROSS-LEGGED on the rug in front of the fire at Granny Neeson's house. James and Nuala were still outside teasing her hens, and Caroline and I had come inside because we'd grown tired of climbing the neat turf stack and, frankly, had already wrecked it, anyway. My whole family, including my father for a change, was visiting Granny to invite her and Aunt Peggy to a station Mass to be celebrated by Father Brendan at our house in two weeks' time.

"Pull off Sinead's head and give it to me," I said to Caroline.

Sinead was her doll and she didn't like boys to touch it, but she also knew I created fantastic hairstyles.

"What will you do this time?" she asked as she popped off its head and handed it to me.

"Plaits, I think."

Her doll had long, shiny hair that felt real between my fingers. I undid the bun my sister had tried to make, laid out pieces of green and purple wool that I'd brought with me, and set to work. I noticed Aunt Peggy's eyes boring into me as I plaited. She was Mammy's older sister and still wore her hair in a beehive, even though my mother kept telling her that she was too old for the style. A lazy eyelid made her left eye look as if it was almost closed, and she insisted we call her "Aunt" because she didn't like "Auntie."

"He's great at doing its hair, isn't he, Peggy?" said my mother.

"So I see." Aunt Peggy's eyes met mine. "Eileen, should he *really* be playing with a doll, do you think?"

"For Pete's sake, he's not playing with the thing. He's artistic, and besides, Caroline likes him to work on its hair."

"All the same, it's not good to encourage him to play with it," said Aunt Peggy, not having listened to a word.

"I'm *not* playing with the damned doll. I *don't* play with them. I don't take the whole doll's body. Can't you tell it's only the head, for Pete's sake?" I held it up by a plait and shook it at Aunt Peggy. "I'm doing its hair, just like I do Granny Harkin's hair."

"Don't dare raise your voice at your auntie Peggy." My mother couldn't get used to the fact she preferred to be called aunt, either. "You must not talk back to your elders."

"If it's not playing, what would you call it then, Gabriel?" Aunt Peggy asked.

"I'm working. I'm teaching myself to be a hairdresser, because that's what I'm going to be when I grow up."

"Well, if that's the case, what's your mother sending you off to school for? Hairdressers don't need to know how to write . . . and hairdressing's a woman's job, anyway."

"It's *not*. I saw men clipping women's hair on TV."

"*Those* aren't men."

I turned to my mother. "What does she mean?"

She didn't answer.

"Those people are effeminate." Aunt Peggy glanced at Mammy before she bent toward me. "Doll's head or not, you shouldn't be fixing its hair because no matter what way you look at it, that's playing. I'll wager those people played with dolls when they were young. Oh yes, you can be mighty sure people like that played at the dolls."

I didn't understand the word "effeminate," but it was clearly something terrible because Daddy looked up from his paper and ordered me to give the doll back to Caroline.

"Look Peggy, our Gabriel's very artistic, and this is a part of being that way," Mammy said. "Go on, Gabriel, finish the hairdo . . . but make it quick, okay? And another thing, Peggy, remind me to show you the artwork he brings home from school when you come to the Mass. His teacher says he's a great drawer . . . and he can sing "The Black Velvet Band" totally in tune. Come on, Gabriel, sing for your auntie." My mother slid forward in her chair. "Sing "The Black Velvet Band" for her."

"No."

"Sing it, *at once*."

I cleared my throat before starting. *"Her eyes are shining like diamonds, sure you'd think she was queen of . . ."*

"Aye, drawing and singing's one thing," said Aunt Peggy. "But this other business needs curtailing. He'll turn out fey if he keeps playing with dolls."

"Fey?" said my mother. "What the hell does that mean?"

"Strange," said Aunt Peggy. There was a little silence. "I mean, it's not as if he plays a bit of football to balance him, does he?"

I saw myself standing in the middle of a swaying seesaw trying to keep it level.

"It's high time you started playing a bit of Gaelic football instead of doing hair, boy," said Daddy.

"I don't want to play football. I've told you that many times."

"Mark my words, it's balance is needed," Aunt Peggy said.

"You'll do as I say," he said. "Knockburn has a junior team, and you'll be on it. Every one of your uncles was on the Knockburn football team when they were small. Luksee, the Harkins were always good footballers, so you can be as well."

"Brendan wasn't much of a footballer," said my mother.

"He can't be used as an example in this instance," he said. "And anyway, besides Brendan, all the rest of us played."

"Sure, you didn't even make the official team, Harry," Mammy said. "Not really . . . at least that's what your mother told me. She said you were only a substitute. In any event, Gabriel's not interested in football, so that's that. Not everyone needs to be chasing after a leather ball."

"He's not interested in machinery, either," said my father.

"He's got his farmyard set," my mother said. *"There's* your balance, Peggy. Continue on with the singing, Gabriel."

"He shouldn't be given a choice, not at his age," said Aunt Peggy.

"Aye, you're right about that," Daddy said. "*Now* you're talking sense, Peggy."

My mother's face reddened, and she rose from her chair. "Let my bit of a boy alone." She pursed her lips at my father, then turned to look at Aunt Peggy, and I was sure they were going to argue. Granny was in the kitchen, and I wished she'd come in and stop them. "Listen, Peggy, when you drop that dandy who won't marry you and meet someone who will and have children of your own, *then, and only then,* can you start to lecture me on what mine should or shouldn't play."

She was talking about Aunt Peggy's boyfriend, who wore cream-colored trousers in winter and had shoes with thin leather soles which Daddy said came from Italy. My aunt's lazy eyelid had popped wide open so both eyes were now perfectly balanced.

"It's not my fault he doesn't want to get married yet . . . and, anyway, you are all against him because he dresses so nicely and takes a bit of a drink now and then." She put her hands over her face, and her shoulders began to heave.

Now I wanted my grandmother to stay in the kitchen until Mammy was finished.

"A drink now and then?" said Granny Neeson, as she came into the room. She held half of an unwrapped currant cake in one hand, a bread knife in the other. "He *reeks* of it sometimes. It's so strong, I could ask him to breathe on my wettest coal, set a match to it, and it would light no bother."

"So Mammy's right, Aunt Peggy," I said. "I'm artistic and can do the doll's hair if I want to, and you shouldn't interfere."

My mother pounced and whacked my ears. "Don't you ever talk back to your auntie Peggy like that, you bad article." Her words grew loud and soft as they hit and bounced against a wall of high-pitched ringing within my head. "When I get you home, I'll beat the living daylights out of you. Give that damned doll back to Caroline. *Now!*"

The half-finished plait unwound as I gave the head back to my sister.

"Let him be, Eileen," Aunt Peggy said. She wiped her eyes with her finger. "He's only a child and doesn't know any better. I shouldn't have spoken."

I didn't understand what had just happened. They were friends again. I was in a complete muddle. I was so muddled, I just couldn't rise or speak.

Lightning flashed across the pencil-lead gray sky, and it thundered and rained heavily on the afternoon Uncle Brendan was flying into Belfast airport. Granny Harkin wheeled her rosary beads between her fingers and prayed as fast as the crazy woman I saw every Sunday at the chapel. She was scared the plane to Belfast would fall from the sky. She couldn't understand how such heavy things stayed in the air during good weather and kept interrupting her prayers with a "Jesus Christ, what was that?" after every thunder clap.

By four o'clock, everyone was gathered for his arrival. Our house had been picked because it was larger than Granny's. The sweet smell of roast beef drifted in from the kitchen.

"Oh, sweet Jesus . . . sweet Jesus and his mother, would you look who's driving in," said Auntie Celia from where she stood by the window.

I ran over to see Mr. O'Kane's eggshell-colored car with the pramlike wheels pass over the cattle grid at our main gate.

"Even worse," said Auntie Celia, "I've just seen Kate the nun's head gawking out the back window."

The nun's name was Kathleen and her religious name was Sister Pious. She was also Mr. O'Kane's eldest daughter, lived in a convent in England, and had been over visiting her parents and collecting pots of money for charity from everyone only two weeks ago.

"Eileen . . . Eileen, you'll have to get rid of that nun fast or she'll find out all about our Brendan's going away," said Auntie

Celia, and she began to wring her hands. "Harry, you know how emotional Mammy gets. She'll be asking Brendan why the hell he went away so quick and why he didn't come home for Daddy's funeral in front of that nun." Auntie Celia said this, even though Granny was in the room with us. "Oh, sweet, sweet Jesus, get rid of them, somebody get them away from here."

"I'll not be talking like that, Celia," Granny said. "Sure, Kate went to school with Brendan. It's good she's here."

"You'll have to answer the door, Celia," said Mammy.

"*I* can't send the nun packing. *I* went to school with her, too. Harry, tell Eileen to go to the door and get rid of them. Listen, Eileen, just keep them standing on the doorstep and they'll take the hint . . . oh, please Eileen, please do it for my sake."

My mother let out a great sigh and went to answer the door. I went out to watch. After saying what a pleasant surprise it was to see her, Mammy said ever so nicely it was a bit of a bad time to call because Uncle Brendan was arriving home for a visit after being so long abroad, and the family were all gathered to greet him."

"Oh, I know that," said the nun. "He phoned last week and asked that I be here. That's why I flew in from Coventry last night. So, I trust you won't mind if we come in."

Uncle Tommy's car arrived between heavy rain showers, and Martin and I spilled out the door in front of Daddy, Granny, and Uncle John. Auntie Celia stayed with Kate the nun and her parents. They wouldn't come out because Mrs. O'Kane said only immediate family should have the honor of first greeting him. Uncle Brendan stepped out of the car wearing a cream hat with a brim and narrow brown band. He looked like my father except he was thinner, and his skin was the same healthy brown as the beautiful man I'd seen on the beach. As he smiled, two lines in his forehead open wide and I could see pure white skin between the cracks.

"I feel like I'm really home with all this rain," he said, and he looked up at the sky.

"Oh, son! Son, you're home," Granny said.

A silence started, broken only when a passing crow cawed. Granny let out another cry as she limped toward Brendan in her new navy blue dress, white cardigan, and matching straw hat.

"Ah, Brendan, son, you've come back to me," she said in a croaky voice I'd never heard before from her. "Oh, why did you have to go away so sudden, son?"

Daddy watched with his mouth slightly open and exchanged glances with Uncle John and Uncle Tommy. Father Brendan put his head over her shoulder as they hugged, eyes closed tighter than a newborn calf's, but didn't speak. After a few moments, he stopped patting Granny's back and pulled back to look at her again, wiped the corners of her eyes with his finger, and kissed her cheek.

"Mother, I've missed you. I've missed you, but it had to be . . . and now I'm home again."

My eyes watered as they began to hug again. Uncle John and my father walked up to him. They shook hands, Uncle John said, "You're welcome home," and Brendan stretched out his arms and pulled them into a huge hug. My father didn't know what to do, his hand hovering an inch away from Uncle Brendan's waist for a second or two before he gripped it firmly.

"Where's our Celia?" Uncle Brendan asked, after they'd separated.

Granny looked about. "Kate the nun's here, so she must have stayed inside with her."

"I'm here, Brendan," Auntie Celia said in a voice almost as high as Caroline's. She pushed past Auntie Bernie and me, her face looking sweaty, and started toward him. "You got bad weather for coming home, but you're looking grand, thank God . . . well, maybe a bit thin and . . . have they . . . have they not been feeding . . . ?" Auntie didn't finish the sentence. She started to shake, her hands fled to her face, and Uncle Brendan rushed to her and wrapped his arms around her, which started my grandmother crying again.

"It's all right, Celia," he said. "It's been far too long." Gently, he took her hands away from her face and she looked up at him like Caroline sometimes looked at me when she wanted something.

"I'm making a fool of myself in front of that Kate the nun. She'll be gawking out the window and wondering why the hell I'm behaving so silly."

"She'll understand," he said. "It's a long time since I've been home. The black sheep's home, Celia."

"Brendan, she doesn't know anything . . . I hope?"

My grandmother stopped a loud nose blow halfway through. "Gabriel, come over here."

After standing beside her, I gathered my shoulders small, placed one foot on top of the other, and dropped my eyes to the ground.

"Say hello to Brendan," she said, and pushed me forward.

"Hello, Uncle Father Brendan," I said. I peeked up at him for a moment. He held out a brown hand and I could see its palm was much whiter. His fingers were thick like Daddy's, and my hand disappeared as brown skin closed around it. I'd wanted to shake his hand like a grown-up, but my hand was lost inside, and all I could feel was his lovely hotness.

"You can just call me Uncle Brendan." He winked at Daddy. "I don't stand on formality here, and besides, it's far too long to say it that other way."

"Okay."

"Isn't he a handsome fellow, Brendan?" my grandmother said. "And look at Caroline, too." She called my sister over. "They look just like you at that age, and they've got Harry's and your brains."

My father laughed and said it was Brendan who had all the brains. James came up carrying Nuala, who looked too heavy for him to hold, and Granny didn't introduce them until Uncle Brendan asked who they were as he picked Nuala up in his hands and grinned at her.

"Oh, Brendan, I wish you'd have come home and made up with your father on his deathbed," Granny said. "Why couldn't you just have come home?"

"These children are just so pretty," Uncle Brendan said. He looked right into my eyes. "Did you know Grandmother says I was one of the best-looking men in Knockburn? Why, I was so handsome, she had to stop the girls from wanting to kiss me."

"And what about me?" said Uncle Tommy.

Everyone laughed, but I was dead surprised Uncle Brendan would talk about kissing girls. He was a priest, and priests weren't supposed to think about women in that kind of way. As soon as my mother approached, he put Nuala down and shook Mammy's hand and then, gripping both of her lower arms, looked into her eyes for a moment or two and finally kissed her cheek. She blushed dead high because she hated kissing anyone.

"Gabriel's good at his books," Granny said.

"You like school?"

I couldn't stop my eyes falling to my feet again. "It's okay, except for Henry Lynch."

"Who's he?"

His voice was so deep and musical, not sharp or rough like the Knockburn men's voices, and laughter rose from the pit of his stomach just like Daddy's.

"He doesn't like me and tries to fight me all the time."

"Look at your uncle Brendan when he speaks to you," said Mammy. "Henry's one of those hooligan Lynchs from the other side of Knockburn. But I'm sure my Gabriel's no angel, either. He's also a bit shy, so Henry takes advantage."

"Are you shy?" Uncle Brendan said.

"Damn the 'bit shy,' " said Auntie Celia. "He and my Martin are not shy when they want to go out and poison trout like we used to do, Brendan." She turned and waved at Martin and Connor to come to her.

"I was shy, too," he said. "Your father had to fight my battles. He always had to protect me." His eyes swept away to watch Martin and Connor coming toward us.

"Oh, many's a scrape I got into on account of you, Brendan," Daddy said.

As Auntie Celia introduced Martin and Connor, she ran her hand through Martin's fringe so that it stood up crisp.

"Take those Scots eyes off the ground and look at your uncle when you meet him for the first time, Connor," Auntie Celia said. "You and Gabriel, the pair of you are just so alike."

I was nothing like Connor, because he did it *all* the time. I saw Kate the nun glide over the gravel toward my uncle, the tip of her large wooden crucifix bouncing against her beige habit. She took Uncle Brendan's hands in her marble-cold hands, but he didn't try to remove them as fast as possible.

"My, but it's good to see you in the flesh at last," she said. "It's blessing enough from the good Lord to receive your letters, but there's nothing like meeting our brothers on the old sod." She looked at Auntie Celia and her lips turned up a little, exactly like the Blessed Virgin's weak smile in any picture of the Holy Family. "Sure there's nothing better than having all your family together, is there, Celia? It's just such a terrific blessing."

"It's a blessing indeed, Sister Pious," said Auntie Celia. "The Lord is most gracious."

Later, when we went into the sitting room, Mr. O'Kane, who now had a whiskey glass in his hand, started telling yarns about the Harkin boys when they were young. Kate the nun kept looking at me. Every time I looked across at her, she was staring, and it made me uncomfortable. I looked away to Uncle Brendan. The more I studied his face, the more I knew Granny was wrong. Caroline and I didn't look anything like him. He was brown, his nose was bigger and straighter than mine, and I put it down to the fact she might have forgotten what he looked like because he'd been away so long. Finally, Kate the nun stopped staring and looked over at Uncle Brendan when he began a story about bringing frogs' spawn into my primary school when he and she were young, which then started the grown-ups talking about children and education after he was finished.

"I teach little black boys and girls arithmetic and English in a bush school with a dark-red tin roof," said Uncle Brendan. He'd looked only at me when he said that. "It's much poorer than your school."

I didn't know whether or not I was supposed to feel sorry about his bad school, so I kept quiet.

"What stage are you at in English?" he said. "Are you doing joined-up writing yet?"

"Yes."

"Martin has gorgeous penmanship," said Auntie Celia. "Just gorgeous."

She asked Martin to fetch a pen and paper and write a long sentence with large words to show him. Immediately, my mother also made me write a sentence and, even though I tried my best to do it like Martin, my writing was definitely bigger and less pretty.

It was even more fun visiting Granny now that Uncle Brendan was staying with her. People were always dropping in to see him, and I enjoyed listening to the stories about the old days, and there were apple tarts and delicious currant cakes for tea. He and my grandmother also visited neighbors' houses, and sometimes asked my mother if I could come along, and she always allowed me.

"Uncle Brendan, when will you be going away again?" I said in the car one evening.

He was sitting up front with Uncle John. We were on our way to visit an old woman with cancer whose daughter had asked Uncle Brendan to give her mother a blessing before she died.

"He's only arrived, so we don't talk about things like that," Granny said. She said it so sharply, my cheeks burned with shame for asking, and it must have shocked Uncle Brendan as well, because he turned to look at her.

"I'm here for a while yet, and then I'll be staying in London for a week or so before I fly out to Kenya again."

"What are you going to London for?" she asked. "Your family's here. Fit you better if you went to see our bishop before you go away and see if he can get you into a parish or one of the schools here."

Granny had just ordered me not to talk about his going back to Kenya, and was now breaking her own rule.

"It's as little as the church could do for all the money I throw into its plate of a Sunday," she said.

Uncle John laughed.

"Can I go back with you? I could teach the boys over there how to do joined-up writing."

"I don't think your teacher would let you go," Uncle Brendan said.

"He should come home where he belongs, shouldn't he, John?" Granny said. "The Lord knows you shouldn't have gone away in the first place. You should have gone to the seminary in Maynooth instead of running to Rome . . . nor did you need to run off to the missions in the arse of beyond, either."

"Uncle Brendan, why did you not come home when Granda was very sick and dying? And why won't Auntie Celia hang your ordination photograph on her wall?"

"Who said she doesn't?" Granny asked.

"Martin."

"Your cousin's telling tall stories," she said. "He'll get a good ear boxing the next time I see him . . . and I'll straighten that out with Celia the next time I see her, Brendan."

Things went quiet until Uncle Brendan began to hum. "Listen, you'll say nothing to her," he said, and he started humming again.

"But *why* did you not come home and see Granda before he died?"

"Your grandfather and I were pigheaded and disagreed about something that happened a long time ago. It's something that only concerns grown-ups and is all forgotten now."

"But Granda wasn't pigheaded."

"Adults have different sides to them, Gabriel," he said. "They can be bad to some people yet nice to others, all at the same time."

"He was your father, Brendan," Granny said.

"Anyway, I had to go away to help the poor people and their

children, and I couldn't get home because they needed me more than Granda did. Granda wanted me to be a priest. He wanted it very much. And he knew I'd have to stay and help people if I were needed in Kenya . . . even if he was dying." He looked out the side window for a moment. "You'll be able to help as well, if you feel the need when you get older." He turned back to me. "Do you think you'd like to help the poor and needy?"

The light from an oncoming car shone as I thought about his answer, and the question. Making new hairstyles was what I really enjoyed, yet I figured if I became a priest, I could also fly away in airplanes to convert souls.

"If I can be a hairdresser and a priest."

Uncle stared out at the road.

"You can't be both," said Granny. "People have to choose in life."

"You don't want to be a farmer like me?" asked Uncle John.

"Gabriel, you don't have to choose between things like that," said Uncle Brendan. "Besides, you've got plenty of time to decide. You mustn't rush into things like the priesthood, because it's a very hard life and . . ." He didn't finish, instead just stared out the window.

"And what, Brendan?" Granny said. She watched the back of his head without blinking. "And what?"

"I've forgotten what I wanted to say, so it can't have been too important." He laughed aloud, though it didn't come from his belly like his normal laughter.

My grandmother lowered her head to look at her hands, and Uncle Brendan watched her in the front mirror. She didn't see him, but he was watching. The car was silent again, then Uncle John started whistling, and I was glad because I knew the quiet was something to do with his going away a long time ago, and his coming back, and the going away again, but I just couldn't think what it was.

———

As soon as I stepped into the old woman's bedroom, a terrible smell filled my nose. She was lying in bed, her skin the color of wet newspaper, staring up at the ceiling with watery eyes. A vase of bright pink roses stood just inside the door because it was night, and flowers were always taken out of the sick room before the person went to sleep. A bottle of soda stood beside her black, cut-glass rosary beads, the light from the bedside lamp making them glitter like rat's eyes, together with a red-edged missal with a curled-up cover on the bedside table. One curtain with big flowers and slim, curling leaves puffed out into the room because of a draft sweeping in from the open window.

"She's riddled with cancer, Father Brendan. Just riddled. It won't be long now," said Mrs. McCloskey, her daughter. "She'll pass soon, please God. The doctor put her on morphine a few days ago. She's stuffed to the gills, but it's making the passage easier."

The heavy smell was morphine, though it smelled more like rotten meat. The draft coming in didn't help much because the room was stuffy with sickness. No one seemed to notice the stink, because they didn't say anything, and I couldn't understand why the woman was saying such terrible things in front of her mother, who was probably listening as she stared at the ceiling. Uncle Brendan searched in his pocket, took out a thin purple scarf like Father McAtamney's, and wrapped it around his neck. He opened a tiny bottle of Holy Water and began to pray as he sprinkled the old woman.

"I won't give your mother any Eucharist because she can't swallow and it might choke her," Uncle Brendan said.

"I understand," she said, as Uncle Brendan laid a hand on her shoulder.

"Let yourself go," he said. "Have a good cry."

Mrs. McCloskey turned to me instead. "Son, would you take a sup of Lucozade?" She nodded at the bottle on the table. "The good Lord knows she'll not see that bottle empty."

I shook my head fast because I didn't want to drink a dying

woman's juice. "That's okay, Mrs. McCloskey. Don't trouble yourself."

"Such manners," she said to Granny. "Why, isn't he just the fine wee gentleman?" She started toward the bedside table. "It's no trouble, son."

"No, thank you."

"Don't be rude and take a glass of juice when it's offered," said Granny.

I looked at the Lucozade bottle. It was half-wrapped in the crinkly gold-orange plastic paper I loved to peer through when someone was sick at our home and had been given a bottle. Its color was brighter than any sunglasses and turned the world instantly happy, making the trees brassy green and the sky brassy blue no matter what its actual color.

"I'm really not thirsty, Granny."

"Nonsense."

"I don't care for Lucozade."

"Since when?" she asked. "*You*, that's always sneaking it when I'm sick. You don't think I know, but I do."

Mrs. McCloskey laughed as she poured some into the only glass on the table. I didn't want to catch this woman's cancer. I thanked her and pretended to sip, but watched the threads of tiny bubbles float to the top instead, and then tilted the glass so they'd think I'd drank a lot.

"Don't spill it, pet," Mrs. McCloskey said.

As soon as they looked back at the old woman, I edged closer to the pink, velvety roses, pretended to smell them, and then chucked the juice into the vase. Uncle Brendan caught me halfway through. He looked at the glass, at me, back at the glass, and then nodded toward my feet a couple of times. I glanced down and saw juice had spilled onto the lino. Quickly, I wiped it away in a great curving streak with my shoe.

"Goodness, you must have been thirsty," Mrs. McCloskey said. "Have another. You're a growing boy, and the glucose is good for you."

"I'm full to bursting, thank you."

"I think one's enough," said Uncle Brendan, and he came over and put a hand on my head.

We went into the parlor, where my grandmother and Mrs. McCloskey joined us a few minutes later. A woman with a shaky hand handed me a cup of milky tea and a slice of cherry and raisin fruitcake. I didn't even nibble it. The smell of sickness was here as well. Father McAtamney arrived and went in to see the old woman, stayed only a minute, and came out and began talking to Uncle Brendan.

"His headmistress tells me he's a smart young fella, though not above the odd trick or two," the priest said, after they'd finished discussing the old woman as if she were already dead.

Granny looked very surprised.

"Yet another Harkin with brains, as well as a few tricks to boot," Father McAtamney said as he winked.

"He says he might go to Africa and cut hair and help in the missions when he's older, Father," said Granny.

"Is it a priest like his Uncle Brendan he wants to be?" Father McAtamney asked. "Sure, he's young enough yet. It'll be a while before you know if there's a call for you. And by then, you'll have discovered the lasses, and you'll want to be out gallivanting with them."

"What's the call?" I asked.

"God calls some boys to be priests when they are older. Just like your uncle here got a call. Isn't that right, Father Brendan?"

"I suppose."

Father McAtamney paused with his teacup before his lips and looked at him for a second.

"How does the call come, Father McAtamney?"

"Into your head."

"Will being an altar boy help me get it?"

In two months, I was to become an altar boy for him. I would get to wear a black soutane and white surplice with lace crosses on its sleeves that my great-great-grandmother had embroidered. Uncle Brendan had worn the same surplice as a boy. Father McAtamney didn't answer my question, instead began talking to

Uncle Brendan about a youth club he wanted to start up in the parish so that the children could learn a bit of Irish dancing and table tennis.

"Father McAtamney says I'll get a call to be a priest, but it won't be for a while yet," I said to my mother as I threw open the kitchen door and barged inside.

She was stacking a milk bottle to cool in the red bucket of cold water inside the larder. "Yes, I'm praying ever so hard you will get a call one day."

"You knew about the call?"

"Yes."

My grandmother and uncles entered.

"The only thing that might stop God calling me is if I dis-cover girls."

Mammy took the teapot and walked up to the stove, but Uncle Brendan told her not to bother because he was "tea'd out."

"You won't be interested in girls or let them stand between you and the call if it comes, will you?" my mother asked.

"No, I won't allow any girl to get in the way of my call."

"Take time to choose what you want to do, Gabriel," said Uncle Brendan, "and remember only you can decide. Being a priest is a lonely life that's full of people."

Mammy's eyes narrowed as she peered at Uncle Brendan, and a strange quiet began, exactly the same kind as had broken out earlier in the car.

CHAPTER SEVEN

O N THE NIGHT OF the station Mass, I insisted on wearing the surplice with the hand-stitched lace crosses because Uncle Brendan had asked me to be his altar boy. As he unpacked the bread and wine, he told me to light two candles already placed on the altar, which was actually our kitchen table that Mammy had taken into the sitting room and draped in her best white linen tablecloth.

"Now, put the bread, water, and wine on the side table and I'll tell you when to bring it to me during Mass," he said.

He watched to make sure I didn't spill it. Martin was allowed to kneel beside me during the Mass, though I warned him he wasn't allowed to touch the little brass bell with the mahogany handle standing between us. Only I was allowed to ring it, and only when Uncle Brendan nodded. Unfortunately, during Mass, I thought he was nodding when he wasn't, and I rang the bell so loudly and often, my mother came up, whacked me on the back of the head, and took it away muttering no one could hear their ears during the consecration.

Afterward, Uncle Brendan walked around the house with a silver bowl and a rattle with tiny holes and blessed every room with Holy Water. The stuff kept splashing on my face every time he sprinkled, and I was obliged to keep blessing myself and say the same prayer over and over until he was finished. Following the blessing, all the women went to the kitchen to prepare the food while the men and Kate the nun sat in the living room.

Martin fingered the embroidery on my surplice. "I know what," he said. "Let's put on a fashion show."

"Good idea."

While Caroline went outside to fetch James and Connor, Martin and I went into my parents' room quickly and searched in my mother's wardrobe for the best things. By the time the others arrived, I'd put on a lilac dress with tiny white sycamore leaves underneath my surplice, and Martin, who'd chosen a black petticoat, was rolling stockings up his thigh. Connor and James refused to wear women's clothes, not even when Caroline begged them to for a laugh, and raked through Daddy's side of the wardrobe for his nicest shirts and ties. Caroline put on a skirt and blouse, and I slipped into a pair of high heel shoes to finish my outfit.

"I'm going to do my face," said Martin. He sat before the vanity and opened my mother's makeup bag. "Are you, Gabriel?"

"Certainly not."

"Suit yourself." He patted face powder on his face and put on lipstick, looked in the mirror as he smacked his lips, and finally kissed at a tissue just like women do. "I still don't feel quite dressed for our show." His eyes darted round the room. "I know what." He went to the chest of drawers, searched about until he found the knickers drawer, and fished out a bra, lowered the petticoat, and put it on. "Strap me in, Gabriel."

After I'd done so, he stuffed two pairs of my father's socks into each cup. "Perfect," he said. He fixed at the petticoat's thin straps as he looked in the mirror. "*Now*, we're talking."

"Jesus, Martin, you are like a woman," said Connor, and he wolf-whistled.

We took turns strutting up and down the hallway with its small yellow, rust, and midnight-blue tiles with bits of white that made them look like marble. As each person walked up and down, the others gave marks out of ten and wrote the scores on sheets of paper. My high heels clicked as I walked, and I stuck out one arm and allowed Mammy's handbag to swing on it, just like I'd seen her do at weddings, but the surplice sleeves kept getting in the way. My right foot slipped out of the shoe as I tried to do a perfect turn at the end of the hall.

"Falling out of a shoe doesn't count," I said.

Martin walked down the hallway in bare feet, sweeping his fingers through his hair and pouting as he held his head at many odd angles. He looked so realistic because of the false tits. James and Connor agreed, but when the marks were counted and he won, Caroline refused to accept the decision.

"I must win because I'm the only real girl here."

"I'm the only one with diddies," Martin shouted. His face colored, and he pointed at the bra angrily. "You didn't even have the gumption to do that, and you call yourself a woman. The judges' decision is final. *I* won."

Caroline's mouth opened, closed just as quickly, and she pushed her ropes of hair behind both ears. "I see . . . very good, Martin. You win hands down." She took off the skirt and patted down her clothes. "Let's have another competition, but first I'll check if the sandwiches are ready."

"I'm famished," said Connor.

My sister left the room.

"That showed *her*," Martin said.

"I think we'd better change," I said.

"Nonsense. We'll do another show," he said, "and we'll inform her she's excluded when she comes back. She'll just complain when I win again." He looked me up and down. "And you should take off that bloody surplice because it looks ridiculous over a dress. That's why I marked you down, severely."

"Why are you rude boys teasing the life out of poor Caroline?" Aunt Peggy called. Her heels clicked faster than mine had done as she came down the hall. "Can't you play nicely together?" Her mouth went goldfish-like. "Your mother's frocks." She turned to James. "What's going on here?"

"We're playing dressing up and Caroline's angry because Martin made tits from socks to make a better woman and won and she didn't."

Caroline smirked from the doorway.

"James, what did you say?"

"Sorry, I meant to say diddies, Aunt Peggy."

"You boys have minds dirtier than public lavatories." She glared at Martin, whose fingers were working furiously behind his back. But I'd tied the knot very tightly and he needed me to pick at it with my teeth. Aunt Peggy grabbed his arm as she ordered us to go to the sitting room. Martin struggled, dug his fingers into her beehive, and a long piece of hair came loose at the top that she didn't notice. It looked like a horse's tail as her head swung back and forth.

"Let me at least get out of this bra, Peggy."

"No."

"You're Gabriel's auntie, not mine, and you have no right to touch me in this manner."

She yanked him powerful hard. We scampered down the hall like lambs, and I could hear the low roar of conversation behind the closed sitting room door as we drew nearer.

"Caroline, open the door and go in," Aunt Peggy said.

As we spilled inside, Kate the nun put her freezing hands to her face. Auntie Celia was the first to laugh, followed by the nun, then Uncle Brendan.

Aunt Peggy let go of Martin, crossed the room to the other door, and called into the kitchen, "Eileen, come in here and be educated for a minute."

"What do you need, Peggy? I'm busy."

"Oh, I think you'll have time. Your son and his cousin are in dresses. Gabriel's wearing your second-best frock, and Martin's in a bra and makeup." Her loose hair drifted back and forth as her head moved. She moved away from the door. "Caroline, it seems Gabriel and his cousin want to be little girls." She snorted. "Shall we send Martin and Gabriel to school in pinafores and bobby socks?"

"Aunt Peggy, this is all a game and I don't wish to wear women's clothes," I said. "We were doing a fashion show."

"So why isn't James in a frock?"

I didn't know the answer, so I looked from adult face to adult face until I came to my father's. His lips were clamped and his eyes drilled into Martin. Mammy looked surprised when she came in, but only for an instant, and then she laughed.

"James *also* knows a very bad word, Eileen," said Aunt Peggy. She shook her head again. "A very bad word." Mammy's eyes followed the swishing horsetail. "You'll have to wash his mouth out with soap. Tell your mammy the bad word."

My mother's smile faded as she looked at James. "What's the bad word?"

"Fart."

The adults laughed.

"I'm forever telling him not to use that word." She smiled again. "James, you must use the word 'wind' instead.

"Oh, no, no, no. No, no. *That* wasn't the bad word, was it?" As Aunt Peggy's head shook, Kate the nun burst out laughing. "James, tell the truth and shame the devil in front of Sister Pious."

He didn't answer. I caught Caroline's eye and bared my teeth.

"Tell your uncle Brendan the disgusting word and he'll ask God to forgive you," Aunt Peggy said.

"I said 'tits.' " James bit his lip as he glanced at me.

Daddy threw back his head laughing from his belly.

"James, where on earth did you hear such a word?" my mother said. "I want the truth now . . . or your uncle Brendan won't ask God to forgive you, and I'll beat you black and blue." She looked at Kate the nun, then at Uncle Brendan. "I'm mortified. He hasn't heard it around here. They've definitely picked it up from that Noel and Jennifer living across the fields." She turned back to James. "One last chance, or you've got a date with a very *big* stick, my boy."

James flinched. "Gabriel told a story with that word in it . . . but he used it only once."

"What was the story about?"

"I don't remember."

"Gabriel, tell your story to Uncle Brendan and Sister Pious right now."

"I can't remember it, either, Mammy."

"I don't believe you, because you've got the memory of a tax-man."

"I don't remember . . . honest to God, I don't."

"Where did you hear the word?"

My mind flashed to the dirty magazines in the loft. "At school."

"Boys-a-boys, they learn quicker and quicker at school these days," Mr. O'Kane said.

All the adults agreed, and the men began to talk amongst themselves again.

"Who said it at school?" When it was something bad, my mother *never* let go. She kept on and on until she got to the bottom of the matter.

"It's so long ago and—"

"You're a sneak, Gabriel." Instantly, she seized my arm, pulled me toward the door, and ordered me to my room.

"Oh, don't be so hard on him, Eileen," said Uncle Brendan. "For goodness' sake, boys of his age are rascals. He did no harm. If that's all the bad words he learns, you'll have little to worry about."

I didn't want him to think of me as a rascal.

"I'm doing it because you're away and don't know him like I know him, Brendan." Mammy's high voice caused the room to quiet, and everyone stared at her. "Well, he has to be shown what's right and wrong . . . and lying is wrong."

Uncle Brendan's eyes moved from her face to the leg of the sofa.

"Oh, I remember now," I said. "It was Henry Lynch. *He* wanted me to say that word in front of the girls. That's why he and his friends pinned me to the ground and tore off my shirt button at the carnival that time."

Mammy was forever saying the Lynchs had filthy mouths, and she wasn't fond of Henry because he caused me trouble. What I'd said was also partly true. Henry had attacked me at the carnival,

though I hadn't been able to tell her he'd taken off my jeans because they were purple, especially since I'd begged her to buy
them in the first place.

"That's not the story you told me at the time. You said Henry
hit you for no good reason. So, you're a liar as well as a sneak.
Well, I'm glad I listened to your father and didn't make a fool of
myself by running to complain to his mother." She pointed her
finger at the door. "To bed, you sneaky liar!"

"I've told you where I heard the word."

"*Bed.*" She pointed at the door again.

Uncle Brendan was still looking at the sofa leg, and Kate the
nun bit into her lip as she watched him. I started out of the room,
making sure I banged the door as I left.

As I lay on the bed, I could hear Caroline and the others talking again. A surge of hot hate rose up inside me. I hated Caroline
and my mother. I hated Aunt Peggy. I hated Henry Lynch. And I
hated my father for stopping Mammy from complaining about
Henry to his mother. My head became tight with hate. I climbed
off the bed, dropped to my knees, and slammed my fists into the
mattress over, and over, and over. When I was finished, the tight-
ness was gone, but I remained on my knees and began to pray.

"Please God, please help me. Please kill Henry Lynch in a car
crash. Please kill him, and I'll say my rosary properly every night.
I'll even think of each mystery like I'm supposed to." I didn't care
if anyone heard me. Finally, I said one Our Father, three Hail
Mary's, and a Glory be to the Father to be sure, just to be one hundred percent sure in case my own made-up prayers didn't reach
His holy ears. After I finished and was getting up, there was a
knock on my door and Caroline came in carrying almost half of
a fruitcake.

"I'm sorry," she said. "I was angry at Martin . . . and I didn't
think James would say the word." She turned down her lips and
her chin crinkled as she gave me the cake. "I didn't mean for you
to get punished."

"Well, I did, didn't I?"

My sister's eyes moved to the cake. "I brought you a big slice."

Fruitcake was my favorite and I knew what she was doing. "So, I see." I pretended to be still angry.

"Shall I get the others to sneak in and see you?"

I nodded.

Caroline walked up to the open door and stopped. "So I'm forgiven, completely?"

"This once, only."

CHAPTER EIGHT

M Y PARENTS HAD GONE to a wedding in Belfast early in the morning and left Jennifer and Noel in charge of us. They were now eleven and due to sit the eleven-plus examination in a few weeks. The eleven-plus was important because, if they passed, Jennifer could go to Saint Veronica's Convent and Noel to Saint Malachy's College. Saint Malachy's was a boys' day school in Desertvale, and Mammy said I would be going there as well because, when it came my turn to sit the exam, she was going to make me practice questions until they were second nature. She also said Noel and Jennifer wouldn't pass because their mother preferred talking about people behind their backs instead of making her children learn, so they'd have to settle for attending the intermediate school. That was fine with Noel. He didn't want to go to grammar school; he wanted to leave school as soon as he was sixteen and join the Merchant Navy, just like his father had done.

"Do you want to see the girls in the dirty magazine again?" Noel asked as Jennifer called James up to the kitchen table to correct his sums. He took a stamp from his pocket, licked it, and pressed it on the envelope.

We were playing make-believe school because that's all Jennifer ever played, and Noel had been writing to his pen pal from County Carlow in the Irish Free State. He had found her address in the pen-friends corner of the *Saint Martin de Porres* magazine. He also hoped to go down there to feel her tits one day. I didn't think it would happen, because she'd asked for his photograph in her last two letters. Noel kept pretending to forget to send it; he told me he needed to have better ones taken, but I knew the honest reason was he was afraid she wouldn't write back after she saw his rotted teeth.

"It's raining fierce," I said, "and Jennifer will wonder why we're going out in it."

"No, she won't. I have to post my letter, and she'll do what I say."

Jennifer had given me geography. It was about different types of rocks, things Jennifer and Noel were supposed to know and I wasn't, even though I was now in the senior side of the school-room also. Noel hadn't mentioned the dirty magazines for a long time because I'd always refused to go to the hay nest when he asked. Now, the idea of looking at a naked girl lying on hay bales seemed more interesting than learning about something I didn't have to know yet, and getting punished by Jennifer. That was another thing about her; nothing was ever done to her satisfaction, because then she could whack me for it.

"Okay, let's go."

Noel informed Jennifer it was his turn to be in charge of me and was taking me with him to the postbox, and then we were going to play other games for a while. As Jennifer peered over James' book, her thick eyebrows moved closer together until a tiny gully formed between them. "He needs to be tested first."

"Afterwards, if Eileen and Harry aren't back from the wedding when we get back."

James said he wanted to go too, but Jennifer said he had two sums wrong and needed to speak to him about them. We left James bawling and ran to the pigsty. Because I was now nine years old and taller, I found it much easier to climb up on the beam. Nor was I frightened of heights anymore.

"Where did you get these magazines, Noel?"

"Somebody gave them to me."

"Who?"

"Somebody . . . stop asking so many damned questions."

Noel opened a magazine, looked through it quickly, and passed it to me. I flicked through the pictures of women taking off their clothes.

"This magazine's best because it has stories and letters from men who write what they'd like to do with women they see walking on the streets."

Noel read a letter from a plumber who described what he'd done to a man's wife while on a house call to mend a leak. After he finished, he spread the magazine on the hay so I could also see another story unfold in pictures. Two dark-haired girls in frilly white knickers and a man in a dark pin-striped suit were sitting on a brass bed. As he turned the pages, the girls' clothes came off until they were nude, then they undressed the man, and finally all of them were in bed together.

As I stared at the pictures, I remembered the beautiful man I'd seen at the beach with the water droplets glittering like diamonds on his healthy tanned legs. I hadn't thought about him since Uncle Brendan's visit yet saw every detail of his face as if it had just been yesterday. I wondered what he was doing at this very moment, right now as I was reading dirty magazines in a stale, dark hay nest.

"That man's giving her a good pumping," I said.

"He's riding her with his cock. That's what your thing's really for." Noel looked at me. "Do you want to see mine?"

"Why?"

"Just to see." he said. Noel unzipped and, as he arched his body slightly and lifted up off the hay and wriggled down his jeans and Y-fronts, I saw the white of his arse glowing in the torchlight. His thing appeared. "Touch and see what happens to it."

"What happens?"

"Touch."

I laid my hand on it and it began to grow. The growing stiffness surprised me and I pulled my hand away. Noel began to stroke it fast.

"Take off your clothes."

"No way. I don't want to, Noel."

"*Do* as I say."

"No."

"Look, it's just to compare," he said more softly. "Come on . . . just for me."

87

As I did, Noel undressed as well.

"I want you to do to me what the woman is doing to the man in the photo, Gabriel."

"I don't want to do that."

"I'll do it to you next, and then you'll see how nice it is. That's why other boys do it to one another. It's just so good."

Noel lay back and placed his hands under his head. The rain crashed upon the zinc like a hundred beating drums in the darkness. Way back in one corner, a steady stream of drops leaked through the roof and fell into something hollow. Slowly, I moved my lips closer and closer until they touched his thing.

"That's it, Gabriel."

His voice was croaky. As he raised his upper body to watch, I got a whiff of his sweaty underarms and began to heave. Quickly, I pulled my face away, leaned over the edge of the nest, vomited.

"What's the matter with you?"

"I want to go home." I sat up and shivered. The hot sourness in my nose and throat stung, my eyes watered, and the smell of my sick made me want to vomit again.

"No. Keep doing me."

"I'm shivering. I *want* to go home and do Jennifer's test."

"Keep doing me."

"You didn't wash under your arms and you stink and that's what made me sick."

Noel sprang up as if stung by a wasp. "Put on your clothes and let's go. We'll come back another time and I'll teach you to play the doctors and nurses game instead. Would you prefer to do that?"

"What is it?"

"You take off your clothes and I'll be the doctor and examine you, then you do the same to me. Loads of boys play that game as well. Would you like to play that?"

"Yes, I'll do that game."

"But this is a secret between us. You must keep it as much of a secret as the magazines." He stared at me fiercely. "If you tell, I'll have a word with Henry Lynch, and then *both* of us will gang up on you."

As Mammy had predicted, Noel and Jennifer failed their examination and had to go to the intermediate school where the pupils wore gorgeous burgundy blazers. After Noel did the other kind of examination on me, I found I liked it very much and began to play doctors and nurses every time he asked. The game always began with a look at the magazines and, as the months passed, Noel got me to do new things to him. After I'd done him, he always did the same to me so we'd be even. I didn't vomit anymore either, because Noel always washed and his skin smelled of fresh soap now.

The nasty part of our game was thinking about Noel's rotten teeth touching me there, and the beautiful part was the lovely pains. I enjoyed the lovely pains. They came after Noel had been playing with my thing for a while. The pains were powerful strong and not like any other pain I'd ever had. They built up slowly inside until they took over and I felt like a prisoner in my own body. The lovely pains overcame all my thoughts, made me forget about everything, though I did not want Noel to go on touching me after they'd ended. Then, my thing would be sore and not sore at the same time. That's the best way I can explain it: sore and not sore at the same time. Other feelings would also come: feelings which made me whip my clothes on, make excuses, and leave, because I needed to get away from Noel. I couldn't bring myself to talk to him about these lovely pains. All I knew was I enjoyed them, couldn't understand why I was having them, or why they changed quickly into bad feelings which made me need to leave until the next time.

Rain had been falling for two days and the river was black and flowing angrily. It had also burst its banks in low places. Many of the fields were waterlogged, and cows stood sadly in matted groups underneath dripping branches, their shins deep in mud, steam spewing from their nostrils like smoke.

The chugging snorts of the old generator at the back of our house made me very nervous. Mammy was worried rain would pour through the leaking roof and mix with the diesel and snuff it out. Sometimes, the lights flickered and solid black lines rolled up the TV screen. Each time it happened, my mother leaped from her chair and cursed Daddy because he hadn't fixed the leak as she began lighting two pearly candles she had waiting on the windowsill.

My sister, brother, and I hated the heavy rain and spluttering engine because it led to arguments after Daddy lost his temper. Nuala was three, didn't understand, and just watched them with huge eyes. At such times I wished I could fix leaks, because they weren't massive yet the arguments were. They always reached a point where Mammy wanted away from the wilderness. That's what she called Knockburn. The wilderness. She'd threaten to take us away from it to live in a town where there was proper electricity and flush toilets, and that sort of talk would make my father even angrier until he'd curse furiously and tell her to clear the fuck away with the bunch of us.

Just after the lights had flickered really badly and Mammy was rising again, someone banged on the front door. Though only five-thirty in the evening, it was pitch-dark outside.

"Who the hell can that be in this weather?" Daddy said as he rose.

"Maybe somebody come to fix the roof," my mother said. She turned to me. "Gabriel, go and see who it is, because I'm in no mood for company. If it's visitors, come in quickly and tell me so I can clear off to my bedroom."

Mr. O'Kane stood at the door as sheets of rain swept past the overhead lamp like the fast-turning pages of a book, the streaky drops changing to liquid silver as they caught in the light. The tiny veins in his cheeks were turned blue-black because of the driving wind, and water dripped like a leaking faucet from the tip of his nose.

"Harry, the Lynch boys went fishing after school and they haven't come home and the mother's beside herself with worry," he said, his voice out of breath as he reached the end. He took a large gulp of air. "I've never seen the likes of the river since I was your lad's age." He nodded in my direction. "We've found a fishing rod, but there's no sign of them. They've already got people combing the banks, but more are needed."

"Fetch my boots and bring them to me in the living room, Gabriel."

"May they be spared and found safe," Mammy said. She paused and watched my father squeeze one foot into a Wellington. "Harry, be careful at the river because we don't need you to get drowned."

I'd been saying my Henry prayers for almost a year now and wanted them immediately undone. I really tried to avoid Henry, but it wasn't possible; the school playground was small, and I'd see him at concerts and other Knockburn events, also. But he didn't annoy me every single day. Some mornings his seat would be empty, and I'd wait sizzling with electricity for fifteen minutes after the bell rang and class began. No one was ever later than fifteen minutes to school, and I'd watch the clock until the big hand passed the quarter, and if he hadn't come by then, I could relax. There were also days when he was at school and left me alone, even if those days were just as filled with worry because I didn't know if he wasn't going to pick on me. Every time I saw him come toward me, my stomach turned into a jumble of living knots. I'd learned not to look him in the eyes when he came at me. The thing was to stand still and stare at his chest until he finished prodding and pushing me about; standing still made me feel ashamed because I knew I was afraid of him. But, later, in the quiet of my bed, I was king as I recited my Henry prayers.

Now, that it might have happened, I realized I didn't want it to happen. I didn't want anyone to die. Wanting Henry dead had been a way of releasing my anger. Also, I had only one more year of primary school to go and then Henry would be history, because I'd pass my exam and go to grammar school where everything would be different. Henry wasn't smart, he was also lazy, and was bound to fail. He'd end up going to the intermediate school, and I'd be at Saint Malachy's with no more fears, surrounded by boys who really liked me.

I felt sweaty cold now. I wanted my Henry prayers undone. My heart leaped at the very thought of the word "dead." I tried to swallow, but couldn't. As I watched my father put on his anorak, my mind screamed to God, begging Him not to have listened, begging Him to spare Henry and his brother. After Daddy left, my mother suggested we say another rosary. I fell to my knees.

"We'll say the sorrowful mysteries on account of poor Henry and his brother, Gerald."

"I don't want to say another rosary," Caroline said. "We've said one already, so we'll just tell God quickly that that rosary was for Henry. He'll know, because they were already in the river at the time we were saying it."

"Shut your mouth, Caroline," I said. Her thinking could be dumb at times. "Don't you want them to find him alive?"

Mammy looked at me as she blessed herself. I prayed harder than I'd ever prayed. I didn't allow my mind to wander as I concentrated on Jesus' agony in the garden and His Crucifixion. I even said the decade my father would have said if he'd been present. Afterward, we waited for two hours, but Daddy didn't come home. Mother sent me to bed. I couldn't sleep. I kept tossing and thinking of Henry in the swirling water, the black-eyed trout gaping, gaping like they'd done when we took them from the river after my cousins and I had poisoned them. I prayed until the wheels of a car passed over the cattle grid at the main gate and then raced to the living room.

"You didn't hate Henry as much as you led me to believe, did you?" As Mammy poked the fire, warm, golden flames sprang up and began to dance.

I searched my father's eyes as he entered.

"They're gone," he said.

"It can't be so." Mammy dropped the poker and it continued

to rattle on the tiles as she sank into her chair. "Tragedies don't happen in Knockburn."

A silence arose, broken only by the sucking noise of trapped water as my father shuffled out of his Wellingtons, his wrinkled trouser bottoms soaked black when they appeared.

"That means the funerals will be on Friday," she said. "I feel so sorry for that poor woman. A drunk for a husband, not a penny to bless herself with, and now a catastrophe to deal with."

I heard, but my brain couldn't take it in. Henry was dead. He was dead in real life. Dead meant no tomorrow. Dead. Dead meant polished coffins with shiny handles that no one wanted. It meant heavy clay and darkness. His coffin was made and lay waiting for him. *Dead.* It had been made while he'd eaten his breakfast. It had been made and lain waiting while he'd read his composition this afternoon in class.

"Where did they find the bodies?" said Mammy.

"They found the wee boy . . . the one who's at school with Gabriel—"

"Henry," Mammy said.

"Aye, they found his body in a very deep part of the river with his brother on top of him."

His body. Daddy had said "his body." Henry was no longer a person. He was his body. Henry and his body had been one and were now separated.

"The water had carried him under, and his sweater was badly snagged in the open door of an old car wreck. I think the brother must have been trying to save him and got exhausted and was overcome." Another short silence started up. "They've taken the bodies to the morgue."

"Was he wearing a red sweater with dogs on it, Daddy?"

"Aye, it was red."

My mother looked puzzled. I saw every Labrador on his sweater. It was Henry's favorite sweater, though it was too small for him now. He'd stretched it until it was thin and very wide at the bottom.

"Thank God it's none of our children," Mammy said.

"I *don't* want Henry to be dead!"

Mammy jumped and clutched her chest.

"He can't be dead. He was at school today . . . and his coffin can't be made yet."

"God wanted Henry and Gerald to come home," she said.

"No, that's not so. It's me. *I* prayed to God He'd take Henry in a car crash, but He drowned him instead. God listened. *That's* why he's dead. He's dead because of my Henry prayers."

The curls of Mammy's auburn hair were loose because she hadn't put rollers in her hair for a few days, her eyes had little red lines in their whites, and she looked old. *Dead.* I stared at Mammy's eyes, saw how the jagged red lines looked like tiny forks of lightning crossing the whites. *Dead. Henry was dead. He was his body. He was no longer a person. Dead.*

"It's not your fault," she said. "God doesn't grant requests like that. He doesn't listen to boys who ask such things."

"How do you know?"

"He knows because boys and girls are always asking for things like that." She nodded at my father. "Tell him that's the case, Harry."

"That's so. Henry had a great big smile on his face when we found him. It was terrific. That definitely means he was happy to go home."

Because Henry had been in my class, Mammy said I had to go to the wake even though I was young. Henry's parents didn't own their home like we did. They rented a council house and paid monthly rent to the government. The walls didn't even have wallpaper. They were painted pale blue, the net curtains were smoky dirty, and there wasn't a picture, not even one of the Sacred Heart or the Virgin Mary.

The grown-ups were sitting with long faces in the living room. Old and young men sat together, some had flat caps with grimy peaks perched on their knees, and everyone spoke in low voices as the women served tea and sandwiches, or passed round silver trays filled with cigarettes. The air was heavy with sadness on account of Henry and Gerald having died so young.

Their bodies were in a bedroom. As I approached, my heart started beating so fast, I thought it was going to burst from my chest. Sweat broke out all over my body and my hands felt clammy. Two gleaming coffins lay on the twin beds, a white one with bronze handles for Henry and a brown one with silver handles for his brother because he was almost a man. A thick yellow candle burned on a table between the beds. Its golden flame flickered back and forth in a draft caused by people as they walked about and peered at the bodies. Mr. and Mrs. Lynch were sitting in rickety chairs between the beds.

"Sorry for your troubles," said my father. He shook Mrs. Lynch's hand and then her husband's.

"Harry, my men have been taken from me," said Mrs. Lynch in a voice above a whisper.

"It's God's will, but it's hard," Mr. Lynch said. His fingers were orange-brown from smoking, a thing he shouldn't be doing because he was poor and on the dole.

Mrs. Lynch was dressed in a black frock and stockings, her eyes swollen with dark rings around them, and her face and hands were as white as Henry's coffin lid propped beside his brother's against a wall. Soon, that lid would be wet and mucky, and worms would crawl over it.

"Come and have a last look at your wee schoolfriend," Mrs. Lynch said.

"Sorry for your trouble, Mrs. Lynch."

I offered my hand, but she didn't take it. The coffin was lined in pale yellow frilly cloth and looked cozy cold. Henry's face was smooth but paler than I remembered, the hair still frizzy and away from his shut eyes, and he was dressed in clothing that was also pale yellow. A white, glossy-backed Holy Communion book had been tucked beneath his clasped hands, and his rosary beads wound like a rope between his joined fingers. I stared at his fingers, at the hangnails and lines of their skin, surprised that his fingernails had

95

been cleaned. I stared and couldn't believe they were the same hateful fingers that had poked, tightened to fists, and smacked me. Nor was Henry smiling as my father had said. His lips were thin and closed tightly, and a piece of cotton wool peeped from one shiny nostril. What's cotton wool doing in his nose? I wondered. Had drowning made his nose bleed? Had he bled in the morgue? His eyebrows were still dark and curly. I wondered why I hadn't before noticed the very thin scar running through his right eyebrow.

I could not take my eyes off Henry's death face that was the same yet not the same. Henry was not a person anymore. He was his body. I looked at the face, spotted a mole I'd never seen before either, and I wondered what he'd say if he saw me looking so closely. He was dead, I was looking at his face, and he'd never know. I was looking at Henry's death face, at the little white scar in his eyebrow he'd have known about, and the cotton wool stuck in his nostril he wouldn't. Henry would never know what his last face looked like. Suddenly, I felt an urge to reach inside and touch his stilled fingers. I grasped the one he'd jabbed my chest with so often, but it was cold, chicken feet–like to the touch, and I whipped out my hand.

"Will you remember Henry in your prayers?" Mrs. Lynch said.

I didn't speak.

"Will you miss your little friend?"

Again, I didn't speak.

"Gabriel, will you never forget your friend?"

My father coughed twice, and narrowed his eyes when I looked up at him.

"I won't, Mrs. Lynch."

CHAPTER NINE

ONE SATURDAY AFTERNOON, IT felt like Henry had reached out from his grave to attack me one last time. His death created a vacancy in the Knockburn under-twelve Gaelic football team, it was late in the season, and the team was doing well in their league. The boys were driven to their games in an old dented minibus, and James was first to see it pass through our main gate. He ran into the kitchen to tell our father that Ciaran Bradley, the team manager, was walking to the door.

"Hiya, Harry," Ciaran said to Daddy. He entered without knocking. "I've just picked up Fergal because we have a game at three o'clock and I'm in a tight jam. I wonder if you'd see your way to letting your eldest boy act as a substitute for us."

"This one's got two left feet and can't play football," said Mammy.

Ciaran had the face shape of a triangle with a broad, bulging forehead and the pointiest chin I'd ever seen. He always wore the same moss green sports coat that rode up at the back because he carried so much loose change in its front pockets.

"A bit of running about will be good for the boy," Ciaran said. He nodded at me as if he were my best friend.

My father ran his fingers slowly through one side of his hair.

"To tell you the God's truth, Harry and Eileen, if you could let him come, I'd be eternally grateful, like. We have two players off sick, and the twin Kellys, our real substitutes, are having extra tuition on account of they're not doing so good on their 11-plus tests. So I'm in a tight jam like, because I can't find anybody else at such short notice."

"I don't have any football shoes, do I, Mammy?"

"We'll get you kitted out with shoes, shorts, and a sweater, Gabriel," Ciaran said.

"Get your bag," said Daddy.

"I've also got to work for my eleven-plus just like the twin Kellys."

"Get your things and out you go to the bus," he said. "You need toughening up and a bit of rough fun will do the very job."

Matters had now gone beyond the point where huffing could help. I fetched my dusty sports bag from the wardrobe and wiped it off, not that I needed to take it because I'd nothing to put into it. As I walked toward the minibus, the boys peered like hens examining earth they'd just raked for insects.

"I'm glad you could come," said Fergal. "You'll be able to say you helped us win the cup if we get to the finals."

The boys were already kitted out in black, white, and gold Knockburn jerseys. Phelem Welsh was sitting next to Fergal, so I sat beside stuttering Anthony. They were very civil and, after a few minutes of teasing me good-naturedly, forgot I was among them and started discussing football tactics.

Throughout the journey, I remained quiet and stared into the passing fields. It was as if the boys were talking from a great distance and I were a spectator. My mind flipped between the moment when I might have to step onto the field and my father's last remark. Thinking of that helped lessen my fear. It made me angry. My father just didn't know or understand me.

It was as if a heavy curtain had suddenly parted and I saw how differently he treated James and me. He treated Caroline far better too, though she was a girl and fathers had a soft spot for daughters. But James was a boy, yet it was me who had to do all the hard work about the house. In winter, I had to split logs that were too thick with a hatchet whose handle was too long. He made me weed lawn borders in summer and cut grass with a push mower that wouldn't cut lard because he wouldn't sharpen it, just like he never mended the generator shed roof. I had to wash his car in freezing weather, using water so icy, my hands turned red and cold. And not once did he say, "Well done, Gabriel," when I'd finished. James was now almost seven, the very age I'd been when he'd first given me these jobs, yet he didn't order him to help me. Nor was my brother scolded when he refused.

The football game was horrid, every bit as horrid as I thought it would be. Sitting beside Ciaran on a damp bench in a borrowed Knockburn jersey that smelled of stale sweat, I watched the boys race like clowns up the field after a sodden leather ball. Now and again, as they reached the opposing team's goal, Ciaran would leap off the bench and urge one or other of the players to sink it into the net for a goal, or over the H bar for a point.

Twenty minutes into the second half, Ciaran decided to try me out because they were winning by such a wide margin. The ball felt cold and slick as it mashed into my chest. I seized it with my hands but, before I could decide what to do with it, a player from the other side smacked hard into my shoulder, tripped me, and tore the oily thing from me as I tumbled to the grass. The ball passed quickly up the field from player to player and was finally lobbed into our goalmouth. Even though we were winning, two of my teammates shook their fists and shouted curses at me.

It didn't help that Ciaran was watching my every move. I felt I had to keep running about like a frisky dog even when the ball was nowhere around, otherwise he'd think I was just plain lazy. His eyes watched as I fumbled my hand-to-toe moves when I did have the ball, and it would never go in the direction I aimed when I kicked. It spun off to the side or, much worse, landed in the hands of a player from the other side. The piercing shriek of the referee's final whistle was sweet music, and I walked off the field determined never to be on one again.

"That wasn't half bad, Gabriel," Ciaran said, his downward-pointed front pockets jingling as he ran up to me. "You're a nifty wee runner and we'll work on the kicking and ball handling skills."

"If he knew how to kick straight, it would help," Phelem Walsh said. "He's got two left feet, hasn't he, Fergal?"

"That's enough, Phelem," said Fergal. "He's never played real football before, and you need to give him a chance."

Phelem looked hurt, and I was happy he was hurt. I was also happy because it was the first time Fergal had stood up for me, even though it was only because Henry was now dead.

The following Saturday, I waited by the window in the living room until I caught sight of the minibus coming up the road and then dashed out and went to the hay nest in the pigsty. I pulled down my pants and tried to read one of Noel's magazines, but I couldn't concentrate. For what seemed like hours, my father, James, and even Nuala called out for me. James called out my name once from nearby the curved climbing tree. I feared he'd come and look in the pigsty, but he didn't, because I next heard him shout to Daddy that I wasn't in the tree as he ran back toward the house again. After the calling stopped, I waited five minutes more in the dark quietness that was interrupted only by the throaty chirps of a curlew in the far-off bog.

"Where the hell were you?" my father said, as soon as I walked into the house. "You've embarrassed your mother and me. You've embarrassed the hell out of all of us. I was so badly done, I offered James, but Ciaran said he's too young."

"You just *don't* get it. You *don't* understand me."

"Caroline, fetch me the fucking sally rod. I'm not going to stand idle while the likes of this answers me back." His eyes flashed like headlights turned on high beam.

As the last one had been broken over James' arse the week before, he sent Caroline to the hedge to pluck a fresh one. I waited with Mammy and him in a nasty silence. It was one of those nasty silences you never want to end because you know something much worse is coming. I kept playing the scene about to take place as I looked over at my mother and tried to reach deep into her eyes, but she looked everywhere about the room except in my direction.

A few minutes later, Caroline arrived holding the thickest brute of a sally rod I'd ever seen. It was thumb thick. I looked at it, then at her. Mammy leaped to her feet, called her a wicked hussy, and ordered her to fetch a proper sally or she'd also get beaten.

My father thrashed me soundly. He thrashed for so long, my mother jumped up and grabbed his arm as he and I spun about the room. Still, he wouldn't stop. He continued thrashing and cursing and thrashing while she accused him of being possessed. I screamed above the din. My legs, lower back, and arse had purply streaks after he'd finished, and I hated him. Every time my trousers touched raw skin, I hated him.

Studying in earnest for my eleven-plus exam started after the summer holidays because I was now in my final year at primary school. I was to sit it in November at age ten on account of the fact I'd first started school a year earlier than everyone else. Saint Malachy's was an excellent college, and Cousin Martin was now a pupil there.

Every afternoon, Mammy sat me at the kitchen table and made me answer questions from hundreds of mock tests within a limited period of time so that I'd be used to the pressure on the day of the real exam. After each mock test, she marked my work and explained the mistakes I'd made. Questions about train distances traveled at certain speeds tormented me because I could never calculate the correct answer. I was just no good at them.

"I want you to take the rest of the day off," Mammy said one afternoon after a very bad score. "You're not getting one bit better at the train questions. You need some time off to clear your head. Your father and James are about to leave for Larne. Go with them."

"Let's do another type of question instead."

"No, it'll do you good to spend time with your father and James in the lorry."

The trip to Larne was long and uncomfortable. We drove for miles along narrow country roads that wound through fog-covered mountains, only stopping once at a lorry driver's café with filthy toilets and which stank of engine oil just like my father's lorry cabin. During the trip, I sat on top of a hard, plastic hump dividing the driver and passenger's seat and watched the great wipers sweep across the greasy windscreen as the throb of the engine beneath vibrated my arse. The interior of the cabin disgusted me with its cream-colored, grimy ceiling and floor of oil-smeared spanners and blackened rags, all of which James didn't seem to mind. Equally nasty were the scratched dials and dust-caked dashboard that I was forced to lay my hands upon each time my father braked sharply. I wondered why he made me wash his car in all kinds of weather yet couldn't clean his own lorry. The fog lifted as we reached the flatlands surrounding Larne, but the views of the faraway harbor looked miserable: the water was life-less gray, the ferries crossing to Scotland dull and tiny.

James adored Daddy and was very interested in the lorry because he asked questions till I wanted to scream at him to stop. His contentment widened the distance between my father and me. My father and I were very different people. He never asked about my schoolwork or the books I read. I never asked about his work. With James, he talked and laughed in an adult way about diggers and English and Irish football teams. As I listened above the throaty roar of the engine, I felt sad I couldn't be more like my brother. I had once tried to talk to my father about these things, but my interest wasn't there. My knowledge of trucks wasn't deep, and it showed because our conversations had always stopped very quickly.

Of course, my father didn't know I felt like this. He would tease me about my not wanting to drive machines. He'd say things that were funny and hurtful at the same time. "Every house has to have a gentleman who doesn't like getting his hands dirty so you're ours," he said often, and I'd laugh and hurt all at once. And ever since the thrashing, I felt so angry inside. I felt so angry he didn't try to understand me. I just couldn't make the feeling go away.

While our father went into the administration offices to sign papers for the new diggers he'd come to collect, James and I walked past a long row of parked ships. Two had strange names that we couldn't pronounce, so I asked a man and he said they were Soviet commie ships. The dark green water smelled of stale pee, and a greasy film of slime, cardboard, and small planks floated between the ships. An old man sat smoking a pipe at the end of a jetty, the tip of his long fishing rod hovering just inches above the water. Out of the distant grayness, a ship loaded with blue and rust-red metal containers sailed toward the harbor mouth.

"Maybe the digger Daddy's picking up is in one of those containers," James said.

"It probably arrived yesterday."

I paused and looked at my brother. He was shorter than I had been when I was seven, yet was so much more confident. James was popular with his friends, they chose him to captain his football team at school, and he was also kind. Only when he was very angry with me did he tease me about not doing things boys were supposed to do.

"James, why do you think we do so many things differently? I don't like doing the things you like, and yet you play football *and* enjoy reading adventure books. And why is it, I always want to play the Indian when we play Cowboys and Indians, even when I know they always lose in the films?"

James threw a stone into the water and counted the number of skims it made. "They don't lose when we play because you're far stronger than me."

He picked up another smooth stone, passed it from palm to palm for a moment, and fitted it between his thumb and finger. The ship was nearer now, and water lapped against the pilings. James stooped and hurled the stone. It popped in and out of the water four times, hopped over a floating piece of wood even. Skimming was something we both enjoyed, so I searched about and found three flat stones. We skimmed, and James won because I couldn't get one to bounce more than three times.

"Hey boys, you're scaring away my bloody dinner," the old man shouted. "Get away o' that." He spat into the water and began to rise.

We ran back to the lorry, where Daddy had already loaded

one bright yellow digger with a white roof and scarlet wheels onto the flatbed and was driving another up the skids. The digger's cheerful colors stood out against the dirty tarmac, dull brown harbor buildings, and the two rusty commie ships. After we'd climbed into the cabin, James slid into the driver's seat, grabbed hold of the huge steering wheel, and began to make truck sounds as he pretended to drive us home. When my father had finished securing the last digger, he came and stood beside the cabin door while he talked to the harbor clerk.

After ten minutes, anger started up inside me again. I burned and wondered how my father could be so selfish as to make us wait like this. Winding down the window, I listened, but already knew he would be telling silly stories about people and things that had nothing to do with diggers, things that meant nothing to the clerk. He looked bored, kept looking toward the office every few moments, but Daddy kept nudging his arm as if the two were best friends. This habit of his annoyed me. I simply couldn't understand why he had to be nudging strangers while talking, or why he had to talk a pile of shite with them in the first place.

"We have to be home soon because Mammy wants to take me shopping for new shoes," I shouted down to him. I struggled to hide my burning. "Let's go."

He looked up for a second before turning back to the man who was glancing at his watch now. "These young ones have no patience," said my father. "I'll 'new shoes' you."

"I have to be getting back to work myself," the clerk said. "Take care an' look after yourself until I see you next time."

"Gabriel, you see that wee man I was talking to just now," Daddy said, after he'd climbed into the cab and started the engine. He curled the tip of his tongue over his upper lip while he turned the steering wheel, glancing often in the long side mirrors and out the front window as he reversed. He'd always start a sentence like this and then go quiet when he was doing something tricky, keeping a person guessing until he'd finished the job, yet another habit of his that drove me crazy.

"What about him?" I said. Again, I stopped my voice from rising. I hated having to dig an answer out of him, but that's what was expected.

"Aye, you see that wee man, there." The tongue curled again. "Well, that wee man would buy and sell his mother. He's also as black as tar. Oh, Jasus, aye, black as tar. That wee man would shoot a Catholic between the eyes as quick as he would look at him. You can't trust the Protestants."

He didn't like the man because he was a Protestant who would shoot a Catholic between the eyes, yet would talk rivers of shite with him.

"*Why* did you talk to him so long, then?"

Politics was very big in our house now because the Catholics were marching in the streets to complain that Protestants were discriminating against us in housing and government jobs. We were also demanding the right to vote. James picked up on my sharpness and gave me a "shut up" look.

"I have to speak civil to the Protestants because I have to do business with them. You'll find that out when you're working. Oh, Jasus, aye, my boy. You have to be civil to them, because they have all the power. That wee man was only civil because I work for a Protestant firm and he thinks I'm a Protestant. He thinks it's safe to talk to me. These Larne boys are a black crowd and wouldn't allow the likes of you and me to live in their town. Jasus, no, they'd burn us out . . . and shoot us in the back as we ran away." He laughed. "Oh, the dirty Protestants have their day of reckoning coming and I can't wait to see it. We're marching in the streets to get the vote and sit in the government. And if they don't let us sit, well then, sons of mine, the IRA will start a civil war and shoot the whole lot of them."

Daddy liked only a few Protestants. He hated Paisley, one of the Protestant leaders, most of all.

"But killing Protestants is wrong," I said. "You told me once, I wasn't to pray for anyone to die. You told me it was wrong. Isn't shooting a Protestant dead just as wrong?"

He didn't answer and started whistling "On Top of Old Smokey," instead.

"Do you like sailing about with your daddy?" he asked after a bit. "I know James does, but do you?"

My father was like that. He always moved to another subject when he didn't want to answer. He did it every time Mammy asked him a question he didn't like. She said that was exactly how he tried to change a subject.

The taking of my eleven-plus was exciting and panicky. Boys and girls sat two seats apart from one another and we were not allowed to turn over the exam paper until told to begin. We were told at nine o'clock exactly and, after the page rustlings stopped, the room became cough quiet. Despite hours and hours of mock tests, my hands shook. The clock's ticks sounded fast and loud, fast and loud. I looked at Fergal sitting a row in front of me and saw he was already writing. A bolt of panic slammed into my body, and I charged through the first question, desperate to answer it even before I'd read it fully. I read "Cow is to herd as sheep is to . . ." Two of the choices were "flock" and "frock." I put a cross in a box and moved on to the next question.

What I'd done didn't hit me until after the exam was over and people talked about the questions and one girl joked about the ridiculous "frock" choice. The word circled and circled in my brain, and I was sure I remembered putting the cross in the box beside it. I couldn't believe I'd been so stupid. Beside myself with fear that I'd done the same thing with a lot of other questions, I hurtled down the corridor to the headmistress's room and told her what I thought I'd done.

To my surprise, she just laughed and said it was just a bit of nerves and everyone made a mistake or two under pressure. She added I was one of the boys whom she expected to "pass with fly-ing colors." My mother wasn't so happy and said I'd be a sorry boy if Fergal got a fat envelope in the mail and I got a thin one when the results came out. (A fat envelope from the Education Board meant you'd passed, you didn't even have to open it, because it was crammed full of grant information, travel pass applications, and other stuff about grammar school.)

On the Saturday in February when the Education Board sent the results, our bandy-legged, Protestant postman walked up the garden path clutching a bunch of envelopes of all sizes and thicknesses. Convinced she saw a small brown envelope in his hands and unable to bear it, Mammy ordered Caroline to open all the letters as she fled to her bedroom and slammed the door. The first fat envelope was *The Far East*, Mammy's mission magazine, the next her new family allowance booklet, and the third bore the Education Board's red stamp.

Seizing the envelope from my sister, I tore it open and took out a bundle of pink, pale green, and white application forms. I ran to my mother's room where she was sitting, fingers stuffed in her ears, on the edge of the bed. Her eyes searched mine, and I looked at the floor.

"Jesus, what will you do now? You've failed. You've failed, and I thought you'd get into grammar school like Brendan and go on to be a priest." She paced between the bed and vanity twice before stopping. "What will he think of you, him that was told you're so brainy?" Her voice was now shriller than a barn cat's at night. "I just knew you'd failed as soon as you came home and told me you'd got that frock and flock question wrong. You're stupid, that's what you are. Well, there's nothing for it now. It's off you go to intermediate school with Noel and Jennifer and the rest of the failures."

Unable to keep a straight face, I told her the truth.

"You cheeky nab." She touched near her heart and sat on the bed again. "You almost gave me a heart attack." She reached out for the forms. "All my novenas have been answered. You're a good boy, Gabriel. I knew you had the brains." She glanced at Caroline. "And you, my lady, *you'll* have to follow your brother's lead and pass when your turn comes." She paused as she riffled through the sheaf. "Did you ask the postman what thickness of envelope he had for Fergal?"

"I did, but he said it wouldn't be right to say," said Caroline.

Mammy's lips thinned. "That's one bad man. Sure it's as little as he could have done to tell a body whether it was fat or thin."

As it turned out, Fergal and Cousin Connor passed, too. My father was proud and told everyone who visited that I was going to grammar school. It was great to hear him boast. It was so great, I forgave him everything and promised myself never to be angry with him again. Uncle Brendan wrote after he learned the news, saying in the letter he was proud of me and inquiring if I still wanted to be a hairdresser like I'd told him once. He added a "ha ha ha" at the end of the question. That made me laugh, and I wondered why the hell I'd ever thought to be a hairdresser in the first place.

Granny Harkin, who always said "plus-eleven" instead of "eleven-plus" no matter how many times I corrected her, slipped me five pounds, but my mother took it from me as soon as she left.

"We'll use that to buy some of your uniform."

She allowed me to keep the ten shillings Granny Neeson gave me, an amount that made her furious on account of the fact my grandmother had pots of money, that I was the first grandchild to pass the exam, and Granny Harkin had given me more. She complained about it to Aunt Peggy, who nodded but said nothing until she got me alone, and then she gave me nothing but advice about how best to study hard.

The last few weeks of August were a whirl of activity as I prepared for Saint Malachy's. Because entry was automatic upon passing the exam, the school didn't interview me, and my first contact came by way of a welcome letter from the headmaster in which he included a copy of the school rules. My mother was not happy to read she had to buy me two pairs of sneakers: a pair for sports, and another for wearing in class because outdoor shoe soles scuffed the polished floor tiles.

We visited the outfitters who supplied the uniforms. The assistant was as polished as his dark wood counter at selling clothing, but Mammy knew all his tricks. He watched her face as he stated the prices, offered other choices when she shook her head and pretended she'd buy the shirts and charcoal pants at a factory shop, and was full of false praise when I tried on the cheapest type of permitted blazer. It was nasty, rough as a cornmeal sack, and had no slits at the back like Martin's.

"I don't think it will do," I said. "Connor's and Fergal's have slits."

"You can get one with panels next time," said the shop assistant. He emitted a horselike whinny as he winked at my mother.

"You're going there to learn, *not* for a fashion parade," Mammy said.

That wasn't exactly true, because Martin, now in his second year, had told me I must on all accounts get pants with flared bottoms. He'd told me that he and his friends were the school's trendsetters, and he'd persuaded Auntie Celia to buy him a pair with fifteen-inch flares.

"What can Celia be thinking?" Mammy said, after I fished out a pair of the fifteen-inch ones from the rack and held them up for her to examine. "They look like curtains . . . and he'll be a clown with those stumpy, wee legs of his."

Things grew even worse when the assistant informed her next that two items she was inspecting, a gorgeous black and royal blue scarf with a thin white stripe and a peaked blue cap, weren't compulsory attire.

Other things occurred as a result of my having passed the exam that I didn't expect. I was allowed to wear long trousers anytime I chose, even during the hot days. My mother told me she would no longer barge into the kitchen when I was sitting in the tin bath on Saturday wash nights. Now I was starting grammar school, she began treating me as if I were already eleven. Neighbors treated me differently, too. They didn't just think I was brainy; they knew it. I had passed a government exam. *That* was the proof. Old people told me I was definitely as brainy as my uncle Brendan, that I'd go just as far if I kept on the straight and narrow like him, that I just had to follow Uncle's example and my life would be "charmed" like his.

PART TWO

September 1970 — October 1978

CHAPTER TEN

I SAW THE BEAUTIFUL GRAY stucco building with its churchlike windows, green copper roof, and massive brass cross rising into the early morning sky as I got off the bus. Adjacent to it was another double-story structure of salmon-colored brick with moss-green trimmed windows and a flat roof that looked far too modern. Attached to the highest gable of the older building was the Saint Malachy's crest, a white bird with outstretched wings symbolizing the Holy Ghost hovering above an open book containing Latin words, the same crest as the one sewn on the breast pocket of my blazer. The other new pupils and I followed the older boys along the long driveway flanked by slender arborvitae, behind which were three tennis courts on one side and a football field with H posts on the other.

"Holy Moses, old Quackers is already here," said Pearse, a fifteen-year-old boy walking with his friend just ahead of Fergal and me.

Quakers was the nickname of Father Rafferty, the headmaster, and I could see an orange-red car parked beside the glass entrance doors.

"Why's he called Quackers?" asked Fergal.

Pearse threw back his head slightly, his thick hair kinking as its ends caught inside the dandruff-flaked collar of his blazer, and laughed. "Because he's a priest and crazy. He's crazy about ancient Greek, crazy about religion, crazy about using his tickler."

"Tickler?" I said.

"His long strap," said Pearse. "It has a piece of steel sandwiched between the upper and lower leather strips so your hand gets an extra tickle for free."

I couldn't believe Pearse was saying such terrible things about a priest.

"You'll be meeting him and the tickler soon enough, because you're now officially prisoners in this shithole for the next seven years." Pearse looked at his friend. "Right, Mickey?"

"Dead right," said Mickey, a boy of about five foot six with an oval face and eyes so hard, they could drill holes in mahogany. Though his legs were bandy like our postman's and his hands were almost down to his knees, he walked tough with his chest puffed out. What's more, he was *already* wearing his indoor white sneakers, which the school rules forbade.

"I wonder which of these motley runts will be the first to get acquainted with the tickler's bite?" Pearse said. He looked at Fergal and me, then glanced over our heads to the other new pupils.

Pearse was from Ballynure, a small Protestant town four miles from Knockburn, where Protestants and Catholics rarely socialized. Eight Catholic families lived in the black stone, two-storey houses in the upper part of Main Street, the unofficial Catholic end of Ballynure, though some Protestants didn't want any living in the town at all. Just before the Twelfth of July every year, a day when the Protestants marched in the streets of towns with drums and fifes to celebrate their victory over the Catholics in 1690, unknown persons painted Union Jacks on the walls of the Catholic houses to upset them.

After it was certain I would be attending Saint Malachy's, my mother had taken me down to speak to Pearse about the school. Pearse's father owned a pub, three rooms on the ground floor of their home, that only Catholics frequented because Protestants who weren't "saved" had their own pub. While we waited for Mrs. Brennan in the gloomy hallway decorated in camel and chocolate-brown paisley wallpaper, the stink of beer and cigarette smoke wafting from the public bar, Mammy kept tut-tutting because she hated alcohol. Later, Pearse had been very friendly as we sat in their parlor with its velvet curtains and heavy chairs with carved claw feet, even made my spirits rise by telling me what a great place Saint Malachy's was, that I'd learn German, Irish, and a host of other fascinating subjects.

"You'll be able to play loads of games as well," he'd said. "There's tennis, basketball, athletics, and rugby."

"Rugby? I can't believe they play *that* Protestant game at Saint Malachy's," said Mammy. She frowned at Pearse's mother.

Before we left, Pearse promised her that he'd watch out for me, and put his arm around my shoulder as we stood outside their pub front door. But he'd behaved so differently on the bus this morning, grunting only a greeting when he got in and then ignoring me, even after I moved seats to sit beside him. He'd also embarrassed me in front of the other boys when the bus stopped to pick up Mickey, because he ordered me out of the seat that he'd been saving for his friend.

Fergal and I stood with about a hundred other boys at the front of a huge gym with a knotted pine ceiling. Honey-colored climbing bars ran up its two longest sides, and the wall opposite the stage was painted dark blue and had a basketball net affixed to it. Behind one set of bars, a wall of large windows overlooked a handball court.

"I hope we'll be put into the same class because I don't want us to be split up," Fergal said.

"Me, neither."

A priest entered with his shoulders thrown back, head tilted toward the ceiling, and the teachers fell quiet. He clutched a clipboard in one hand, and lifted the bottom of his flowing soutane like a woman does a long dress as he ascended the short flight of steps to the stage framed in gray velvet curtains. After adjusting his spectacles, he peered out for a moment without smiling.

Within five minutes, Father Rafferty welcomed us to the school, informed us that we were a privileged bunch of boys, and reminded us of the rules about hair length, proper uniform, and wearing sneakers indoors at all times. He called out boys' names, ordering them to stand in line across the width of the gymnasium as each class formed. Fergal's name was called out first and he took his place in Class 1B. More names were announced and the class grew. Fergal kept popping out of the line to check if there was still room for me. The class grew larger and larger. Just as I'd about given up, my name was uttered, and I walked past Fergal to squeeze into the narrow space between the last boy called and the wall.

After I heard Connor's name being called for Class 1A, I didn't hear another thing because I became too busy deciding whether I should be glad I was in the same class as Fergal or jealous my cousin had been put into an "A" class. One-A sounded far higher than 1B and, if that were the case, my mother would not be pleased.

As I was trying to decide, a woman in a short pleated skirt with the fattest legs I'd ever seen told us to follow her. Her skirt was far too short. The class filed in silence along the corridor, passing closed doors with little side windows through which I could see boys seated at desks, the only noise being our creaking sneakers and the teacher's stockings rubbing where her fat legs kissed.

"My name is Miss Brown and I'm your form mistress," she said, after we'd seated ourselves behind box desks with hinges running across the top and graffiti covering every square inch of wood. Fergal sat beside me, and neither of us could believe graffiti existed at Saint Malachy's. Miss Brown's little nostrils flared. "You're my little men, and I intend to see you all do well under my tutelage."

Her shining, pale brown eyes met mine and she smiled again, a smile so warm and special, I knew from that instant I'd do everything in my power to please her. She took us to the stationery store and walked us throughout the school, pointing out the different classrooms and laboratories, teachers' staffroom, headmaster's office, and the empty cloakrooms that smelled of dirty feet. A sneaker with a broken sole lay on one of ten highly varnished benches running its length. Each boy was allocated a peg with a number written beneath and told to hang on it his shoe bag (bags sewn from old curtains or bed sheets), which contained our out-door shoes that we'd been carrying with us. Again, she told us about the rule not to wear our indoor shoes out-of-doors.

Back in the classroom, we were shown how to make a timetable and also told a bell would ring every forty minutes to signal the end of a class. As I stared at the timetable I'd made, I was amazed to think I'd learn nine subjects every day and still have time to take two breaks. Introductions were next: Miss Brown told us to stand in turn, announce our names and where we came from in a loud Saint Malachy's voice, and ask one question. When my turn came, as the words tripped out, my voice was alive with trembles that wouldn't stop. I could not lift my head, or halt the damned trembles.

"Speak up a little, Gabriel, and look at the boys when you speak," Miss Brown said. "Remember, I said in a loud Saint Malachy's voice."

I took a deep breath and looked up just like she'd said. Twenty-one heads of all shapes and sizes watched and waited for my words yet it felt like a thousand. I gripped the sides of the desk until I thought it would splinter and began to speak.

"Very good, Gabriel, but you forgot your question," she said, after I'd finished.

She'd praised me and no one had laughed. "Miss Brown, are the boys in class 1A smarter than us?"

I held my breath in order to hear her answer better.

"An excellent question, Gabriel. Boys, I want you to know that 1A and 1B are one and the same with regard to intelligence. One and the same."

The bell rang soon thereafter, and we were led to Latin in a room called Group Activities 1 where she left us in the hands of Mr. Carmichael.

The Saturday after my first school week was very hot. House mar-tins swarmed about the house and garage, their high-pitched twit-ters filling the sky as they prepared to leave for warmer countries.

As I watched their darting flights, I wondered if some of these same birds would go to Kenya and build their nests on the eaves of Uncle Brendan's school because he'd told me they had house martins as well. Thoughts like that made me feel close to him despite his being so far away in a country I knew nothing about. A week ago, he'd sent me a lovely letter wishing me well at Saint Malachy's, and had enclosed a photograph of his new school extension that I'd pinned to the bedroom wall.

"Gabriel! Gabriel!" Nuala ran into the backyard. "Mammy says you and Caroline must take James and me for our last sum-mer bath in the river before tea. You must do it now."

I placed my arms on her shoulders as she looked up at me. Nuala's front teeth crisscrossed slightly and made her smile imp-ish, and her every request always began with a "must."

"We must, must we, Nuala?"

During the summer months, if it was warm, our mother liked us to bathe at the river because it saved her work. I always picked the same spot for us to bathe, right where a high bank of rust red clay reared up on one side, prickly rings of gorse carpeted the other, and the shimmering water sang as it trickled over the stones. No one but cows chewing cud on the lip of the high bank could see us naked. When we got there, it was always Caroline's job to shampoo and rinse James' and Nuala's hair, and mine to make sure they washed their arses, necks, and inside their ears.

After we'd bathed Nuala, she got out and disappeared among the gorse clumps, returning a few minutes later clutching a hen's egg that she gave to me. The egg was yellowish, peppered with tiny white spots, and I wondered how a hen had managed to escape its coop and make its way down to the river to lay it.

"Were there any bones nearby?" I asked, thinking a fox had caught the thing and it had laid the egg in fright before it died.

Nuala shook her head so fast, her wet, curly hair flew away from her face.

"Take me to the spot."

As we were searched about, Noel appeared from behind a

dense gorse bush. He took the egg, smashed it against a mossy stone, and a terrible stink arose from the runny mess. Nuala jumped back pinching her nostrils.

"I was looking for you, and your aul doll said you were here," he said. "How'd the first week go?"

"I've got a really gorgeous form mistress."

Noel looked at my sister. "Go back to the others and tell them Gabriel's coming with me. We'll be back in a wee minute."

I watched Nuala scurry across the clearing and disappear just as Caroline called out she'd caught a fish with her hands and wanted me to see it. I started toward the river, but Noel seized my arm.

"Let's go to the bridge."

"Let's see the fish."

"It's only a bloody trout she's tickled. You've seen a trout before, haven't you?"

I shrugged and followed him. As we walked along the river-bank, Noel and I compared timetables. Even though he was over twelve, he didn't study German or Irish because his school was an intermediate, not a grammar one like mine, and he had to study nasty subjects like woodwork and metalwork. We came to a deep part of the river where the water was pitch black and rusty-colored froth clung like soapsuds to the trailing brambles and grass. Near the edge, something peeped out of the water's still surface.

Noel stooped, grabbed, and pulled a sack toward him. Water rushed from its loose weave as he held it up. After it had trickled to a steady drip, he laid it on the grass and opened it. "Just as I figured. Take a look."

I bent down and peered inside. At first I thought it was a pile of black and white rags but, as my eyes focused, I saw the rags were pups. A bag of drowned sheepdog pups curled around a glistening black stone, their eyes closed as if in sleep.

"Some farmer's bitch had a litter and the bastard's drowned them," Noel said.

He drew the twine around the neck of the sack and tossed it

into the water again. I watched the sack float for a moment before sinking beneath the blackness. The rusty froth rocked back and forth until the last ring of ripples vanished and the water stilled again.

"We should find out who did it and report him to the RSPCA," I said.

"What good would that do? Sure, the river's full of bags of dead kittens and pups. Come on, let's go."

I couldn't stop thinking about the pups on the way to the bridge. As we drew near, through gaps in the trees, I could see Fergal's house about two hundred yards farther up the brae. I heard his voice and saw he was playing ball with three other boys on the road. I wanted to show him the sack of pups and called out his name as I waved, but he didn't look. Only the smallest, a fry of a boy acting as goalie, looked back for a moment before turning back to the game.

"Shut your fucking mouth. We don't want them coming down here." Noel checked to see if the boys were coming. "We'll go to the pigsty, instead."

"I can't. We're expected home for tea soon."

The bridge had two arches whose stone ceilings stood five feet above the riverbed. Water flowed entirely through the far arch and only partly through the nearest, leaving a two-foot strip of stones and grainy sand where people could walk to the other side without getting their feet wet.

"We'll go under the arch," he said.

After climbing over a fence of sagging barbed-wire that ran across the mouths of the arches, we walked into the cool, dim shade. Noel stopped halfway inside. A car passed overhead, and I listened to the whoosh of wheels and whine of its engine as it picked up speed to climb the hill. The noise faded, replaced by the babbling, cheerful water. Without saying a word, Noel unzipped his jeans and pulled down his underpants to just above his knees.

"Quick, do me here."

His voice sounded hollow underneath the bridge. I couldn't believe what he'd asked. We always started our play with doctors and nurses. Now, he was skipping that bit and wanted the last part first.

"We can't do this here." I watched in scared fascination as his thing grew. "It's not dark enough . . . and we haven't done our doctors and nurses examination."

"We haven't got time, and I want you to do it now. Nobody will see us. Only this one time in daylight, Gabriel. I'll do it to you, too. Take down your trousers and kneel before me."

I sank to my knees. Noel's white legs and jutting thing looked so out of place among the crumbling lime and moss on the bridge's walls.

"I don't want to do this, Noel. I'm feeling so sad about the pups."

It didn't seem right to do it here, especially since my brother and sisters were playing farther up the river, and a bag of beautiful, murdered puppies lay sunken in the water. Noel put his hand around the back of my head and pulled my face toward his middle. Moments later, his hands left my head at the same time as I heard a loud gasp from the entrance. I turned, expecting to see James. It was Fergal. He stood, fringe clumped with sweat, staring at me kneeling in front of Noel's thing. It was so unreal, I thought it was a dream. I sprang to my feet and looked again. He wasn't there. I heard him grunt as he scrambled up the ditch. As fast as my thoughts, I whipped up my jeans and spilled over the barbed-wire fence. I managed to grab the back pockets of Fergal's pants as he plunged through a hole in the hedge.

"Fergal, wait a minute." My heart knocked so loudly, I thought he'd hear it as he reversed out and stood before me. "Noel and I play doctors and nurses. We examine each other for fun." My lips were dry, so I wet them with my tongue. "You caught us doing the last bit first and . . . come and play with us, if you want."

Fergal shook his head. "My cousin said you were shouting for me. That's why I came down, but I'm not playing any game like that."

"Why not?"

He shrugged. "I'm going home to my cousins. I'll see you on Monday morning."

I don't know why, I think it was his gaze and voice, but I was scared of him for the first time in my life. I needed to make things right.

"Noel found a sack of drowned pups and I'll show you where they are."

Fergal looked into my eyes without blinking. He did not blink once. I met his stare, though it was powerful hard to meet it.

"No, I've got to go."

I watched as he passed through the hole in the hedge, and then stood staring at the empty space for a long moment. When I returned underneath the bridge, Noel was gone. Just his footprints, and my footprints, and the hollows where my knees had sunk into the grainy soil remained.

CHAPTER ELEVEN

FERGAL SAID NOTHING MORE to me about what he'd seen. As the days passed, I convinced myself he'd seen very little, though a part of me kept asking why he hadn't wanted to take part in the game. His words had had such a hard edge and that troubled me. I was so troubled, I asked Noel the following Saturday while in our nest if boys really did play this game together.

Noel switched on the torch and propped himself up on one elbow. "Of course, they do."

"Why did Fergal not want to do it? Why did he say he didn't want to play 'any game like that'? That's exactly the words he used, Noel."

He didn't respond for a moment. "Lots of boys do it, so you needn't worry. Some do it only with girls. Others do it with boys and girls, both."

"So there's nothing wrong with doing it, then?"

"Not one single thing." He switched off the torch. "Fergal just doesn't want to do it."

I felt so happy, I forced myself to stay after the lovely pains passed and the other feelings, the ones which always made me jump up, dress, and leave came over me. I ignored them, and forced myself to stay because I wanted to continue pleasing Noel. After a while, he began to make noises. Soft noises like cries. Cries that grew louder and deeper. His body started to tremble and he called out, "I'm coming, I'm coming." I pulled away, fumbled about until I found the torch, and switched it on.

"First time you've been able to make me do that," he said.

"Do what?"

"Come." He sat up and I saw creamy liquid upon his stomach. "I couldn't help it."

"What is that on your belly?"

"That's spunk. Only older boys can make it. You can't yet."

"What's spunk?"

"A man rides a woman until his spunk comes out and it mixes with her egg to make a baby."

"Why did you make it come out?"

"You can't stop it. It's a feeling that comes over your body and won't stop."

Everything clicked instantly in my brain. I knew exactly what he was describing. "Is it like a lovely pain?"

His face scrunched. "Yes, that's a good way to describe it . . . and your aul doll will explain all about it when she gets round to telling you about sexual intercourse."

I waited for my chance to ask my mother about sexual intercourse. It came the following bath night, after I'd washed and was sitting in front of the fire while she read her magazine. Two hours earlier, Daddy had left the house after they'd argued. The disagreement started because he was going out to the pub with his friends, she hadn't been out for a long time and was fed up, and told him he was a married man and should be taking her as well because she was his wife, not his slave. She said also he had to change his ways because I was at grammar school now and beginning to understand more about the nature of adult relationships.

"Exactly what did you mean when you said to Daddy I'd be understanding more about adult relationships now that I'm at Saint Malachy's?"

"Oh, I meant all sorts of things." She flipped a page.

"Would it include things like . . ." I paused and looked at Caroline, "how a man's spunk mixes with the woman's egg to make a baby?"

Caroline, who was brushing Nuala's wet hair to untangle the knots, laid the wire hairbrush down and pushed Nuala aside. She had dared me twice to ask after I'd told her what Noel had said. My mother closed the magazine slowly.

"Spunk is a filthy word, Gabriel." Her nostrils widened. "Filthy."

"Why is it filthy?" Caroline asked.

"Shut up, you, or I'll send you to bed this instant." She turned back to me. "Don't ever use that word again."

Mammy ordered James and Nuala to bed. She peered into the fire, watching its orange and mustard tongues flutter and lick the crackling coals for a moment, and finally eased back in the armchair. "Caroline, check and make sure James isn't listening in the hallway."

After Caroline returned, Mammy said, "The pair of you, go and sit on the sofa."

We sat rigid at opposite ends of the couch as our mother studied the dancing flames again. Her lower face glowed in their light, and the muscles at the side of her mouth began to twitch.

"It's time to tell you the facts of life, because you're at Saint Malachy's now." She rose and switched off the television. "Caroline, you're smart and will be experiencing little changes to your body shortly, so I'm going to tell you also." She took a deep but slow breath. "Son, you may hear a lot of awful words to describe the private parts of your body from the boys at school. They use words like that because they haven't been told the facts of life properly by their parents. Those boys have learned about the sacred act of sexual intercourse the wrong way. And never forget that sexual intercourse is sacred. It's a gift given by God for the purpose of bringing new life into the world."

My mother sat stiffly as she explained about the changes which would occur to my penis and Caroline's vagina. She explained the actual doing of the sacred act. She used words like "engorged" and "spermatozoa."

"Now God also allows sexual intercourse at other times other than when the woman is trying to conceive. He allows it when a woman isn't ovulating . . . but she *must* use the rhythm method. If she uses that method, then the Catholic Church says it's okay *not* to produce a baby."

"Isn't there another way a woman could avoid conception?" I asked.

"How might that be so?" Mammy's voice had risen at the end of her question.

"Well, if the man lies flat on the bed and the girl climbs up and sits on his engorged penis, then that would stop the spermatozoa coming out, wouldn't it?"

Her jaw slackened for a split second. "I'll wash that dirty mouth of yours out with soap. How on Jesus' good earth did you come up with such a filthy notion?"

"It's a law of physics that things don't flow upward."

"Oh . . . oh, I see. I see . . . very good. Physics doesn't apply in this case, Gabriel."

"Can a blind man's penis get engorged?" Caroline asked.

"Of course. Now, that'll be all the questions for today, I think."

"How can a blind man get like that if he can't see his wife?" I asked.

"You'll understand the mystery if you get married . . . though, of course, I'm still hoping you'll be the priest in our family."

"Are you going to get Daddy to explain the other part to me?" I said.

"Other part?" Mammy cocked her head.

"About men doing it together?"

"Jesus, Mary, and Joseph, what are you saying? Haven't you been listening? Men don't do the sacred act with other men. That's unnatural."

Icy tingles passed instantly from my hipbones to the top of my spine, the hair on the back of my neck rose, my ears exploded in bells.

"Only women have eggs . . . forbidden . . . abomination . . . eyes of the Church . . ." Her lips moved faster and faster, "Unnatural . . . mortal, mortal sin . . . abomination . . . hear such a thing?" She stared at me as if expecting an answer. "I said, where did you hear of such a thing, Gabriel?"

My mind raced faster than the tumbling pieces of James' kaleidoscope.

Abomination. "I don't remember, Mammy." *Forbidden.*

My voice was weak and false. It was as weak and false as my lie. *Unnatural. Forbidden. Abomination.* I couldn't say I heard boys talking about it at school, because it was unnatural. That thought caused me to realize no boy did talk about it at school. How could I have been so stupid? *Mortal sin. Abomination.* An image of the man at the beach popped into my mind, and I saw myself crawling underneath his towel. I'd wanted to see all of him. It was unnatural to have wanted to see him naked. Another image flashed, the one of Fergal watching me kneel before Noel at the bridge.

"Tell me the truth, Gabriel. Who told you about this wickedness?"

I looked up and met her gaze. It was as hard to look at her as it had been to look at Fergal that day. Noel had lied. God forbade it. I would go to hell if I died. Fergal had known it was an abomination. Was this why he looked at me strangely in class sometimes, or was I just imagining that? More chills raced up my spine, yet inside I was frying. My mind leaped from Fergal to the polished altar rails where I knelt to receive Holy Communion every Sunday. I was a sinner receiving Communion. It was hell for me. Roasting flames and bodies that never cooked. Another surge of sweat came as soon as I realized I could never confess such wickedness to Father McAtamney. Not even in the pitch-dark of the confessional could I whisper this evil. Even more terrifying, I'd have to go on receiving Our Lord in a state of sin because I was too young to refuse and my mother would insist even if I did. Mortal sin would pile upon mortal sin till I could hardly breathe.

Clawing every ounce of strength, I raised my eyes to her face.

I felt transparent as glass. I was sure she saw my every thought, yet had to continue as if everything were normal.

"Mammy, I made a stupid mistake. I just thought sexual intercourse was such a wonderful gift from God that it was for all kinds of people to enjoy together."

"Well, now you know better."

CHAPTER TWELVE

T HE NEXT TIME I saw Fergal, I could barely look him in the eyes. It was almost impossible and, when I did, it was torture. Even though I'd seen him countless times since that day at the bridge, my new knowledge changed everything. I felt such shame, I was sure I reeked of it and he could smell it. And I was also sure the other boys could smell my shame, too.

School and the classroom became a living hell. If I thought Fergal was acting cold or moody toward me, I suffered a thousand agonies. I would check constantly to try to see if he was upset with me about anything, to see if he was still my friend. If he chose to sit beside another boy in the classroom, I became convinced it was because I was an abomination. If I saw him and the boy he was sitting with snickering in class (and I checked often to see if they were), I was sure it was about me. I was sure he'd told him about what he'd caught me doing. I'd brace for odd looks and the teasing to begin. I couldn't even talk to anyone about it, and felt so alone in the crowded classroom. Instead of concentrating on my lessons, I'd try to count the number of times Noel and I had done it, kept asking myself why I'd allowed it to occur in the first place.

It got so bad, I began to avoid Martin and his gang of three friends. I'd fallen into the habit of meeting them by the handball court where we'd play a couple of games. If the court was already taken, we usually went to an empty classroom and ate our sandwiches while we chatted. It didn't matter to them I was only a first-year, or that I wasn't in the House of Cork. (Our school used

a four-house system for competitive purposes at sports and examinations, the house accumulating most points winning a trip
abroad at the end of the year, and I was in the House of Belfast.)
It didn't matter to his gang, because I was Martin's cousin and he
their leader. The other members were Giles, Niall, and David.
Giles was the most colorful and, until I'd learned about the
wickedness of my acts, I really enjoyed him. Although only thirteen, he was already six foot, skinny, and extremely funny. He
refused to trim his patchy sideburns or wear his hair regulation
length and, as a result, was forever hiding from Father Rafferty.

But he was also girly. Some of the other boys had nicknamed
him "Pansy" before I came to Saint Malachy's. He didn't care.
He'd even given Martin and the gang permission to call him by
that name, telling them the more it was used, the less ammuni-
tion it gave the other boys, because then they'd see it wasn't hurting him and the joke would be on them. The gang hadn't been
able to bring themselves to use the name, had compromised
before my arrival at the school and nicknamed him "Pani"
instead.

As gang leader, Martin had us make our school ties in loose,
exaggerated knots, roll up our blazer sleeves, and strut about the
corridors and around the edge of the football field as if we were on
fashion parade. Until I found out about my mortal sin, I'd loved
to strut with them. Until then, I hadn't cared much about Pani's
girlishness or the name-calling. Now, I didn't feel like strutting
anymore.

For the first time, I was glad I didn't have fifteen-inch flares,
because they looked ridiculous and made Martin and his friends
stand out from the rest of the boys. I began to think the name-
calling and wolf whistles were directed at me as much as at Pani.
The boys could smell I was different, in the same way a healthy
dog can smell another is sick and snaps at it because it wants the
sick one to leave. So I didn't strut for six days. On the seventh,
Martin was standing outside my history classroom when the lunch
bell rang, the top of his indigo toothbrush peeping from his breast
pocket because he always brushed after eating.

"What's the matter with you, Gabriel? We wait for you every day and you never come. The others are beginning to think you don't want to associate with us anymore."

"That's not true." I glanced at the wall because his rolled-up blazer sleeves and exaggerated tie knot annoyed me.

"What gives, then?"

"I just don't like all the name-calling. It's got under my skin. I can't hack it."

"*Please*. I've told you before you shouldn't give a hoot what these heather-breeds say."

Heather-breed was Martin's name for country boys, a name that hurt because I was from the country, too.

"*I* care, Martin. I really do."

"Anyway, you know as well as I do that most of the insults are directed at Pani, *not* you or me."

Martin paused as Fergal and two other boys came out of the history room. Fergal's eyes riveted on Martin's indigo toothbrush. One of the boys had his arm around Fergal's shoulders, which made me turn cold inside because of what I'd done to Eamonn Convery, a quiet boy who'd tried to be my friend in chemistry class two days ago. As we were sitting on our stools at the lab desks, Eamonn had put his head near to me and rubbed his hair playfully against mine. I'd wondered why the hell he'd done it and warned him not to do it again. I warned him in front of two other boys. He'd turned scarlet, and I felt dead sorry as soon as I saw his mortification, but didn't apologize.

"You simply must stop being so sensitive, Gabriel. I'm always telling you that."

"Please put that toothbrush in your inside pocket."

My cousin looked puzzled.

"I don't think . . ." Two more boys came out of the room and I stopped talking until they'd passed. "I don't think it's only Pani they're calling a pansy. It could . . . it might be some of the rest of us as well."

"I don't give a damn about the heather-breeds." Martin's face puckered. "Half of them can't even speak proper English, for

Christ's sake. It's what you believe about yourself that matters. You mustn't allow these people to ruin your life." He paused as he swept his lemon-bleached bang off his forehead. "For Christ's sake, Giles *wants* people to call him Pansy. Besides, let them call us any name they want. They'll be the idiots when they see it doesn't bother us in the slightest."

I liked Martin when he acted like a big brother. In fact, I was jealous of Connor in this regard. Often, I thought how wonderful it would be to have an older brother to act as my protector, just as Uncle Brendan had said once how Daddy had always protected him.

"These farm boys are jealous of us, Gabriel. Look how some of the seniors roll up their blazer sleeves as soon as school is finished and they're walking out the gate to the buses. Who do you think started that? We did, that's who. Our group started the whole thing. They want to look so hip when they chat up the Saint Mary's Convent girls, but don't forget *we* started the craze." Martin pointed a finger at his chest. "The heather-breeds follow *us* when it matters."

It made sense, but I still needed time to think and told him so. I needed time to analyze, just like I analyzed everything, turning it over and over in my mind until all angles were examined. For the next few days, I thought and analyzed, and the more I did, the more I realized he was dead right. Martin didn't give a damn if they called us names. Pani didn't give a damn, either. Neither did David or Niall, so why should I? He was also right about me being too sensitive. I was far too sensitive, and that needed to change.

Another amazing thing happened over the course of the next few days. My mind stretched Martin's opinion to apply to the other terrible thing. I was being far too sensitive about that, too. Yes, I had committed a sin. But I hadn't known it was a sin. I hadn't known it was an abomination when I'd been doing the acts. I was being far too sensitive, because God would understand if I asked him to. What had happened was unnatural, but God knew I wasn't evil.

The hardest part to analyze and overcome was the confessing aspect. I could never tell a priest. The very thought of confessing always brought Uncle Brendan to mind, which set me back every time because it stirred the shame. I thought about how clean living and holy he was. I could never tell him, or any other priest. As I analyzed that problem, it popped into my head that God was all about forgiveness, too. God would forgive what I couldn't tell a priest. I would talk to him directly, ask Him for forgiveness, and no priest would be required.

At my bedside, for the next ten nights, I got down on my knees and chanted the Act of Contrition. I did it faithfully. I did it swiftly too, before James came into the room and asked what the hell I was doing. I also talked in my own words to God, told Him how sorry I was, that I'd never do it again.

An astonishing thing happened as I was doing it one evening. He came to me. He came and spoke inside my head in a beautiful fatherly voice. He spoke in a beautiful fatherly voice and told me I was completely forgiven. I heard Him clearly, as clearly as the pealing bells of Derry city. He asked only one price: I had to tell Noel it was over. I had to stop avoiding Noel and tell him it was over.

"Your aul doll said you were down at the well," said Noel. He walked toward me with his hands in his pocket. "Do you want to go to our nest today?"

I was fetching drinking water from the well. "No, and I won't be going to your nest anymore. I won't be doing the caper with you again, Noel."

Lifting the buckets, I started quickly across the field.

Noel looked surprised as I hurried past him. "What are you talking about?"

"You heard me."

"Why?" He followed me.

"You know *why*."

"I don't."

I put down the buckets so hard, water sloshed over the sides. I looked him in the face. It wasn't hard, because I now despised his ugly face with its brown front teeth. Everything about Noel was ugly. He was a thin body of ugliness and filth, and I wished he were sixteen and leaving to join the merchant navy.

"I know the facts of life. What we've been doing is unnatural and a mortal sin. Men don't do that sort of thing. It's an abomination in God's eyes. You'd better drop to your knees and ask His forgiveness, just as I did."

"They do so."

Decayed front teeth flashed as he smiled.

"Sexual intercourse is sacred and for making babies."

"Lots of men do it together. *That's* the God's truth."

"It's a mortal sin, and I'm *not* going to do it with you again."

Noel's face contorted to resemble a hideous mask.

"Did you tell your aul doll about us?"

I picked up the buckets and started walking. "No, I didn't tell my mother." Water sloshed over the rims and soaked my jeans.

"Just make sure it stays that way. Because if you do, I'm going to come over and tell her exactly what you did to me . . . and more importantly what you got me to do to you." He moved in front of me, then started a running reverse as we advanced across the field. "I'll tell her every detail, and she'll believe me because I'm older than you." His eyes pierced mine. "Do you understand that?"

I didn't respond.

"Do you understand?"

He was the one who'd offered to do it to me, but I'd permitted him. I had definitely permitted him. Did my permitting make me as guilty as him? I wasn't sure. Now, I really wanted him out of my sight.

"I understand. Go away and leave me alone."

"I'm glad we see eye to eye."

He started quickly across the field, and I watched as I continued homeward. He lit a cigarette, its blue smoke whipping behind his head as he exhaled, and slouched toward an arching gap in the ragged hedge. His camel-colored jacket merged with the turning leaves as he passed under the narrow arch. My shoulders and arms throbbed from carrying the buckets, but the pain was lovely. Never would Noel touch me again. Not so much as a finger of his would touch my clothes, and this lovely pain would bear witness to my promise to God.

My first school examinations occurred in mid-December. I sat with two hundred boys in the huge gymnasium with its wall of windows that let in the bleak gray light. No two members of the same class were allowed to sit within ten feet of each other in case they cheated. Teachers stalked the narrow aisles with folded arms and slow-swiveling heads, hoping to catch a boy or two succumbing to temptation, because trust was taught, not practiced, at Saint Malachy's.

Toward the end of the term, the results flooded back and it became quickly apparent I hadn't done well. With the announcement of each result, clusters of boys sat tallying averages during class breaks and then compared with one another to ascertain who was in the lead. Latin, Irish, and mathematics were my downfall. I failed them miserably, my other results were average, and I ended up in sixteenth place out of a class of twenty-two. I finished ten places behind Fergal, which ensured I had my first ever terrible Christmas.

The report card arrived on a snowy late Saturday afternoon at the end of January and gave rise to fresh misery when Mammy resurrected the worn comparisons with Fergal. I stared at the list of results, results already burnished painfully into my brain, and my class position in each subject. They were written immaculately in black ink. Only one other thing appeared in the report card, in blue. "Only a mediocre student," was Father Rafferty's comment, written in dusty blue fountain pen ink in his chicken-scratch hand.

"What the hell does 'mediocre' mean?" my father asked.

"Nothing good, that's for sure," Mammy said. "Fetch me your dictionary, Gabriel."

I ran to my bedroom and fetched it, though not before checking.

"Average or inferior." She looked aghast at my father.

"Jasus, you're making a fool of us. You're no good with your hands, and now you're proving you're no good at the books, either." He picked up his newspaper and crackled it fiercely as he opened it. "Aye, that Fergal's a far smarter pup than you."

The very mention of Fergal's name sent my mother ballistic. She threatened I wouldn't get my nose out of the bedroom if I didn't swear to improve.

"What are we going to do with you?" Daddy said. "Luksee, if you can't learn your books, you're neither good to man or beast."

"I'll do better next time," I said in a low voice, as my mind screamed at him to shut his fucking, fat mouth.

"Mammy, I will do better, I promise." I turned to her and froze him out. "Next time, I'll pass all my subjects, beat Fergal, and end up in the top ten of the class."

"See that you do," said Daddy.

"May I be excused?" I said to her.

"That's all your father and I want, Gabriel. We want you to be in the top section of your class because you've got the brains." She paused and ran her eyes over the report card again as if it might somehow have changed for the better. "I'm going to go and see Father Rafferty and have a wee chat with him. Maybe there's something we can do to help you." She glanced at my father. "We'll go and see the priest."

"I've got no intention in this world of going to see any priest."

"He's your son, too."

"Luksee, I'm not going near that priest and that's that. He's got to pass his books on his own."

She went alone. She'd said I should go as well, and I tried to persuade her it was a bad idea because the headmaster would probably want to talk to her without me being present. She didn't agree until she spoke to Auntie Celia, who informed her she'd gone up with Connor, and the priest had taken him inside for a second or two and then made him wait outside while she and

Father talked privately. Unfortunately, Father Rafferty couldn't put a face to my name and told her she should have brought me along. His not being able to place me had been the way I wanted it. Boys avoided him as he walked along the corridors; we darted into classrooms or under staircases, speaking to him only when summoned, or when he couldn't be avoided.

Mother explained to me that he went through my report card line by line before he consulted a big burgundy book in which teachers had written detailed comments. Miss Brown had written I had tremendous potential, but Father Rafferty told my mother he wasn't convinced. He also informed her that he'd "watch my progress with much interest" and, as she repeated his words with emphasis on "interest," a new fear entered my heart.

CHAPTER THIRTEEN

For my form-mistress's comments, I was grateful. They dispelled my mother's fears I might have to be removed from the college in disgrace because I couldn't keep up with my classmates. Miss Brown was magnificent. She smiled and joked with me more than she did with the other boys, and I was more lighthearted and relaxed in her English and history classes than I was in any other class. She was also lenient when she caught me talking, rendering halfhearted scoldings and calling me a chatterbox, which always brought me into line.

The other boys didn't care for her as much, and I took it personally if I overheard them muttering she was only a "damned Protestant." That she was Protestant was true, but this mattered nothing to me, and certainly had nothing to do with her ability to teach. Their attitude was biased. I also disliked it intensely when they called her cruel names like "Thunderthighs" because of her fat legs.

Martin had her for second-year history and she was partial to him, too. At lunchtime, if our gang happened to be passing the staff room and she was coming out with her friend, Miss Quinn, she'd stop and chat for a few moments. "Gabriel, Martin, and these boys are excellent young men," she'd say, and I felt so grown up.

Fergal and I didn't sit together much in Miss Brown's or any other class in the second term. It was by unspoken agreement. Suspicion and jealously stalked the friendship because he was now the yardstick of success in my parents' eyes. Each time I informed my mother I'd done well in a class test, I wasn't congratulated until she'd learned I'd trounced Fergal. Competition between us was fierce, unspoken, concealed by smiles and little jokes with jags. I didn't care he was more popular with the other boys. I was fully prepared to yield superiority in sports, but academic superiority was an entirely different affair.

Fortunately, I didn't have to yield to Fergal on the sports arena, either. Mr. O'Dowds, the head of physical education, discovered how fast I could run around the bases during a game of rounders and recruited me to the athletics department. Thus, whereas Fergal trained for the junior football team, I spent two lunchtimes a week with other athletes practicing the one hundred and two hundred meters under Mr. O'Dowds' watchful eye. It was so wonderful to be decent in one sport. It was so wonderful, I spent part of Saturdays practicing at home with James as my competition. Even my father seemed pleased I was good at one sport, though also admitted to knowing next to nothing about athletics.

I began winning races at interschool athletics meetings and brought back glittering medals. For the first time in my life I had boys slapping me on the back. "Go, Dynamite! Go, Dynamite," they'd shout when they saw me in the corridor as we changed classes. I'd acknowledge them very coolly. Boasters were detested at Saint Malachy's, but inside I shivered with pride, lapped up every word, wanted more.

Amongst all the newfound recognition, Fergal and I battled in quiet ferocity when it came to schoolwork. When results of class tests or homework essays were graded and handed out, I made a point of asking him how he'd done, and what comments the teachers had written in the margins. If he wouldn't tell me, I figured it couldn't be good, yet still I had to be certain. More than once, I got Martin and the gang to keep watch while I sneaked into the classroom at lunchtime and rummaged quickly through his schoolbag to find out exactly what had been written.

For the most part, I did better. Only in useless subjects like Latin and Irish did he do better. Still, I'd rage about it quietly. I'd rage and could hardly bring myself to talk to him. Of course, I hid the anger behind smiles because always, always lurking deep within my brain, was my fear of him remembering and revealing the incident underneath the arch of the bridge.

In the same manner my athletics wins attracted the magnificent nickname and welcome attention, so, unfortunately, did my soaring grades eventually attract unwelcome attention. I found myself a target of verbal attacks during school breaks. At first, the insults were just plain dumb. Silly taunts like "Harkin is a sneaky stew," or "Harkin's a dynamite stew" (stew was Saint Malachy's slang for someone who studied too much), but it got more serious. Soon, stuff about Miss Brown and me began to appear on desks and other places. Nasty things like, "Harkin tries to ride fat Miss Brown but can't because his cock's too small" appeared beside the anonymous Shitehouse Poet's latest verses on lavatory walls. I tried to wipe them off, but discovered they'd been written in indelible ink. I also tried to block out the comments, using Pani's theory of not allowing their sting to affect me, but it was impossible. Pani had abilities I didn't possess, because the comments still hurt, even though I told myself over and over that my decent nickname countered them.

Calling a boy horrible names gives better mileage than calling him good ones, and quickly the taunting started up on the bus ride home, too. Journeying by bus had never been a good experience from the beginning because of the complicated travel arrangements. I was one of fourteen boys living in Knockburn which, because it was a rural mountainous area, wasn't well served by public transportation. Around seven-thirty every morning, four other Upper Knockburn boys and I gathered in rain or sunshine at the corner of the Ballynure main road to catch a bus carrying factory girls to their work as machinists in the village of Muckamoney. The homebound journey was even more chaotic. A fleet of old and new buses, caked mud on their sides and "wash me please"s on their greasy back windows, collected us from the town square, where boys purchased candy and single cigarettes from a nearby shop. It was Belfast Zoo at feeding time: sixth-formers flirted with convent girls while fourth- and fifth-years taunted Protestant schoolboys in dark uniforms much like our own, except their crests weren't religious and the ties had red, not blue, diagonal stripes.

Our bus terminated in Ballynure, where Pearse's father had his pub, and, because it was still too early to connect with the evening bus taking the factory girls home, the Education Board organized a taxi to transport those of us who lived in Knockburn. On top of that, my bus had the questionable honor of being known as the rowdiest bus leaving Saint Malachy's front gates. No less than four times since my arrival, Father Rafferty had kept us behind after morning assembly to lecture and threaten us because of complaints from bus drivers and members of the traveling public.

"Gabriel Harkin's a big lick-my-arse," Paddy Flannagan, a fellow in my class, shouted down the bus one afternoon. "He wants to screw Thunderthighs, but isn't man enough."

I was speaking to Aidan, a thirteen-year-old with whom I'd struck up a bus friendship, but the rest of my sentence collected behind the backs of my front teeth which had snapped shut as soon as I'd heard my name.

"Ignore him," Aidan said. "Mickey's put him up to it."

I glanced down the bus and saw Paddy sitting two rows from the long back seat where Mickey sat. A short, wiry boy with an elfin face and squirrel eyes, he was allowed to sit near Mickey and Pearse at the back of the bus. Mickey was fifteen, mean, and I'd been wary of him ever since my first day at Saint Malachy's when he'd turned and drilled his mahogany hard eyes into my face as we'd walked along the school driveway. Even some upper-sixth boys were scared of him, and they were eighteen and in their final school year. They were scared because Mickey loved to fight and give powerful head butts which a person could hear, and they also drew gallons of blood.

"Gabriel Harkin's a mammy's boy and wants to be a priest like his uncle Brendan," said Paddy in a singsong voice. "Got any priests you can get to come and give us a vocations talk, Father Gabriel?"

Laughter rushed down the bus, as if trying to catch up with the taunts. He was making fun of the fact I attended vocation meetings. I loved to talk to priests from different orders who came to the school to tell us about the religious life. Saint Malachy's had a strong tradition of producing priests, and Father Rafferty liked junior boys to attend these meetings on the grounds they might receive an early call. Even Paddy went sometimes, though only because he hadn't done his homework and needed to cut class.

Now, I wished I'd kept my mouth shut and not boasted to a few boys that Uncle Brendan would give a talk when he came home from Kenya. As soon as my parents had received the letter in which he'd mentioned he was coming for another visit, I told a few of the boys I'd ask him to give us a talk. I'd said it without writing to ask Uncle Brendan because I figured I'd be able to convince him when I saw him, and I also knew Father Cornelius, the vice-head and head of vocations, was always looking for priests to discuss missionary work. I'd said it to impress, to have the boys in my class look up to me, and also to make Fergal jealous because his family had no missionaries. But it got out of hand because somebody informed Father Cornelius of my plan, and he came to me asking for Uncle's address so he could write and make arrangements. Then came the letter from Uncle Brendan saying he'd changed his mind and had to go to San Francisco instead. It was a nightmare: I had to tell Father Cornelius before he wrote to tell my uncle what a marvelous idea it was, and I had to tell the boys it had been a mistake and he wasn't coming after all. Finally, Mickey and the others got wind of the whole thing and began to tease me about priests and vocations.

"Hey, Gabriel, why do you really want to be a priest?" said Dermot Hagan, a sixth-former, in his very uncouth voice. "You'll not be able to put your hand up Thunderthighs' skirt and cop a good feel if you become clergy."

"Gabriel would rather put his hand up Father Cornelius' soutane," someone else said.

It was a joke among the senior boys that Father Cornelius was a poof. I heard them joking about it, though they said he liked blond-haired boys and I was dark. More ignorant laughter broke out. I tried to block out the whole thing by riveting on hundreds of small, impressed diamond shapes on the plastic seatback ahead. I willed the boys to lose interest in me, to move on to somebody else. I willed, and stared at the impressed plastic diamonds.

I didn't even hate Paddy. He was only mean when Mickey was around. Otherwise, he was a decent chap when you talked to him one-on-one. He was the class clown and popular. Paddy was also a natural at sports because of his wiriness, and that's why Mickey and the others liked him. They used him. They put him on their team when they played indoor football before classes began in the mornings.

Senior boys intimidated me. From my first sight of them, they'd looked like grown men. They were old, seventeen and eighteen, the backs of their hands were hairy, and they had long sideburns and manly voices. I was deferential because that's what they expected. They made sure juniors feared and rendered them respect, shouldering us aside in the corridors as they thundered by, and ignored us in favor of older boys when we tried to buy goodies at the tuck shop. My deference was one difference between Paddy and me. Nor did he fear them, either.

"Hey, Mickey wants to know if you'll give Father Cornelius a feel," Paddy said.

Paddy, I could handle. Mickey was different. Mickey was in on the baiting, my prayers went unanswered, and it wouldn't end now until we got off the bus at Ballynure. My eyes burned. I'd been staring at the plastic diamonds so long, I'd forgotten to blink. Paddy laughed again. So did Dermot Hagan, and Pearse, and Jim Hegarty, a senior with a donkey bray whom I didn't like. I hadn't liked him ever since he'd drawn the boys' attention to my new schoolbag. On the first morning I'd taken it with me to school, he'd come up to me as we were waiting for the connecting bus outside the factory gate.

"What the fuck is this?" he'd asked.

"My new schoolbag, Jim."

"Hey, fellas, come and take a gawk at this fucking spectacle."
Ha ha ha. "Harkin's carrying his brains in a fucking mobile
library." Ha ha ha.

After the boys had formed a circle to gape at my bag, he seized
the strap and affected straining noises as he tried to lift it. The
boys roared. Fergal laughed, too.

"Mickey thinks you want to be a priest to hide the fact you're
a poof," Paddy called down the bus.

My ears rang like the tuning fork on top of my music teacher's
piano. Bad scenes whizzed before me: Noel and I in the pigsty;
Fergal witnessing me on my knees at the bridge; Henry pointing
and calling me a sissy; my knee prints on the sand.

"Ignore them, Gabriel," Aidan said. "If you react, you've lost.
They're baiting you. They want you to react, and won't let up if
you do."

Aidan didn't know what Fergal knew. His eyes flicked
upward, and I turned to see Mickey standing in the aisle beside
me.

"Move over," he said to the two second-year boys in the seat
across the aisle. They obeyed instantly, squeezing into the wall of
the bus as if trying to become part of its lining. Mickey sat down
sideways, leaned toward me with a hand on each knee, and smiled
as if he were my best friend.

"Pearse and me think you shouldn't let that wee runt treat you
like that," he said out of the side of his mouth. He took a quick
drag of his cigarette and expelled the smoke brutally. "Sure, he's
that short, his arse is barely above the ground. Come back with
me and beat the shite out of him."

Mickey's tone was silky compassion, his face ruthless callous-
ness. All he wanted was a scrap of flying fists and gallons of blood.

As I regarded his dry, cracked lips, I wanted to slap his mouth
so hard, the blood would fly from him. Another thought instantly
replaced that one. I wanted him dead. I wished he'd drop dead
right on the filthy bus floor and I'd dance on him. A murderous
thought came next. If I had a knife, I'd stick it in his gullet and

kill him. Right here, right in front of all the boys, I'd stick it in his gullet and kill him. The viciousness of my thoughts made me lightheaded. How could I have such thoughts? I felt no longer in control.

The thoughts circled and circled and wouldn't stop. They were every bit as insistent as other thoughts I had quite often. Thoughts I did put into action. Thoughts like stepping on every third flagstone as I walked down the street, or the compulsion to reach a certain tree or gate before the count of ten. I acted on those because, if I stepped on every third flagstone or reached the tree before the count ended, I'd definitely get the grade I wanted on an exam, or whatever else I needed at the time. Those thoughts were also insistent, and wouldn't leave my mind until I did what they demanded. They compelled me to do them. The thoughts about killing Mickey circled in my mind in the same way and terrified me because I feared I'd turn them into acts if I had a knife. Sweat broke out all over my chest and back, and I felt my shirt stick to my skin in places.

"Come on, Gabriel," Mickey said. "Let's whip the runt's arse."

Mickey's voice brought me into control. "I don't think that's a good idea. Thanks for the advice, but I don't want to get into any trouble with the busman for fighting." My voice would not stop trembling.

"That's okay. We'll form a wall to shield both of you." He narrowed his mahogany eyes and curled his lips so that the cigarette dipped from one side. "The bus driver will never see yous and yous can go at it till your heart's content."

"I'll leave it all the same, Mickey. Someone might tell him."

Mickey's eyes bore into mine, and I saw his disgust enter and mix with their existing hardness.

"Get back to your seat, Mickey, and leave Gabriel alone," a voice said. "Go and pick on someone your own age."

It was Finbar, the bus prefect, and I could have wrapped my arms around his waist at that moment. A boy of quiet authority, Finbar had facial scars from old acne and some boys called him

"Colander Head" behind his back. He was in the upper-sixth, expected to do very well in his final exams, and go on to Oxford University.

"I'm not fucking well doing anything to him," Mickey said, yet arose with alacrity. "I was only chatting to you, wasn't I?"

I remained quiet.

"And what might be the nature of your little chat?"

"Oh, this and that."

"It wouldn't have anything to do with trying to get a scrap going, would it?"

"No."

"I'm glad to hear it, because I'd be exceptionally disappointed if it did."

As Mickey swept his fringe aside with a defiant jerk, a cord in his thick bull neck stood out. He stared sullenly at Finbar, just long enough to show defiance but not arouse anger, and strutted down the bus pushing back his shoulders to show the other boys what a hard man he was because he'd stood his ground.

"Don't let him get to you," said Finbar.

My eyes rested on an apricot prefect's badge the size of a thumbnail on his lapel. It was shaped like a shield and had the word PREFECT printed in gold upon its shiny face. The quiet power of that sweet apricot badge.

"How many more points have you won for our house since I last spoke to you?" Finbar asked.

"Thirty."

"Naw, Harkin's a fucking yellowbelly," Mickey said down the aisle. "He's too fucking scared to fight."

"Well, keep it up," said Finbar, and he winked. "I want to go on another trip before I leave school."

CHAPTER FOURTEEN

A s I FELL TO the ground I tried to protect myself with my hands, but didn't succeed and landed hard on my arse. The senior boy was to blame. He'd emerged from the doorway next to the school oratory at high speed, saw I was in his way, and shoved me aside. Some of the seniors were behaving more boisterously than normal because there were only a few weeks to the end of the school year, and I think they sensed the teachers' grip on authority slackening. It certainly seemed that way: exams were over, and teachers arrived later in the classrooms after lunchtime because many of them had strolled into town on account of the beautiful weather.

"Ugly pig," I said.

"What did you say?" the senior said. "I'm going to teach you a lesson you won't forget."

Before I could respond, he'd seized the lapels of my blazer, spun me around, kicked my arse, spun me around once again, and finally sent me slamming into the rough stucco façade. He came up to me and put his face near mine so our noses touched, though I felt nothing until the last of the shock passed and the first thing I smelled was the sourness of his fetid breath. Sharp pains began to radiate one after the other from the bones of my arse like shunting railway carriages.

"I'm sorry, I'm very sorry," I said.

He flung me away from him. I doubled in pain for a moment before composing myself under the inquisitive stares of boys crossing the paved yard between the old school building and the salmon-colored brick extension.

"Some sort of punishment's in order because enough is enough," said Pani, after I'd explained to the gang what had occurred. As he shook his head to underscore contempt, his curtain of long hair swept away from both of his cheeks to expose unruly sideburns and too large ears.

It was lunchtime, and all of us were in the art room except Martin; he'd gone to brush his teeth. We'd been trying for ten minutes to come up with a good means of revenge but couldn't settle on anything decent.

"He's a fifth-year," said Niall. His upper lip quivered as he pondered for a moment. "That's it. Let's watch and see if he leaves the school grounds at lunchtime. Only the sixth-years have permission to do that, but we know others do it, too. If he tries to leave, we'll locate the teacher on duty and report him."

"That's chicken-brained, that is," said Pani. He put a piece of driftwood he'd been toying with back among the rest of the still-life objects upon the table. "Teachers are animals. They hate snitches as much as they hate boys who give them trouble. It's *us* who'll get our heads knocked about." He rolled his eyes at Niall. "Wise up, for Christ's sake."

Niall's eyes fell to his warty hands. He was very self-conscious about the warts and was forever picking at them. He was also the most thoughtful member of the gang, and this had been his first suggestion. Pani was out of line, though I didn't say so because I knew he loved to act the boss when Martin wasn't around.

The door slammed open, and my cousin entered. "I've got the perfect plan, Gabriel. We'll give him a scare. We'll tell him to report to Father Rafferty for kicking you."

"That's bloody brilliant," said Pani. "Let's find him and tell him." He started to roll up his blazer sleeves in preparation for our strut around the school to look for the boy. "That'll definitely scare him shiteless."

We didn't find the fifth-former until next day. He was playing soccer in the all-weather pitch during the lunch break. David came with me while Martin, Pani, and Niall watched intently from a corner of the school building.

"Hey you," I said, as I walked toward him with my chest out and shoulders pushed back till they ached.

The fellow looked at me, then at David, and finally nudged his friend.

"How's your arse?" he said, after I drew up to him. "First-years have to show respect for their betters." He glanced at David. "So do second-years, for that matter. And if you don't, well then, you have to be taught the hard way, simple as that." A smart-arse grin painted his face.

"You'll be able to tell that to Father Rafferty at three o'clock tomorrow in his office," I said.

"He'll tell you if he thinks your plans to teach juniors respect are sound or not," David said.

The fellow's smart-arse grin disappeared as fast as his cheeks changed from pink to pale. "Ach, yous are only joking me, aren't yous?"

"Do I look like the type who would joke about a thing like that?" I asked.

The question sealed our plan, and we walked away leaving the two conferring with another boy in the middle of the pitch as the ball passed back and forth. The next stage of Martin's plan required me to find him before three o'clock next day and inform him I had indeed been joking. However, as gloating knows no limits, I decided to keep him in suspense until the two-fifteen bell rang for change of classes, my last opportunity to see him before three. I'd even done my homework and found out 5B, his class, would be assembling in Room 12 at that time. As the bell rang, I was standing in front of Mr. Kelly's desk while he explained to Barry Shaw and me why our crystal-growing experiment had been a miserable failure. With one eye on the teacher and the other on the door, I watched the rest of my physics class leave.

"Sir, may I be excused because we have German next and Miss Devine asked me to see her before class begins?"

"This'll only take a few more minutes."

I didn't hear another word about how to successfully grow crystals. Five minutes later, I hurtled along the empty corridor, the only noise being the grating screech of my rubber soles as I negotiated corners. I arrived at Room 12 with a roaring stitch in my side. Peering discreetly through the side window, I scanned inside, but he wasn't there. I loitered for as long as I dared, hoping he was perhaps late for class, but he didn't arrive.

Throughout German, I shifted about in my chair so much, its wooden seat irritated my arse and made it itch like mad. I dashed out at the first peal of the three o'clock bell. My class had taken place in the salmon-colored extension while the headmaster's office lay in the older section of the school. The corridors teemed with boys whose faces I scoured as I threaded my way. As I reached the gymnasium doors, I saw the fellow enter the headmaster's office.

Throughout geography and the following class, I kept watching the door, waiting for Father Rafferty to peer through the side window as he always did before entering a room. He didn't come. Just as I was beginning to relax, the door was tapped gently during religious education class on Friday morning, and his birdlike secretary entered, spoke with the teacher, and I was told to present myself at the headmaster's office at lunchtime on Monday.

As the gang decided moral support was in order, they accompanied me along the corridor at the appointed hour, though melted into the shadows of the trophy cabinet in the vestibule adjacent to Father Rafferty's office as I walked the final five yards to his door. Pani, owing to his unlawfully long curtain of hair, opted to view from a more discreet distance and planted himself by the gymnasium doors some twenty-five feet away.

The headmaster was an expert in torture. He kept me squirming for exactly seven minutes before I heard, "Enter." He looked me up and down as I closed the door, inquired as to the reason for my visit and, after I'd explained, ordered me to stand with clasped hands before his desk. He read a little more before leaving his office without a word, and returned moments later with a big burgundy book.

"I note we've made some progress since the Christmas term examinations." The priest pushed his shiny spectacles up his nose. "I expect your summer exam results are still reflecting this."

"So far, Father."

"Young man, look at me when I'm addressing you. Saint Malachy's boys exhibit leadership qualities. They do not glance at the floor like beggars receiving alms when addressed."

"Yes, Father."

I looked at the priest and had to admit that, while he had an overall cold demeanor, now that I was really close, I saw a flickering of kindness in his crinkly face. As his attention returned to the burgundy book, the chicken scratch words "only a mediocre student" thundered in my mind, followed swiftly by the thought as to where exactly he kept his leather tickler with its sandwiched piece of cold steel.

"Young man, do you hope to be successful here?"

"I do."

"Pardon?" His salt and pepper eyebrows arched behind his gold-rimmed glasses as he looked up and thrust his head slightly forward.

"I do, Father."

"What might success constitute in your mind, exactly?"

"That I will do excellently in all my examinations, Father."

The eyebrows arched even higher. "Is that all, young man?"

The way he'd said "young man" was most off-putting as I raked my brain.

"And to be consistently good at sports, too."

"Pardon."

"And to be consistently good at sports, too, Father."

"And that is *all* success means to you?"

I looked at him and couldn't think what else he wished me to say. The silence grew excruciatingly.

"What about character and integrity?"

"Character and integrity are very important."

"And they're very much lacking in your case, are they not?"

There ensued a lecture about liars and lying and the virtues he expected Saint Malachy's boys to consistently demonstrate. I only half-heard because my mind was preoccupied with the tickler. A few minutes later, he came around to my side of his boxy desk, slipped his hand into a slit in his soutane, and pulled out a limp piece of ancient leather. Within the space of sixty seconds, he'd administered three powerful whacks on each palm, their echoes chasing the little silences between each slap as they bounced off his varnished pine door, and I'd been efficiently dismissed. As I started toward the gymnasium where the gang now stood, Pani propelled himself from within the shadow of its recessed doors.

"How'd it go?" he asked.

Martin's and Niall's eyes were riveted on my hands. Before I could reply, Father Rafferty's door opened, Pani streaked across the vestibule in three gigantic leaps and barged out of the swing doors, the rest of us pursuing in his wake. I emerged into the sunlight feeling very dark.

"The pain will pass quickly," Martin said.

The ultimate authority had punished me. No one in our gang had been punished by him, not even Pani with his illegal hair. My cousin laid an arm around my shoulder, but the lump in my throat would brook no acknowledgment of his kindness.

CHAPTER FIFTEEN

THE BALANCE OF THE summer holidays passed quickly. In the middle of August, Martin and I spent a week touring towns in Donegal with Uncle Tommy, Auntie Bernie, and their two children because they wanted to investigate renting a summer holiday cottage near the seaside on a permanent basis. On our first day at the beach, Philip, my uncle's five-year-old son, begged him to swing him round and round so he could relive a carousel ride he'd been on the previous afternoon. While pretending to read my novel, I listened to Philip's joyful screams as he was swung ever faster and was reminded of my own pleasure when Uncle Tommy had swung me like that so long ago.

Shortly before my return to school, my mother summoned us to the kitchen table for a family discussion, a most peculiar event in itself because she'd never before called such a thing. As my siblings and I settled at the table, Daddy came in, sat opposite us, and my mother came and stood behind him and laid her hand upon his shoulder. The scene reminded me of sepia photographs I'd seen of wanly smiling husbands and wives dressed in their Sunday best, except my father was the one who sat.

"Children, your father and I have made a great decision which will affect our lives forever. It will involve a great deal of sacrifice. There'll be a lot of hardships for a time. For example, we won't be having a lot of meat on our dinner table, not even stewing steak on Sundays, and we'll have to go without new clothes for a while."

The stewing steak I wouldn't miss, because I'd always thought it tasteless, and felt as if I were chewing string rather than meat, anyway.

"Your father's leaving his job. He's going to buy a digger and start a business. We have some money saved, but not enough, so we need to borrow more from the bank. That means we have to cut back on expenses."

"What sort of digger, Daddy?" asked James, his voice lilting with anticipation.

"A JCB."

"Can I drive it?"

"We'll see." My father glanced at me and smiled, but I looked away.

He outlined his plan to work for the local farmers, adding he'd apply to do government jobs when he had enough money to purchase newer equipment, and finished by stating we'd be millionaires in a very short time. Mammy scoffed at that, though it was clear she was delighted.

The digger, a rusty, tractorlike machine with a cab and wide, front bucket whose uneven edge glinted in the sunlight, arrived two months into my new school term. Daddy was very proud, so proud I arrived home from school the next day to find it had been resprayed. He'd done a brilliant job, because it gleamed like brand new in the low autumn sun. It didn't stay like that long, however, because he began to work the thing mercilessly. He worked for hours enlarging the farmers' bits of fields, removing trees, stone fences, hedges, and ditches so they could use hay balers and combine harvesters instead of doing the harvest manually.

In my second year, I'd been put into class 2B and Miss Brown was still our form mistress. Connor moved from the "A" stream: Saint Malachy's required boys to choose a second European language in addition to German in year two and, choosing French over Spanish, he had to join my class.

Throughout that year, I continued to excel at athletics and schoolwork, even finished first in my class after the Christmas examinations, but still I had to endure taunts on the bus ride home. Mickey and Pearse continued to gang up on me, as well as a few other boys, though I seemed earmarked for the elephant's share. It didn't happen every day. Some days they seemed to forget about me, or they got caught up in other mischief, and there were also days when they had to stay late for sports training and I could breathe easy. But on the other days, days when I thought Mickey appeared to be in a bad mood as he boarded the bus, I'd slink down in my seat so that even the top of my head would not be visible to him. The ploy usually didn't work, and there was no one to protect me anymore. Finbar had left for Oxford, and the new bus prefect was as useful as a spare head. He was just as frightened of Mickey as me and turned a blind eye to his bullying so he wouldn't have to confront him.

One afternoon, toward the end of that year, I was summoned to the back of the bus where the older boys sat. I was immediately suspicious and didn't want to obey until Paddy came up to me, crossed his heart, and swore it wasn't for anything bad.

"They want to ask you a question," he said, "and besides, if I were you, I wouldn't risk annoying them by refusing to go down."

No sooner was I before them than Pearse and two other boys grabbed my arms and legs and held me while Mickey poured something on my clothes. Instantly, the bus stank to Zeus' throne. People pinched their noses and thrust the upper windows of the bus wide open.

"Harkin's shit himself," a voice said above the furor.

The driver stopped the vehicle and came down the aisle, demanding to know who'd released the stink bomb. No one would admit to it, and he was at a loss what to do. Finally, he ordered me to come with him and made me stand by the open door for the rest of the ride to Ballynure.

"The boys got you good," Fergal said as we started up the road.

"You call that animal behavior good?"

"Don't take it so seriously."

"How'd you like it? I'll have to hang my uniform outdoors tonight."

"All the same, you have to admit it's amazing how Mickey was able to concoct a stink bomb in chemistry class."

"Remind me to check and see if he passes his chemistry exam at the end of the year."

Fergal laughed. "You're getting far too touchy about everything."

"How would you like to be picked on constantly?"

He didn't reply.

After that incident, I began to sit in the front seat of the bus for the rest of the year. I did throughout year three, also. I didn't care if a bunch of first-years surrounded me. My bus friend, Aidan, and a few other boys who liked me sat beside me sometimes; so did Paddy, but only when he needed to copy homework from me.

In my third year, sixth-formers like Jim Hegarty, who'd teased me about my large school bag, left for university, though it didn't help my situation much. The teasing still continued because, although a new group of boys became sixth-formers, they were either scared or friendly with Mickey and Pearse, who were sixteen and even more powerful now.

"They threw bricks through Brennan's pub windows the other night and it serves them right, Ruth," someone said at the delicatessen which lay on the other side of the high supermarket shelving.

The woman was referring to an attack on Pearse's father's bar, an event that was also big news in Knockburn. My mother and I were in the canned fruit and vegetable aisle, and the shelving prevented her from determining who the customer was. Mammy, who was examining a can of pineapple chunks, narrowed her eyes even more and shook her head.

"I quite agree. Did you also say you wanted a pound of streaky bacon?"

"Provided it's lean." A brief pause ensued. "Ruth, my poor Trevor's scared witless. I'm frightened to death for him. They're so scared they're erecting a higher fence around the police station and festooning it with even sharper wire just to make sure those IRA savages don't lob bombs over it. What's this place coming to, I ask you? It's not right in a civilized society. We're living amid savages who know no bounds . . . oh, Ruth, that bacon doesn't seem too healthy. It looks more tan than pink."

"The bacon underneath came in this morning, so I'll give you that instead." Another silence arose, fractured intermittently by the sound of metal clinking against metal. "Every last one of those IRA scum should be lined up and shot on sight. Yes, sir, shot on sight. *Then*, there'd be no need to intern them."

My mother, who'd moved across the aisle to baked beans, dropped a can of them on the floor. I picked it up and handed it to her. "Jesus, Gabriel, listen to that bitch's badness." She put the can, a very expensive brand, into her basket. "These are wicked women. Listen, pretend to be searching for something in case somebody comes into the aisle while we listen to the rest of this badness."

"I'll tell you something else for nothing as well," said the clerk. "A prison officer friend of my Sammy says they're learning Irish in prison. *Irish*, if you don't mind. They gabble to one another in it, just so the guards won't understand what murderous plots their other IRA scum friends on the outside are planning. And you know what else Sammy says?" She emitted a shrill laugh. "He says the British government told some of the prison officers to learn it. Imagine that? He also says the sounds that come out of the mouths of those IRA thugs when they're speaking Irish are nothing short of primitive. Aye, my Sammy told his boss in no uncertain terms that the flames of hell will be mighty cool before he'll agree to learn that excuse for a language."

My mother accidentally felled part of a stack of spinach cans.

"Let's leave now," I said.

"That bitch is evil personified."

"I'm a slice or two over the weight. Do you want me to take it off?"

"No, that's grand."

"How can we be expected to share power with Catholics? It's

just not right. The British government's out of its mind if they think they can foist this new initiative on us. Sammy says there should be an Ulster-wide strike to protest it. 'Let's close down the roads and the power stations and remind the British who controls this place,' he says. And Sammy's dead right, you know?"

"Oh, Ruth, wouldn't it be a grand lesson for those Knockburn people if they couldn't get down here to shop," said the customer. "That would teach them a lesson, wouldn't it?"

The clerk laughed. "It would be worth it just to see the look on their faces."

Ballynure was a Protestant town, and Hamilton's was its only supermarket. It employed one Catholic, their coal deliveryman, out of a staff of twenty. Relations between Protestants and Catholics had been strained in the province for a while. We were incensed because internment without trial had been introduced in 1971, and the only people imprisoned had been Catholics. A year later, the British army had shot thirteen innocent people dead at an internment protest rally in Derry, a rally that my parents had attended, and the government in London had since been condemned internationally for their poor handling of Ulster's affairs. In reaction, the British had imposed an initiative to share power with moderate Catholics. This, in turn, incensed the Protestants. The hard-liners, secure in their privileged Protestant birthright to rule, didn't want Catholics to have any say in the province's affairs. Their anger, which had previously been confined to the cities, was spreading to smaller towns and villages, and judging by the broken pub windows, Ballynure would be no exception.

"Oh my, but it would be great value to be at the roadblocks to see their faces when they're turned away and can't get down here for their milk and eggs," the clerk said.

Mammy's face was now as purple as the label on a can of kidney beans she was examining.

"Many of those Knockburn men are in the IRA, and those that are too old are offering shelter to them that's on the run," said the customer. "And I can tell you *exactly* how their faces would look. My Trevor says if looks could kill, he'd be a goner ten times over. He sets up the police roadblocks to search their cars for guns, and he says they'd shoot bullets through their eyes if they could when they're stopped." Her voice lowered slightly. "Between you and me, though it doesn't do to say, Trevor would love to give some of them a damned good hiding. But he can't, of course. I mean, he wears the uniform, doesn't he?"

"Since when has wearing a uniform ever stopped the police?" Mammy said, and she laid down the can of kidney beans. "I've listened to quite enough of this."

She emerged from the aisle like a battleship at full throttle.

"Hello there, Mrs. *Harkin*," the clerk said. She'd emphasized the surname so the other customer, a very bony woman who looked like she had cancer, would know at once we were Catholics. "It's such a gloomy day. Do you think this rain will ever stop?"

"It is so very gloomy out, isn't it?" the bony customer said.

"Family all keeping well, Mrs. Harkin?" said the clerk, as she handed the customer her package.

"It's not only rain makes this day gloomy," Mammy said. "I'll have four rashers of streaky bacon and a soup bone with plenty of meat on it."

"I'll see you soon, Ruth," said the customer, and she walked away.

The clerk picked up the first slice of bacon with her tongs.

"Oh, no, no. I don't want from the top," said Mammy. "I want the fresh bacon. Good, pink rashers . . . just like those you gave to your previous customer."

The clerk became so flustered, she gave her five rashers instead of four.

"I asked for four," Mammy said, after the bacon was nicely wrapped and laid upon the counter.

"That's all right, Mrs. Harkin. My mistake. I'll only charge for four." She took the money, whisked the change out of the till, and handed it to her. "Have a lovely day, now?" she said, and walked quickly into the back room.

"I can smell the Protestants' fear," said my father, after Mammy recited what we'd overheard in the supermarket. "They're scared because they know this is only the beginning." He slapped the arm of his chair. "The British will force them to share power, and then they'll withdraw from the place in two or three years. Sure, Ulster's no good to England anymore. She's made her money off the Paddies. She doesn't need us anymore now she's in the European Common Market."

"I think we're better off under Britain than we'd be under that useless bunch in Dublin," said Mammy. "Those people can't run a country. Everybody's out of work down there."

"Aye, we'll show these Ballynure people a thing or two. We'll push them and all the Protestants into a united Ireland . . . and those that don't want to live in a free Ireland can pack up and clear off to England."

"Though, you've got to admit not all the Protestants are like those women. We'd have to be fair to the good ones if we do get a united Ireland, Harry."

"I'm in a suck about what's fair or not fair for them. Have the Protestants worried about what's fair for us since 1690?"

"If we respected our differences, then Ulster would be a far better place," I said.

"Gabriel, shut up," said Mammy. "You're too young to be politicking."

"Politics my arse," said Daddy. "It's the IRA who'll solve our problems. Mark my words, it'll take more IRA bombs and less words before the Protestants see the error of their ways."

CHAPTER SIXTEEN

THE HARDSHIPS WE'D BEEN warned to expect after my father started his business had not been exaggerated. He'd been working for over a year to farmers and there wasn't a lot to show for his efforts. We still didn't have great meat on the table, and I needed a new school blazer because I was now five eight tall. More than a handful of farmers pleaded poverty and settled their bills in dribs and drabs, while some of the craftier ones didn't even bother to pay at all because they hoped my father would get embarrassed of always having to ask for his money and just write it off. Even several Knockburn farmers were dishonest in this way, yet were always first in line for Communion at Sunday Mass.

Of course, my father was also partly to blame. He was slow to learn what Mammy had been forever telling him, namely not to do work for farmer friends because friends and business didn't mix well. He drained their bogs, ordered quarry stone by the ton at his own expense, dug manually when the digger couldn't be used because the soil was too soft, and accepted excuses or nothing when it was time for them to pay. He was a social person, loved talking and laughing with people, and useless at ferreting out money. Not even Mammy's sharpest rebukes could change him. He preferred resending bills with NOW 90 DAYS OVERDUE, PLEASE REMIT or NOW 110 DAYS OVERDUE, PLEASE REMIT in red ink. He'd even ordered a rubber stamp with the PLEASE REMIT shite on it.

Unfortunately, red-inked stamps, empty promises, and crafty excuses didn't help pay the bills, and Mammy kept telling him the business wasn't breaking even after expenses and the monthly bank payment had been deducted. One month, there wasn't even money to cover the loan and my father, either because he was too proud or too scared, wouldn't go to speak to the bank manager. Mammy went, after scraping together six pounds to show good faith, and returned very happy two hours later.

"I can't believe how decent some Protestants can be," she said. "He was as refreshing as an ice cream on a hot day. It's a pity there aren't more Protestants like him in this country. He understands farmers are slow payers. He also said the bank's taking a long-term view of your business . . . which, of course, is more than I am."

"It's a pity the bank doesn't have a Catholic bank manager," Daddy said. "It's easier dealing with your own than having to deal with Protestants."

"Nonsense. You don't want to talk to anybody, neither Catholic nor Protestant. Sure, you won't even talk to the farmers. And let me tell you something for free, there are many of our own kind who'd sink us faster than some Protestants. If we had more Protestants of the caliber of your bank manager in the government, there'd be no need for the bombings and killings taking place in Belfast. That man can see we're facing discrimination. He wants to give Catholics a fair shake and is caught up in the spirit of this new power-sharing initiative the British started."

"He's covering his arse. Behind our backs he wants it to fail, just like all the Protestants want it to fail. They're all the same as Paisley at the end of the day. They know it's the first installment in a united Ireland scheme."

"You and your united Ireland. Don't let me hear you mention a united Ireland again. Having that won't pay our bills. We need money, not a united Ireland. It would fit you better to press those useless farmers to pay up. And don't expect me to be going to the bank manager again. If you can't speak to the bank about your debts, then it's high time you went back to lorry-driving."

Mammy was thrifty, but still couldn't make ends meet on his earnings some months. Behind my father's back, because she knew he'd be livid, she approached Granny Harkin for small loans to buy essentials. She swore me to secrecy when I caught her in the act of asking, and I promised, provided she told me what was going on. Borrowing pained her something fierce, and then came the month when she had to miss a repayment to Granny Harkin. She couldn't bring herself to ask her for even more money, so her next approaches were to tight-fisted Granny Neeson and Aunt Peggy. She always got a few pounds, but not before much sermonizing that she shouldn't have allowed my father to give up his real job. Every time Aunt Peggy said "real job," I could smell Mammy smoldering as she blithely regarded Aunt's starchy beehive.

The strain cast great shadows over the table at mealtimes, and I began to resent my father as a consequence. I resented his inability to badger the farmers for his dues and his ability to find a pound or two to go out for a drink with some of them on Saturday nights, even if he did drink only sodas.

"I can't take this anymore," Mammy said, after I refused to eat the sloppy, yellow eggs she'd prepared to go with the mashed potatoes one evening.

It disgusted me. I had to eat eggs every Friday because I hated the bony, smoked fish she served, and now I was expected to eat them on Saturday night, too. I pushed my plate aside, turning up my nose exaggeratedly. What had precipitated her outburst was Caroline had followed my example. In addition, Mammy was annoyed with her because she wasn't doing well in her eleven-plus mock exams, her breasts had grown large almost overnight, necessitating the purchase of bras, and money had also to be found for her new school uniform, whether convent or intermediate. On top of that, Nuala was six now, tall for her age, and in need of new shoes.

"Why can't you get off your backside and go and collect what's due you?" she said to Daddy.

His eyes ignited, but he continued eating.

"I'm harried trying to scrape money together to clothe every one of yous. I don't dare buy a new stitch for myself."

I retrieved my plate and pretended to eat the putrid slop. Caroline took my cue and did the same, while Nuala bounded off her chair.

"This useless man of a father of yours. All he does on a Saturday evening is preen to go out when he should be staying home."

Still, he continued to eat.

"What do you need to be going out to a pub for? I don't get out to enjoy myself, so why the hell should you? If it's out you want to go, then pay a visit to those bloody farmers."

"Why the *fuck* don't you go and ask them? That's all you fucking well do is complain. That's why I want out of the fucking house of a Saturday night. To give my head a bit of peace and get away from *you*." The table shook as his fist slammed into it.

Caroline's chair scraped loudly, and she vacated the table in a mass of swaying ringlets. Even though I was now older, these moments still upset me greatly because they instantly transported me back to childhood. I felt defenseless, and weak, and all my school accomplishments seemed so insignificant. My stomach churned with tension when all I desired was cozy security.

The more I watched my parents argue, the more I swore I'd never marry. It was beyond my comprehension how they'd fallen in love, married, and had children, only to spend their lives insulting and threatening each other now. Although always on my mother's side, as I watched her begin to pace prior to her inevitable stampede to the bedroom, I swore to myself no woman would ever possess me. I was going to have no millstones like women and marriage so I wouldn't have to deal with constant arguments.

"You're not looking after your children, Harry. They're not being properly fed. Your responsibility is to us, not to be out spending."

My father leaped up, chin, lips, and temples twitching, hands clenched to fists. He snatched his dinner plate and hurled it on the floor. "Why don't you go out and find a job like other decent Knockburn women? You gave up your bookkeeping job because you wanted to have children, but there's plenty of women who had as many as you and they're *still* working at the shirt factory." A twisted smile formed fleetingly. "Oh, that's right, I forgot. You're too stinking with pride for things like that . . . just like the rest of the fucking Neesons."

We scuttled into a corner, where Caroline and I formed a feeble barrier between our parents and James and Nuala. I wanted to get away, but Nuala was watching me, her tiny crisscrossed front teeth exacerbating her vulnerability. I reached out and pulled her toward me.

"Try and count the number of geese and goslings on the wallpaper and tune everything else out," I said.

She gripped my forearms, and her cupid lips began to move quickly as she counted. My parents didn't usually notice us when they were this angry but, as if driven by animal instinct or habit, we didn't dare move a muscle. I stood still, scarcely permitting myself to breathe, waiting, waiting for the moment when one of them might decide to use me or any of my siblings to score a point.

"Well, I'm bookkeeper enough to know you're making no money, and also bookkeeper enough to know we'll be listed in the *Gazette* if you don't do something about it fast."

To have your name listed in that paper meant you were a failure. You were a bankrupt, an unmentionable disgrace, because all the neighbors could read about your debts.

"And for your information, I'd have a job if you had books worth keeping . . . and don't you dare bring the Neesons into this, either. You owe the Neesons more than you think, if you want to know." Mother paused to let her truthful words sink in. "If your mother had reared you right, you'd stay at home with your children. But she didn't raise you right. You're that useless, you can't even wash a dish or make a cup of tea."

Nuala abandoned her count. "Mammy! Daddy! Be friends, please."

My father glanced at her for a split second before he focused on my arm draped around her. "And him. You've turned him into one useless chap. He's just another Brendan. He can't even use a fucking shovel."

"Shut your trap," Mammy said.

"He can't even come out on a Saturday afternoon when I ask for help. He used to help me, but now he does nothing. Every time I ask him, he runs to you, and then you come saying he's only a boy and has his books to study. Books, my arse. He's fucking useless. He's for nothing, if you want to know. He can't even mix with the other Knockburn lads. All he wants to do is run about with that fancy boy Martin, learning his affected ways."

"Leave Gabriel alone."

"I was out working when I was his age."

"And where has it got you?"

Sometimes I wished she wasn't so quick. Daddy's facial muscles twitched rapidly, and I thought he was going to hit her. He'd never hit her, but sometimes I thought it must definitely come when she said things like that. He stood rock still. Nuala's fingers pinched into my flesh.

"Well, I'm sick of the whole damned lot of you, and I wish I could do what other men in my situation do and just clear off for good." He went to the door and yanked it open. "Eileen, you can go to hell. You can just go to hell . . . and take him with you."

He slammed the door as he left, and its ringing echo engulfed the kitchen. I remained frozen as his footsteps receded. Seconds later, the car engine revved, was followed by a ferocious screech of gears, and he drove off.

"I'm not going to be like him when I grow up," I said. I stooped to help pick up the shards of broken plate. "All he does is rant and go out to pubs."

"*Don't* you dare say a word against your father." Mammy paused with a piece of plate in her hand.

"But it's true. He's always picking on me. Always wanting me to do dirty work I don't want to do . . . and you heard what he said about me just now."

He would get no more love from me. He was Daddy to me no

longer. The word "Father" was a better way to address him. Used in England but not so much in Ireland, at least not in Knockburn, it was ideally remote. I was removed from him, and it was just the perfect word. I resolved to think of him only as Father in my mind from now on. Of course, I realized I'd still have to call him Daddy to his face. I'd have to use it when he spoke to me directly, otherwise my mother would notice and pass remarks after a time. Nor could I address him as Father in front of Caroline and James because they'd die laughing at its ridiculous formality. No, I couldn't avoid calling him Daddy to his face, but he was only Father in my mind from now on.

Mammy stood and gazed out the scullery window. "He's got a point, Gabriel. You should offer to go out and help him. Your father's working like a dog and does need help by times. You could help him pick up stones and do a bit of shoveling some Saturdays." She turned back to look at me. "He's never refused you anything when you've asked and we could afford it."

To be perfectly honest, avoiding going out to help Father had become one of my priorities because I was definitely work-shy when it came to doing manual labor. I hated it. The priests at Saint Malachy's said *all* work had dignity and pleased God, and it wasn't only the Protestants who had a work ethic. I couldn't buy that load of junk about all work being dignified. I couldn't buy it because I couldn't see what was so damned dignified about breaking your back. I couldn't see what was supposed to be so dignified about digging drains and ditches with a shovel and pick. Nobody would do it if they didn't have to. Manual work is hard and demeaning, and I felt people should just be honest, admit it, and stop saying ridiculously good things about it.

"It's true, Gabriel, and you know it's true. You *should* offer to help. Your daddy's a very good man. He doesn't drink. He attends Mass. And, while it's true he can't make himself a cup of tea, I hope you turn out to be as good a man."

Her ability to reverse herself and stand up for Father was truly astonishing. Just when I thought she hated him, just when she was threatening to walk out and take us with her, she'd turn on a penny and praise him. Jesus, it was such a source of bafflement. It baffled me to bits. I noticed Caroline could change like this, too. One moment a thing was black, the next it was white, and you didn't know where the hell you stood.

CHAPTER SEVENTEEN

Tiny scarlet nets were etched into the whites of my sister's eyes as she stood before my mother in a disheveled state. She'd just got in from school, and the two uppermost buttons of her blue-and-white-checked blouse were missing, a long ladder ran from the middle of her right stocking to disappear underneath her tunic, and her hair was uncharacteristically tangled.

"I'm telling you I didn't provoke them," Caroline said. "None of the girls ever speak to those horrible boys when we're waiting for the taxi to take us home."

"You definitely didn't smile and give him a wrong idea?" said my mother.

"I *didn't*. They called us 'Fenian whores.' They're always calling us names, but they'd never tried to touch me until this afternoon. Those Ballynure school pupils hate us only because we're Catholics. That's exactly what it's about. Even the girls swear at us, and they egg the boys on, too. That's why the brute lunged and tried to grab my breasts."

"It's disgraceful," said Mammy.

"His hand was inside my blouse and he was grabbing me. I had to get away. That's why my blouse is torn." Caroline began to cry again. "Honest to God, Mammy. It wasn't my fault."

"All right, I believe you." Mammy patted Caroline's head twice.

"I'm sorry about the blouse," Caroline said amid sniffs. "I'll sew the buttons and my stocking tonight."

"We'll get it sorted," my mother said. "They're a bunch of

scum and something needs to be done. You must tell Sister Margaret-Mary about this tomorrow. She'll contact the police."

"What can the headmistress do?" my sister said. "The police won't listen to a nun. Sure *they* hate us Catholics, too."

Caroline was now a teenager and in her third year at Saint Veronica's Convent in Carntower. Every evening she had to catch a connecting bus near the steps of the Ballynure clock tower and her uniform, a royal blue frock and blazer with a crest comprised of a cross on its breast pocket, was the giveaway she was Catholic.

Arguments between Protestant school and Saint Malachy's pupils were forever breaking out, too. Sometimes, it was the Protestants who started them; sometimes, it was Saint Malachy's boys. The whole thing was dumb. It offended me because I was now a fourth-year and had befriended a Protestant schoolboy. Nigel lived in the Protestant fringe surrounding Knockburn and traveled the last part of the morning journey, a ten-minute ride into Ballynure, to catch the same bus as Caroline to Carntower. A ram of a chap with a thick neck, round face, and ginger hair (the latter unusual for a Protestant, I thought), Nigel was also in his fourth year and played rugby at Carntower Academy, a brilliant Protestant school. One morning, he chanced to sit beside me on the bus. We nodded and smiled, got talking, and I learned in the course of our first sit-together that Protestant schoolboys could be very mannerly.

I hoped he'd sit beside me the next day, and he did. I began reserving the seat for him, albeit very discreetly. I never said a word to him about what I was doing, but Nigel knew I was keeping the seat. I knew by the way he grinned as he walked down the aisle. The more we talked, the more we got to like each other. Even our mothers, who'd seen one another in Hamilton's supermarket but never spoken, began to talk on account of our friendship. Nigel fascinated me, and fast became a source of fantasy. In bed, after I'd said my prayers, I'd imagine us entering into a lasting friendship where I'd visit his house, he'd visit mine, and we'd talk about every subject under the sun. I imagined us talking about the real differences between Catholics and Protestants, not obvious stuff like religion, but rather about what made us dislike each other, and what could be done to improve relations. Of course, he and I never discussed such a prickly subject on the short bus ride, but nevertheless, sitting beside him every morning talking about school stuff was one of the highlights of my day.

Another fascinating thing about Nigel was his uniform. The blazer was stunning: red and white stripes against a purplish-blue background, and he wore a matching cap and scarf which was compulsory wear. All was so classy, and made my own uniform so drab in comparison. The Saint Malachy's boys took offence at the Carntower Academy uniform, grumbling its colors were the same as those in the Union Jack just to provoke the Catholics. It didn't matter to them that the school and its uniform colors were hundreds of years old.

Over time, some boys noticed I was keeping a seat for Nigel, and the pathetic nonsense and stories soon commenced. Nigel and his uniform provided new fodder for Pearse and Mickey, and of late Mickey's younger brother, Willie, who was a third-year and fast becoming a bully in his own right. They didn't bother me during the morning commute because they were either too sleepy or too busy copying homework. It was always during the evening ride home when Mickey would send Willie down to bat me on the head for sitting beside a Protestant. Nor could I do a thing about it, because Mickey was behind it all.

After the bus dropped us off in Ballymore every evening, a taxi was waiting by to take us up to Knockburn. Eventually, somebody got it into his head to torment me during this ride as well. Six of us had to arrange ourselves in the backseat of the vehicle. It was so packed, I could hardly breathe let alone move, but every evening, within five minutes of starting the journey, I experienced such painful stabs in my thigh, my eyes instantly watered. No matter how many fractions of an inch I tried to shift my leg away, I would soon feel the stab again as something sharp pierced my flesh. It was impossible to ascertain who was doing it. I complained one evening, more than one boy laughed, and then I understood the whole attack had been planned.

The stabbing was all the more painful because I didn't know what to do about it. I couldn't appeal to my parents or teachers: Father would just turn a deaf ear as he always did; Mammy wouldn't understand, and always agreed with him whenever he told her not to interfere because I had to fight my own battles; and appeals to the teachers who mattered at Saint Malachy's were most unwelcome.

Saint Malachy's was Irish Catholic boys' school down to its consecrated foundations. Boys were expected to be tough, assertive, to show no feminine qualities because that was an inexcusable sign of weakness. Naturally, we had to respect such feminine qualities in women. In women, such qualities weren't weaknesses and had to be respected, because women were our mothers and would eventually be our wives one day. Saint Malachy's boys dared not worry about facial spots, dared not show affection for one another, dared not giggle too shrilly. Most of our senior male teachers had come through this system, were now gentlemen with wives, yet some still took pleasure in punishing boys in ways that bordered on perverse. So I couldn't approach the teachers who held real power with my problem because I was fourteen now, and unyielding manliness was demanded.

Not all the Saint Malachy's teachers behaved like this, of course. There were decent teachers as well, but they were low in the pecking order. So I had to learn to bear the stabbings in silence or find my own solution. I knew something had to be done. I couldn't tune it out like I did with the verbal abuse. This was physical. I had to act. Trouble was, just when I'd narrowed it down to a particular suspect and observed his movements carefully, I'd find out I was wrong.

"You know damned well who's jabbing me in the leg, don't you?" I said to Fergal, after the taxi dropped us off at the crossroads one afternoon.

The ride had been particularly painful, and the gloomy

weather compounded my frustration. It was damp, and the silent hedgerows, interspersed with middling-sized, ragged hawthorns, seemed otherwordly because of the enshrouding mist.

"I do not indeed."

I stopped and cast my satchel down on the road. "*How* can you go on saying that? How can you lie to me when you know someone is sticking something sharp into my leg?"

Although Fergal and I talked every day, we were actually estranged. Our boyhood friendship was as tattered as a tinker's clothing. We knew it, denied it, and chose instead to fill the walks home with phony conversation. Fergal was a ruddy complexioned, very average pupil, one of those jovial schoolboys one sees peering from an old class photograph whose face is familiar but whose name is always forgotten. Competitiveness and parental jealousies had distanced us to chasm proportions over the years. We lied to each other habitually about the silliest things: whether or not we were studying for a class test, or whether we were doing research or not for some project. Both of us knew we lied, and yet we went through the motions and asked the questions, anyway.

More than once, Fergal had called me a poof in the bus when it was noisy and he probably thought I wouldn't hear his voice. But I heard him. I'd know his voice anywhere. His voice had been around me since awareness, and you never forget a voice that's been around that long. He'd always apologize when he guessed by my frostiness I'd heard him, and I *did* forgive him. I'd forgive him on account we did go back to awareness. But trust was an entirely different matter. Circumstances had rendered trust between us irrevocably dead. We were in a schoolboy's dilemma. We couldn't terminate the friendship. We couldn't do what adults do when a friendship's over, because we were only schoolboys who had to walk home together and go through the charade every day.

"How would you like someone to do that to you every day, Fergal? It's sore as hell, and my leg's full of tiny red holes."

Fergal looked at me for an instant before diverting his gaze up the road where he could see nothing. The clinging fog lent a ghostly appearance to his body, made him appear so different, like someone from another time.

"It's Kevin McDermott . . . he says you're a big stew and you deserve it for talking to that black Protestant from Carntower Academy."

"Is he using a needle?" I picked up my satchel and started up the road.

"A compass."

That it was Kevin surprised me, because he was very civil. It was also ironic he called me a stew. Kevin, with his long teeth and Cheshire Cat smile, looked as devious as God ever intended sneaks to appear. He was in the same year as me, consistently first in his class, and *all* the boys complained it was easier to pull wisdom teeth with chopsticks than to get him to share his homework.

"How do you think Kevin manages to always come first in his class?" I said.

"Because he's a stew."

"Exactly. So how can he have the nerve to call me one?"

"I believe, it's more to do with the Protestant thing."

"Nigel's not a black Protestant. He should get to know him before he makes judgments."

"Hmm. I don't think you should be reserving seats for Prods, if you want my opinion. They're all the same. Nice to your face, but stab you in the back when it suits them."

"Like Kevin's doing, you mean?"

He sighed. "You know what I'm saying, Gabriel."

"But you fancy Cathy Simpson who waits near our bus line in the evenings?"

"That's different. She's a girl . . . and I only like her because I'd like to ride her, so it's okay."

Fergal was unfazed by his glaring hypocrisy. It had to do with the fact he was completely oversexed. Sex was what he and many other boys in our class talked about most of the time now. They talked tits, hard-ons, riding girls, homework complaints, latest soccer results, more tits and hard-ons. It was all big talk because, if a girl approached Fergal, he'd bolt. Although only one year younger than him, I wasn't obsessed with girls or their body parts. I liked girls, but I wasn't obsessed. I liked looking at a girl overall, not just at her tits and arse. And the way they talked about hard-ons, about how this girl or that one made them get really stiff, was ridiculous. I woke up stiff as well sometimes, but I didn't go on about it as if getting stiff was the only thing in life that mattered.

"I don't think you should say that sort of thing about Cathy, either," I said.

Cathy Simpson was one of the really pretty girls, and I knew she wouldn't give the likes of Fergal a second glance. She didn't look Irish Protestant in the slightest, either. Her silky blond hair fell to the small of her back, and she tossed it beautifully as she got out of the school bus, just like a horse does its mane in full gallop.

"If you like a girl, what does her religion matter?" I said.

"I would never go steady with her. She's a Prod. You only ride the Prod girls."

Kevin liked to play chess at lunchtime. Next day, I went to the physics laboratory where they met, took him aside before he began a game, and asked point-blank why he was stabbing me with a compass. At first, he denied it vigorously. "How could you even think I could do such a thing?" he kept protesting as he tried to look me in the eye. I told him I knew it was he because some-one had informed on him. He looked away, pretending to watch an upper-sixth fellow wiggling his index finger against the tip of his nose as he pondered a move, then turned back and mumbled an apology.

"I won't do it again, either," he said, and flashed me his Cheshire Cat smile. "I promise."

I was more than happy to leave it at that, but two days later, the stabbing recommenced. Three gentle stabs the first day, back to the old intensity and frequency the next. The following evening, I made sure to be in Kevin's vicinity as we bundled into the taxi. At the first stab, I took my own compass out of my pocket, negotiated my hand toward his leg, sank the entire point into him, and withdrew it quickly. His cry shrank to a gasp as the others complained loudly about his shifting about in the packed car.

I didn't feel a sliver of pity. Not one sliver. Yes, it was a savage act, but I had to protect my body. I had to make him stop. If I didn't protect myself, who else would do it? It worked, too. Kevin stopped the attacks. And even more astonishingly, he began to respect me. It was a slow-built respect, beginning first with chats about homework which then moved on to include other stuff.

Father's big break came around this time. He'd applied six months previously to be entered on a government "select list" for subcontract work. A new business contact, who was Protestant like his bank manager, had recommended Father's company, and a letter arrived unexpectedly advising him that the company was required to assist in a multimillion-pound road building project. The job involved the construction of a bypass around a large Ulster town, and Father was to be one of ten subcontractors working for the main firm, a large company with its head office in London.

After signing the contract, which would pay about two hundred and fifteen thousand pounds throughout its duration, Father took a copy of it, as well as the letter of appointment, to our bank manager and requested a massive working capital loan. Mr. Frazer was delighted, persuaded his head office in Belfast to approve it, and two brand-new lime green excavators with Japanese names and metal tracks, two lorries, and another rubber-wheeled digger stood in our backyard six weeks later. Father had the lorries sprayed royal blue and gray, and the words HARKIN CONSTRUCTION LTD., KNOCKBURN written in black lettering on all the cabin and excavator doors.

It was a proud moment for the whole family. We were on our way. There were no more poverty-pleading farmers to be dealt with and, in our familial euphoria, it didn't matter one iota that the power-sharing experiment brokered by the British government between the Protestants and Catholics was close to collapse. The hard-line Protestant majority had called for a province-wide strike and had the muscle to carry it out. They threatened to bring Ulster to her knees, closing ports, roads, and disrupting the national power supply, if Britain didn't back down and kill the plan. But that didn't matter to us. What mattered was our juicy British government contract.

CHAPTER EIGHTEEN

CLASSROOM 6 WAS LARGE and had a matte white ceiling, eight overhead sphere lights, and pale gray walls. Despite four gaping windows, it remained dingy, even on sunny days, because of a five-foot cypress hedge flanking an abutting narrow strip of paved yard. A blackboard ran its entire width at the front, two steps back from the teacher's desk, and the only other furniture comprised thirty box desks arranged in three-row pairs running down its length. Plump Mr. Smith, whose sloe-black hair highlighted his acute dandruff, always sat during the lesson, and rose most lethargically only when obliged to write new French verbs on the blackboard. French was also the only class where Connor and I sat together at the back of the room.

"Do you know what I'm going to be doing this weekend?" he said one Friday near the beginning of May.

"What?"

"I'll be getting the feel. Rosellen McKeever's going to let me feel them."

Connor, like Fergal, talked a great deal about sex. He was also prone to exaggeration, so I looked up from my textbook and gave him a lingering, dubious glance before resuming my reading. It was a waste of time because my cousin didn't see it. He never looked at a person directly.

"I am, *honestly.*"

Connor was as unlike Martin as a brother could be. His heavy, dark eyebrows, sunken eyes, and very large nose put him on the poorer side of handsomeness. I knew Rosellen (as youngsters, Martin and I had played mud-pie baking and tennis with her and her friends), so the idea he'd be feeling the tits of someone I knew intrigued me greatly. I gave him the benefit of the doubt, and listened as he explained she'd asked one of her friends to tell him she had a crush on him and wanted to meet at three o'clock Sunday in the plantation running behind Connor's house.

"It doesn't mean you'll get to touch anything," I said.

"But that's where she took other boys to get the feel."

That, and his specificity about time and place, convinced me it wasn't a lie. On Monday, just before lunch, we had French again and I couldn't wait for it to come around. Connor had been playing matters very close to his chest all morning. He'd smiled knowingly in maths and English every time he'd noticed me looking in his direction, which made me determined not to ask and let him see how much I needed to know. Connor loved you to pry news from him because it allowed him to feel he was doing you a big favor when he did eventually get round to telling. I knew his game. If you pretended you didn't care, he'd soon trip over himself to tell you, but it nearly killed me not to ask.

"Aren't you going to ask about it, then?"

Paddy Flanagan was now ten minutes into his murdering of a translation of Madame Pompadour's visit to the hairdresser.

"About what?" I continued moving the pencil on each word of my own translation as Paddy haltingly advanced three words, reversed ten, and advanced two.

"I got the feel."

"Oh, that's right." I stole a look at Mr. Smith, who had his nose stuck in the textbook, his head shaking slowly.

"We went deep into the plantation and lay on a bed of pine needles."

"Oh, that's nice."

"She lay back and made it obvious straight away I could undo her bra. God, Gabriel, I got so bloody stiff." He paused for a moment. "Do you want to hear every detail?"

"Suit yourself."

A little into his description, Connor's hand touched my thigh. At first, I thought it was an accident. It happened again, and then he began to stoke my leg. I was surprised, yet every cell in my body began to pulsate. My thing rose instantly. While I didn't whisk away my leg, I knew also I ought to make some kind of protest. So I glanced up at Mr. Smith before scanning the room, though it was perfectly safe because of the deep box desks and our position at the back of the class. His stroking ceased. I made sure not to flinch as his hand moved to my fly, rubbed and pressed tenuously for a moment, and then began to unzip it as he continued talking about Rosellen. I didn't hear another word of French translation.

"You can touch me as well," he said out of the side of his mouth.

Immediately, I reached over, our wrists crisscrossed, and began to undo his fly. As soon as I felt him there, I was mortified. I was mortified because he seemed so much longer than me. A few minutes later, Mr. Smith's chair scraped the floor as he pushed back, rose, and approached the blackboard. Our hands retreated, and I fumbled to put myself in order as the new verbs and nouns of the day appeared.

As soon as class ended, Connor told me to follow him. He took me into an end cubicle in the lavatory where we masturbated as urinals flushed rhythmically in the background and boys rushed in and out. After we'd finished, I couldn't wait to get away from him. For the rest of the day, guilt lingered like a bitter aftertaste because I remembered the promise I'd made to God. I'd broken my promise at the very first temptation. I'd committed the abomination again, and enjoyed it. I loathed myself. In my bedroom that night, I sank to my knees and said a slow Act of Contrition and vowed never to do it again.

Connor and I pretended it had never happened next day, but in bed that night, a thousand sexual thoughts overwhelmed me. I relived the whole event, remembered Connor's every squeeze and touch. No matter which way I turned in the bed, I couldn't stop the crackling excitement until finally I surrendered. As soon as James started to breathe deeply, I took tissues I'd already placed under my pillow and put them by my thigh, made a little tent under the bedclothes with one hand, and abused myself senseless with the other.

The guilt rushed back after it was over. Once more, I recited a slow Act of Contrition and promised Him I'd never do it again. Two days later in French class, Connor began talking about what he'd done to Rosellen, his hand moved to my fly, and I raised no objection. Afterward, when I got him alone, I told him that what we'd just done was an abomination.

"Well, don't you agree with me that it's an abomination?" I said.

"No."

"Don't you feel guilty and sinful because we're boys?"

"I don't think there's any problem so long as we think about feeling girls while we're doing it."

"Look me in the eye and say you truly believe there's nothing wrong with it."

"So long as we're thinking about feeling girls while we're doing it, I think it's fine."

His eyes hadn't darted away as he'd said that, and I loved his reasoning. It made a lot of sense. So, I continued doing it with him. I told myself this wasn't the same thing Noel and I had done, because Connor and I were thinking of girls as we touched each other. It was much more difficult to push aside the mortal sin aspect, and the fact I was also breaking my promise to God. Eventually, though, I managed to reconcile this dilemma by concluding everyone breaks a promise to God because that's the nature of being human. That, together with my slow recital of the Act of Contrition, entitled me to unquestioned absolution.

Granny Harkin visited Auntie Celia every weekend, and I started to go in with her. The purpose of my visits was now to see Connor as much, if not more, than Martin. We'd go upstairs on the pretext of discussing schoolwork. One Sunday afternoon, I arrived to learn Auntie Celia wouldn't permit Martin to come out of his bedroom. In June, he was to sit his O levels (the "O" being an accepted abbreviation for "ordinary"), and had done extremely badly in the mock examinations.

O levels were a set of major exams given by the Northern Ireland examination board, the courses were of two-year duration, and they were vital for two reasons. First, if passed, one could proceed into the sixth-form to begin Advanced level (A level) courses, successful completion of which guaranteed a place at a university. Second, universities applied to during the final year of school looked at one's O level grades, together with the headmaster's report, in deciding whether to accept or reject an application.

Connor and I were studying nine O levels apiece and had another year of preparation before taking them. Martin was studying five because he wasn't as bright, and both he and Pani were lazy. They'd passed only three mocks, and Martin's teachers were concerned. Apparently, at a PTA that week, they'd informed Auntie Celia he'd most likely fail, and she decided to take drastic action. She confined him to his bedroom and warned him he'd have to make extra efforts at his studies if he wished to continue attending the Saturday night dances that he was now attending weekly.

Her strategy was very inconvenient because Connor and I couldn't do anything upstairs anymore out of fear Martin would walk in and discover us. Instead, when I visited, we started going off to the plantation where he'd first felt Rosellen. I made sure never to initiate. I'd always allow Connor to make the first move, which he always did by beginning a story about what he'd recently done with Rosellen. So long as he talked about her, everything was fine, and we couldn't possibly be poofs, because poofs were effeminate and talked girlish, just like the actor on the sitcom *Are You Being Served?*

Uncle John turned into the kitchen clutching the side of his fat tummy, and Auntie Bernie, her face almost as white as her bead necklace, followed behind. Two weeks ago I'd visited Granny Harkin and she'd complained over tea that her usual letter from

Uncle Brendan had been extremely short. Uncle John said he now knew why. It turned out Father Pascal, the head of the missions in Kenya, had called Uncle Tommy to tell him Brendan had had a bit of a turn. Unfortunately, Uncle Tommy hadn't been at home, so Auntie Bernie took the call and panicked as soon as she'd heard the word "turn" (she was phobic about medical problems and was continually checking her raised facial mole), and had run to find Uncle John.

"I told Bernie we ought to consult with you because you'd know what to do," Uncle John said.

Mammy pulled a chair from under the table. "Sit, John."

"What'll we do?" he asked.

Uncle looked up at her like a little boy awaiting an answer and Auntie fingered her necklace, a thing she always did when she was out of her depth.

"Exactly what kind of a turn, Bernie?" my mother said.

"All I know is Father Pascal used that word." Auntie Bernie began to tug at the necklace. "You know what I'm like. As soon as I heard him say "turn," I was finished. My ears buzzed and I could hear nothing else for a while, and when I did come to my senses, he was saying Brendan was in Nairobi. The only thing I managed to glean is Brendan's been acting strange. He ordered Father Pascal not to tell the family because he didn't want to cause us any more trouble." She paused. "Strange? Can you imagine? Well, Father Pascal didn't agree, which is why he tried to call Tommy."

The emergent creases of displeasure in my mother's forehead were faint yet unmistakable as Auntie Bernie had uttered her last words. Electricity and the telephone had arrived in Knockburn, we'd had the latter for six months now, and Mammy had called Uncle Brendan's mission, as well as the order's main house in Nairobi, to give them our number as the primary contact.

She recovered quickly and, picking up the phone, dialed the order's house and demanded to speak with Father Pascal. It transpired Uncle Brendan had been broody and withdrawn from the community for months, but started behaving erratically one morning when another priest caught him throwing the Bible and other religious paraphernalia about the sacristy of their little church. The community doctor diagnosed nervous strain, prescribed rest, and he was sent to recuperate at the order's Nairobi home. Uncle had agreed on condition we, his family, not be informed of his illness. Next, my mother insisted on talking with Uncle Brendan. When he came on the phone, I could tell their conversation was stilted. After replacing the receiver in its cradle after she rang off, double-checking to make sure it was down properly because she wasn't used to it yet and was terrified the call might not have terminated and she'd incur huge charges, Mammy shrugged as she rolled her eyes.

"I'm sure you got the gist of that," she said to Uncle John. "You're not to tell your mother under any circumstances, and he wants no one flying out. He says he's almost recovered."

"Didn't he say what caused the breakdown?" asked Auntie Bernie.

"No."

"These turns don't happen to a body out of the blue, do they, Eileen? I mean normal people can't just—"

"All he said was he's been under pressure and flipped. That's all I know. He made no attempt to elaborate on what caused the flipping."

CHAPTER NINETEEN

"Sure, let him go."

"It's a lovely piece," my mother said. "How much?"

"Thirty pounds. It is a lovely wee piece of Belleek china, isn't it?" said Auntie Celia. She set the nine-inch Celtic cross down on the shelf again, placed the tip of her index finger on her lips, and smiled appreciatively at the ornament glittering in the overhead light. "I don't mind saying it's one of the nicest pieces I've seen for a long, long time."

My parents and I were in her shop. Mammy was looking for a wedding present for a neighbor's daughter and, as she was showing her stuff, Auntie Celia had also informed them she was allowing Connor to go with Martin to his first dance at the Fortress Inn. The dance hall was literally an old fort at the north end of Duncarlow Main Street, and the Indians, a very popular band whose music I loved, were playing. I'd known they were playing, of course. Martin had told me at school, and we'd hatched a plan for me to bring my parents into the shop, where he'd get Auntie Celia to soften them up so they'd let me go as well.

"And it's such a bargain," said Auntie Celia.

"I don't know her so well to be buying a Belleek cross of such intricacy," my mother said. Her eyes darted along the rows of ornaments. "What about that glass cat up there? How much is that?"

Auntie Celia glanced at Father before reaching for the item. "Harry, you were out at the dances when you were Gabriel's age."

"That *definitely* means I should be allowed to go."

Auntie checked a price tag underneath the ornament before

handing it to my mother. "Eight pounds and fifty-five pence? Sure, let him go. After all, it is *the* Indians."

"Eight pounds and change for a glass cat."

"He can go as far as I'm concerned," said Father. He winked at me.

"That's not glass," said Auntie Celia. "That's best Irish crystal, that is."

"Would those wee glass bubbles I see inside its head make it any cheaper, do you think?"

"Bubbles? Let me see that."

"Anyway, Gabriel's far too young for dances," said Mammy. "Next year, maybe."

A bell rang as the shop door was opened and a short woman entered with a panting spaniel on a leash. Auntie Celia greeted her as she advanced to the counter. My mother picked up a china vase, squinted and read the tiny price tag on its base, and shook her head as she laid it down again.

"Harry, what do you think of that china toast holder with the red and yellow rose pattern?"

"Nice."

"*Nice!* What do you mean nice? Will it suffice or not?"

"For God's sake woman, pick something."

Recognizing Martin's assistance was urgently required, I took advantage of their skirmish, walked quickly to the back of the shop, opened the little door, and mounted the narrow stairs leading to their flat. I found him blow-drying his hair in the bedroom. An open bottle of peroxide stood upon the vanity beside its white top and a fine-toothed comb. Scarcely before I could seat myself on the edge of the bed, the hair dryer was whirling full blast on the floor, singeing the carpet, and Martin had whipped off the towel around his neck and thrown it over the bottle. What's more, his neck had turned splotchy pink, the way it always did when he was dead embarrassed. So it wasn't just lemon juice he used on his fringe to make it blond, I thought. Old Pani was right. He accused Martin of using bleach every time my cousin arrived at school with his bang blonder than usual.

"You're far, far too early, Gabriel."

"Only by fifteen minutes." I crinkled my nose. "What's that chemical smell?"

"Chemical smell? There's no chemical smell. Listen, has my mother asked Auntie Eileen if you can go?"

I explained they were at an impasse as I allowed my eye to travel pointedly toward the crumpled towel.

"Go back at once, keep them on the subject, and I'll be down in a jiffy." He shot a glance at the towel, part of which was now wet, and nearly ripped my arm out of its socket as he escorted me out of the room. "Quick, or they'll have made up their minds *not* to let you go."

He arrived within minutes, just as Mammy was expressing a fear that if she let me go out to this dance, it might open the sluice gates and become a regular occurrence. Martin's bang was the brightest I'd ever seen. It was platinum, and he'd tried to tone it down by covering and mixing it in with his normal dark blond hair.

"I'm tired of this," I said. "I'll be a fifth-former soon and you're treating me like a child. And Connor's allowed tonight. I'm just tired of never getting to do anything."

Auntie Celia approached. "Martin, you've kept the lemon juice on your hair far too long again. I keep warning you about that."

Father stared at Martin as if he were an alien.

"Auntie Eileen, anyone who's anyone is going to see the Indians. Let him go."

She hemmed and hawed and finally relented, though emphasized twice it was just on this one occasion. Martin whisked me upstairs to show me his new jacket. It was made of royal blue and canary yellow plaid and was gorgeous. Connor came into the room as I was trying it on and Martin was readjusting his fringe, checking every few seconds in the mirror and moving his head from side to side.

"I really think I might have overdone the lemon juice this time. What do you think, Gabriel?"

"You definitely have," said Connor.

"Shut the *fuck* up, you."

"It matches the yellow squares in your jacket nicely," I said.

Connor laughed as I walked up to the vanity and peered in the mirror. The jacket was dead slimming, my backside didn't show at all, though my plum button-down shirt looked extremely dowdy now. In fact, it looked depressing.

"I can't go tonight," I said. "I'm wearing rags. I look pathetic."

Connor jerked his head rapidly at me behind Martin's back to indicate I should follow him out of the room. I waited a few seconds before leaving.

"My room's got the double bed, so you'll be sleeping in my room after the dance, dummy," he said.

I decided my shirt would suffice.

Entry to the Fortress Inn ballroom was an adventure. After crossing a pebbled courtyard surrounded by thick, crumbling walls, I arrived before a massive arched gothic door that I passed through into a room with gilt ceilings and a wooden floor that creaked. The room, maybe a formal drawing room, had been regal once, but now looked scruffy and reeked of stale smoke. At its east end, we passed through a pay kiosk and turnstile and went down a flight of concrete steps, further jarring my sense of romance about the place, and then entered a cellar containing the cloakrooms, juice bar, and a snack area. Another flight of concrete steps led to the ballroom.

Martin wouldn't take off his jacket, even though the place was stuffy and packed with people. Overhead lights struck a great revolving glitter ball comprised of hundreds of tiny mirror squares in the center of the ceiling, and condensation trickled down large mirrors running along the two longest sides of the room. At the front of the ballroom was the stage where the band, clad in brightly colored Indian outfits and trailing head feathers, was singing, "*Son, don't go near the Indians,*" as they whooped and danced about with tomahawks.

Parallel to one set of long mirrors ran a three-deep wall of women with highly glossed lips and perfect hairdos. On the adjacent dance floor, a line of men in dark clothing, not a single bright plaid jacket evident, jostled one another as they filed past the women. After observing for a little while, I saw how the system worked: if a man spied a woman he fancied, he'd extend his hand to her, and she either clutched or continued chewing gum and ignored it. Jealousies broke out among the men now and again because one or two had extended hands to the same woman, though this was always resolved by a dirty look or shove or two.

"I want to dance," Martin said. "Let's go up the line."

Connor declined because he was waiting for Rosellen to arrive and was afraid she might see him in the line. The queue of men moved in fits and starts. About a quarter way up the room, Martin asked someone to dance and was accepted. I struggled to both stay in formation and scrutinize the women as I continued to advance. The women examined each man's face intently, some whispered behind their cupped hands amongst themselves, and the whole scene would have been comical if I hadn't been so anxious to find a dance partner to prove to Martin I was equally as good as him. Finding myself near the end of the line, I grew desperate. I spied a young girl smiling and extended my hand. To my cringing dismay, her smile vanished, and she regarded me brazenly for an instant before lolling back her head to look up at the ceiling. Utterly jellified within, I closed my eyes and allowed my body to be propelled forward by the chest and malleable stomach of the man behind me.

Near the stage, I stood watching the band but heard no sound as I analyzed exactly what could have gone wrong. I didn't know whether to blame my horrid shirt, the two yellow pimples on my face, or the ugly goose down sprouting above my upper lip. One thing I did know for certain, I had to acquire a bright plaid jacket, and fast. I couldn't bear joining the line again that evening, and managed only to recover fully when Connor began telling me later in bed what he'd done with Rosellen in the secrecy of the car park.

A week later, I pleaded with my mother to be allowed to go to the Fortress Inn again. She complained vociferously at first before giving in. With some anxiety, I walked the gauntlet to the strums and croons of Philomena Begley and her Rambling Men. I spied a good-looking girl halfway down and, after a quick look about to make sure no one was watching, extended to her my quivering hand. She accepted. It seemed to me that I floated her onto the dance floor. Dressed in a flared lemon skirt and black nylon blouse that highlighted her ivory skin, her short dark hair glistening as if dipped in oil, a cloud of pale freckles on either side of an impish nose, she was the most beautiful girl I'd ever seen. We smiled at one another politely as we danced, looked about the hall a little, smiled again, looked about some more. The music stopped. Another number didn't commence, and I realized the previous song had been the end of a set and the band was taking a breather.

Gritting my teeth, I slid my arm gingerly around her waist. Martin had told me the end of the set was a critical moment: if a girl liked you, she didn't flinch and everything stayed good; if she hadn't yet made up her mind, she behaved like a nervous filly, shuffling a little but staying; and if she hoped to catch something better during the next set of dances, she'd say a crisp "thank you" and flee back to assume her position in the three-deep wall of women.

"I'm Lizzie. What's your name and how old are you?"

I was prepared for this question, because Martin had also told me this was another critical moment. Too young and they walked. Lizzie stopped chewing her gum as she awaited my response. A girl's age was so damned difficult to guess.

"I'm sixteen going on seventeen."

"You are? Me, too."

She slipped her arm around my waist. My eyes darted about, scanning the crowd for Martin, Connor, for anyone from school, but there was no one to witness the victory. The next set was slow, and we waltzed about the dance hall. Presently, I spied Connor dancing with Rosellen and winked. He nodded only slightly. My cousin liked to act cool when with his girlfriend.

Minutes later, I saw two fifth-year boys at the back of the room, so I steered Lizzie closer, taking pains to ensure I wasn't being too obvious. As we danced by, I rested my chin on her shoulder, stroked her glistening hair, and gave them a cursory nod. Out of the corner of my eye, I saw one boy stop chewing his gum as they both watched like bemused cattle. I ran my hand slowly up and down Lizzie's back, and she pulled back her head and smiled. She was the same age as these boys, I only a little over fourteen, yet it was me who had her. After the set, I asked if she'd like a soda, she agreed, and we walked down the concrete steps to the café hand-in-hand, every follicle in my scalp tingling.

"I'm dying for a fag," she said after we'd finished our sodas. "My brother's got some in his car. Do you want to come out with me?"

We went outside and searched for the car, walking up and down between rows of vehicles whose roofs glinted in the moonlight. Eventually, she spotted it and we drew up to a rusty contraption with a piece of hay bale twine holding its bonnet shut.

"What do you want?" her brother said. He was snogging in the backseat.

"Give me a fag or I'm getting into the front seat to court my new boyfriend."

"Like hell, you are."

Grumbling, he fumbled in his pocket, handed an entire packet and a box of matches to her, and she took two cigarettes. After lighting one, she placed the other carefully into her skirt pocket and led me to the other side of the fort, where couples were leaning in embrace against its thick stone walls. Above, the upper branches of two massive sycamores stretched over its battlements, while the mottled trunks of others glowed dimly within the dusky park stretching down to the river.

"God, what I would give to know the names and histories of the chieftains who stood behind these battlements in its heyday," I said.

"What's a battlement?"

"Those notched walls above us." I pointed upward.

Her eyes drifted up. "Oh, those things. I hate old forts and castles. They should just knock down this pile of stones and make a bigger dance hall." She took a long drag of her cigarette and looked up at the stars as she expelled smoke. "You want a puff?"

To decline didn't seem very manly. I took it, trying to hold it skillfully between thumb and forefinger, and pointed its lighted end toward my palm like I'd seen boys doing at school. As she observed, I took a great drag, threw back my head like her, and inhaled deeply as I looked at the stars. Suddenly, they blurred, and my entire chest felt as if a car had driven over it. I couldn't breathe. I began to cough like a consumptive. I coughed so much, I doubled over to try to catch my breath.

"Never smoked before?" I felt her cold fingers relieve mine of the cigarette.

I tried to answer, but remnants of smoke snagged within my lungs made me cough violently again. I shook my head. After a few moments, the coughing stopped but the sour aftertaste remained.

"You've got to take it slowly." She demonstrated. "Like that."

She gave it to me, I tried again, and this time it was a little easier. It still tasted vile, but I didn't cough. We chatted, shared the cigarette until it was finished, and then Lizzie leaned into the wall and looked at me expectantly. Nervously, I slung my arms around her shoulders. She put her arms around my waist and drew me closer. I put my lips to hers and we kissed as the percussion from the drums throbbed through the walls. Her lips felt dry and firm. She forced my lips apart with her tongue and wiggled it about inside until she found mine. I opened my eyes and saw hers were firmly closed, causing me to feel peculiar, as if I was a voyeur, because I was drinking in her face while she was unawares. I wished to withdraw my mouth, though instinctively knew it would be rude. Closing my eyes, I began pushing my tongue against hers, all the while thinking about the smoke and warm saliva being exchanged. The kiss was nasty, and I was much relieved when she withdrew her mouth.

"You've French-kissed before, haven't you?"

"Yes."

Another French kiss ensued, which proved no less horrid. By the fourth one, however, I'd acclimatized, but she wished to return to the dance hall. We had danced only two sets when the band stopped playing and asked everyone to stand for "The Soldier's Song." (The Fortress Inn was a Catholic dance hall, so the Irish national anthem was played.) The custom was to stand rigid and not talk during its rendition, but I turned to Lizzie and asked if I could see her again despite not knowing if I'd be allowed to another dance. She agreed, and we left for the juice bar after the Anthem finished, borrowed a pen to exchange addresses, and I had to be very vague when she pushed me for an exact date.

As my mother had feared, those initial nights at the Fortress Inn proved indeed to be the opening of the sluice gates. Because it was now summer vacation, it proved not as difficult to persuade her to let me attend, and we reached an agreement whereby I was permitted to go on alternate Saturdays and stay overnight at Auntie Celia's.

Despite the dismal Ulster economy, worsened by a successful militant Protestant strike which had destroyed the power-sharing experiment and resulted in the British reimposing direct rule, Father's business was growing and, consequently, he had money. As a result, he always gave me three or four pounds to spend at the dances.

Caroline became annoyed I was permitted to attend dances regularly. Although just thirteen, her large breasts made her look much older and, thus, she felt she should be allowed to go to them, too. Mammy wouldn't hear of it. She was scared the older boys, or even grown men, might take advantage, and told her she was still too young. This infuriated my sister. She accused our mother of being hypocritical because, if our parents went out at night visiting relatives, they left the two of us jointly in charge of James and Nuala, signifying thereby that Caroline was old enough for that large responsibility.

On one occasion when my parents were out, Caroline and I disagreed because she kept picking unnecessarily on Nuala. It spun out of control when she called me "Fat Arse" because I was extremely sensitive about my backside. Boys at school teased me about its size, and Caroline knew this. I hit her very sharply across the face before fully realizing what I'd done. Later, I apologized profusely, and she took full advantage of my remorse by insisting the only way to forgive the attack was for me to ask Mammy to let her attend a dance. The following Saturday, I asked, promising my mother I'd not let Caroline out of my sight, and to my amazement she agreed. Because Caroline was going, Father agreed to pick us up after the dance, which was a terrible downside because that meant I couldn't stay at Auntie Celia's. This made me extremely nervous that the sluice gates might have opened permanently for my sister, too.

Caroline and Lizzie liked each other instantly. The three of us danced together the entire evening, except for the slow dances, when Caroline was obliged to join the three-deep wall of glossy-lipped women. Toward the end of the night, Caroline insisted we join Martin and Sabina, his new girlfriend who worked in a factory shop, for a final soda. A few minutes later, I signaled to my sister that we had to leave because I didn't want Lizzie to witness the spectacle of Father picking us up. He was already parked in front of the dance hall's main gates. Caroline climbed into the front seat and I was glad because I didn't wish to sit next to him.

"Did you enjoy your first dance?" he asked her.

"It was fantastic and I'm definitely going again."

Father made no attempt to drive away. "I don't know about that, my girl." He peered over his shoulder and winked at me. "Did your big brother here look after you well . . . or was he too busy consorting with the ladies?"

I looked at him dourly. Father winked and acted jovial only when it suited him. The driver of a car waiting to exit the gates honked.

"Of course, I looked after her," I said, "and can't you see you're blocking the exit?"

His jokes angered me because they were always on his terms, always when he decided to crack them. We had nothing in common, and I was finding it impossible to talk to him about anything now. Any conversation between us was plastic as hell. Sometimes, I had to ride in the car with him alone, I had no choice, and we'd travel for miles in a smothering silence, occasional car rattles being my only amelioration because the radio was broken, and I'd close my eyes and will the journey to end.

Unfortunately for Caroline, that night proved to be her only outing, and I was back to spending alternate Saturday nights at Auntie Celia's, where Connor and I would discuss his exploits with Rosellen in the warmth of his cozy double bed. One evening, a few weeks before the new school year was due to begin, Connor suggested at the dance that we take the girls for a stroll to the river at the bottom of the sycamore-pocked park. The idea appealed greatly because it was such a warm night, but Martin wasn't interested. He wanted to stay at the dance, which didn't please Sabina because she kept hinting how a walk to the river would be fun. However, Martin wouldn't renege and, behind her back, told us to scram quickly.

The moon was almost full and lit up the mottled tree trunks as we made our way to the river. I could hear murmuring couples stretched out in the grass behind those with the greatest girths. At the bottom of the park, we helped the girls climb over the barbed-wire fence and followed the bank until we came to a quiet clearing where I could see the river's shining blackness. Its ruffled water looked as if it had been transformed to a blanket of sparkling diamonds. Here, we separated without any exchange of words, Connor and Rosellen taking one corner where they sank to the grass, we to the other.

Following his example, I pulled Lizzie close to me after we lay down. The grass was soft, cool, and all was perfect save a cluster of gnats that began to feast on my neck and face. Our first kiss was noticeably different. Lizzie thrust her tongue into my mouth as before, but there was added urgency now, and her hands slipped down the back of my jeans and fished out my shirttail.

"Isn't it nice to be outside?" she said, as her nails crossed my bare back and scraped its flesh.

"It is . . . it is lovely, isn't it?"

"You can stroke me, too . . . if you'd like."

Connor and Rosellen were still locked in an embrace, though he was on top of her now. I pushed Lizzie gently on her back and eased myself on top as well. Her legs spread open quicker than an oiled barn door. As Lizzie's eyes were closed, I stole another glance at Connor and saw one of his hands was dipped inside Rosellen's blouse. I kissed Lizzie and allowed my hand to travel along her neck and down to her right breast, which I squeezed, immediately feeling the coarseness of bra fabric beneath her satin blouse. She emitted a low sigh and thrust her hips gently, while her free hand moved to my hair and she began to dig her finger-nails into my scalp.

I felt on fire as she raked my roots. I French-kissed her deeply while unbuttoning her blouse, slipped my hand inside, and cupped her sheathed breast. Its corseted firmness was immediately off-putting. Perfume wafted from her exposed cleavage, its sweet-ness stronger than I'd ever noticed before, and evoked a memory of Auntie Bernie's perfumed stink from childhood. Suddenly, Lizzie's body felt delicate and weak beneath me. I felt every quiver of her soft limbs, I felt the restrained thrusts of her urgency, and needed to get away. I wanted to rise and run, but couldn't. I was the man, with the man's duty to see things through. All about me, her sweet stink that repelled even the gnats because they were no longer swarming. All about me, her sweet stink that was at once of flowers and not of flowers. I wanted to rise and run, yet felt my fingers reach underneath and struggle to release her bra as she arched her back.

Lizzie's eyes opened slightly. "Easy, you horny sod."

I tried again, and still it wouldn't undo. Her arms were thin as a heron's legs. Moans drifted over from Rosellen and Connor. Lizzie's painted lips stretched to coyness, and her rouged cheeks and curled eyelashes clotted with mascara now looked bizarre. I smiled upon her, felt not the tiniest stirring of my spongy thing.

"I think we should go back to Martin and Sabina."

"Wh . . . what?" Her hand froze on my back.

"Yes, we must go back."

"What's the matter?"

"I don't want to lose control."

Her mouth gathered for an instant, and then she made to rise.

"We're going back to the dance," I said to Connor and Rosellen, as Lizzie brushed her skirt with her hand.

They didn't respond.

Much later, as soon as Connor began to discuss his exploits with me in bed, my thing ballooned faster than a flat bicycle tube being pumped. I was stunned at its impertinence. After we'd finished and I'd recited my customary Act of Contrition, I lay with my eyes wide open, listening to the calm rise and fall of Connor's sleeping breath, bewildered utterly by my thing's absurdity.

CHAPTER TWENTY

Almost from the beginning of the new term, circumstances improved for me at school. I was now a fifth-year, the taunting in the bus stopped because Mickey and Pearse had left, and Willie, Mickey's aggressive, younger brother, focused on other boys and didn't confront me because his shield was gone.

As their teachers had predicted, Pani and Martin failed their O levels, though Father Rafferty allowed them to come back and repeat. This was an added bonus because it was terrific to have them in some of my classes.

Early one Sunday afternoon, a few weeks into the term, Father came home from second Mass and announced at the lunch table that an IRA man was coming to stay with us for a few weeks.

"I *don't* want any IRA volunteer staying under my roof," my mother said. She set the gravy boat down in front of Father very hard. "It's far too dangerous . . . and the house renovations aren't finished yet, so where would we put him?"

Her excuse was weak. Renovations were complete, we had a larger living room, another bedroom and bathroom, and a kitchen with the latest German equipment. Only a few weeks of decorating remained.

"The fellas asked me at the chapel gate, and I couldn't refuse," said Father. He began to slice into his thick T-bone steak. Red blood and oily water oozed and pooled beside his cabbage.

"I support the cause as much as the next person, but we have our children to think about, Harry. What if the army launches a raid in the middle of the night and finds an IRA man here? What'll happen then? They'll cart you away and intern you in

Long Kesh. What'll happen to the business? What'll happen to us?"

"They'll *not* raid here. Luksee, they won't think we're harboring anybody precisely because we have children in the house." Father looked at each of us in turn as he chewed his meat. "They'll be our cover."

"I don't want any strange man under my roof." Mother paused as she stared at her plate. "Just when we're making a bit of money and beginning to have a life, now along comes this. We don't know what terrible things this man might have done. He could be one of those men who blew up the soldiers a few weeks ago, for all we know."

A month previously, the IRA had placed a bomb under a road culvert in lower Knockburn, and five British soldiers had been blown to bits. The Protestant customer at the Hamilton's supermarket delicatessen was dead right when she'd said Knockburn was nationalist, but dead wrong when she accused most men of being IRA volunteers. Knockburn people were decent and didn't support the use of violence in the main, but many were also fed up because the Protestant hard-liners wouldn't give an inch and refused to give Catholics any say in the running of the province's affairs. Some young men were so frustrated, they had turned to the Provos (a group which had split from the more peaceful Official IRA) as a last resort. The Provos believed violence was justified to banish British rule and, in addition to bombing and shooting in the largest towns and cities, had stepped up their campaign in rural areas. Because of this, many IRA volunteers were on the run, and there was an unspoken code that every man and woman in Knockburn was expected to provide refuge for volunteers if asked.

"Harry, I don't want anyone ruthless sleeping under my roof. He'll be a bad influence on Gabriel and James . . . he might try to recruit them into that way of life." The rapidity of Mammy's speech underscored her panic. "And Gabriel needs peace to study for his O levels. As it is, he's had to contend with all the noise generated by the renovations."

"I wouldn't worry about his being recruited to the cause,"

Father said. "James, maybe." He looked at my brother and winked. "Aye, James, maybe, but not Gabriel."

"What about those English people you sometimes bring here to talk business?" Mammy said. "If he hears their accents, he'll spread the word and maybe arrange to have them kidnapped . . . or even worse."

"Luksee, there's a fella by the name of Seamus Regan coming to stay, *end* of discussion. He'll be here in a few weeks' time and I don't want to hear another chirp from anyone. Not another chirp."

"Well, he can sleep in an outhouse," Mammy said, clearly stung that such a major decision had already been made without discussion.

" 'Deed by Jasus, he'll not. He's out fighting for his country, so he can sleep with Gabriel or James in their bed."

I was looking forward to having my own room after the decorating was finished and certainly did not wish to share my bed with a strange man. Moreover, the thought of his legs and arms touching any part of my body during sleep caused me to wince.

"I'm *not* sleeping with him. He can share with James. I don't care if my room's not completed yet, because I'm moving a cot in there tonight."

"I'm almost as big as you," James said. His face darkened, like it always did when he felt he was being put upon. "I'll take the cot and sleep in your unfinished room."

"I don't want a stranger in my house," Caroline said.

Now in the mid-throes of puberty, Caroline was most self-conscious about a new spurt of growth that had left her gangly in appearance. She had the full breasts and hips of a woman and the forehead pimples and gait of a girl.

"Gabriel shouldn't have to sleep with him," Nuala said.

My little sister took my side in everything, even when I was wrong.

"What the hell's the matter with you?" said Father. "You should be proud to help a man who's fighting so you'll have decent jobs in a free Ireland."

"A fat lot of good the fighting has done us this far," said my mother. "The Protestants just dig in their heels and it's we who are suffering."

"I don't agree with the IRA's bombing and shooting," I said. "They're killing innocent people as well as the soldiers. They're giving Catholics a bad name. As it is, most Protestants think we're all a bunch of savages and murderers."

"The Provos are very bad, and Gabriel shouldn't have to sleep with one of them," Nuala said.

Mother looked at her absentmindedly. "A body can't even go into a shop in Belfast or Derry but the army and police are pawing at us, searching our bags for incendiary devices."

"We shouldn't really invite him here, Daddy," I said, pushing the word "Daddy" out of my mouth. "Let them find him somewhere else to stay. I'm sure there's many a house would be glad to have him."

"Shut your mouth. Sure, you're no Irishman. All you do is back the dirty, thieving English. You'd rather have English rule than a free Ireland."

His rabidity wasn't even slightly true. I wanted justice, also. Justice was the same as breathing. I just didn't see the sense of hating every Protestant in order to obtain it. Father and James believed Protestants who didn't want to live in a united Ireland should leave. It was absurd to think they'd do such a thing. The Protestants were now every bit as entitled to live in Ireland as we were. They'd been living here since 1690, and that entitled them to stay.

"You don't want a united Ireland," Father said. "You're the enemy every bit as much as them."

Father was right and wrong. Certainly, I didn't want a united Ireland.

"How dare you accuse me of being the enemy? That's below the belt, that is. You know it's true that the Southern Irish government can't look after their own people properly, so how the hell could they manage us? They'd make a sow's ear of the North. They can't even build motorways . . . or provide free university education for their citizens. And the Catholic Church controls everything down there. I hate Paisley every bit as much as you, but you have to realize that other, decent Protestants can't accept an Ireland where the Catholic Church pokes its nose into political affairs."

"That's enough, Gabriel," said Mammy. "Just remember your uncle Brendan's a priest."

"Don't you dare say anything bad about the Irish republic," James said.

"It's ridiculous that we can't criticize what's rotten and useless down there out of fear we're acting disloyal," I said. "That makes no sense to me and—"

"You're too fucking English," Father said. "Always backing them when all they've done is rob us of our land and kill us. Why can't you be a real Irishman?"

"I agree," said James. "Always sitting beside that Protestant Nigel in the bus every morning, talking a load of shite with him, and him as black as the ace of spades."

"He's *not* a bigot."

"His mother's very nice," Mammy said. "A very decent woman."

James had three deep furrows in his forehead, exactly like Father's when he was angry. "Daddy's right. You *are* a disgrace."

"Aye, you tell him, James," said Father. "*You're* the sort of Irishman this country needs."

Banging down my fork and knife, I leaped from my chair and stomped outside, where I stood sulking and cursing against the side of the house. I knew I was behaving like a loser, but there was nothing else to do. Half an hour later, Nuala came out and eventually persuaded me to return inside, where I found things had calmed. James and Caroline were arguing about whether or not Marc Bolan from T-Rex was effeminate because he wore eyeliner, and Father was reading the *News of the World*, getting his fix of salacious scandal from an English newspaper that Mammy had to always stuff under the couch when Father McAtamney paid us a visit.

My mother and I were traveling in the car and had just finished the rosary. We'd been visiting Granny Neeson, who'd been having dizzy spells. The visit had been awkward because Aunt Peggy was in Scotland visiting Colin (her fiancé of two years now), who was doing a company audit over there, and my grandmother had perked up enough to complain to Mammy that Aunt Peggy was wasting her time. "Taking a vacation to visit the lovely highlands, my backside," she'd said, "as if I'm dying in a bubble. What incentive does he have to marry her, I ask you? The man's happy enough to stay engaged, so she'll never get him to marry her because she's over in Scotland acting as his wife now, anyway." An awkward pause had followed during which my mother, thinking I couldn't see her because I was reading a book, tried frantically to alert her to drop the subject by vigorously shaking her head. And Granny did drop it by remarking she was definitely on her deathbed this time, though I'd known exactly what she'd meant. To ensure the subject was permanently changed, Mammy began to lament about the IRA man's arrival, which Granny countered by telling her not to bother her with trifles while she was on her deathbed, and finally the two sat in brooding silence until it was time for us to leave.

"I've been meaning to ask you, but it always slips my mind," Mammy said as a car that had been unnerving her on account of its being too close to our tail passed by. "I don't hear you talking too much about the girl you meet up with at the dances. What's this her name is?"

That was a lie. She never forgot names.

"Lizzie."

"That's right. Her."

"Oh, she's out of the picture."

I hadn't even mentioned her to my mother until Caroline, after I wouldn't ask if she could attend another dance, huffed and told her I had a steady girlfriend. In all honesty, I'd dumped Lizzie because she'd outlived her convenience. She'd been convenient:

I didn't have to walk up the three-deep wall of women and risk rejection and, albeit unknowingly to her, in addition to Mickey's departure from school, Lizzie had also helped end the taunting on the school bus. My reputation had improved markedly among the boys as a result of having a girlfriend, even more so when they found out she was older than I, to boot.

But Lizzie got more and more troublesome. It was nerve-wracking being with her because I felt nothing sexual. My thing never stirred on those rare occasions when I couldn't make any more excuses, and Lizzie and I would go to the back of the Fortress Inn to court in the dark. It would remain relentlessly shriveled. It remained relentlessly shriveled, yet turned hard as oak whenever Connor touched me. *That* preyed on my mind because there was no denying it. I could fool myself that I was thinking about girls when Connor and I were doing things, but my sponginess down there let me know exactly how things stood when I was alone with Lizzie.

"Well, I'm glad to hear it," my mother said.

"Why?"

"You're far too young to be going steady with girls."

I listened to the low hiss of the car tires on the wet road. Outside, the fields were full of darkness. Rhododendrons shone blackish-green as the headlights struck them when my mother negotiated bends. At one point, a hare darted from the hedge and stopped abruptly, transfixed by the bright lights until my mother lowered them.

"Are you still thinking about the priesthood?" she asked.

My body stiffened. "I don't know." The tires hissed again, and I stared out at the pitch-dark fields. "Do you really want me to be a priest?"

She chuckled, the way she always did when she was about to say the exact opposite of what she was really thinking. "If you feel it's not for you, then that's the way it must be." A silence, but it was dead prickly. "And there's always James, I suppose. Maybe he'll be the one."

"Why is it so important?"

"Oh, it's the most wonderful thing in the world for a mother to have a son entering the priesthood. I can think of no greater honor. Think how very proud your Granny is of Brendan."

"Well, seeing as you mention that . . ." I thought fast and spoke slowly to make sure nothing I would say would set her off, "Granny told me quite a while back it was Granda far more than she who wanted him to be a priest. Granda pushed from the first day he set foot in Saint Malachy's." I paused, but no response seemed forthcoming. "And Granny didn't want him to go to Rome, either. She was sad when he went there instead of Maynooth . . . and she also said he wouldn't have gone to Rome or the missions if it hadn't been for Granda's stubbornness."

She gave me a sidelong glance. "When did she tell you this, and what else did she say?"

"Shortly after Uncle Brendan went back to Kenya. I came upon her sitting crying on Granda's chair one day. She called me to her and held me really tightly, so tightly in fact, I could hardly breathe. She said her heart was scourged." I paused again. "She also said I was Uncle's special nephew."

"I see. Why didn't you tell me about this back then?"

"Well, after Granny stopped crying and let me go, she asked me to imagine my future grave and then made me swear on it not to tell a soul about what I'd caught her doing." I glanced at Mammy's profile. "And you'd also warned me a long time ago never to speak of that to her again, so I deemed it best not to say a word." I cleared my throat. "What really did happen between Uncle Brendan and Granda?"

"Brendan was a young man like you and James . . ." She stopped talking and I hardly dared breathe lest the moment would be killed, "No, he was far older than you at the time. There was an argument about something which threatened his becoming a priest, and your grandfather was livid and . . ." She fell silent again, ". . . they were both so headstrong. It happened so long ago, I can't remember the exact details."

"Try and cast your mind back."

"It had something to do with his going steady with a girl for a wee while. Your granda felt very threatened by that."

"Was Uncle Brendan serious about her?"

Another short pause. "I don't know."

"Was she nice?"

"I never met her."

"But, he became a priest in the end, so why didn't Granda speak to him?"

"People have arguments, and stupid pride won't let them back down, I suppose. Now it's too late for them to make up, anyway."

"I don't understand. It seems such extreme behavior for a little thing that didn't matter in the end. There must be something else. There has to be."

"Well, extreme or not, that's what happened and that's all there is to it." Again, she peered sidelong at me. "Why? Are you thinking I'm lying or keeping something back?"

The directness of her question threw me.

"No."

"I'm glad to hear it."

"It all seems so petty, that's what I mean. Uncle Brendan should have come home to see him when he lay dying. That was definitely wrong of him, wasn't it?"

"Yes." She sighed. "People can be so headstrong ... even when it's to their detriment. That's what happened. Both men were pig-stubborn." She looked at me intently now. "Promise me, you'll always think well of your father and me. And also promise, you'll never act so pig-stubborn if something should ever happen and we have a terrible argument one day."

"We'll never argue like that."

"Promise me, anyway."

"*Mammy*, watch out, the *ditch*."

The wheels of the car caught on the grass verge and I could feel it veer toward the hedge. She shrieked as she turned the steering wheel sharply. The wheels slid, and we jackknifed slightly before the tires caught the road surface and the vehicle rectified itself again. We traveled in silence for half a mile or so.

"Well, do you promise me?"

Her persistence shocked me, especially since I'd assumed she'd been thinking about our narrow escape.

"So long as you don't push me like Granda pushed Uncle Brendan." I smiled at her mischievously. "Otherwise, *I* might have to run away, too."

"May God forgive you for thinking I'm pushing you, Gabriel."

"I was just kidding . . . though I must admit I find it so difficult to agree with the Church's views on certain subjects."

"We all do," Mammy said, and she laughed, which meant she was relaxed again. "That's normal. I've even had the odd difficulty." She laughed once more. She put on the indicator to turn right. A sheep's eyes glittered ghostlike from behind a fence as we swung into the side road. "What's the certain subjects, by the way?"

"Oh, minor subjects."

"Like?"

"Take contraception, for example. It's ridiculous to me that the Church won't consider its use."

"Jesus, that's not a minor subject. *That's* major. Using contraceptives is a mortal sin. How can you even question that?"

I sighed, stared straight ahead, shook my head inwardly. I was taught to question things at school. I was taught to look at all kinds of problems with the honed mind of a Saint Malachy's student. Yet, when I dared to question the Church's position on this matter in religious education class, it was just plain taboo. It was taboo by the priests, taboo by my mother.

"Practicing artificial contraception is a mortal, mortal sin."

A mortal, mortal sin. One mortal more than an everyday mortal sin. What Connor and I were doing was also a mortal, mortal sin. That thought whipped up a chill that surged up and down my body.

"It's killing babies, Gabriel . . . and very, very selfish."

"What about the poor people in Africa? I don't think God means for those people to have large families and live in poverty, do you?"

"The missionaries teach them all about the rhythm method."

"You mean to say Uncle Brendan goes around teaching about the rhythm method as part of his work?"

"Oh, I'm sure he does. Africans have to be taught that the pope forbids contraception, too."

"How would *he* know anything sensible about contraception?"

She didn't respond immediately. "You must always accept what the pope says. You must accept without question. He's God's representative on earth. He understands the divine plan. He knows everything."

She was like a bloody machine gun. Everything spewed out, it was so ingrained.

"Gabriel, never let your uncle Brendan hear you speak like this. I certainly hope you haven't been putting mad views like this in the letters you send him."

"What if I have?"

"Because craziness like that would be enough to give him another nervous breakdown."

"That's ridiculous."

"Are you writing things like this in your letters to him? Here I was thinking I was rearing you the right way, that I was rearing you to be a good Catholic, and now I find I'm rearing a heathen."

She became a repository of sniffles and tears. My mother became such when she wasn't getting her way.

"Please don't cry anymore."

"Jesus, *how* can I not cry? My heart's broken."

"I'm sure the Church is probably right."

"The Church is infallible, and don't you ever forget it."

CHAPTER TWENTY-ONE

THE IRA MAN ARRIVED to stay for ten days while final arrangements were being made to spirit him off to America. My bedroom was finished, so James had to share a bed with him. Seamus was stocky, in his late twenties, with a disarmingly boyish face and tight auburn curls. He didn't fit my image of a vicious IRA volunteer, though admittedly, I didn't have much information as to what they were supposed to look like. The world within which the IRA operated was shadowy, populated with faceless men who did their deeds in secrecy, and no one dared openly admit they knew any volunteers.

My feelings toward Seamus and the IRA were ambivalent. I did not agree with their violent methods, yet I was also outraged by the shootings and killings which Protestant paramilitaries were perpetrating on innocent Catholics in Belfast, and wanted protection for them. Murder is another mortal, mortal sin, and I would have preferred that none of these organizations existed, but my history books demonstrated that peace and justice don't come about sometimes until brutal acts have been committed. The old Knockburn men also said things like this, and they also said the Protestants were stubborn and indifferent to injustice.

Seamus had a hearty laugh and big hands with spotless nails and perfect white crescents because he manicured them. His spotless nails and perfect crescents intrigued me because they appeared so at odds with the worrisome life of a man on the run. Although not formally educated, his mind was sharp as a flicked whip. He could help James with his mathematics homework, something I couldn't even do on account of I was so dreadful at it.

Though I had determined to act coolly toward him, his enthusiasm to join in our draughts games and talk about books warmed me to him.

He read voraciously. He read Protestant, Catholic, and any British newspaper he could lay his hands on. He read my Shakespeare and O'Casey plays, Caroline's poetry books, and Hardy, Austen, and Joyce novels. Once, he sent me to the Ballynure library, two small rooms over a hardware shop, with a list of Russian and American authors that made the old librarian scratch her head because she hadn't heard of some of them.

"You must read Steinbeck's *Grapes of Wrath* when you get the time," he said. "That's what I call a book."

"What's it about?"

"It's about the working man and subjugation. The people in that book were treated the same as the Irish are now. They were forced to leave their land by the enemy, though granted it wasn't the Ulster Unionists doing the forcing." He laughed at his own joke. "But their enemies pushed them out of their homes for the same reasons. They pushed them out for greed and power. That's why the Protestants and English are pushing us about like the people in that book, Gabriel. We're disenfranchised, just so the rich Protestant farmers and corporations can make money." He looked at James and me gravely. "Be sure to read that book soon, and tell your friends at school to read it, too."

"Are you on the run because you killed soldiers?" James asked.

Seamus' lips quivered for a moment before stretching into a boyish grin. "You ask too many questions, young fella. It would fit you better if you asked your maths teacher more questions instead of me."

The man was just so good-humored, you couldn't dislike him.

"But did you, Seamus?" James asked.

Father peered over his newspaper, and I could see he was astounded at my brother's insolence.

"It's bad manners to ask people questions they don't wish to answer," my mother said.

"The lad's okay," Seamus said. "Let's just say I've done a few wee things I don't care to crow about. We'll leave it at that, shall we?"

A murderer was sheltering under our roof, and yet was so intelligent, so good-natured, and had such beautiful hands, you couldn't help but bond with him.

My fifth year at Saint Malachy's got even better when Pani got a car. It was ancient, and he hung two furry, yellow die from the windscreen mirror and set a tiger with a scarlet tongue and nodding head on the ledge of the backseat. He parked it in a narrow driveway leading up to the school, near a public housing estate that had been built by the Unionist government in a scurrilous attempt to stop Saint Malachy's from expanding, and we'd sit in it at lunchtime listening to pop music on Radio 1.

Martin, Pani, and I also sat together in every class we had in common. We sniggered, whispered, and didn't listen to a word the teachers said. I don't know why exactly, but I was becoming most unruly. I think it was for a combination of reasons: my troubles on the bus were over, I was anxious because I wasn't feeling much for girls when I thought about them sexually, and I'd also got the stupid idea in my head I was far smarter than everyone else in my class.

Now that Pani had his car, Martin convinced him to take us to other dance halls and discos farther afield. My mother didn't object, because Caroline and I were spending long hours in my bedroom, studying supposedly, but actually discussing a raft of teenage problems such as acne, my fat arse, her crushes, ABBA, and my fat arse again. With regard to ABBA, I devoured every magazine article I found, and fantasized regularly about being invited to join the group. Blond Agnetha with her straw yellow hair and throaty voice became an obsession, though not in a sexual way. I daydreamed I was conversing with her, and she was always captivated by my intelligence. At other times, I'd strut about my bedroom, a pair of rolled-up socks serving as a microphone, singing the words to "Waterloo" as it belted from the record player.

Acting was another passion, and I got a part in our school drama department's production of *Twelfth Night*. I'd tried out for the part of Malvolio, but got Viola. I'd acted in small plays we'd written in second-year English class with Miss Brown and enjoyed it. But acting in front of class peers is one thing, and their parents quite another. I was shy, but Mr. Casey, the head of drama, believed I had talent and said I'd be very successful in the role. Of course, Father was highly skeptical about boys donning women's clothes for a school play. My mother's theories that it was so lucky I'd got a part at all and how grand it would look on my future university application forms did not persuade him.

"Why did he have to cast you as the woman?" he asked. "Why couldn't he give you a man's part?"

"Because I'm good at the role."

"What will anybody going to it from Knockburn think?"

"It's only a play, Harry," said the IRA man. He set down his newspaper.

Because the production was contemporary, I was to wear an old polka-dot dress, and was standing on top of a chair because Mammy was altering it to fit me. The first dress rehearsal was the following evening and she'd left my costume to the last minute. I sighed exaggeratedly because we'd had this same tiresome discussion before, and Father's ignorance of Shakespeare and his plays was very dank. Even Seamus, now in his final two days with us, didn't say a word. I could see he understood, even though he'd had no formal education.

The phone rang. My mother took the pins she'd stored between her lips out of her mouth, handed them to me, and went out to answer it.

"Besides, I'm not the only one," I said. "I've told you that Martin's playing Olivia and has to wear women's clothing throughout the *entire* play."

Father's look spoke volumes, though nothing further was said.

Mammy returned a few minutes later. "That was Brendan on the phone and he didn't sound like himself at all. I hope to God he's not relapsing."

"What do you mean?" asked Father.

Seamus had taken up his newspaper again and his face was now hidden behind its pages.

"He was vague and rambling. I asked how the missions were doing and he said, 'Only so-so.' Then I asked how he was and he says to me, 'I'm a bit depressed, if you really must know.'" She glanced at Seamus' paper. "I swear to God that's what he said, Harry."

"Any word of him coming home?" Father said. "Sure he's long overdue. A gallop home would soon put any depression nonsense out of his head."

"He's coming in May. He didn't say for how long . . . and then, without as much as pausing for a breath, he asked how your mother's health is. He said he'd been thinking about her a lot of late." She fell silent for a moment. "Do you think he's had some sort of premonition about her?"

Mammy was very superstitious. It was so chronic, she wouldn't even allow a pigeon to rest on the roof of our home, just in case it might really be a dove because doves on roofs always meant a death in the family. She chased them away with stones, even broke one of the front windows once because she was such a lousy shot.

"Don't be stupid," said Father.

"I didn't want to tell yous, but I woke up in the middle of the night very recently and I heard something wailing," Mammy said.

She was also terrified of hearing the banshee.

"I didn't want to say anything to scare yous, but now Brendan's saying things like this."

"Don't be crazy," I said.

"I'm telling yous that wailing came from nothing belonging to this earth," she said. "May God strike me dead if I'm lying, but it was at the corner of the house one second and far away the next. I'm telling yous that's exactly what the banshee does."

Father laughed, and her shoulders pushed back.

"Brendan also said he has something to share with us, but I couldn't wheedle out of him what was to be shared."

"I hope he's not badly ill," Nuala said.

"That did cross my mind," Mammy said. "Cancer runs on the Harkin side, Harry." She made one of those sudden shivers people make when they're discussing something uncomfortable. "Didn't one of your uncles die of cancer when he was about Brendan's age?" Mammy answered her own question before Father could reply. "But then, there's such a paucity of priests for the foreign missions, I'm sure God wouldn't take him." She'd regarded me as she said that. "He said something else very strange. He said he loves us all, and hopes we love him too, and then he asked me to throw in an extra wee prayer for him when we're saying our rosary."

"What's so strange about that?" said Father. "If anybody's got God's ears, it has got to be you because you're hardly ever off your knees."

Seamus chuckled, and immediately crinkled his newspaper noisily to disguise it.

"That's a stupid statement for Uncle Brendan to make," Caroline said. "As if we'd dare *not* love a priest."

"All the same, it was a bit peculiar, Harry . . . and he finished his call very odd, too. Brendan always finishes with a 'May you find peace in Christ's love,' but he just said 'bye' this time. *Bye.* That was it, honest to God. No, something's up. He never fails to say the 'May you find peace in Christ's love' bit."

Because rehearsals took place after hours, Auntie Celia and Mammy made arrangements to pick Martin and me up after school. They rotated duties so that one week I stayed overnight at my aunt's house, and then the following week Martin stayed with me. This proved very advantageous because sex was now an important part of my life. I thought about it nearly all the time, just like Fergal, whom I'd criticized for the very same thing a few years ago. In addition to doing things with Connor, I masturbated two or three times a day, and at least once nightly, too.

"What part of sex do you think about most when you're wanking alone at night?" I said to Connor in bed one night.

"Riding." He reached over and seized my thing. "Why? What do you think about most?"

This was my cue to begin to fondle him, also. I allowed Connor to initiate always, even though I was as eager as he was.

"The same thing."

That was a lie. The truth was I could not get a hard-on when I thought about a girl, not even if I gave her huge breasts. No matter how much I concentrated, my thing wouldn't respond. I couldn't get it beyond a soft firmness, and always had to resort to thinking about a man to get it successfully stiff. Once it was up, however, everything worked fine. It was just that the means employed to get it to that point felt very false, and preyed more and more on my mind.

"I've often wondered how a woman feels when it's being done to her," Connor said.

"You have?"

"You know the way teachers tell us that if you do something rather than just read about it, how it helps make you understand the thing even better? Let's take you and tennis, for example. Because you play it, you understand what's going on at Wimbledon far better than if you'd just read the rules. Isn't that right?"

"Aha, but what does this have to do with riding?"

"Well, think about it. If a man does it once, don't you think he'd know better how the woman feels? Don't you think he'd be able to satisfy her more? He'd know exactly what she's feeling and be able to please her better as a result."

"Yes, I see what you're getting at."

"Well, how about you try doing it to me, Gabriel? Only this one time, mind."

215

"*Me* ride you? I don't know. I think it would . . . I'm not sure."

"Oh, let's try. If it makes us better when we're riding girls, why not? Right?"

"I suppose that's true."

Connor rolled over on his tummy, stretched out his legs like a toad in mid-leap, and I climbed on top of him. A second or two later, I yelped and leaped out of bed.

"Jesus, my thing's hurt." I pulled back the curtain and examined it in the dusky orange glow of the street lamp.

"What are you talking about?"

"Jesus, switch on the light, quick." I looked down and saw blood. "I'll bleed to death. What'll I do? *What the fuck* will I do?"

"Shush . . . shush, you'll wake everybody."

"It's full of blood vessels down there, and we won't be able to tell Auntie Celia what happened." I looked at my thing again. "Connor, what'll I do? What the fuck will I do?"

He seized his school pants off the floor, pulled out a tissue, and wiped my thing. A car with a broken exhaust passed noisily down the street, and suddenly my whirling imagination conjured up images of wailing ambulances, peering doctors, and hot-faced explanations.

"Oh, it's just a little scratch, Gabriel. Look, it's almost stopped bleeding."

He was right. The bleeding had slowed, but my foreskin was torn. "That's the last of *this* sort of carry-on. We shouldn't have tried to do that in the first place. It's not fucking right."

"It's time we stopped the whole caper. I've been thinking that for a while now, if you must know."

"You mean, never to do anything again."

"I'm sixteen and shouldn't be doing this anymore. We should be concentrating on girls full time. If we don't, we might turn ourselves into queers."

"You said it didn't matter, provided we thought about girls." I felt extremely queasy.

"I'm older than you, and it could begin to take over if I'm not careful."

"Do you think so?"

"Definitely."

"Connor, I want to ask you something . . . have . . . have you ever thought about boys when you're wanking? You know . . . just for a wee change now and again . . . when you're tired of thinking about girls, maybe."

"Don't be bloody crazy! Only fucking homos do that. I always think about girls. Are you trying to infer I'm already a homo?"

"No, I'm not."

"Why do you ask? Have you thought like that?"

"Jesus, no way. Only homos think that sort of stuff."

"Well, we're both all right, then. We're stopping in time."

We climbed back into bed, Connor switched off the light, and I lay cold and wooden beside him. The clock's tick in the hallway began to accuse me. Tick-tock; ho-mo; ho-mo; ho-mo. Sporadic traffic passed up and down the street: parents and sleeping babies and happy girlfriends and boyfriends driving by in cars. My world was ripped and torn. Tick-tock; ho-mo; ho-mo; tick-tock; ho-mo; ho-mo; ho-mo. Connor's breathing settled into rhythmic slumber. I wanted to stop the clock, but couldn't because Auntie Celia would hear me try to open its casing. Ho-mo; ho-mo; ho-mo; ho-mo. "I'm *not* homosexual," I screamed within. Ho-mo; ho-mo; ho-mo. I turned on my side and stared at the dusky glow of the wallpaper. I'd never initiated things. Connor was the one who always started things. Ho-mo; ho-mo. Now he didn't want to do it anymore because he was scared he'd be homosexual. Ho-mo; ho-mo. I lay on my back, passed my fingers over the cold sweat on my chest, took a deep breath. Another surge of warmth swept over my body. Ho-mo; ho-mo.

I experienced a fierce urge to leap from the bed and cry and bang my head against the wall. I wanted to cry and bang my head hard to stop the thoughts. But banging my head was useless, crying was feminine, and I'd still have to get up in the morning and go on. I sat up and watched Connor's placid breathing. Up and down, pause, up and down. How can he be so selfish? I wondered. Nothing would be changed in the morning, except he and I would arise and never touch each other again. I could stand it no longer. I had to get up. I rose very gently, but still felt dizzy. I thought I'd faint. Leaning my hand on the wall, I took a few slow breaths and went into the hallway now silent and dark as mortal, mortal sin. I felt my way along the wall, past the clock, past Auntie Celia's room where I could hear Uncle Frank snoring, and went into the bathroom.

I switched on the light, looked at my face in the mirror, and despised the image gawking back at me in the stark brightness. Falling on my knees before the toilet bowl, I knelt and tore at my hair as I prayed and beseeched God to come and help me. I prayed and beseeched for ten minutes, making up the prayers and pleas as I went along. And He came, just like He'd come to me so long ago. He was my maker, my one true friend. He came, and His soothingly masculine voice spoke inside my head. He stopped the whirling thoughts. He told me I was good, that I was not to be so hard on myself, that I was His child. I was His child, and if I was careful and changed my ways I would not end up a homosexual.

CHAPTER TWENTY-TWO

FATHER CORNELIUS RAISED HIS bushy eyebrows behind the heavy black-framed glasses as he stood near my desk and regarded me. He held my paper high for a moment before allowing it to drop on my desk like a piece of putrid garbage.

"Your essay hinted at promise in the first few paragraphs, but as usual didn't deliver in the end. You really are going to have to pick up your socks."

Next, he turned and addressed Martin beside me. "This *does* show promise, though I'm cognizant of the fact you've had the benefit of a repeat year to reach the passing standard." The eyebrows raised again, though not as high, and he returned my cousin's paper very decently before walking away.

"Fucking homo," I said to Martin.

My cousin didn't reply because he was too busy reading and salivating over the juicy comments. Pani heard and sniggered as the priest approached Paddy Flanagan.

Father Cornelius was vice-head and we'd had him for English literature for three months now because Mr. McGovern, our regular teacher, had been arrested by the British army and was now interned on a ship in Belfast Lough, accused without any evidence of being a member of the Official IRA. Mr. McGovern admired the Officials because they were also socialists, he'd never hid his admiration from us, but we didn't believe he was actually in the IRA. Neither did Father Rafferty, because he was fighting to secure his release. He told us he was sure the government would release him in due course, but in the meantime he'd appointed

Father Cornelius to teach us because we were sitting our exams in June.

"Nice effort," the priest said to Paddy, who grinned dead cheesy.

It stung like hell-fire that someone like Paddy Flanagan was getting more "nice efforts" in English literature than me, but I knew I'd show everyone what I was made of when I took the O levels. I'd show all of them when it mattered, not in some damned essay marked by someone who wasn't even our proper teacher. What mattered, and every boy knew it, was the last-minute cramming a month or so before the exams. I would cram like hell, pass every subject, and show them I was both a terrific actor and student.

Father Cornelius knew I was a good actor, already. Sometimes he came in to watch the evening rehearsals, and hadn't been reticent about coming up to the stage afterward on two occasions to tell me that I made a very convincing Viola.

"I really think I'll become an actor," I said, after I'd finished my last bite of sausage. It was a week and a half before the curtain was due to rise. I was happy with my performance in the main, the only glitch being a number of lines that wouldn't stick no matter how many times I went over them. "They've got the Lyric Players in Belfast, so I think I'll apply to them instead of university."

"As if they'd take you," James said. He rose from the table and put his plate in the sink. "They only want good-looking people."

Caroline and Nuala giggled. James began examining his face in a shaving mirror that our mother kept on the windowsill. He squeezed a creamy pimple. Since puberty had struck, my brother was obsessed with his oily face. I'd even caught him sneaking into Caroline's bedroom behind her back to slather her astringent lotion on it, though he might as well not have bothered.

"You certainly couldn't be one with those big yellow things," I said.

He looked at me over his shoulder. "Daddy, what do you think of our Gabriel becoming an actor?"

"I'll 'actor' him." Father wiped milk from the corners of his mouth with the edge of his hand. "Fit you better if you were out helping me. Luksee, if you want spending money this summer, you'll have to work for it. I'm not dishing out money to you to go dancing or run round the country with that clown of a cousin of yours and get nothing in return. Damn the bit, not at your age. I've got a job starting this summer, we're making the grounds for a big factory, and you can help out. Why should I take on another man and pay him when you'll be at home?"

"Gabriel will go gladly," said my mother.

There was no point in arguing when both were in agreement.

"You can hire Martin, too," she said. "They'll be good company for each other." She nodded at me. "Yous'll have more money for spending when yous go on holiday with Tommy in Bundoran." She chuckled. "I'm sure Celia pays Martin very little when he helps out in her shop, anyway."

That part was true, because Martin was forever complaining she paid him peanuts.

"Martin and his flat feet and wee stumpy legs would be no good to me on a building site," said Father. "I need strapping men."

"You can try him out," she said.

"That's a point," I said. "How much will you pay?"

"After deduction of living expenses, I'll give you twenty pounds."

"I'm only fifteen. I don't have to pay living expenses . . . and if I have to, then you'll just have to pay me the same rate as you're paying the rest of your men."

Father laughed before taking another gulp of milk. The manner in which he drank tea or milk at home infuriated me. It was loud and uncouth. He never made such noises when we dined out in public.

"You drive a hard bargain, Gabriel. Aye, we'll make a businessman out of you yet." He laughed at his wit. "I'll tell you what, I'll pay you twenty-five pounds a week."

"Each?"

"Aye."

"Mammy, I want twenty-five pounds a week for chores as well," Caroline said.

"Harry, that's far too much," said my mother. "What would our Gabriel need so much money for?"

"I'll be doing a man's work."

"I'll give it to them." Father took another noisy slurp, then wiped his mouth. "But I want a decent day's work out of you, and there'll be no boss's son favors, either."

After being excused from the table, Caroline and I went to my bedroom where, instead of studying, she complained about the wages issue for a while, and then agreed to listen to the lines of the play that I was having difficulty with. This time I recited them perfectly. Thereafter, I crept out to the hallway and called Martin to learn if he'd be interested in working for Father. At first he was very hesitant, grilled me as to whether the work would be hard or dirty and if the workmen were friendly, until I told him the wages. Immediately, he hung up to tell Auntie Celia he was quitting her shop.

For the past four years, Uncle Tommy and his family had rented a house in Bundoran, a seaside resort in Donegal with amusement arcades and a dance hall. That night, instead of my usual sexual thoughts, I feel asleep thinking about the fun Martin and I would have there. I was awakened abruptly by loud banging.

"Open the door," a man said. "Open up, now."

I glanced at the clock and saw it was three-fifteen in the morning.

"Open! Open now, or we're breaking this door down."

I detected an English accent.

"Who is it?" Mammy said.

"British army."

She emitted a clipped shriek. "What do yous want at this time of the night?" Her voice was very unsteady.

"Open this door or we're kicking it down."

I ran into the hall as she was opening it. Instantly, a swarm of soldiers with painted black faces and rifles swept inside. Some went into the bedrooms, five headed to the living room and scullery, and three opened the trapdoor in the hallway and climbed into the attic.

"You've got one minute to get dressed," one said from inside Father's room.

"What the hell's this about?" he said. "Why are you raiding my house?"

"Where's the other man?" the sergeant said to my mother.

"What other man? There's no other man here." She was trying to stay calm, but her voice was all over the place.

I knew it was Seamus they were asking about, but their intelligence was useless because he'd flown to America weeks ago. Nuala ran from the bedroom in her primrose pajamas, closely followed by Caroline, who was clutching her dressing gown tightly at the throat.

"There's a soldier searching under our bed," Nuala said.

"There's nothing of interest to you in those drawers," Father said.

Pots crashed onto the kitchen floor. Thunderous steps walked across the attic.

"Rip up all the boards until you find their guns," the sergeant said aloud.

"Yous damage anything in this house and we'll set the law on yous," my mother said. Her voice was much firmer now. "Where's your warrant?"

"We don't need a warrant to search for terrorists." The sergeant sneered. "No warrants needed to search safehouses."

"What's this, Sarge?" a private said. He came from the living room, my duffel bag in one hand, the polka-dot dress and wig in another.

"That's my *Twelfth Night* costume."

"Your what?" the sergeant said.

"My costume for a Shakespeare play we're doing at school."

He looked at the frock again. "That's no costume, mate.

Shakespeare costumes don't look like that. They're old-fashioned, they are."

"It's a fuckin' disguise, Sarge," said the private, "I'm telling you it's a disguise."

"It's his fucking costume," James said.

"Keep quiet, James," my mother said. She turned to the private. "Stop cursing in front of my children."

"Is this a disguise, ma'am?" the sergeant asked, as if she'd be fool enough to admit it was.

"My son told you what it is, and none of my children lie."

The sergeant stared at her, then at the garment, as he decided how to respond. "Where's the terrorist who's staying here? Does this belong to him?"

"Call the priest and you'll find out it's a costume for a school play," she said.

Father came out of the room, and was followed by a private who hadn't painted his face like the others. His skin was so black, it looked blue-black, which made his teeth dazzlingly white and perfect. One tail of Father's shirtfront wasn't tucked properly into his trousers, his fly was only partially zipped, and his wavy hair stood on end. Another soldier walked up to him, and both men seized his upper arms.

"Let go of me."

The sergeant turned to Father. "Do these items belong to the terrorist?"

"You heard my wife. There's no other man living here. Let go of my arms."

"That's not what our intelligence confirms," said the sergeant.

"Your intelligence is bloody useless," said James.

"You have no right to be bursting into someone's house at this time of the morning," said Father. "And your guns are frightening my children."

"I don't give a ball of blue what your intelligence confirms," my mother said. "The only other man staying here was his brother. He argued badly with his wife and stayed here weeks ago."

The sergeant was so surprised by her answer, he took a step backward. China rattled as a cabinet was moved in the living room. Wood cracked like gunfire in the attic.

"So it was your husband's brother, then?" The sergeant's tone was softer now. "Who's this vicar you're talking about? Is he local?"

"He's not a vicar. He's a priest. He's headmaster of Saint Malachy's." Mammy laughed short and deliberately. "Oh, yous have made a grave mistake coming here and raiding an innocent man's house. Yes indeed, a grave mistake."

"How would he know?" the sergeant continued.

"Who?" Mammy said.

"The vic . . . the priest, I mean." Clearly, it was dawning on the sergeant his intelligence might be erroneous, and he seemed nervous a mistake had indeed been made. "Give us it, then."

"Give you what?" said Mammy.

"The number." He looked at the soldiers holding my father. "Get him into the truck."

"Let go of me," Father said. His eyes bulged in his crimson face. "I'll walk out of my own door in my own good time. I'm *not* going to be taken from my own house like this in front of my children."

"Yes, leave my father alone," I said. "He's done nothing wrong, and he'll walk out on his own if needs to go out."

The soldiers lifted him inches above the floor and he struggled and swore as they moved toward the front door. Father clawed at the doorjamb, but the soldiers were strong, had momentum on their side, and whisked him outside. It was astonishing to see my father, a man always in charge, a man who never asked for advice, carried in such an undignified manner.

"Yous have no right to do that to my husband in front of his children. Where are yous taking him?"

"The phone number," said the sergeant.

Mammy advanced in a burst of steps toward the telephone table, whipped the directory out of its drawer viciously, banged it on the tabletop, and began flicking through it. The pages snapped crisply, two ripping at their corners as she turned them. After she'd located the number, she thrust the book at the sergeant. "There it is," she said, "beside Father Rafferty's name . . . and I'll tell you another thing for free as well, the priest won't be pleased you're calling him at this ungodly hour of the morning."

The sergeant dialed.

"Where are yous taking my husband?"

"Ballykelly barracks."

"What for?"

"For questioning. We must. It's routine in cases like this, ma'am."

"Even if you know your intelligence is for nothing?"

The sergeant didn't hear her comment because he began to talk. After a few moments, he started to apologize and kowtow to Father Rafferty, who was clearly grilling him because the sergeant gave his name, rank, and battalion.

"Now that this has been cleared up, I'm sure yous won't need to take my man away," my mother said as the sergeant laid down the receiver.

"I can't do that, ma'am. I'm very sorry, but I'm under orders to take any men living in this house to the barracks."

"Well, we'll just lie in front of your Land Rovers and you'll not be able to take him," she said. "Gabriel, James, everybody out and lie on the ground in front of the wheels."

We started to move, but two soldiers standing by the door blocked our exit.

"Ma'am, we'd just have to remove you if you did that," said the sergeant. "Please understand that orders are orders."

"They're orders that'll land the pack of yous in a pan of boiling frying-oil by the time I'm finished," Mammy said, though she made no further attempt to advance. "Coming here brandishing guns and wrecking the homes of civilized people. If there's as much as a scratch on him when he comes home, yous'll have me to answer to, personally."

My mother had come from nervousness to ferocious defiance all in the space of minutes. And it was all show. She knew as well as I did her threats had no bite, because the Ulster government consistently covered the army's blunders when it came to harassing Catholic families like mine.

The ensuing twenty-four hours were an accumulation of foggy occurrences: the phone was always ringing, relatives and neighbors visited offering long faces and sighs, and the teapot was never off the boil. Mammy's moods swung in an arc like a wrecker's ball: laughter and jokes one moment, frets and wails the next. I was also apprehensive for Father, especially after some of our visitors began narrating secondhand stories about the torture of prisoners at many army barracks throughout the province.

Finally, news came that Father was being released because the government could neither obtain nor find proof he'd been operating a safehouse. At nine o'clock the following evening, he arrived home. The army had issued him and five others travel passes and had put them on a public bus to Derry, where Uncle Tommy met him. Wan and tired, he was very happy to be home. He was so happy, he kissed and hugged my mother tightly, something I'd never before witnessed. He kissed Nuala and Caroline too, and finally hugged James and me. As Father and I embraced, I could feel his rapid heartbeats and felt so awkwardly happy.

CHAPTER TWENTY-THREE

I POKED PANI DISCREETLY IN the ribs as soon as the boy read the line, "Still we were coupled, and inseparable." He was reading aloud from *As You Like It*, and every time there was an opportunity for a bit of double entendre, I seized upon it. Shakespeare was good for that sort of thing, and I hardly ever missed one. I'd make eyes at Martin and Pani, nudge them, or make smart-arse comments at the mention of things like "codpiece," and we'd kill ourselves till we were flushed in the face.

"Shut up, Gabriel," Martin said. His shoulders shook, and he clutched his sides. "Father Cornelius will throw us out of the class, and we can't afford that."

Pani passed from a snigger to a snort. In the row behind, one of two stews, certain to get grade A's in all twelve O levels he was taking, demanded in a loud whisper that we keep quiet. The priest looked up.

"Marcus O'Reilly, why are you talking?" he asked.

Everyone turned to stare at the youth. A rose-colored patch started where Marcus' long, pale neck ascended from his shirt collar and extended up to his stricken face. It was almost more than I could bear not to burst out laughing.

"It's Gabriel, Father," he said. "He was talking so loudly, I couldn't hear my ears."

"I'll see you after class," Father Cornelius said to me. "Marcus, you continue with the reading."

As I watched Martin and Pani file out of the room, I didn't feel so cocky. Father Cornelius kept me waiting while he continued to read. I wished there was another class lining up at the door, but the stairwell was as noiseless as inside the room. Downstairs, I heard a door bang shut. Without saying a word, Father Cornelius rose and walked to the door, closed it rudely, and returned to his desk, where he recommenced reading.

"Come up here, Harkin," he said, after a few minutes.

I went and stood before him.

"Why are you trying to ruin yourself?"

"I'm not, Father."

"Don't think I haven't observed your fondness for crudity in class. Do you think I'm stupid? You're obsessed with baseness." He looked fiercely into my eyes, and I withdrew my own as quickly as an admonished dog. "I've checked into your overall performance and, aside from a favorable comment from your drama teacher, it appears it's every bit as bad as your sense of humor. Judging by how you performed in your mock exams, I believe you're going to fail your O levels. You're going to fail, just like your cousin, only more spectacularly. Do you really want that, boy?"

"No, Father."

I'd done very badly in my mocks, and he was probably one of seven teachers who'd wanted to speak to my mother at a PTA meeting held a few weeks ago. Thankfully, she hadn't attended. She and Father had argued when he refused to accompany her, so she'd accused him of shirking his responsibility, decided to retaliate, and didn't go, either.

"Stand erect! Spread your feet and put your hands by your sides." His black-brown eyes ran with searing deliberateness up and down my body before he turned again to my face. "Every bit of my being wants to send you to Father Rafferty, *boy*." He paused until the echo of the emphasized word was devoured by the silence. "Do you know what that means?"

"Yes, Father. I'm really sorry. I'll be better behaved from now on."

"What does it mean if I march you to his office now, *boy*?"

Priests at Saint Malachy's addressed us as "boy" at such

moments in order to ram home their absolute power. His stressed use of that word rendered me small and insignificant faster than a stinging whack on my hand.

"It means I'd be thoroughly punished, Father."

"Punished and perhaps suspended. And do you know why? I'll tell you why. I'll tell you exactly why, though you already know. Because other teachers have written in the burgundy book you've been troublesome all year. Troublesome and impertinent." He paused again to let it sink in he'd been checking the burgundy book. "Is there a reason for this disruptive behavior, Gabriel?"

Gabriel! Suddenly I was Gabriel again. He'd succeeded in scaring me, and now the second chance was coming. Immediately, I transported myself outside the classroom. I imagined running down the stairs toward my next class.

"I've been a bit silly, Father, but I'll stop now." I made sure my tone dripped with apologetic meekness.

"When good boys of your age behave as you are doing, Gabriel, there's usually something behind it. Do you have some problems or confusions, perhaps?"

A hot body flash culminated in my face. "No, I haven't . . . I haven't got any problems or confusions."

He sighed. "As I said, the only people with good words to say about you are Mr. Casey and your physics teacher. The former said you were an excellent Viola . . . which I've already commended you for. However, that's an extracurricular activity, and I'm *sure* I don't have to tell you the Examination Board doesn't take prowess as a budding thespian into consideration." His brows rose to look at me quizzically while he placed his white hand on the table. The black hairs on its back stood out in relief, and I was struck by its largeness. For no logical reason, I thought his hands more resembled a farmer's than a priest's.

"I will apply myself diligently from now on, Father Cornelius. I promise. Now if I could—"

"How did it feel to play the part of Viola, by the way?"

"It was a challenge."

"Yes, indeed. I've often wondered about what effect it has on our boys to be obliged to play female roles just because we're an all-boys school. Tell me, did it feel strange in any way?"

"I didn't think much about it, Father. It was just a role."

"Of course, it was a role. But how did it *actually* feel to dress in women's clothing?"

My eyes moved reflexively to his soutane. "It was just a role, so there was nothing to really feel. Father, I'm very late for my next class."

"Miss King has you now, does she not?"

"Yes."

"I notice she's also entered a comment in the burgundy book." He paused. "You're quite right to worry about tardiness, but I'll have a word with her. She'll understand."

Suddenly, his hand moved, and he began to stroke the side of my buttock with the velvety gentleness of a baby's touch. The hairs on my leg began to crawl.

"Father Rafferty is a most unforgiving priest, isn't he?" he said. "Will you promise me you'll apply yourself from now on? I know how bright you are, and I'm concerned about you." The strokes became firmer.

"I shall, Father."

My voice sounded high and girly. His hand arced toward my fly and I stepped back quickly.

"Come here, Gabriel."

"Father, I need to—"

"Come and stand here." He pointed to the spot.

I obeyed, and the fumbling recommenced.

"Father Cornelius, someone might come in and catch us doing this."

The words I'd used didn't sound right. They were words I should never have needed to say to a priest. Priests didn't do these things. The stuff boys said about Father Cornelius were jokes. They were jokes. Everybody understood that at the end of the day. The words I'd used just now sounded like collusion. My mind played madly with the words, flinging some away, fitting different, better words I should have used. Suddenly, I felt the classroom air cool skin it should never have been cooling in the first place. The word "boy" echoed in my head and mixed with the dough of the different, better words I should have used and hadn't. Chair legs scraped. He eased to his hunkers as he muttered, "Don't worry. No one comes up these stairs at this time of day." I stared at the cresting waves of gray hair running across the back of his head, waves almost like Father's, waves almost like Uncle Brendan's. I stared until my parched eyes stung and reminded me of where I was. I turned away, gazed out the window, and soon the images of boys playing in the football field became gray and blurred.

After he'd finished, Father Cornelius began to put me in order, restoring my trousers neat and perfect, and then patted my thigh as if to make me whole again. He sat back in his chair.

"Look, Gabriel, I got completely overcome and lost my self-control just now. This shouldn't have happened."

"Why me, Father? Is there something about me that told you I'm not normal?" My voice was flat and distant, everything so real and unreal."

"No."

"Why'd you ask if I was confused?"

"There's no such thing as 'not normal' in God's eyes." Father Cornelius cast his eyes to his lap and began to massage his left temple with the hand that had touched me.

"But something about me must have showed I'm maybe not normal? What was it?"

"You're a bright young man, Gabriel, and you'll grow up and find yourself a lovely girl one day. Don't ever think you're not normal. Don't even consider such a horrible thing. The only thing is that you're too sensitive behind your belligerence." He paused. "Now, let's not give another thought about what's just happened here. It must be forgotten. It must, because it can't be undone. That was the devil at work between us."

So that was it. I was still too sensitive. I just couldn't get rid of it. It oozed from me like a stinking perfume.

"You must stop acting the class clown. Do you hear me? It

must stop." Father Cornelius sprang from the chair unexpectedly, and raked his hair as he walked up to a window. He pushed it open and took a deep breath. For a moment, the terrible deafening silence returned as he stood gazing out at the football field. "Look here, *boy*, this incident's over. It's to be forgotten immediately, you understand." He swung around and stared at me. "Do you understand?"

I didn't speak.

"I said, do you understand, boy?"

"Yes, Father."

"Good." He came back to his desk. "Let's say an Act of Contrition together and receive our forgiveness from the Higher Power." He fished out his purple stole from a pocket in his soutane and sat. "Kneel before me and let us pray." His big farmer's hand trembled as he laid it upon my shoulder.

I moved my lips as he recited the long version of the Act of Contrition. At its conclusion, he made a large sign of the cross in the space between us.

"You may now leave. I'll speak to Miss King."

I returned to my desk, eased my satchel off the floor, and started down the room. I was different. The boys had been right. They had always been right. Henry had known I was different. Aunt Peggy had known and warned my mother. Noel had known I'd allow him to do things with me. So had Connor, yet he was now normal just like every other boy. My cousin and I now acted as if nothing had ever occurred between us. We acted as if nothing had ever occurred, yet what we'd done was uppermost in my mind every time we spoke because I wanted it all to occur again.

"Oh, boy," Father called out as I reached the door.

I closed my eyes and waited without turning back to look at him. I waited for the final words. There were always final words in awkward situations.

"Work diligently, no more fooling in class, study hard, and maybe, *just maybe*, you'll scrape through. Otherwise, you and I will pay a visit to Father Rafferty with all that that implies."

The velvet-dressed threat, the caution wrapped in compassion. Anger heat surged through my body. Every cell sweated anger at his overriding power.

Pani and Martin were dying to know what had transpired. We were sitting in Pani's car, and I didn't much feel like listening to ABBA this lunchtime. I wanted to be alone and replay, analyze, work out other endings that could have been if I'd only said different, better words. I needed to sort out my thoughts before the end of lunchtime, so I could go to my next class and forget everything that had happened.

"I'm on a warning." I rolled my eyes toward the ceiling, when what I really wanted to do was let them plummet to the floor. "Next time, it'll be Father Rafferty's office, maybe even suspension. He made me promise to stop clowning and to knuckle down to my work."

Pani looked hard into my eyes. I couldn't last the scrutiny and turned away to look beyond the boxwood hedge to a small crabapple tree.

"Bastard," he said.

"You're lucky he likes blondes," Martin said. "Maybe you should settle down a bit, Gabriel. It is getting close to the exams, and you know what happened to Pani and me last year."

Pani guffawed as he reached out with his long middle finger to turn on the tape player. He had slender pianist fingers. I shivered as Agnetha's dulcet voice snaked out from the cassette. For the first time, I took no pleasure in her singing. As her voice was chased and finally engulfed by the heavy synthesizer rhythms, I felt compelled to leave the car, to get away from all of it.

For a while, I strolled aimlessly. I found myself near the arborvitae flanking the football pitch, where my obliviousness was eventually pierced by the sound of low voices and tobacco smoke, the stink reminding me of my failures with Lizzie. I walked the corridors, passing the tuck shop (a storage cupboard, really), where junior boys were trying to buy goodies. A red-faced, blond boy, a first- or second-year, fought his way to the counter, shoving larger boys who could have flattened him. He wasn't sensitive. He wouldn't allow Father Cornelius to do what I'd just allowed him to do. The boy turned and saw me, instantly stopped pushing, fearing perhaps I'd pull him out of the queue and lecture him because I was his senior.

Finally, I retreated to an empty art room. I stared out the large windows at senior boys filing past an orderly line of juniors waiting to go into the school dining room for the second sitting. A row of pretty watercolors of foxgloves, seashells, and driftwood lay drying on the long bench running up the length of the room. God made pretty seashells with smooth, pearly interiors, and He also made me.

"Why the hell are You doing this to me?" I cried out. "What have I done to You? Why have You made me different from everyone here? Is it some kind of sport? Am I just fucking sport to You, God?" The art room resumed an indifferent quiet. I felt like ripping apart one of the seashell paintings. "Jesus and Mary, why can't You intercede for me? Why can't You make Him make me just like the other boys? Do You want me to fucking-well hate and spurn You, too?"

But God knew I would never spurn Him. He knew He was in every molecule of my being. He was my life force. Moreover, fear wouldn't allow me to turn away from Him. I was too frightened, because then I'd really have nothing.

For the next few weeks, it was impossible to look Father Cornelius in the eye. Class became purgatory. Out of the corner of my eye, I saw him watching me. I wouldn't look at him directly unless it could not be avoided. When he asked someone to read aloud and everyone bent their heads to their texts, I caught a flash of him watching, and each time my heart froze thicker than a fort's walls with hate. I could not hate God, but I could hate Father Cornelius.

When he watched me, I wondered if the devil was inside him

again, if he'd try to get me alone. I wished him dead. I wished him dead when he directed his stupidly clever questions at me to force my participation. Asking his stupidly clever questions as he sat in a soutane and off-white dog collar, his white farmer's hands resting on the desk, forcing my participation. I wished him dead as I pushed the words from my throat, keeping my tone pancake flat so no one knew a thing, and all appeared normal between us.

He did succeed in quelling my boisterous streak, but still I didn't feel like studying. I didn't study, and I tried to turn back the twisted deviancy pursuing me within, pursuing me as relentlessly as foxes pursue newborn lambs in the spring. And the more I bridled and spurned, the more the deviant yearnings clung to me. Worst of all was nighttime. I would lie in bed after saying my prayers and the image of a sixth-former would come to mind, followed by another, sometimes even a teacher or a handsome passerby I'd seen on the street that day, and I'd fantasize a little and then pray them away. But the deviancy was patient and lurking, lurking till I was prayed out, and then it would storm back until, broken and loathsomely willing, I'd seize upon one favorite image and my fevered hand would become a piston working and working until the moments of ecstasy came, followed always by oily, black, despairing guilt. Oily, black, despairing guilt spliced with "why me, God?"'s shrieked into the downy pillow.

I'd curse Father Cornelius, but deep within I knew he wasn't the only one to blame. What he'd done was sinful, but my desires had their own deep roots. I'd also try to bargain with God. I'd make desperate promises, promises to lead a good Catholic life if He'd just see His way to spare me, just see His way to turn me normal; if He'd just allow me to get aroused around girls so I could marry and have children one day, I'd be utterly His.

He must have partially heard my bargaining, because my old English teacher got released from the prison ship a few weeks later and Father Cornelius was gone from my sight. There were no more daily reminders. Now, I had to see him only from afar, bear him if we chanced to meet in the corridor when, as a well-bred Saint Malachy's boy, I was required to greet him courteously.

As time passed, I also developed a solution to the nighttime yearnings that assuaged my guilt and fears. It was a powerfully simple solution. As I performed the night act, I'd allow myself to think about a man right until the cusp of orgasm, whereupon I'd quickly substitute him for thoughts of some naked girl whose face I could never see, but whose breasts were always succulent and firm. In that way, I was thinking about a woman as I carried myself through, which meant everything was normal. I also convinced myself this was a great test God wished me to pass. He was testing me, making me go through this painful phase, and all I had to do was struggle, pass, and all would be fine.

CHAPTER TWENTY-FOUR

IN THE MIDST OF all my fictitious fornication, Father Brendan arrived. Auntie Celia had arranged to pick my mother up on the afternoon of his arrival because she wanted someone to accompany her to the airport. Apparently, Uncle Brendan had informed her that he didn't wish Granny to be present, which Mammy found extremely strange.

When James and I arrived home from school that evening, our mother was sitting rigid on the living room sofa beside Uncle Brendan, and Auntie Celia, despite her wide hips, was in a narrow parlor chair staring out the window. Mammy's coat was still slung over the back of the sofa, and the curly horns of a midsized ebony carving protruded still from its brown paper wrapping.

"We've just got in a little while ago," Mammy said. "Your uncle's plane was late."

"James, I wouldn't recognize you," Uncle Brendan said. He rose, shook my brother's hand, and peered over at me. "And Gabriel . . . my God, you're as tall as me. You're a man now."

Auntie Celia watched intently as he shook my hand and then, as if on a whim, embraced me. I felt embarrassed as the hug dragged on. Women, much less men, never hugged for long in Northern Ireland, and I kept patting his back as I waited for his withdrawal. When it came, I saw his eyes were misty.

The shyness I'd felt when I met him first so many years ago returned. I also felt terribly shabby in my uniform: my blazer was worn, my pants gleamed from two years of sitting on wooden school chairs, even my skin looked anemic compared to his nutmeg tan.

The intervening years had been good to Uncle, and I would never have guessed he'd been ill—not that I really knew what to look for, because I'd never met anyone who'd had a nervous breakdown. He was even more handsome than I'd remembered, his frame lean, with no tiny paunch like Father had lately acquired, and the silver wings adorning his hair made him look noble. Instead of clerical garb, he wore jeans, a wine-red T-shirt, and sneakers.

"I have to go off to football practice in fifteen minutes, so what is there to eat?" said James.

"Make toast and scrambled eggs," said my mother. She glanced at me. "The rest will have to make do with Chinese take-out because I haven't had time to cook."

Uncle Brendan's eyes followed James as he left the room.

"God, Eileen, I've been in Kenya far too long. Your children are no longer children."

Mother sniffed as she pushed a wayward strand of graying hair behind her ear.

Auntie Celia emitted a mournful sigh before saying, "Gabriel's in the same class as Martin and Connor now."

It was as if she'd forced herself to speak, and what she'd said also sounded wrong. It sounded as if I were an intruder in my own class. Uncle Brendan smiled wanly. He was about thirty-five, and better preserved than any man of his age in Knockburn. Here, most men over thirty looked far older, their faces weatherbeaten from hard farmwork or manual labor in all kinds of rain and wind. The idea of silver wings appealed greatly, and I wished I could sprout them then and there until I remembered my hair was brown and flat, not black and wavy like his or Father's. Black, curly hair also peeped from Uncle's open collar, much denser than Father's, and I hoped to acquire that Harkin attribute, though, as I slipped a finger discreetly into the gap between two shirt buttons, things didn't feel promising.

"Martin's older than Gabriel. How can that be?"

"Don't you remember?" Her tongue flicked out and moistened her upper lip. "Don't you remember I wrote and told you he didn't pass his exams. Your prayers and masses didn't work too well in Martin's case . . . though now we know why, of course."

"Oh that's right, I forgot."

"No, your prayers didn't work too good." Her eyes narrowed and she stared at him as if to reinforce her blame.

"What with my illness and problems with my calling, Celia."

Mammy coughed. "Listen, Gabriel, you might as well know your uncle Brendan's left the priesthood."

I looked at her incredulously. No one left the priesthood. I didn't even know it was possible to reverse Holy Orders.

"Yes, it's true, Gabriel," he said.

"Why?" My mind's eye sped all over the place: I saw Granny Harkin crying as she talked about him one instant; I saw him administering last rites to the old woman with cancer; I saw myself serving at his Mass on the night he'd said it in our home. I also knew leaving the priesthood was the ultimate disgrace to visit on any Catholic family.

"Why must you leave, Uncle Brendan?"

Auntie Celia turned to stare out the window again.

"It's a long question to answer, but basically I'm being called to do other things with my life. The priesthood's not for me. It's wrong. It has been wrong from the beginning. I've been fooling myself."

His eyes burrowed into mine and I recognized his pain, saw immediately it was important for me to understand.

"What'll Granny say?" I asked, careful not to allow my tone to reveal any lingering shock.

Auntie Celia's chair protested her body's sudden movement with a high-pitched creak. "It'll kill your granny *before* she gets a chance to make any comment on it."

"For God's sake, Celia, please don't say that," Uncle said. "I have to be honest with myself."

"Oh, honest, indeed." Her tongue flicked over her lip again. "You should have made sure you had a call in the first place. Priests don't get made in a day. You had plenty of time to change your mind at that seminary in Rome you ran off to."

My mother gave Auntie Celia little ratifying nods, but she didn't see them because she was trapped in Uncle Brendan's stare. He was giving her one of those brother-and-sister stares that meant nothing to Mammy, yet communicated a thousand messages between the two of them. I recognized the penetrating, frozen eye lock. I used it on Caroline, James, and Nuala when I needed to rebuke or communicate with them in a stranger's presence.

For some reason, I thought about all the money my mother had sent him over the years for masses. Masses for two deceased grandfathers. Two pounds when she was taking her driving test for the fourth time. Masses when Father was starting out in business. I'd even sent him a pound for a secret petition. He'd never asked in his subsequent letter what my petition was for. He'd simply written and said he'd received my money and would say three masses for its granting, even though a pound only paid for one. I considered whether his leaving the priesthood might have diluted its effects, but dismissed the thought as quickly.

"It's God's will, so we'll just have to hold up our heads and learn to deal with it," said Mammy.

"Are you getting married to a girl from Kenya?"

Uncle Brendan laughed grimly. "Nothing like that, Gabriel."

"Thank God for that small mercy," said Auntie Celia. "Yes indeed, thank God for that small mercy . . . because if a darkie woman had been in the picture, I'd definitely have to sell up and clear off to Belfast where nobody knows me." She rose, walked up to the fireplace, and rested her hands on the mantel very mannishly. "Brendan, you are very misfortunate, and the terrible thing is, it always comes home to roost with us. It comes home to roost with your poor family." She spun around to face him. "Daddy's dead and gone, but you can be very sure he'll be spinning circles in his grave after you add the effects of this to the results of your first charade."

"Celia, that's *quite* enough," my mother said. She rose and quick-stepped halfway toward her. "That's quite enough."

The atmosphere was palpable now.

"Eileen, I've been in a daze ever since he told us coming down from the airport, but now I keep thinking of my poor father and mother and the hurt Brendan's already caused our poor family."

A decent cough would have floored me. In one utterance, Auntie Celia had transported us back to the time when poor Uncle Brendan had gone out with a girl and upset Granda, who'd badly wanted a priest in his family.

"And Eileen, let me also inform you that you just can't understand things from my stance." She shook her head as she laughed falsely. "You can't understand, because you're *not* his sister." She'd spoken as if Uncle Brendan weren't present. "You won't have to face the people knowing they're laughing because one of the Harkin boys has left the priesthood."

"What are you talking about? *I'm* married to a Harkin. I carry and sign my checks by the Harkin name. I believe that makes me one of yous in people's eyes." Mother laughed shrilly. "Oh yes, that's more than sufficient to cover me when the muck starts to fly."

"Please don't say things like this," said Uncle Brendan. "If I'd known it was going to cause this amount of trouble, I'd have stayed away for good. Then, you'd all have been none the wiser."

Auntie Celia's mouth opened to respond, but closed again.

"I know you're upset, Celia. You're my only sister and have every right to be. I'm so sorry I have to inflict such pain on the family." He turned his head from her as if it were too painful to look at her a moment longer. "There's no woman involved, and I'll be single for life. The simple truth is, I should never have entered the priesthood." Uncle Brendan paused. "When I took Holy Orders, I thought I had a vocation. But I didn't. I was fooling myself and trying to please someone else. That was wrong." Uncle rose, walked over to the sideboard, and began to stroke the reddish breast of one of the shiny bird ornaments I'd always liked. He emitted an odd little chuckle as he picked it up and examined it. "Why, Eileen, I remember these pretty birds! I remember Mother and I spent a whole day searching china shop after china shop to find just the right wedding present, and she tired of it and said I was being far too pernickety because Harry wouldn't look at them more than once, anyway." He chuckled again. "I'll bet she was right, too."

Mammy's eyes and droopy mouth mirrored her confusion as to why he was talking about ornaments at a time like this, but she recaptured her tongue quickly. "They're lovely birds. I could see you took care in picking them." Her eyes cut to Auntie Celia. "I'm very fond of my budgies. And I'm sure Harry is as well, but you know how men are about things like that. Men never pass remarks on an ornament, whether its quality or not."

"Cockatoos," Uncle Brendan said.

"Pardon!" She shot another glance at Auntie Celia.

"They're cockatoos, Eileen," said Uncle Brendan.

She gazed at the birds as if seeing them for the first time. "I see . . . very good."

There was an awkward silence as all eyes focused on the ornament.

"I was just as careful about deciding to leave the priesthood." He set the ornament down carefully and continued to observe it. "It's taken me a long time to leave, precisely because I didn't want to hurt or disgrace the family. But the truth is, it's been gnawing at me since the second year of my ordination. At first, it was doubt I fought against. I reckoned everyone suffers a little doubt, so I just put down my head and worked harder. But then doubt was replaced by the certainty I'd made a grave mistake. I'd gone in because I felt guilty about letting everyone down, because Father wished it, and because I thought it would make everything right again."

Auntie Celia sat tight-lipped, eyes still riveted on the cockatoo.

"I didn't have these feelings in the seminary. I don't know why I didn't have them. Maybe I was still suppressing the thing . . . or maybe I was in denial. I knew I'd made a mistake when I saw you all on my last visit, but I'd already resolved to stay in and continue serving and do the right thing because I also knew I wouldn't be the first priest who'd made a mistake. That much I do know, because I've met enough of them." Uncle paused. "Celia, believe me when I tell you that I've fought against doing this. I've fought it and fought it every hour of every day until my mind knew only frustration and despair, and *still* I had to go on for the sake of my pupils. I was in a despair so deep and shapeless, I'd never known it could exist in the human condition. I honestly don't know how I got out of bed in the morning . . . or how I made it back to bed at night. And I prayed and prayed, until even that failed, and God abandoned me completely, and I thought it would be better if I just ended—" He stopped abruptly, and the corners of his mouth trembled. "Well, I had a breakdown instead."

The air was viscous now as my mother toyed with the collar of her blouse and Auntie Celia stared at him, her mouth agape. I pondered which would have been the bigger disgrace to her. Would it have been his leaving the priesthood, the going out with a darkie girl, or the big unmentionable? None of them probably thought I knew about the big unmentionable, but I did. I could feel my heart beat faster as it tried to pump blood that was surely as viscous as the air separating all of us. The thought of Uncle Brendan far away in his sun-filled mission, rising and praying and pushing away the shapeless despair that he never knew could exist in the human condition as he tried to deal with the big unmentionable, filled me with a curious mix of pity and selfish relief. Deep in the spring of my being, I was relieved Uncle had troubles, also. I felt a burst of immeasurable closeness to him, and would have crossed and put my arm around him if it wouldn't have appeared peculiar at that moment.

"I've left, and we have to deal with it," he said. "I've come through a breakdown, and I'm *not* going to allow it to occur again. Life for me is outside the priesthood. I know it'll be difficult for all of you for a while, but I must move on. I'd like you to accept my decision, or at least stay silent if you don't." He returned to the sofa and stared into the hearth.

"Brendan, I knew you had a breakdown, but this other thing . . . I had no idea." Auntie Celia went to him. "I didn't know you were having thoughts of that nature. Listen, I've been very selfish. You're my little brother, and we'll deal with it. We'll work through this." She paused and shook her head at my mother. "I had no idea it was so bad."

"Yes, we'll pray and stick together," my mother said.

"You're family and we'll support you no matter what happens," Auntie Celia said. "My God, just let anybody dare say a word against you . . . or give you so much as a sidelong glance when I'm around. I'll throttle them, I will. You're a Harkin. We'll get through the coming scandal. Why, we'll laugh and wonder what all the silly fuss was about a year's hence, because people will be busy feasting on some other scandal, please Jesus. That's usually what happens, and this one will be dropped like a dog drops an old soup bone for a fresher one. It'll all be forgotten." She placed her hand on top of his, and they looked into each other's eyes and forgot about Mammy and me for an instant. "Are you really all right now, Brendan? You're not having these dark thoughts anymore, are you?"

"I'm fine now."

My mother asked if he had any plans for the future, and Uncle said he wanted to do a social work course in America. Neither Auntie Celia nor she knew anything about social work and listened intently as he explained it in detail. After he'd finished, Auntie Celia nodded at the clock and suggested she and Uncle Brendan start doing the rounds to inform the rest of the family, because everyone would now be home from work. My mother offered to accompany them twice while they debated their itinerary. Each time, she met with no response until finally, after my aunt muttered it wasn't necessary because she'd done far too much already, Mammy insisted. Auntie Celia and Uncle Brendan went out to the car as my mother whipped on her coat in the kitchen and searched about for her purse.

"Get your father to take Caroline to the Chinese when they get home," she said.

"Do you not think it might be best for them to be alone? They'll be able to talk as brother and sister."

"Oh, they *don't* want to be alone." She ceased rummaging in her purse for a moment. "You heard her ask for my support."

"But that's only when the neighbors are told. Now, it's only family."

"Don't be ridiculous . . . and don't say a word about this to your father, either. Not one word until I get back, so he can be told properly." Auntie Celia's car revved, and Mammy began riffling in her purse furiously as she complained about my aunt's lack of consideration. Finally, frustrated, or perhaps panicked by the sound of the reversing car, she foisted the purse on me and ran out the door.

They returned after nine. Caroline, James, and I ceased studying and ran from our bedrooms to the living room, where Father was watching TV. My mother peered at him, then at me, as she tried to determine whether I'd said anything. Father and Uncle Brendan clasped hands, hugged, and then Uncle asked if he'd heard the news. Mammy's face softened at the sight of Father's blank looks, and the story commenced, an abbreviated version this time, because it had by now been told so many times, he'd perfected it.

"Aren't you going to say something, Harry?" my mother said, after Uncle had finished.

"What am I supposed to say? It's not as if it's the end of the world." He looked at Uncle Brendan. "Whatever makes you happy is all that matters. If you weren't happy being ordained, then you did the right thing." He studied the TV screen for a moment before turning back to him. "Brendan, you have to do what's right for yourself, and to hell with what the neighbors say."

"It'll be hard because of all the talking and gloating the neighbors will do," said Auntie Celia.

"Let the neighbors say whatever the hell they want, because they're going to do it, anyway."

Auntie Celia solicited Father's opinion about the best way to tell Granny Harkin, but Uncle Brendan said he'd still prefer to do it alone. The subject was then dropped as Father began chatting to Uncle Brendan about his business. He launched into the usual litany about his useless workers, and how some of them wanted to work and collect the dole on the sly at the same time.

Before he left, Father took Uncle out to see a new shed he'd constructed to store his equipment, as well as the gleaming new track excavator he'd just purchased. It was my first time to see it, too. James, anxious to show off, climbed into the cab, started it, and moved the long arm about until Father ordered him to stop. I hung by the big doors and watched, observing by their easy manner that the two brothers had a great deal of love for one another, though Father's was well disguised by machismo, of course.

"I can't stop that one from driving my machinery," Father said. He jingled coins in his pockets. "James is a character."

Uncle Brendan turned to me. "Can you operate it?"

"He's just like you, Brendan," said Father. "Gabriel's better at the books and has no time for my machines."

"It takes all types to run a world, Harry."

We watched the taillights of Auntie Celia's car streak out the gate and disappear up the road.

"Poor Brendan, this is going to be such a hard cross for him to bear," Mammy said.

"Hmm." Father went to his seat and picked up the paper.

"You know, she's right, of course. This *could* kill your mother."

"Let's talk no more about it. Sure there's not much scandal in that nowadays with the way the world's going."

"Tell *that* to Celia. She squawked like a half-shot crow this afternoon. She said it would have been better he'd never entered the priesthood in the first place." Mammy paused to await Father's response, but he offered none. "Did he talk much about being a priest when he was Gabriel's or James' age?"

"I don't remember."

"It was your father's pushing," she said, clearly displeased by his unwillingness to be drawn. "Pushing never works. It's either in them to be priests, or it's not."

"Quit your talking."

"I'm telling you. Your father pushed, and now the cock's come home to roost. He should have accepted Brendan wasn't meant to be a priest. Brendan started associating with that girl, and *that* was the sign for your father to behold." Mammy looked about fleetingly to see what we were doing: Caroline and James had settled down to watch the news, and Nuala and I were setting up the draughts board. She must have suspected I was listening, because her eyes returned quickly and caught me watching her.

"Mammy, I'm glad you told Auntie Celia to catch herself on and forget the past," I said. "It was disgraceful. Making such a big deal about the fact Uncle Brendan disgraced her and the others just because he had a quick fling before he went to the priesthood."

"Your auntie was raving herself to distraction," said my mother. "It was the shock talking. I thought she'd been far too quiet on the journey down from the airport."

"She overreacted, just like Granda overreacted, right?"

"Don't speak ill of the dead, Gabriel."

"I think Granda was very uncharitable, because he got what he wanted in the end."

"Your granda saw it as a threat because the woman was handsome, with big, sparkly eyes, a smile to match, and always clad in the latest fashion."

"You told me once that you never met her."

Mammy's face reddened. "Once or twice, but not for very long."

Father glanced up from his newspaper.

"Was she from around here?" Caroline asked, and moved closer to Nuala and me.

"No."

"Do you think Uncle Brendan regrets letting her go?" she said.

"I have no idea. That's your uncle's business and not our concern."

"Things don't add up," I said. "Granda's deep bitterness makes no sense. I told you that before."

"You've been told already your Granda was pigheaded. Isn't that right, Harry? Look, tomorrow's a school day, so off yous go to bed. It's been a long afternoon and I need a bit of peace. Besides, *you* should be studying instead of trying to play Sherlock Holmes. It doesn't need much detective work to investigate the shambles you made of your mock exams."

That remark silenced me.

"Nuala, you go to bed. The rest of yous to your rooms and study, *now*."

I sat at my desk, knew she was raking up Uncle Brendan's past with Father now we were gone, and it proved too great a temptation. I sneaked down the hall and stood by the living room door. Indeed, Father was talking, but the TV's volume had been turned up and I couldn't hear a thing. I put my palms on the door and pressed my ear closer. Suddenly, it burst open and I spilled inside.

"What the hell do you think you're doing?" my mother said. "Are you snooping? That's the only thing you're good at these days, as well as failing exams."

I gawked idiotically at her as Caroline's door opened in the background.

Mother's eyes diverted to the door. "Take a good look at your sneaky brother. He's nothing but a good-for-nothing snoop." She looked back at me. "Get to your room this bloody instant and get that nosy beak of yours into a book, and *don't* let me see it again until you're at the breakfast table tomorrow morning."

CHAPTER TWENTY-FIVE

T HE SCANDAL WASHED INTO every Knockburn home and surrounding Catholic town. My mother reported daily how she
noticed people whispering as they came out of the shops, in line
for confession, behind graveyard headstones, and how they always
gave themselves away by becoming silent or talking about the
weather as she passed by. Auntie Celia said her shop sales were
up, though only for incidentals: farmers' wives, who'd always gos-
siped behind her back that her china selection was limited and
daylight robbery, had the gall to come in on the pretext of shopping for wedding gifts and, when they'd finished asking their
pointedly indirect questions and saw they were getting no information, all but the most brazen felt obliged to buy a carrot or two
in order to save face.

"Are you upset about what Uncle Brendan's done?" I asked
Granny Harkin.

Uncle Brendan was staying in Belfast with an old school
friend, and I was visiting her for the afternoon. She placed a large
slice of warm, home-baked rhubarb tart on a plate and set it before me.

"I won't, Granny, but thanks, anyway."

"My crust's nice and crunchy this time."

I shook my head adamantly. Granny would go to her grave
without ever knowing why I didn't like to eat jam or pies made
from the rhubarb that grew in her little patch. It seemed uncharitable to tell her that I knew what she did there. Her rhubarb tarts
had become a long-standing grievance between us. A grievance
arising from my own stupidity when, forgetting myself once in her

presence at a wake, I accepted a slice of her neighbor's rhubarb tart. It hadn't mitigated matters when I informed her the offending slice contained much more strawberry than rhubarb, or that I'd taken just two small bites and set it aside as soon as she reminded me I detested rhubarb.

Granny shook her head as she gave Uncle John, sitting in grandfather's old chair beside the range, my slice.

"So you weren't terribly surprised by Uncle Brendan's decision, then?"

"Why should I be surprised? Life's short enough, and Brendan must do with it whatever God intended. If that means social work, then he's got my blessing."

"You're educated," said Uncle John. He wiped crumbs off his lips with his gnarled fingers. "I can't make heads or tails of what Brendan says about this social work business, and I didn't want to appear ignorant probing him too much while he was explaining it. He says it's counseling. He says people get counseled when they have mental problems, or lose limbs in an accident, or when they have problems of . . . well, you know, of an intimate nature." He paused. "Now, Jimmy Kelly didn't get counseling when he had his arm yanked off by the combine harvester last year. He got nothing from the government."

Granny, who had the pie dish in her hand and was about to rise, set it down on the table again. "Exactly what is this social work, Gabriel? And, more to the point, will he be able to make a living at it?"

"It's done more in the big cities." I didn't wish to appear ignorant about the subject. "There's lots of counseling going on in Belfast, and people do make a living at it."

"What's the world coming to?" asked Granny. "City people always were peculiar. Imagine running around airing things of an intimate nature to strangers. If things like that need airing, they should be aired only behind a closed bedroom door." She shook her head like a sage. "Did anybody's limb ever grow back as a result of this counseling is the question I want answered."

"He'll have to stay in America after he's finished his schooling if he wants to make a living at it," said Uncle John. He slapped his tummy twice. "Only the Yanks would pay good money for a stranger's advice."

Uncle Brendan and I were standing in the meadow underneath a solitary beech tree near the grave of Granda's old carthorse. He'd asked me to join him for a walk because he was leaving soon for America to speak to university contacts and other people about courses and places to live.

"I hope you're not disappointed in me, Gabriel." It was the first time he'd spoken to me directly about his leaving the priesthood.

"It's your life."

"So you're fine with my decision?"

"If you want my opinion, I think Auntie Celia was out of order when she said Granda would be spinning in his grave."

"If you're thinking even slightly about the religious life, I trust I haven't put you off it."

"That was a long time ago."

"A long time ago?" He laughed softly. "Next, you'll be telling me, you're very old. I remember you telling Father McAtamney once you were going to be a hairdresser *and* a priest. It seems like it was only yesterday." He fell silent. "Of course, you wouldn't remember that."

"I remember, Uncle Brendan. I've always had a good memory. Sometimes, I wish I didn't." I placed my foot on the mound of gray fieldstones I'd erected years ago as a marker for the old horse. "Many things have happened since then to make me change my mind about the religious life."

"Really. What sort of things?"

"Girls, for a start."

That sounded false, because it *was* false. Without any warning, a heavy pressure built inside my head, my eyes misted, and a tear popped and began to trickle. I could feel it trace down my cheek, and wheeled around quickly to look in the direction of a cluster of old farm buildings in the distance.

"What's the matter?"

I couldn't speak, and continued to focus on the bowed slate roof of the barn as I willed myself into control. "Nothing . . . nothing's the matter."

"Are you thinking about your granda?"

"I want so much to be involved with a girl and get married and have children someday, Uncle Brendan." I turned back to look at him. "I really want that so much."

He appeared surprised. "There isn't anything to prevent you from doing so."

"Don't you want to marry and be a father one day, now that you've left the priesthood?"

Uncle stared at the grave for a long moment. His Adam's apple rose and fell as he swallowed. "I'm sure it must be wonderful to bring up a child." His voice wavered. "I'm sure there's nothing more wonderful than to watch your own flesh and blood grow up to become successes." He walked up to the stone wall behind the tree, laid his hands on its top, and stared beyond to a twenty-foot-wide band of tall firs marching like soldiers up the side of the hill. "I was about eight years old when the forestry commission planted those trees yonder. They were so small and delicate, and your father and I used to jump over them. Now, they're almost fully grown. I never got to see their in-between stages." He peered at me. "Were they beautiful in their in-between stage, Gabriel?"

I was amazed he was asking about trees when I'd been talking about wanting to be able to love a woman enough to make children with her. "All the times I've come up here, I've never given those trees a second thought. They've . . . they've just always been." I walked up to him and observed them.

"That's very true. We take everything for granted. Even young people take things for granted. We don't notice changes in things because we see them every day." He laughed, then looked sidelong at me. "I bet it's the same with your school things, too.

You probably haven't even noticed how much you've learned since you first started Saint Malachy's because you've been doing it incrementally every day."

"Uncle Brendan, may I . . . I'd like to ask you something."

"Ask."

"Did Father Cornelius . . . did Father Cornelius teach you when you were at Saint Malachy's?"

"He wasn't there in my time. Isn't he the vice-head?"

"Yes."

"Why, is he one of the strict priests?" Uncle chuckled.

"He taught me English for a while." My mouth began to quiver, and the pressure in my head returned. Before I could control myself, I'd let out a dry gasp and become a mass of heaves and sobs.

"What's the matter, Gabriel? Son, what's wrong?"

He draped his arms around my shoulders and drew me to him. My forehead touched his solid chest, it felt so wonderful, and he stroked my crown until the hacked sobs began to ease. I could feel his rapid heartbeat, just like I'd felt Father's heartbeat on the occasion he'd been released by the British army, but it wasn't in any way awkward as those moments had been. Another burst of sobs threatened, I steeled myself into a semblance of control, and withdrew apologizing. His gaze remained fixed on me as I hung my head and sniffed myself to composure.

"What's bothering you? Tell me. It's better to get it off your chest. Believe me, I know all about things like that."

"If I confide . . . if I tell, will you promise not to say a word to anyone?"

He remained silent as he considered the request. "It depends on what it is."

"I must have your word, or I can't tell."

"You can trust me to do the right thing, Gabriel." He patted the top of the wall. "Sit here and tell me."

I hoisted myself on the wall and immediately felt the corky dryness of the lichen underneath my moist palms. The stones were warm from the afternoon sun, and their heat radiated into the seat of my jeans as I sat telling him about Father Cornelius, and how I was too sensitive, and how the priest had detected this and somehow knew he could do wicked things to me. I couldn't bring myself to tell him about Connor, or that I fantasized about doing things with men. Throughout, he made no attempt to interrupt me. I suppose years of teaching taught him not to do that, but his face had certainly paled by the time I reached the end.

"Don't you believe me?" I said, caving in to my one overwhelming concern that this was a priest and a teacher I'd just told him about.

"I do. Of course, I do. I'm just amazed you haven't told your parents. They could have done something about this."

"They don't understand things like this. Mammy believes priests can't do any wrong. She can't even watch a man and woman kissing on TV. She changes the channels. And Daddy would never understand a man doing things to another man, much less a priest." I shook my head. "When I was younger, he couldn't understand why I was allowing boys to bully me at school. So how could he deal with this weakness?"

"They would understand because this is a serious matter. I know Knockburn's a small place and people live very sheltered lives here, but what happened to you is abuse, Gabriel. Your parents would understand that." Uncle fell into a reverie as he looked away to the marching firs. "Look, you'll have to tell them," he said finally. "I'll be with you and I'll make them understand. We'll get it all sorted out."

"No . . . no, I don't want that. I know my father better than you know him in things like this . . . and you promised."

"I promised to do the right thing, and this would be the right thing."

"Please treat me as an adult. Treat me the same way you did when you told me you'd left the priesthood."

"This involves great wrongdoing on Father Cornelius' part."

"It's very painful for me, and I wish it to go no farther. I didn't even plan to tell you. It just came out. But now that it's out, I'm feeling better, so there's no need to do anything more."

"I understand, but again this is very serious."

"I *expect* you to understand how I feel because you should know all about pain." I hadn't meant to sound so harsh, and his head jerked back as if I'd punched him across the face. "I'm sorry. I didn't mean to say it like that."

He placed his hand on my shoulder. "Your pain came out because it's been preying on your mind." He sighed. "If this is how you wish it, then I'll agree on one condition. I'll agree, provided you consent to my speaking to Father Cornelius."

"No, Uncle. No, please."

"I must insist, because I'm older and wiser in this regard. You must trust me here. I will respect your wishes, but this, you must agree to. You can be sure he's doing this to other boys as well, and that must stop. Father Cornelius is very sick and needs treatment."

The words "sick" and "treatment" cut into my brain like a sweeping scythe. I knew at once I'd been right not to tell him about Connor or my urges. I, alone, would have to war against the sickness. I, alone, would have to cure myself.

I was in the biology laboratory when the school secretary came in and informed my teacher that I had to report to Father Cornelius' room. En route, I visualized the scene about to play out. The classroom door was open, and he was seated at his desk, white-faced, white-knuckled, Uncle Brendan standing over him.

"Gabriel, I've had a long chat with Father Cornelius and he has something important to say to you."

He waited until I drew up beside them before nodding gravely at the priest. My heartbeat echoed in my ears.

"Please accept my apologies for what I have done," Father Cornelius said. "I've acted disgracefully. It was never any fault of yours, and I'm sorry for the anguish I've caused. May God forgive me for this terrible act." He stopped speaking, and lowered his head to stare at the top of his desk. "Will you accept my apology and forgive me because I'm weak?"

"Forgive you because you're *sick*, Father Cornelius," Uncle Brendan said. "We've discussed this, and you've recognized you are ill. Doing this to young boys is an illness and *must* be so acknowledged."

"Yes, I'm ill."

"Do you accept Father's apology?"

"I do."

"Father Cornelius has agreed to resign his post at the end of the year, and he will travel to England where he'll seek treatment for his illness. I don't believe they'd understand the nature of this condition in Ireland, so it's for the best he travels across the water and remains for a while. Not another word shall pass our lips about what has transpired here today. Not a soul shall be any the wiser, and Father's otherwise exemplary teaching record will not be tarnished." Father Cornelius' head raised at that. "And when the treatment is over, he'll come back to Ireland if he so desires, request the diocese to place him somewhere as a curate, and that will be the end of the affair."

"Thank you, Brendan."

"It's Gabriel you must thank."

Now that I had told someone about what had happened and there'd been a resolution, I felt so much better. I discovered I also lost the hate I'd had for Father Cornelius. Only a thin slice of resentment lingered because Father Cornelius would get treatment for the sickness, and I had to nurse mine, alone.

A few weeks later, Uncle Brendan left for America and I began to study in earnest. The number of things to revise was endless: novels had to be reread, quotes learned from poems and plays, German and French vocabulary expanded (Latin and Irish I gave up on, figuring they were dead languages, anyway), and the Books of Genesis and Luke had to be reviewed for religious education. Subjects like mathematics and the sciences couldn't be crammed, so I left those to luck and my mother's novenas. A pass in mathematics was mandatory. It was one of four core subjects that had to be passed, failure in any one translating to automatic rejection by all universities and relegation to the inferior polytechnics.

A warm, sunny third day of June heralded examination month. Throughout the three weeks and two days of examinations I surprised myself, raising my hand often to request extra writing paper in a number of subjects, and I felt extremely confident after it was all over. Only in Latin, Irish, one part of a physics paper (calculation of velocities), and two chemistry questions (inorganic and one reaction equation) had I had nothing to contribute.

CHAPTER TWENTY-SIX

Dressed in a faded T-shirt and old jeans with a gaping hole in the right knee, I joined Father's workforce at six-thirty one morning. I sat in the back of his transport van, its musty stench of oil reminding me of his lorry cab on the trip to Larne harbor many years ago. On the way into Duncarlow to pick up Martin, we stopped to pick up his workers. When we arrived in the town, my cousin was already waiting outside Auntie Celia's shop, a bright orange lunchbox tucked under his arm.

"Jasus, does gentleman Jim think he's going to be working in the site manager's office?" Father asked.

Martin was dressed in a pair of gorgeous, immaculately pressed parallels with one-inch cuffs, a matching college sweater with narrow, twin maroon bands on each arm, and wedge-heeled shoes just like the Bay City Rollers wore on *Top of the Pops*.

"Aye, I dare say that'll be management, Harry," said Dessie, one of Father's longest-serving excavator drivers.

The other men sniggered. There wasn't much room in the van; Martin had to squeeze in beside two hefty, dozing laborers, and one grunted irritably because he trod on his foot.

"Didn't Gabriel tell you to wear your old clothes?" Father said. He stretched his head back to hear Martin's response as we sped out the main road.

"These *are* old clothes, Uncle Harry."

"Dessie, it must be great to live in a town," said Father. "You don't have old clothes because you never get a chance to wear them out."

"One half of the world doesn't know what the other's up to," said Dessie.

Father laughed and I was livid. Martin and I exchanged confirmatory glances that the whole bunch was beneath us and of no consequence. When we arrived at the factory site, as Father had previously pointed out, we were given no special treatment. Our duties consisted of raking and gathering fieldstones in the long expanses of raw earth, which were to be transformed into lawns, running alongside the factory building. He sent Martin to work with a crew at one end of the factory, me to the other.

A sour stink wafted from the soil and grew more and more unbearable as the sun grew warmer. Flies buzzed about my face, sweat trickled into the corners of my eyes and stung, and my lower back ached. I kept checking my watch, but its hands never seemed to move forward. After what seemed like an entire work day, the first break of a mere fifteen minutes duration came around, and I left my position to locate Martin. I found him dusty and a little cranky. However, at lunchtime, I saw his arms and short legs barreling down the site toward me.

"You told me *this* would be an easy job. Your father's working me to death." His face and neck were redder than Vesuvius in eruption.

"It is tough, isn't it?"

He ranted as we walked down the road toward the only large tree capable of providing any shade in the entire site. Martin didn't even lower his voice when other site workers passed by. My blood began to rise. We reached the tree, and Martin whipped the lid off his lunchbox and took out a sandwich, cut daintily into a triangle and with its crust removed as if he were on a picnic. He took a bite and put the sandwich down, then thrust his curled fingers in my face savagely.

"Look at my hands and nails," he said. "My nails are black, my hands are blistered. Look at my sandwich. It's black . . . and I'm sunburned."

"The sun *is* nice and strong. It's such a pity you didn't bring some lemon juice for your hair."

That silenced him for a moment.

"This is just plain ridiculous. My body's not designed to endure this torture. It's not worth twenty-five pounds a week. It's not even worth a hundred."

In all honesty, I was seething at Father, also. "It's not my fault. I just didn't understand how lawns get made. I didn't realize stones and rocks had to be gathered or that the damned soil is to be leveled by hand."

"Why hasn't he got machines to do this? If Uncle's making so much money, why hasn't he got machines to perform this slave work? I can't be expected to do this for the entire summer. No, it's not on. You must tell him that I wish to do something else."

"Quit whining. You're behaving like an old woman. It's only for six weeks, and we'll have lots of money to spend on holiday."

"How dare you say that? And there won't be any holiday if this sort of slavery continues, because *I'll* be in the hospital."

We fell into a broody silence during which I ate and watched three shirtless men wearing white construction hats erect guttering on the factory roof. I tried to avoid looking, even turned my head away a few times. It didn't work. No matter how hard I tried, I kept reverting to take furtive peeks, and was disappointedly pleased when they finally left.

"I didn't mean that, Martin," I said. "I'm sorry."

"So you should be."

Another flash of temper charged from my brain demanding articulation, but I managed to keep my tongue in check. Martin could be just as sharp as his mother on occasions and, also like her, didn't mean it. He dusted his trousers and scraped acrid clumps of soil off his shoes with a twig for a little while, something I found hilariously idiotic because he was going back to do more filthy work.

"I am sorry, Martin."

"Accepted." He wiped his sweaty bang and swatted at a fly, but missed. "I am, too. I realize it's not your fault."

All too soon, the lunch break was over and I went back to my area and didn't see him again for the rest of the afternoon. Later, in the van on the way home, Father asked him how he'd enjoyed his first day as he winked conspiratorially at Dessie.

"I'm sure I know every kind of rock and stone that's to be found in Ireland, Uncle."

Father and Dessie roared like idiots, while Martin tightened his lips and shook his head.

Next morning, Auntie Celia was standing alone outside her shop.

"Harry, he's not coming today. What did you do to him?" She started to laugh, but thought better of it and killed it. "He told me last night he wasn't going back to work, but I didn't ring you because I thought he was tired and would change his mind. But he was grafted to the bed this morning. I couldn't get him to budge."

"That's quite all right, Celia," Father said.

"Gabriel's hardier." She stuck her head halfway inside the side window, looked at me, and smiled. "He says it's his allergies." She withdrew her head outside again. "Between you and me, Harry, I think he doesn't want to admit the work's too much for him. He's not as sturdy as Gabriel, you know?"

"I'll find someone else for tomorrow," Father said.

"Are you sure?"

"I am. I must be going now because time's money."

As we hurtled out the road, Father remained silent for a while. "Your cousin's allergic to work, that's what's the matter. He's one useless lump of a chap. Just plain useless, and I always knew it."

"Don't talk about him like that," I said. "You should have machines to do this slave work."

"Quit your talking. You'd think I was a millionaire the way you're raving."

My luck changed two weeks later. Father commenced a road repair project on the outskirts of Castlebenem, a pretty Protestant village in the heart of rolling countryside, and I was sent there to labor. Castlebenem was also horse country. Girls and boys of my age, smartly dressed in jodhpurs and white shirts, rode by with poker-straight backs and upturned chins.

It didn't trouble Father's workers that these people looked down on us. They didn't know any better. It irked me something fierce, however. I didn't want to be seen in that light, so I made a point of trying to befriend one girl who usually smiled as she rode by. She was of medium build and, while she had silky, straw-yellow hair like ABBA's Agnetha, she wasn't good-looking because it framed an oval, country-red face. Her feet looked mannishly large in the stirrups, too. Indeed, when Father's workers first saw her approach, the girl's hair caused a commotion and attracted much ribald commentary, until she drew closer that is, and then they fell silent and picked up their shovels again.

The next morning as she approached, I braced myself to speak. "That's a lovely horse you're riding."

The horse's chestnut thighs came to a halt.

"Pardon."

"That's a lovely horse. What's its name?"

"Stroller."

The horse's velvety flanks quivered for no reason other than its progress had been impeded.

"Isn't that the name of a famous show jumper?"

"No, it's the name of my horse." The girl's eyes narrowed for a moment, undoubtedly because she was surprised a laborer would know anything about show jumping. "I'm Fiona McFarland. Who are you?" After introducing myself, she stood on her stirrups and swept her eyes over the gawking workers. "This seems like awfully hard work."

Her accent was English, like that of a BBC announcer, and she didn't look nearly so plain anymore. At the same time, I wondered if there must be an unwritten universal rule that horsy girls always resemble their horses, in the same way many dog owners look like their dogs. The beast's flanks stopped quivering, he began chafing at the bit, and I was sure he sensed my nervousness. He began to reverse and she yanked the reins.

"I'm only doing this work for the summer," I said, and upped the ante. "I'm still at school. My father has the contract to do this job."

She didn't say anything, because the horse was still reversing. While I took a few discreet steps farther into the ditch in case it lunged forward, I considered if I should repeat what I'd said in case she hadn't heard.

"He's a trifle frisky this morning," she said. "I'm a student, too."

"Where?"

"Granderson College."

Granderson was a prestigious, coeducational Protestant school about four miles from mine. The Saint Malachy's junior and senior rugby teams played there, but because we specialized in Gaelic football and rugby was a Protestant game, they were superior and always thrashed us soundly.

"You sound English."

"I went to boarding school over there for a time. But I kept beseeching Mummy to persuade Father to allow me to come home, and last year he relented."

Clearly, the girl was filthy rich, because only filthy rich Protestants attended boarding schools in England.

"Are you boarding at Granderson?"

"Not for much longer. I hate it because I can't ride every day." She looked over her left shoulder because someone had started up the steamroller. "I've told Mummy, I'll take A levels there, but only if they agree to my commuting daily." She laughed, and its rich tinkle was instantly absorbed by the screech of the great rollers crushing and flattening the road's surface. "I've had enough of cold dorms and bossy monitors."

I laughed to indicate agreement, and at the same time wondered why the hell I was laughing because I knew nothing of cold dorms and monitors. "So, you're starting A levels next term, too?"

"No, I'm sitting O levels this coming year, but you've got to work on parents a few years in advance, don't you think?" She glanced over her shoulder again.

Out of the corner of my eye, I saw Father approaching, so I stepped from the ditch with alacrity, thrust my shovel into a pile of gravel, and began to spread it about. Fiona took the hint. She kicked the horse gently in its sides and it started to walk away.

"I see the boss is coming. Well, cheerio for now."

"Were you talking to a horsy lady?" Father asked. He watched as the horse broke into a canter.

"Yes. So what?"

"Who's her people?"

"She said she's McFarland."

"Jasus, you go straight for the top drawer. The McFarlands are big people round here. Her father owns every blade of grass you can set your eyes on hereabouts." He looked at me and laughed. "Well, get back to your work because lost time is lost money."

I loathed the way Father referred to rich people as "big" people. Knockburn people always referred to wealthy people as "big" people, and in so doing subconsciously categorized themselves as little people.

From that morning, if Father was not in the area or was at another job site, Fiona stopped when she rode by and we'd talk snatches at a time. Road repairs progressed quickly due to a long stretch of excellent weather, and by the beginning of the fourth week of July, the crew had moved three miles outside the village. Late one Tuesday morning, Father arrived in a great hurry from his factory site, informed me he was running late, and that he had to take our foreman to a meeting with the Department of the Environment in Belfast.

"I want you to keep an eye on my men," he said. "If you see them skiving, don't be afraid to tell them to get back to their work." He winked to reinforce we were bound in a secret conspiracy. "Keep them hard at it, Gabriel, because lost time is lost money."

I didn't want to be in charge. As it was, the men were already suspicious of me because I was the boss's son; often, conversation would stop abruptly if I was in the vicinity, and the recently employed or more nervous workers would scatter like town pigeons. I needn't have worried, because all that was required to keep the spades and picks busy were periodic walks about the construction site, though I was very self-conscious about doing so and always pretended I was looking for something. By four-thirty, Father still hadn't returned. Already two of his laziest workers were consulting their watches, the tracings of fret already on their grimy faces, but I wasn't worried, because he always got back before knocking-off time when he was away like this.

At five o'clock, as I was about to make one final patrol, a woman called out my name. It was Fiona, and she waved as she cantered across the field to enter a small paddock containing red and white horse jumps. I watched for a few minutes until an urge overtook me, and I scrambled down the low bank, climbed over the barbed-wire fence, and ran across to her.

"I didn't know you practiced around here." I drew up to Stroller and patted his sweaty neck.

"This is our home farm," she said. "Our house is over there." Following the direction of her extended arm, I saw the red-brick chimneys and slate roof of a house rising above a band of trees in the near distance. "I'm practicing for a gymkhana outside Londonderry next week."

Even though she was Protestant, and I knew Protestants said "Londonderry" instead of "Derry," nevertheless it riled me. I avoided asking where exactly it was to take place, because that would have meant I'd have to say "Derry," and then she might get annoyed at me for the opposite reason.

"Could I have a go on the horse?" I said.

"Your father must be away." She grinned as she dismounted.

"There's only half an hour of work time left and you know I've always wanted to try riding him."

Fiona took off her riding hat and placed it on my head. It fitted perfectly. For the first time, I realized we were exactly the same height and, now we were eye to eye, I also noticed her nose was a fraction off-center and her irises were far more greenish than blue.

"You've got an audience," she said.

I turned toward the road, where five of the workers were leaning on shovels watching us.

"Give her a good, hard riding," one of them shouted.

The others laughed coarsely.

"The amazing thing about *double entendre* is these people think it's only they who get it," she said. "What shallow lives they lead."

"Very shallow."

After struggling in a most undignified fashion into the saddle, I straightened the hat and peered down at her. It was surprising how high I was, and more than a little frightening. Fiona took the slack of the reins and led me around the paddock.

"Could I try on my own?"

"Well okay, just grip the reins, dig your heels into his sides gently, and he'll start walking."

It was a treat. One of those occasions where I felt like a god. I was in supreme control, though admittedly my feet wouldn't stay in the stirrups, but the combination of the creaking saddle, the horse's docile power, and the coarse, oily touch of its mane was exhilarating. After five minutes or so, I tried a canter, but my buttocks kept slamming into the saddle until Fiona showed me how to move in rhythm with the horse's pace. Every time I thought I'd finally mastered it, I'd suddenly forget the rhythm and be back to arse-slamming.

"You catch on quickly," she said, after I'd finally succeeded.

"I want to try one little jump before I dismount."

"I don't think that's such a good idea, Gabriel. That requires a lot of skill. The next step is usually to try a gallop."

"Just one tiny jump."

"I don't know."

"Just a really tiny one."

She walked up to a jump and regarded it for a moment. She removed two bars so that it stood only eighteen inches high and looked at it again.

"What exactly must I do?"

"It's very low now, so just canter toward it and he'll know

what to do. Remember, your buttocks will rise off the saddle as you go into the jump."

After lining up the horse, I sized up the jump and then smacked my heels into his rubbery sides a few times until he broke into a canter. On the approach, I imagined I was in a major competition and the jump was four feet high. Because I knew the men were watching, my body tingled with pride. It didn't matter that the horse was definitely in charge, and I clutched the reins and watched the clumps of chocolate mane rising and falling on his bobbing neck. The horse began to ascend, I saw white cotton clouds, my arse rose off the saddle, and then all became tangled confusion. My foot slipped out of one stirrup, my torso swayed backward and then listed to the side, and I began to fall. Somehow, I cleared the jump with one foot immersed fully inside its stirrup. I slid some more, finally hit the ground, and was dragged across the grass until the horse halted abruptly. Looking toward the beast's front, I saw Fiona had grabbed the reins. I set about freeing myself with as much dignity as I could muster.

"Are you all right?"

My legs shook as I stood up, in the background I heard Father shouting, and like an idiot started to brush grass stains off my dirty jeans. "I'm fine. Not a scratch."

"I really shouldn't have let you jump. You're very persuasive. I was awfully silly."

"Don't think anything of it. It's me who's foolish by trying to be Eddie Macken on my first try."

"Gabriel, come here," Father called.

"He's furious because I was left in charge of his men." I started away quickly. "Thanks for everything. I'll see you again."

Father's fury gave strength to my legs, and I sprinted out of the paddock and across the field.

"This is what you do when my back is turned," he said. "Get into that bloody van."

"Aye, you'll not be representing Ireland any time soon with a performance like that," one of the men said. "What do you say, Harry?"

Father didn't reply. I was getting the silent treatment.

"What do you think I caught him doing this afternoon?" he said to my mother as I sat at the table. Nuala was already seated, and Mammy was setting down a lamb casserole. "I go off to Belfast and leave him in charge, only to come back and catch him on top of a bloody horse." He regarded me murderously. "Aye, we're making money when he's acting the gentleman, and all my workmen are leaning on their shovels watching him."

"Don't be so dramatic. It was almost quitting time."

My mother's face remained impassive for a moment longer, and then she laughed.

"What the hell are you laughing at?" Father pulled a chair out roughly and sat. "He's fucking useless."

"I'm not useless and you're overreacting. I've been doing a damned good job. All *you* want me to do is watch over the men and snitch on them when they're not working. That's no job, and I'm no bloody snitch."

His eyes widened simultaneously with his mouth. "I'll take James to work instead. I'll ask him when he comes home from football practice. That's exactly what I'll do. *He's* sensible."

"Harry, that's enough," Mammy said. "He made a mistake."

"Why don't you take James? You've always made it abundantly clear you prefer him, anyway. You've always treated us differently." I leaped off my chair, jabbing my index finger at him. "I've never been good enough at anything in your eyes."

"That's enough of your backchat," my mother said. "Don't talk back to your father like that."

"I'm *not* talking back to him. I'm telling him how things are. It needs to change. Uncle Brendan understands me far better than him and he lived away in Kenya when I was growing up. *He* listened and knew what to do when I needed help."

As soon as the words were out, I knew I'd gone too far. My mother's gape confirmed it. The momentary silence filled with enough energy to light up every home in Knockburn.

"What are you talking about?" she asked.

Father's chair squealed, and he lunged at me. "Don't you

fucking well talk to me like that. Who do you fucking-well take me for?"

I dodged his grasp and ran around the table, but he gave chase. It was surreal. Caroline watched by the sink, her hands immersed in soapy water because she was washing a pot. Nuala clutched a gold crucifix around her neck that I'd bought for her at a church mission. The chain had turned a dull orange within two weeks of its purchase and Mammy said it was made of cheap tin, but Nuala never took it off. I dashed toward the door, but somehow his foot connected with my arse before I reached it. It didn't hurt and I didn't stop.

"Clear off to America and let him feed you, if that's how you feel," he called after me.

I hung about the yard muttering curses as I kicked at stones and invented ways to make him pay. After I'd calmed down, I went and sat on the trunk of the curved climbing tree now dying because diesel oil from his machinery had seeped into the soil and poisoned its roots.

Half an hour later, Caroline came out. "He's calmed down, but I must say the things you said in there were a bit strong, Gabriel. He makes no difference between James and you."

"How'd you know?"

"Oh, stop."

"Well, to hell with him."

"Mammy told him you're anxious because the exam results will soon be out." She paused. "That's it, isn't it?" She laid her hand fleetingly on my shoulder.

"I don't know what it is, Caroline. I'm just so angry at him all the time."

"Well, don't be. Look, he says you're to come in."

I went inside, and Father just said I wasn't fired and the matter was over as far as he was concerned. He didn't speak to me for the remainder of the evening though, and that meant he was still disappointed in what I'd done. Mammy kept biting her lower lip and sighing every so often, stuff she did when she was excessively tense, and I caught her glancing at me under her eyes a few times, too.

Next morning, I got up, but never felt less like going to work. At the breakfast table, Father was back to his old self. He told me the jobs I had to do on the site that day, even joked I should stay away from the horses. It was as if nothing had happened. I still harbored a grudge, but I had to admit his attitude was a quality I admired in him. Father never allowed anything to fester; he forgot unpleasant incidents quickly, and always forgave readily.

That evening, my mother maneuvered until she got me alone after supper and began to grill me about what I'd meant when I'd said Uncle Brendan once helped me. I was fully prepared, and concocted the excuse that I'd wanted to hurt Father at the time and had made the whole thing up.

"Well, you hurt your father very much when you said it. His skin's not as thick as you seem to think, Gabriel. Granted, he doesn't show his feelings much, but that doesn't mean he doesn't have any. And if you hurt him, you hurt me, too. You'd do well to remember that."

"I'm sorry."

"You promised me a long time ago you'd never turn on your father or me." She paused. "Do you remember?"

I remembered. It was the same time she'd lied about never having met Uncle Brendan's girlfriend.

"It was in the car one evening," she said. "Remember, we discussed how pigheaded your granda had been about Uncle Brendan."

"Oh, you mean the night you told me you'd never met his girlfriend?"

She ignored the provocation. "You won't do this again, will you?"

I clenched my teeth as I nodded, and she also said the whole affair should be forgotten, and the quicker the better. However, she didn't mean it, because, when I got my paycheck on Friday, I discovered an entire afternoon's pay had been docked. When I asked about it, she said I shouldn't be gallivanting about on horses belonging to Protestant girls on my father's time, and it had been deducted to teach me a lesson about responsibility.

CHAPTER TWENTY-SEVEN

As soon as I laid down the receiver after talking to the head-master's secretary, I felt Father had a point. I was useless. I really was. I passed down the hall to my mother's bedroom where she was waiting, Nuala perched on the edge of the bed beside her.

"I passed four."

"Away o' that," she said. "What did you really get?"

"An A in religious education and Cs in English, chemistry, and German. The rest were Es and Us."

"How many unclassifieds?" Nuala asked.

"Five, if you must know."

All those days I'd raised my hand in the examination hall to request extra writing sheets flashed before me. The essay booklets which the Examination Board had provided hadn't been enough. I'd needed more paper, and for what? A bunch of unclassified grades.

"This is abominable," said Mammy. "Abominable. An absolute catastrophe. What can I tell your father?"

"I don't know what you'll tell him."

My mother's face twisted into a shape befitting a Notre-Dame cathedral gargoyle. "By Christ, if that Fergal or Connor passes, he'll have some choice words for you."

The stirrings of acidic criticism right on cue. She was so pre-dictable. I said nothing, continued merely to regard her brutish face as I tried to decide whether to repeat the year, or die. Dying seemed preferable. She was still ranting five minutes later when the phone rang. Caroline called that Auntie Celia was on the line. My mother started from the room, though not before pausing for a second shot.

"She's phoning to boast about how well your cousins have done, I have no doubt."

Martin passed, but Connor didn't. I felt relieved, though not completely, because there was still Fergal to go. Poor Martin hadn't passed French this time either, which meant the universities would not accept him, and he was now doomed to attend an inferior institute of higher education no matter how well he did in his final exams two years from now.

However, the news mitigated my catastrophe in Mammy's eyes, because she decided to ring Fergal's mother. Caroline, Nuala, and I listened, scarcely a breath exhaled between us, until my mother's voice rose from dolorous to animated. It transpired that Fergal had done worse: only three passes, though no unclassified grades. In comparing mediocrity to atrociousness, she'd found solace, though continued to whine about what the neighbors would say.

Her incessant fear of telling the neighbors about my failure was ridiculous. It infuriated me. I felt no sympathy for her self-inflicted predicament and had to leave. I walked to the twin-arched bridge where I hopped up on its wall and dangled my legs over it. Halfway down its stone façade, a sturdy sycamore protruded from a fissure, its roots clinging with silent tenaciousness to the caked limestone binding, defying both gravity and oblivion in its need to survive. It seemed at once admirable and pathetic.

I left the bridge and strolled along the riverbank before returning to the house. Father was already home and reacted surprisingly civil. There were no banged fists on tables or "I saw it coming"s, though I'd fully anticipated and deserved them. He simply looked me squarely in the eyes as he gave me a backhanded compliment, saying I would have to do better next time because I had the brains. "Is my dinner ready because I'm famished and could eat a horse," was his next remark.

Uncle Tommy, Auntie Bernie, and their two children, Philip and Anna, were already at their summer bungalow on the north side of Bundoran town when Martin and I arrived to begin our holiday. After supper, Martin and I went to our room to change to go out. Auntie Bernie summoned us into the living room when we came downstairs again and laid down the house rules, chief of which were that we were not to eat in cafés that looked suspect, or use any public lavatories. Philip caught practically every bug going around, and my aunt, already neurotic about her own health, was terrified of infection. Satisfied with our promises to obey the rules, she turned next to Martin and skimmed her eyes over his clothes.

"Those will get filthy."

We were going to the amusement arcade, and Martin had donned a pair of white jeans and matching balloon-sleeved shirt open to his sternum. We'd been to the beach that afternoon, and he wanted to show off his tan. His body was in reality boiled-lobster red, except for his orangey-brown face, and that was only because he'd put on countless applications of fake suntan lotion. Martin's skin didn't tan like mine. It was too fair, but he refused to accept defeat. He swallowed great quantities of pills supposed to kick-start his melanin deficiency, but which succeeded only in making his insides rattle as he strutted.

"Oh, one last thing, don't be talking to those bold hussies I see hanging around the arcades," Auntie Bernie said as we edged toward the door.

"Don't heed everything she says," said Uncle Tommy, and he winked at us. "Bernie, they're fellas wanting a bit of fun, for Christ's sake."

"That's exactly why I'm saying it. Boys, I'm all for you having fun, but fun does not entail experimentation of any kind . . . not while you're on my watch. You hear that, Martin. No experimentation, and no alcohol, either. You're only seventeen and have another year to wait."

We discovered the larger amusement arcade situated on the north end of the town was the most fun. It had a dizzyingly high helter-skelter, a decent ghost train ride, and dodgems. Martin and I got into a dodgem and were soon pursued by two girls. The driver, an olive-skinned girl with a long neck swathed in love-beads, teased him good-naturedly each time she crashed headlong into us, and also outmaneuvered him deftly when he tried to retaliate. After the second ride, as we were exiting our car, she and her friend approached.

"I hope I didn't cause too many bruises," she said. "If I did, I'm a nurse and I'll be delighted to help bandage you up."

"You can help by driving me to the local hospital," Martin said.

"I'm Sheila, and this is my friend, Bridget."

The girl was stocky, had a small purplish-red blister on her chin that she'd tried to conceal with makeup, and prominent front teeth sank into the fleshy inner lining of her jutting bottom lip.

"Are you lads game for a go on the helter-skelter?" asked Sheila.

I declined, and Bridget wasn't keen. Instead, we opted to take a ride on the electric swing boats, but that was also a mistake because the cars crisscrossed at increasingly ferocious speed and seemed to miss one another by a hair's breadth, judging by the rush of air in my face at the swing's extremity. During the initially sedate part of the ride, I learned the girls had been best friends since nine years old, that they were nursing auxiliaries who intended to become nurses one day, and this was the last evening of their vacation. Bridget had a soft-spoken Donegal accent, appeared to be interested in me because she kept asking questions while simultaneously touching my arm, and her unfortunate teeth seemed to be at the back of her mind, because she tried hard not to smile.

Martin and Sheila were already waiting when we arrived back at the base of the helter-skelter. They had decided in our absence we'd eat fish and chips at a nearby café and go on to the dance at the Astoria ballroom afterward. As it had been a long time since

I'd been with a girl, I found it enjoyable dancing and smooching on the dance floor. The only unease occurred when I found myself looking also at attractive men. One in particular, a tall football player type with proud, pushed-back shoulders, caught my eye, and I kept sneaking peeks. If he was dancing, I watched to see if the girl would stay with him, hoped she wouldn't, and felt genuine relief when I saw her walk away at the end of the set. It was ridiculous, I knew it was ridiculous, but I just couldn't stop watching him.

"As it's my last night here, why don't you come back to my B&B for a little while?" Bridget said to me at the end of the dance. "The landlady's a bit of a witch, but she'll be in bed by now."

"Ahm . . . I think . . . ahm, let me see what Martin wants to do."

Sheila had already asked Martin, and I could see he was also hesitant. However, the girls insisted, adding we had to go back with them because it was their last evening in town, we were having such fun, and it was far too early for the night to end. The terraced house was situated two streets from the seafront, and the heavy salt air eclipsed the fragrance of crimson and white roses growing in rusty urns by the front door. No sooner had we passed inside the dim hallway than the girls began to take charge. Placing one finger before her lips, Sheila removed her pumps, signaled to Martin to take off his shoes as well, and led him up the creaking, carpeted stairs while Bridget guided me into a damp-smelling living room. She switched on a lamp perched on a small doily-covered table next to a bay window. A matted sheepskin rug lay before the hearth, and two armchairs and a crushed-velvet maroon sofa were pushed against walls awash in photographs and a Sacred Heart picture with its de rigueur flickering lamp.

After settling me on the sofa, Bridget excused herself and went upstairs. As soon as she returned, I noticed immediately she'd retouched the makeup around her blister, opened her blouse one more button, and, most disturbing of all, the bra was gone. She sidled close to me.

"Don't worry," she said. "We just had to be extra-quiet coming in. The old dragon won't hear us now."

"She doesn't allow male visitors?"

"What do you think?" She puckered her mouth and glanced at the Scared Heart picture as her fingers raked my hair. "If we hadn't already paid the old bag, we'd have left after the first night."

Bridget drew her face close for a kiss, but its application proved quite difficult because my tongue kept curling around her jutting teeth. It became quickly apparent nursing auxiliaries from Donegal on their last night's vacation could be very horny because, growing impatient with my reticence to explore, she grabbed my hand and guided it inside her blouse as we continued to negotiate another kiss. Her skin felt warm and interestingly firm. An embryonic curiosity began to compete with my reluctance. She swung up her legs and eased back fully on the sofa. After taking off my shoes, I eased on top of her, cupped my hands around her breasts, and squeezed. They felt mouthwateringly ripe. The alternating soft pliability of breast and rough hardness of nipple were the most exciting things my hands had ever touched. I explored the textures with my fingertips, utterly astonished because I had never known a woman's body could have such manly roughness amid its feminine softness.

She sighed from deep within and my body was suddenly ablaze. I dropped my head and sped my lips voraciously from one rough nipple to the other, back and forth, back and forth, spurred by her continued groans of pleasure. I felt myself grow stiffer and stiffer as each touch and moan merged to unfathomable ecstasy. But she was not yet finished with her womanly tricks because, emitting yet another charged sigh, she thrust her pelvis up hard against my rigid maleness. The front door opened and someone stumbled into the hallway softly singing. Bridget ceased raking my hair, her neck and shoulders stiffened, until the drunken stranger passed by the door and started up the stairs. We kissed more passionately as my incited fingers reached underneath her skirt, dipped inside her knickers, and plunged into unfamiliar liquid warmth. Never had I felt such liquid warmth. I kissed, feasted, probed until the singing commenced again, aggressively intrusive now, piercing our fragile intimacy. The melody transformed to hoarse yells because the fellow couldn't get his key into the door lock. A woman shouted to stop the racket, followed by a deathly silence during which Bridget shoved me to the floor, and then chaos erupted.

"That's the second night in a row, you drunken cur," the woman said. "Get out of my house. You're waking the household with your cat screeching. Get out. Get out, or I'll summon the Gardai to haul you to jail."

Footsteps thumped down the stairs and the front door was flung open. Bridget and I adjusted our clothing with ferocious speed.

"Jesus, I can't get my blouse buttoned properly," she said.

The door slammed shut.

"Who's got the light on in there at this hour of the morning?" the woman said.

Neither of us spoke, and we riveted on the ajar door. It opened wider. A severe-featured woman entered clad in an electric blue satin nightgown, her hair tucked into a hairnet. "*You*, again. I might have known."

Rapid footsteps started down the stairs. The landlady spun around to peer out into the hallway. "Halt. You in the white. Halt, I say." She tore out of the room.

"I was visiting a friend and I'm just leaving," Martin said.

The sound of male laughter rushed in momentarily from the street as the door was reopened. I scooped up my shoes and said good-bye as I dashed out of the room.

"Donegal trollops bringing Ulster trash in here," the woman shouted from the threshold. "Next time I catch curs like . . ." I swept by her at enormous speed and almost sent her careening out into the street, "Aah, Jesus, what's happening?"

I caught up with Martin at the end of the street where I found him pacing up and down in an excitable state.

"Where's my shoe? I dropped my shoe on the stairs," he said. "Christ, what'll I do?" He ran his fingers rapidly through his hair. "Gabriel, go back at once and fetch my shoe."

"No bloody way."

"You must."

As I stooped and tied my own shoes, he paced and cursed and paced. We walked back to the B&B in hopes the woman might have thrown it out into the street in anger. She hadn't. The upstairs lights were still burning, and I could hear Sheila, Bridget, and the woman shouting at one another.

"It's gone, Martin. She called you 'Ulster trash.' You won't get it back now."

My cousin went to the door and raised his hand to the bell, but didn't ring it.

Despite such a precipitous ending to my first true sexual adventure with a woman, I knew exactly what people in love meant when they compared it to walking on wooly clouds. The next six days in Bundoran were beautiful because I'd touched a girl and my body had responded as it was supposed to. I wasn't sick, after all. Every afternoon, I lay sunbathing on the beach fantasizing about touching Bridget's breasts, until I became excited and had to roll over on my belly lest Auntie Bernie or anyone else would notice.

On the final night, the wooly clouds dispersed when I spied the attractive football player type with the proud, pushed-back shoulders at the dance hall again. I hadn't seen him since that first night, couldn't take my eyes off him as before, and I didn't have Bridget to save or distract me from myself. I spent the entire evening watching him from a discreet distance, and later in bed, after Martin was sound asleep, abused myself thinking about him. The last-minute substitution of Bridget's soft breasts and rough nipples didn't alleviate my guilt this time. Affliction stalked me still. It would not be denied. I could never let down my guard. A fresh terror, a terror that I might not win this war, loomed in my consciousness.

A letter from Uncle Brendan awaited me on my return home. He was beginning studies at Berkeley in September and, after expressing commiseration about my poor academic showing, he added it was understandable on account of my ordeal concerning "poor, sick Father Cornelius." Not even his subsequent words of encouragement that I'd do better the following year cheered me up. I was sick and in need of curing. At that instant, the fresh terror etched permanently in my mind. I was as sick as Father Cornelius; Uncle Brendan didn't know I was as sick as him, and would never know. Fearing my mother might come across the letter as she cleaned my room and read it, I took it outside and burned it, watching the edges of its feathery, gray-white ashes glow scarlet as they ascended to die in the breeze.

CHAPTER TWENTY-EIGHT

Humbled by my examinations debacle, and extremely grateful to Father Rafferty for permitting me to return to Saint Malachy's, I set about working diligently at the college from the first day. I was determined to pass my exams and not permit my terrors to interfere with the goal. Pani and Martin had moved on to the sixth-form, and I was lonely in my classes now, although we continued to meet up with each other at lunchtime.

Early in the new term, my bruised ego sustained an additional knock when the issue of my fat arse reemerged. As is usually the case when someone joins a new class, a bully must be reckoned with, and he set about making my life a misery. A skinny youth with body odor and badly cut hair, Roland taunted me unmercifully about my arse and addressed me as "poof" and "queer boy" when he wished to speak to me. His cruel references to my arse made me frantic because I suspected it was too large and, notwithstanding Caroline's assurances that it wasn't "all that big," I banged it mercilessly against my bedroom wall, and also tightened and squeezed it as I lay in bed in hopes of diminishment. Finally, I ceased taking off my blazer altogether, always wore a sports jacket on social occasions, and permitted no one even a side glimpse if I could help it.

"Hey, poof, come over here, I need to speak to you right now," said Roland.

We were three months into the year now, and I was at my desk rechecking mathematics homework during the first short break. Five other classmates were present and, as was my usual response to his provocation, I ignored him.

"Fucking yellabelly," he said.

I watched under my eyes as he strutted up to the blackboard, picked up a stick of chalk, and began to write. After he'd finished, the boys laughed. I looked up at the board. The words HARKIN IS A FAT-ARSED QUEER confronted me.

"That stays on till the teacher wipes it off," he said. "Otherwise, I'll have to give you a good hiding."

The boys laughed again. The hoarse resonance of their laughter was unbearably humiliating this time. It mocked my years of docility in front of Mickey and all the others who'd ever taunted me. A keg of resentment, my mind exploded, and I bounded cursing from the desk.

"You fucking-well remove that, *now*."

My hands clenched to balls. His eyes fell on them. Curiosity, tinged with doubt, flashed in his eyes.

"Oh, fuck you." He threw back his head contemptuously and turned to walk away. I seized him, spun him around, and punched him in the chest. The punch was so violent, it propelled him through three rows of tubular-legged desks, his arms rising and legs buckling as he sped backward, and he landed on his skinny arse in the middle of the room. He picked himself up quickly, though made no attempt to approach me.

"I'm leaving this room for exactly one minute, you bastard. If those words aren't off the board by the time I get back, I'm going to make you *lick* them off."

I walked hurriedly around the perimeter of the football field. The boys in the classroom stopped talking when I reentered. Both the words and Roland were gone. Without acknowledging its removal, I sat and commenced rechecking my mathematics homework.

A sea change occurred from that day: the boys accepted me as one of them, and even Roland, once his bruised ego recovered, tried to befriend me. I thought about what a few old Knockburn men had said about political violence, how sometimes it was necessary in order to focus an enemy's mind, and how the strategy seemed to work in a school environment, too.

The demise of that problem gave rise to new energy to alternately pray away, suppress, and continue the battle against my sickness. In a state of great vigilance, with countless relapses and fresh starts, I managed to see my repeat year through. When the exam results were published they were nothing short of astounding; a coveted string of A and B grades and not a single unclassified. Even Father Rafferty was impressed, because he deigned to call and congratulate me at home, something I'd never known him to do. Connor and Fergal were marginally successful and left school. Fergal decided to help his father on the farm until a better job came along, and Connor, who'd spent the summer working in a pub in London, applied for a bank position there and got it.

I moved into the sixth-form to begin the first of my final two years at Saint Malachy's and chose to specialize in history, English literature, and economics. Becoming a sixth-former was an unofficial rite of passage: we had our own common room replete with a careers reference library, plump sofas, magazines and daily newspapers, and teachers began to treat us as adults. No longer was it assumed we were present in class against our will; we were now proven young men bound for universities throughout the United Kingdom and Ireland.

A few weeks before the end of the first term, Uncle Brendan, who was coming home for Christmas, informed me he was arriving a little earlier so he could attend the annual prize-giving, where I was to be presented with an award for my turnaround. I greeted his news with mixed emotions. I looked forward to seeing my uncle, but didn't relish the prospect of receiving such a prize in front of him. The award, a new category at Saint Malachy's, recognized the "Best Improved Pupil of the Year" and reminded me, quite frankly, of a raw period I wanted to forget.

On the actual night, I stepped across the stage to much applause and received my prize, a gilded goddess of the Grecian style atop a plinth of polished Connemara marble. The irony that she was yet another woman whom I didn't wholeheartedly desire did not elude me.

"It's really quite an honor to have a new category created just for you," Uncle Brendan said, after I'd turned back from receiving congratulations from a woman seated on my other side, who was also undoubtedly hoping her own son would never have to sully his hands holding it. "Once your name's inscribed on her and she's set in the trophy cabinet, you'll be immortalized in the school's annals."

I peered at my twenty-three-inch-high goddess. "A dubious honor, is it not?"

"Honor, notwithstanding."

A few days later, in the privacy of Granny's home, he reiterated how proud he was of me and remarked I was a survivor because of what had happened, and how very fortunate I was because it could have wreaked havoc on my impressionable young mind. He paused, and looked to see how I was taking his remarks, trying to gauge if I wanted or needed to discuss the matter further.

I remained utterly impassive.

"If you ever feel a need to discuss Father Cornelius again, Gabriel?"

"That's water under the bridge and I don't wish to be reminded of it again. Not ever." I swept my eyes from his. The idea entered my head that I could jolly well ask him about his past, too. "By the same token, I'd like to know something about the woman you dated before entering the priesthood, Uncle Brendan. No one seems to want to talk about her, or why there was friction between you and Granda about it. You can tell me about that because I'm an adult now."

He didn't reply immediately, and when he did, said, "I won't insult your intelligence by lying to you. It was a painful stretch in my life and, while there were some good things that came out of it . . ." Uncle paused while my grandmother came in to collect the empty teacups, lingered for moments fluffing up and adjusting the sofa cushions, and returned to the kitchen. "As I was saying, it's a period I wish to forget."

"I understand exactly what you mean."

"No, really, Gabriel. I have no wish to discuss my past with you or anyone else."

Though disappointed he wouldn't confide in me, I didn't probe any further. After all, the man was now happy with his new life. Contentment glowed beaconlike from his richly tanned face. He was the yardstick of happy manliness which I aspired to become.

That God had helped Uncle Brendan overcome his unhappy state compounded the glimmer of hope I harbored with regard to the war raging just beneath my own, much paler skin. Indeed, the hope glimmer that Bridget's ripe breasts and liquid warmth had stirred within me passionately had transcended its own importance with the passage of time. There were days of optimism and days of denial. That she'd aroused my blood signaled the certainty I'd turn out normal on optimistic days. But there were more denial days, days when doubt as black as a winter midnight crammed inside my head. Days when my obsessing alter ego convinced me that I had to be homosexual because I had not tried to repeat the experience with girls. It feasted on my doubt and intelligence, filled me with angst that it had indeed all been a fluke, that I wouldn't get aroused if I tried with another girl, and thereby assured its utter accuracy because I avoided further contact lest it prove to be the case.

It was also becoming increasingly difficult to ignore or reason away the terrible desires. I was sixteen now, and they were relentless. No matter how much I swept them away, they returned seconds later to beat me down, corrupting my every thought, even in the sanctity of the classroom. There were two of me: good Catholic Gabriel who wanted to be normal and lead an exemplary life, and dark, degenerate Gabriel who lived only to lust. Sometimes, in the common room, I'd look out the window and watch the sun disappear behind a wooly, navy-blue cloud, and the cloud's core would stay dark but its ragged edges would be gilded like my unwanted goddess. That's what I was. I was a gilt-edged cloud with a core of darkness.

The only way to vanquish dark Gabriel was to submit to his degeneracy, so I masturbated and the temporary calm would come. Then, a day arrived when, as I conjured up the habitual, last-minute figment of Bridget's breasts, I found myself unable to climax. I tried again, but the moment of gratification disappeared as fast as a gale-driven cloud. It happened the following day, then on the third, and the next, and my mounting panic was stoked all the more by a recent knowledge Connor was now going all the way with his girlfriend in London. I wanted to talk about it desperately, but there was no one, so I bore the corroding panic in silence. Sometimes, I felt so hot inside, I'd sweat profusely, and the only way I could think to truly relieve myself was to run about the house hurling china and furniture. It was impossible to do so, of course, so I'd run each time to the secluded spot by the river where we used to bathe as children and scream away my terror at the bemused cows chewing on the lip of the high red bank.

Toward the end of the year, my social life blossomed. Another perk of being a sixth-former was that we could attend parties called sixth-form socials at other schools. Martin and Pani, now in their final year, and I went to my first social at Saint Clare's College in a coastal resort some ten miles from our school. It was a cheerful event monitored scrupulously by smiling nuns in off-white habits, who, circling the dance floor perimeter like beneficent tigresses, were ready to pounce should a dirty-minded grammar school boy try to kiss one of their precious charges.

Two other unremarkable socials followed. An unexpected invitation came to attend the Granderson College do. It was the first time Saint Malachy's boys had ever been invited to a Protestant social. Schools of different denominations rarely met, and when they did, it was always at athletic and debating competitions, and we had been invited no doubt because our senior rugby team was doing surprisingly well and gaining respect in the hallowed circles of Protestant school sports departments. Father Rafferty was delighted when informed; in his eyes, we'd probably crossed some invisible barrier, and he swooped into the common room to strongly recommend a contingent of us attend *and* to behave in exemplary fashion when we did.

"I'm not going," Pani said, after I'd told him I knew a pupil there. I spiced it up by adding she'd spent the entire summer teaching me how to ride, though omitted to say it was on her horse.

"I think we should go," Martin said. He turned down the volume on his Neil Sedaka tape. "It would be an education."

Pani adjusted the windshield mirror so he could peer into it. "Education, my arse," he said. "No way am I going there." He examined his parting and began to pull out premature gray hairs.

"You can always hide the car in a dark corner of the car park where nobody'll see it," Martin said.

He'd articulated exactly what I'd been thinking, both of us having chalked Pani's reticence down to embarrassment about his old car with its noisy exhaust and freshly minted dent on the passenger door that screeched unmercifully when opened.

"It's got nothing to do with my car," Pani said, a long hair poised between his fingers as he looked savagely at Martin. "I just can't abide the thought of hanging around all those snotty Prods."

Martin worked on Pani and got him to change his mind. On the night of the social, as we drove up the winding drive, Pani's car headlights struck the enormous pale gray girths of old beeches and miles of sprawling rhododendrons. They were endless. Just as we were beginning to think they'd never terminate, he turned a curve and a rambling Georgian mansion with ivy-covered gables confronted us.

Pani emitted a great rush of air through his front teeth. "It's just like Queen's University."

We thundered into the half-full car park, and Martin, his face already mottled because of the car's exhaust, started to peer about him. "I suggest you park over there." He jabbed his finger excitedly in the direction of a less well lit area. Pani ignored him, and drove toward a bay next to four girls climbing out of an orange BMW 2002.

"Pani, not *here*," I said through gritted teeth.

"Both of you go to hell."

Pani reversed into the bay so fast, he caused the driver exiting from the BMW to whip her leg back inside and shut the door.

Martin lowered his head. "I'm not getting out of this tin can until *they* go inside." He pretended to search for something at his feet. "I'd never survive the screech of this fucking door."

The driver got out, glared in at Pani for a moment, and joined her friends who were busy adjusting hair and patting wrinkles out of their skirts. She complained, all turned to look at Pani's car for a moment, and finally started toward the entrance. Martin waited until they'd disappeared inside and opened the door, its screech even more monstrous given the school's regal setting.

"How many times have I told you to do something about this?" Martin said. He placed both hands around the back of his neck and flung out the ends of his hair so that it flowed evenly over his collar. A car entered the parking lot. "Jesus! Jesus, quick, somebody's coming. Come on, Gabriel. We'll see you inside, Pani." Martin didn't wait for me, either. He spirited across the car park in his bottle-green flared pants, slowing to a walk only when he'd reached the narrow path leading to the entrance.

"You could have waited," I said, as I ran up to him.

"That car's a fucking disgrace."

"Well, hurry up and pass the driving test and you can take Uncle Frank's car."

His face splotched. Martin had already taken the test, twice. He was a good driver but, just as my mother had been, couldn't handle the conditions of the driving test. The pressure made him forget to put on his signals when turning, and he could never execute a three-point turn. It took him five maneuvers, and he couldn't understand why it mattered how many it took so long as it got done without bumping into things.

We approached the door, where we checked our reflections one last time in its glass panes. "Is my hair still nice at the back, Gabriel?"

"It's fine."

The social, like others we'd attended, was set up in the gymnasium. Within a minute of entering, Fiona, whom I hadn't seen for almost two years, called out to me from across the room. She wore a checked midi-skirt and dazzlingly white blouse with abundant ruffles that set off a hunter green twinset, a single strand of pearls around her neck being her only adornment. Her hair was still yellow-blond, though boyishly short now, and her face was still country-red because she wore no makeup. I was excited she'd even remembered my name. Pani arrived, and I made the introductions.

"How's old Stroller?" I asked.

"He's turned into a fine jumper . . . and I've got a gray now, too."

Martin's eyes lit up because he realized I hadn't been lying about her owning horses.

"Mind if I try him out as well?" I asked.

She remembered my riding fall because she laughed while affectionately smacking my arm. I could see Pani, despite his vitriol about mixing with Protestants, was suitably impressed.

"Sure, but no jumping this time." Fiona chortled, and so did my cousin.

Indeed, Martin was suddenly buzzing around her like a bee around a flower. He remarked about her elegant necklace and asked her to dance. I could see Fiona's surprise because it was still very early, but she accepted and led him away to join a band of ladies dancing in a dusky corner. Within two minutes, she returned with these girls, introduced them, and all of us chatted until, as always happens in such situations, people begin to engage in side conversations.

"Have you decided which universities you'll apply to next year?" she asked me.

"Whoever will take me."

"I'm serious."

"I'm thinking of reading law at Trinity or Queens."

"None of the English universities?"

The idea of attending an English university both terrified and attracted me. My adventurous part longed to quit Ulster and leave all the petty bigotry behind, but the quiet part was intimidated I'd be taken advantage of by strange men in London, or some other big city. I'd read of such things in the English press, how perverts sought out "dilly boys" who sat on the steps of the Eros fountain at Piccadilly Circus. Reports like that filled me with dread. It was impossible to share this with Fiona, because she'd been to school in England and would laugh at such foolishness.

"Shall we dance?" I asked.

She looked surprised, though not so intensely as when Martin had invited her.

"So you haven't applied to an English university, then?" she said again.

Suddenly, it struck me she might think I was just a narrow-minded Catholic because I wasn't considering colleges in mainland Britain.

"Someone I know goes to university in Cardiff and likes it very much because it's a beautiful city. Maybe I'll apply there . . . and perhaps to Durham, also." Our eyes locked, and she smiled. The more I looked at her, the more I began to forget the disturbingly boyish hair and plainness. "And you?"

"I'm planning to read economics anywhere but here. The older I get, the sicker I am of all the fighting and bigotry. It's too tiresome. I'm leaning toward Cambridge, Bristol, and the London School of Economics."

She was a privileged Protestant, and I admired her directness in alluding to the quagmire of Northern Irish politics so assertively. Not once during that summer when we'd first met had we mentioned politics. We'd talked only horses and school.

"All good schools," I said.

"If I end up in Bristol, and you in Cardiff, then we'll likely bump into each other because there'll only be the Severn Bridge and a few miles separating us." She grinned mischievously.

"I didn't know that."

The set came to an end, and I stood beside her utterly unsure what to do. I liked her and was intrigued to know more, but the fact she was a girl weighed on my mind, as did the fact I hadn't experienced any reassuring surge of physical attraction. Before I could decide or take my cue from her, a thin girl in an emerald satin dress brayed Fiona's name from across the gym as she slithered toward us, and I knew this was probably a secret arrangement they had to aid one another in just such situations. Girls did this sort of thing. Fiona made no attempt to leave. About ten feet to my right, Pani looked similarly perplexed; he was standing by a girl's side, thrusting his head back every now and again to adjust his mop of unruly hair, a habit of his when he was uncertain. Fiona introduced Heather and we chatted politely for half a minute or so. No signal came forth and, after an "absolutely lovely to meet you," she turned and slithered away again. I decided to take a risk, slipped my arm around her waist, and Fiona sidled up to me immediately.

From that moment, all barriers fell. It was as if we'd seen each other every day since that summer. We danced, helped ourselves to food from the buffet table, chatted, and danced some more. Toward the end of the evening, after learning she'd traveled to the social with Heather and another friend, I asked slyly if I could see her home. I knew she'd decline because she was an impeccably bred Protestant, and would naturally suggest we make another date.

She consented without hesitation, which put me in a terrible pickle; I hadn't asked Pani, and there was the dreadful matter of his car. I excused myself, walked frantically around the gym looking for him, all the while cursing myself for my damned stupidity, and found him near the coffee urns. He was chatting to the girl I'd seen him dancing with earlier. As soon as propriety permitted, I butted in and dragged him aside.

"We're taking Fiona home. I'll do the same for you when I get my license and my parents let me borrow the car."

"You sly dog."

I was relieved the first obstacle had been so easily overcome. I glanced about as I braced myself. "Ahm, Pani, what excuse should we use about your car when she hears it, do you think?"

I felt bad, but also knew it couldn't be ignored, especially since Fiona had told me as casually as if she were talking about the weather that she was having *both* horses shipped to England when she went over to university. That's how damned rich her father was, and now I was seeing his daughter home in a cacophonous deathtrap.

"Don't push it."

"I didn't think she'd accept a ride home on the first night." His girl was looking at us quizzically now.

"Come to think of it," he said, "where does Fiona live, exactly?"

"Castlebenem."

"Are you out of your fucking mind?" Pani looked over at the girl, his eyes widening as he mouthed he'd be right over, the lips stretching into a smile. When he turned back to me, the smile was gone, replaced by bulged eyes and a creased nose snarl. "We'll have to go through a bad Protestant area to get there." His voice had lowered even more precipitously when he said "Protestant" on account of where we were. "And it's late. We could end up with cut throats if the UDA have set up an illegal checkpoint to try and snare Catholics."

"Oh, don't be silly. We won't get snared." I laughed to disguise my unease.

While Fiona chatted to some friends after the social ended, the three of us discussed the problem clandestinely. Martin sided with me, and Pani eventually gave in. Outside, Fiona's glance at the dented car door hinted strongly that I'd been right to be concerned. Its tooth-aching screech, notwithstanding Martin's burst of loud coughs as he whipped it open, confirmed the matter. We climbed in and roared our way across the car park to join a line of exiting cars.

"Sorry about the noise," I whispered. "Giles said the body shop didn't do a good repair job on his exhaust."

"I'm sorry, Gabriel, what did you say?"

Boys and girls gawked in at us as they crossed in front of the car or walked alongside it. The line moved slowly, then came to an eventual halt. Unable to peer straight ahead or fake it a second longer, Martin said something about searching for Radio Luxembourg and lowered his head to the radio.

"You know damned well it's preprogrammed," Pani said.

He pressed on the button and the Radio Luxembourg jingle came on to accompany the metallic snort of his muffler, thus obliging Martin to continue staring at the radio, or lift his head and look out the window again. He chose to lift his head and look out, though also began to hum. After what seemed like hours, the traffic started to move and the muffler's snort grew to a roar. I apologized again, and lamented Pani's laziness for getting neither it nor the car door mended, this time in a voice a little louder than my former whisper. To her credit, Fiona joked she noticed only the condition of horses, not cars.

As our liking for one another was mutual, Fiona and I began to date. I took her to other Catholic school socials and, because Pani was seeing the girl he'd met at Granderson also, we went to dance halls attended by both Catholics and Protestants. The more I got to know Fiona, the more I determined to make a go of it. I didn't tell my mother that Fiona was Protestant, because she didn't believe in interfaith dating, and would have insisted I terminate the romance immediately. In early July, I passed my driving test. Two weeks later, Father purchased a new fire-engine red Mercedes saloon, added my name to the insurance, and I was allowed to borrow it, which meant I could see Fiona even more.

Caroline, who was now out at the dances, accompanied us quite often. Unfortunately, the fruit of deceit being ultimate discovery, my sister forgot one evening in my mother's presence and let it slip that Fiona came from Castlebenem. It didn't matter to Mammy that Fiona was a pupil at exclusive Granderson College, that she owned *two* horses being shipped to England in the near future, or that her father owned every blade of grass around the village. She was the other sort, and *that's* what registered.

"It's just not done, Gabriel," she said. "Harry, put your foot down and stop this craziness."

"He's only young once, and Gabriel has more sense than to get serious with a Protestant."

"These things get serious." Shallow lines had formed recently above my mother's eyes and mouth, and they suddenly deepened to fissures as she squinted and clamped her lips shut to a fraction just above the point of bloodlessness. She twisted her torso around sharply toward the television with not the slightest intention of watching it. "We'll have no Protestant hussies about here, thank you very much." She whipped round to me again. "There's more than enough of your own kind."

"I'm seventeen. I'm not bloody well marrying her."

"You must give her up because I'm not allowing the bitch to darken my doorstep."

"Her people's very big," Father said, "with pots of money."

"I don't give two hoots of a tawny owl who or what her people are. She could be royalty, and she's still not coming about here."

Father arched his brows as he peered at me to indicate he sympathized.

"I'm *not* giving her up."

"Jesus Christ, you're just as pigheaded as Brendan," she said. "Just the very damned same. Just every bit as determined to bring people trouble. Is that what you're planning to do? To follow his example and disgrace yourself, and us, into the bargain."

"You're overreacting, Eileen."

"You can just go to hell, because I'm washing my hands of you, Gabriel," she said as she rose.

She slammed the door so hard, the windowpanes reverberated as she left the room. I couldn't believe she'd invoked Uncle Brendan's name to suit her own selfish needs, particularly when she'd been so understanding in his time of need. Her double standard and bigotry infuriated me. And Fiona was fun. I didn't feel threatened in her company. She was my salvation, and I wasn't giving her up.

For the first time, I felt hatred toward my mother. I resolved not to back down, no matter the cost. A moral stand had to be taken against her bigotry. I stopped talking to her. It lasted for weeks, becoming so bad, a room would literally grow tense as soon as one of us entered and saw the other was present. Only Father didn't notice; or if he did, he made a good job of pretending he didn't. The silence was poisonous, but so was her bigotry. Matters came to a head during the seventh week when she burst into tears at the supper table.

"You're driving me mad," she said. "You're destroying me. You'll drive me into a mental institution."

"It doesn't have to be like this, Mammy. I would like to speak to you, but I can't accept your attitude about Fiona."

My delivery was dry and awkward, as if my tongue needed oiling, but nonetheless I'd spoken. We began to talk again. I won the battle, because she abandoned any further attempt to sanction me. I was permitted to see Fiona on condition I wouldn't get serious and eventually marry her. This condition, together with a promise I would not bring her home, concluded the issue because my mother felt she, too, had won.

CHAPTER TWENTY-NINE

THE ADVENT OF MY final year at Saint Malachy's brought a major decision because university applications had to be completed by early November. The application process was centralized and administered from England, allowed five university choices in descending order of preference, and one was obligated to attend one's first choice upon acceptance by that institution. I felt enormous pressure. Martin was now studying at a fashion institute in London and loving it. Fiona and Pani (who was repeating once again because he'd only passed one exam and not even a mediocre institution would accept him) couldn't wait to quit Ulster. They tried frequently to persuade me to leave, too. Fiona, knowing I hated Ulster politics just as much as she, couldn't understand my hesitancy. I longed to unburden myself, but could not. Of course, I wanted to leave as well, but was so afraid because I still fought and submitted to my sick urges daily. Belfast beckoned as a violent refuge. Going to university amid its bombs and shootings appeared to be my safest option because there weren't homosexuals lurking on its street corners, that sort of activity being illegal in Ulster.

At school, Father Rafferty astonished me and awarded me the ultimate Saint Malachy's honor. He created me head boy. As such, I was in charge of the prefects, and the dispensing of fairness and compassion now truly mine. The tiny apricot shield, that varnished symbol of power and fairness I'd first seen on Finbar's lapel years ago, was affixed to my blazer.

An Italian family migrated from Naples to our school town because of the freedom of workers to move within the European

296

Common Market. They opened a pretty café where Pani and I took to drinking cappuccinos, and afterward, we'd drive around town in his car until lunchtime ended. Unfortunately, our jaunts in his old motor terminated abruptly one morning. As Father Rafferty recited the Angelus at assembly, an enormous bang rocked the gymnasium, dust and plaster rained down upon us, the wall of plate glass adjacent to the handball court rattled, and other windows shattered. A minute later, Father Shaw, the vice-head, barged through the door, mounted the stage hurriedly, and conferred with him.

We were informed a bomb had gone off in the council housing estate abutting our west wing. The estate was a sore point with Father Rafferty; it challenged his priestly obligation to turn the other cheek, because it had been hastily constructed by the Protestant-dominated town council with the sole purpose of preventing Saint Malachy's from purchasing the land for expansion. Part of the estate's surrounding lawn ran alongside the school's driveway where Pani parked his car. As soon as assembly ended, we ran to the driveway and saw his vehicle was damaged beyond repair.

Bedlam existed at the driveway entrance. I stood rooted to the ground as I observed events unfold. It was akin to watching a war film: Pani wailed the loss of his car; policemen shoveled stuff into trash bags, soldiers crouched pointing guns, and ambulances screamed their hurried approach. Later that day, we received additional news that a part-time Protestant policeman, who was also our government-appointed truant officer, his Catholic wife, and four-year-old child had been blown to pieces in the massive car bomb. I realized at once that it had been body parts I'd seen the police shovel into the trash bags. The hideous reality of Ulster life confronted me starkly now. This man may or may not have been bigoted, but he was also married to a Catholic, and had walked our corridors in the execution of his duty to monitor Catholic school truancy.

The carnage troubled me so much, I told Uncle Brendan about what I'd witnessed when he called the following weekend.

There was a silence after I'd finished, and I began to think we'd been cut off.

"No, I'm still here," he said. "I was just thinking about all the horseshit young people have to put up with over there."

If it hadn't been so heavy on my heart, I would have laughed and teased him about using such a Yankee term as "horseshit." In the brief silence that followed, I could hear a woman's voice.

"Is there a woman with you?" I asked.

"What woman? There's no woman here. You know, Gabriel, someone should take a stick to the politicians and beat them about the head until they agree to work together and reach a solution so everyone can live in peace over there."

"Now that you're gone from here, it's easy for you to say that, Uncle Brendan."

"Ulster's a sick place, Gabriel."

The "sick" word again, only this time in another equally, wrenching context.

"Its people are very sick." Uncle paused, the line crackled, and I could hear the woman's faint voice again. She spoke with an English accent, this time I heard her complaining about her husband, and I knew at once we had a crossed line. "Get out of that cesspit because the only thing it's good for is sucking the souls out of the youth. I don't want to see that happen to you, because you've got a good soul." Uncle Brendan paused. "You're dear to me, Gabriel."

I didn't know how to respond to his last words. Not even my parents said that kind of thing.

"Go to university in England and broaden your horizons. Get away from all this evil. You'll eventually settle down with Fiona, or another nice girl, and have those children you want."

Shocked by the bombing and influenced by what Uncle Brendan had said, I began to give more serious weight to going across the water to attend university. However, his advice was also a double-edged sword because his parting aside about my marrying and having children stoked the flames of my anxieties further.

The situation was that Fiona and I had progressed to the petting stage, but in all honesty, it gave me no great pleasure. The lusty urgency I'd experienced with Bridget in the living room of the Bundoran B&B had never been repeated; I was able to get an erection all right, but it wilted quickly, and I would not allow her to touch me. Luckily, Fiona didn't appear very eager to touch my thing, anyway. She even spared me anguish in that regard when, feeling it my manly obligation to probe her body further, I slipped an unenthusiastic hand underneath her skirt one night.

"I'd rather not go any farther than this if you don't mind," she said, and clamped her hand around my wrist.

Her words could have been set to music and sung. We'd been cuddling in the car, following a night of celebrating because she'd come second in a gymkhana, and I drew my face from her breasts and gazed at her in feigned bewilderment.

"I've always regarded that step for committed relationships. I hope you don't think me prudish, but I think we need more time."

I affected injury to my masculine pride. "And I always thought Protestant girls were easier than Catholic girls."

Fiona didn't laugh.

"It was a joke."

"You're okay about us not having full sex, then?"

"I respect your decision and agree with it fully."

About this time, Sean arrived at the school and, despite myself, I experienced my first real crush. I was besotted, and loved and hated these strange, new feelings. A six-foot, amber-eyed chap with a lush mouth and gentle disposition, he was a football player and had transferred to our sixth-form from a boarding school to be near his recently widowed mother. We didn't share any classes, didn't speak other than to say hello, and I was overwhelmingly attracted from the moment I set eyes on him.

That attraction changed to infatuation when I first watched him step onto a football field. Our senior Gaelic team began winning

games, and the entire school, even pupils and teachers not re-
motely interested in the game, became wildly enthusiastic because
there was a real possibility Saint Malachy's might win the All-
Ireland title. One Saturday afternoon, Pani and I attended a game,
standing on the sidelines swathed in our school scarves and wav-
ing wooden rattles, and I saw Sean run onto the field. He was
magnificent in the royal blue, gray, and black Saint Malachy's
jersey.

I was so smitten, I saw no one else on the field for the rest of
the game. An epiphany occurred, and my head filled with romantic daydreams. I dreamed of impossible things: the two of us attending events and parties together; or of meeting him at such
functions whereupon he'd be completely captivated by me, just as
I'd always imagined in the past that Agnetha from ABBA would
have been, and we'd talk and laugh to the exclusion of everyone
else present.

Of course, the baser needs demanded satisfaction, too. And
vivid fantasy being sustained only by acute detail, I stole furtive
looks at his person in the common room throughout the day.
Actually, I feasted. I feasted on his beautiful hands, and devoured
how his fleshy lips parted so endearingly as he sat deep in con-
centration, how his dark chest hair tufted just above his shirt and
tie. His rich mouth captivated me. I yearned, like some heroine in
one of Caroline's ridiculous romance novels, to know how it
would feel to be kissed by it. I'd stare and wish and yearn, poised
at the same time to retreat to the safety of my textbook should his
warm, amber eyes unexpectedly flick my way.

When our eyes did accidentally touch, I'd see instantly there
was no reciprocity, and a great internal crash would follow my
retreat because the spell was broken. I'd feel miserable about having such depraved thoughts, and that in turn would lead me to
think of Uncle Brendan and how truly sick he'd find me. I'd stare
at the pages of my book, squirming at my sinful sickness, until the
crisp text blurred to gray nothingness. I'd squirm because no
healthy Irish boy, certainly no boy sitting alongside me in the common room, harbored such vileness. I wondered what Sean would

think if he could read my mind. Would he even say hello and smile as he did occasionally? That he was gentle was undeniable, but would his gentleness make such a leap in the rabidly homophobic environment of a Catholic sixth-form common room?

I knew the answer already, but still I continued to ask these questions. The answer was he'd be horrified. Horrified, like Father, and Mammy, and Uncle Brendan. Horrified, I'd even allow my mind to ponder him in such a perverted way. Mortification would rise and shrivel my insides, making me so agitated, the air would become stifling, and I'd have to leave the room.

In early November, a mutual friend who studied physics with him told me Sean wanted to read medicine and had named one of London University's colleges as his first university choice. As soon as I could, I barreled to the career's guidance library and riffled through the college's prospectus to see if it also had a law school. It didn't. A few days later, after scrutinizing the London collegiate system, I completed my own application, listing University College London as my first choice, and submitted it to Father Rafferty so he could attach his headmaster's report. My major decision made on a whim.

The rest of the year was spent studying for final exams, fantasizing about Sean from across the room, and thinking about how he and I would grow much closer in London, because we'd be part of a relatively small bunch of Irish students in a strange city. Also, I thought about Fiona visiting me from Cambridge on those weekends she didn't have a gymkhana, and how we'd be able to experience all of the city's marvelous sights together. Naturally, my analytical side brought up the glaring contradiction of wanting to be with Fiona and Sean simultaneously, but I shrugged it aside because I needed them both and a way would be found. The customary sixth-form socials in the final term compounded that contradiction when, locked in Fiona's arms on the dance floor, I'd see Sean waltzing in a girl's arms. I'd watch, seared by the reality my passion for him was unsustainable, scornful as a jilted lover.

We were attending a fund-raising dinner dance for Action Cancer in an elegant restaurant, an old, converted stable with a plethora of farm implements on its whitewashed walls, outside Antrim. Mr. McFarland had had a few whiskeys and was navigating the conversation into dangerous political waters. With a silvery mustache stained yellow and orange-brown from tobacco smoke, he was a small-built man and looked older than his fifty-five years, his ordinariness compounded by his wife who was so tall and glamorous.

He leaned across the round table as he puffed on his fat cigar. "I'm sure you'll agree, society needs a strong police force or else chaos results," he said. Fiona glanced at me and rolled her eyes. "If these people respected the rule of law and agreed Ulster's an inalienable part of Great Britain, then maybe, just maybe, we could talk to them."

"Darling, we're having a lovely evening with Gabriel and everyone," his wife said. "Let's not get all depressed by horrid political discussions."

Mrs. McFarland knew how to enjoy her gin and tonics and was a good conversationalist. She was president of her chapter of the Women's Institute, the group who'd organized the event, and I'd bought a ticket to please her after Fiona told me how important the event was to her mother. She knew I was the only Catholic here, and I smiled broadly to convey my appreciation of her attempt to circumvent her husband's boorish conduct. The only others present were one of Mrs. McFarland's colleagues, the woman's chinless husband, and Fiona's two horsy friends, Sandra, and another girl whose name I kept forgetting.

"Yes, Father, let's drop it," Fiona said.

A couple started to rise at a nearby table and I watched them, noticing in the process that a man with the ruddy disposition of a farmer seated next to them was observing me. I turned back to our table and sipped my drink. Every time I looked back, the stranger was staring. On the fourth eye touch, a great jolt passed through my body, my breath quickened, and a nervous excitement sprang up inside me.

"Sandra's going over to the gymkhana at Cardiff Castle, Gabriel," said Fiona.

"How nice."

"Cardiff's such a pretty city," said Sandra. "You'll love its civic center. The ground was bequeathed to the city by one or other of the earls of Bute. It's absolutely loaded with magnificent architecture."

"How nice, but maybe I won't be going there because it's only my second choice now."

"Yes, Gabriel changed his mind at the last minute and listed London first," Fiona said.

They resumed talking about the gymkhana and I looked at the ruddy-faced man again. Another spasm of excitement whipped through me, and my thing started to grow. I was getting a hard-on while at table with Fiona, and a very plain man in a tweed jacket was the cause.

"Mummy needs us to help her collect the raffle tickets," Fiona said. "You'll be okay with Father and Mr. Armstrong for a short while, won't you?" She looked doubtful.

"I'm sorry. What did you say?"

"I have to leave you alone for a moment and want to know if you'll be okay with Father."

"Of course." I squeezed her hand reassuringly.

I was happy her father didn't interrupt his chat with Mr. Armstrong to include me, but I also couldn't relax because I felt I ought to remove myself from my exciting predicament. As I rose, I felt the stranger's stare, but didn't look toward him. I walked to the lobby and retreated into a corner. I stood four feet away from a group of people chattering around a coffee table, next to a window with floor-to-ceiling, mustard-colored curtains overlooking a little shrubbery. Within two minutes, the stranger approached, stood a little apart from me, and stared out at the dusky bushes. The air grew charged. I felt myself grow stiff again. A magazine of tiny shocks passed through my body.

We stared at each other, yet looked away as soon as our eyes touched. The rumble of conversation and a woman's laughter punctuated the clammy space between us. I could scarcely breathe. Our eyes touched and this time locked, but still he didn't speak. I willed him to speak. As the seconds passed, I grew frantically impatient, thinking Fiona and her mother were perhaps finished with their tasks. I turned to him and, pretending to point to something outside lest anyone sitting at the coffee table should notice two men suddenly talking together, I asked for the time. It was idiotically asinine, but the only ploy I could devise. As he consulted his watch, my eyes darted over the crowd, searching for Fiona or anyone else from our table.

"Almost nine-thirty."

"What's your name?" I asked.

"John . . . and you?"

"Mark." I flashed a vapid smile.

"What do you do?"

"I'm a farmer."

"Hereabouts?"

"Yes."

"Are you married?"

"No, I live with my mother."

"Do you have a girlfriend?"

"No. Is the blond one yours?"

"Yes. Her name's Fiona. She's a nice girl, and a good show jumper."

I was spouting off like an idiot. It was pathetic. His eyes opened wide, and my heart sank because I'd probably frightened him off by talking about Fiona.

"That's good." He looked about the foyer. "Hold on to her, because a decent woman's difficult to find."

"They are, indeed."

We continued talking ridiculously about women for a minute or so, the two of us a foot apart now, my head swiveling like a guard on a watchtower. I thought I saw Fiona's mother approach in the crowd.

"Shall we go somewhere?" My audacity horrified me as soon as the question had been asked. I'd crossed a line. All ambiguity was irretrievably gone. I gripped the coarse curtain fabric discreetly between my fingers and began to rub it to remind myself this was a real situation and I'd just propositioned a man. He regarded me as if I'd lost my senses.

I thought to flee. At the very cusp of the instant, he smiled, then shot another glance about the foyer. "Okay, you go out first, and I'll follow."

I went outside, walked around the perimeter of the hotel, and waited. A bout of paranoia beset me. For moments, I believed he might fetch the bouncers to pulverize me. Footsteps approached. It was him. He was alone. Without a word, he walked up to a clump of nearby rhododendrons and, after checking to see the coast was clear, disappeared into their dim bosom. I followed swiftly. What followed amid the dusky, jagged limbs was a flurry of excited fumbling that culminated in my gratification, whereupon, in a despicably selfish manner, I bounded out of the thicket and ran toward the restaurant without even so much as a thank-you. I hurried back to the table, where everything was as it should be; skeins of cigar smoke twisted toward the ceiling, and Fiona was still busy. The poor man didn't appear again, nor did I wish to see him. Presently, Fiona returned and stroked my arm as she looked at me. I couldn't look back, and pretended to search for something on the table.

"You've been very quiet," she said, after I stopped the car before the front door of her home later.

"I haven't."

"It's Father, isn't it? I know it's because of my father. What did he say to upset you?"

"I'm tired and need to get home to bed."

She sighed as she opened the car door. "Don't be so sensitive to Father's remarks."

"I'm not bloody well sensitive. Stop accusing me of that."

A golden retriever bounded from the darkness and drew up to her, but she was too startled to greet it. "You don't have to be so touchy, Gabriel."

"I'm sorry . . . your father was a little annoying."

"He doesn't dislike you, and it's going to happen again when he's tipsy. It's the Unionist in him that comes out when he's like this. He can't help it, and you know how much bitterer older people are about these things. I'll bet your father isn't all sweetness about politics, either." She chuckled. "I bet he'd say something Nationalist to me, if I were ever to meet him."

I still couldn't look at her. "You're right. Let's pretend it never happened."

"Let's." She leaned over and kissed my cheek. After she got out of the car, she bent down and peered inside for a moment. "It'll all work out, you'll see."

CHAPTER THIRTY

THE MEMORY OF WHAT had happened at the fund-raiser proved not as fleeting as the encounter. Renewed fear, self-doubt, and panic piled up like trifle layers, and proved more pervasive than that which I'd experienced on the endless night when Connor had ended our playing forever. This occurrence could not be regarded in the same light as the trysts with my cousin, or my innocent infatuation with Sean. I had crossed a ghastly threshold, and I had crossed it irrevocably. No longer was I an innocent party, no longer was consenting sex with an adult man a figment of passionate imagination, and no longer could I assuage the guilt by clinging to my ultimate defense that I was the passive participant.

The bald truth was, I had desired and initiated an illicit encounter. I had seized an opportunity to lure and seduce a stranger while out with my girlfriend. I had gratified my urges with a man, and enjoyed it. The thrill of a strange man's intense gaze, the necessary furtiveness, the exploring, all had been intoxicating, savored like nectar. I had played the seducer, had come to the role as naturally as a lamb stands on its feet minutes after birth, and the depraved aspect of my being desired its despicable satisfaction again.

I became paranoid of anything related to homosexuality. If I overheard anyone talk disparagingly about homosexuals at school, I believed they were doing so because they thought I was a queer and knew I was listening to them. And homosexuality confronted me from every corner. Not even my own home was spared. Newspapers and magazines spilled scandals about the acts of homosexuals. *The Naked Civil Servant* aired on TV in the presence of Father, James, and Caroline, and I cringed as the main character, an articulate, effete man, cavorted on the screen. I wanted to turn it off, but couldn't for fear of drawing attention to myself.

"What kind of filth are you watching, James?" Father said, after the main character announced assertively in a courtroom that he was homosexual. "Turn the TV off, or find something else to watch."

I was happy the embarrassment was removed, yet also wounded because Father had articulated his prejudice. His disgust made me even more determined to save myself. I tried to reject every sexual thought about Sean or other men with renewed ferocity. When the thoughts came, I tried to replace them with thoughts of Fiona, and the wonderful times we'd share together across the water. It proved no match. The fantasies and illicit thoughts were powerful and entered my mind at every opportunity. Exciting, hateful fantasies about kissing men with taut bodies and strong hands; poisonous, arousing thoughts about lying with them in the hay nest above the abandoned pigsty.

These rushing thoughts would not be contained, because deep within I wanted them. I wasn't strong enough to resist. I could not resist my poisonous thoughts because I had now acted upon them and tasted the forbidden. I began to fear myself. I feared being alone at a dance hall, because depravity would almost certainly overwhelm my sense of morality. I feared I'd scour these places hunting for available men, and when found, would initiate encounters. Good, Catholic Gabriel had no defender. I was now against myself.

So I avoided going anywhere alone where I'd be tempted. If I went to dances, I always went with Fiona and seldom left her side. One night, at a dance, I went to the lavatory and a young man entered. Notwithstanding there were many free urinals, he came and stood beside me, and I noticed him turn often to look at me. My blood churned with excitement. I clenched my teeth, stopped in midflow, and left hastily.

When I got back to Fiona, I put my arms around her and

hugged her hard. I'd successfully resisted and was ecstatic. "I'm so happy to be out with you tonight, darling,"

Fiona threw back her head and regarded me curiously. "What's got into you?"

"It's wonderful to be together. You and me . . . just us, don't you think?"

"Yes, it is. I'm surprised you pick this moment to say so."

For the rest of the evening, I kept looking out for the young man, and was disappointed when I didn't see him. My victory had had no substance. The aftertaste of having missed out on an exciting adventure was as present as the aftertaste of an artificially sweetened soda on the tongue just after one has taken a drink of it.

It took every ounce of willpower to apply myself to my studies. When sexual thoughts came, or I felt a surge of overwhelming panic that I was indeed becoming a homosexual, I pushed them away as best I could. If they persisted, I'd simply masturbate and continue. Analyzing them to oblivion was useless because I just got caught up in a web of circuitous "what if" arguments that squandered precious study time. As before, masturbation proved to be the tranquility key. When exam month arrived, cold fear became another potent ally: cold fear of failing Father Rafferty's trust; cold fear of disappointing Uncle Brendan and my parents; my own cold fear of failing the examinations again.

In such a way, I saw myself through to the last exam. My final paper was part two of economics. I knew I'd done well in the first paper and that the possibility of an A grade was not out of the question. Three evenings before the final exam, I went to my room and, as was my usual habit, threw myself upon the bed to study.

The pressure of the exam triggered something in my mind because, without warning, a storm of panic overwhelmed me as I thought about the vile creature I was becoming. What was the point studying to get into law school when I was destined to be homosexual and hated by everyone? I jumped off the bed and began to pace. I fell to my knees and prayed. Still, the panic wouldn't leave. I pulled at my hair and pinched my arms and legs intensely to distract myself. Nothing helped. Finally, I opened the bedroom window and began hurling textbooks and pages of notes out into the lawn.

"What are you doing, Gabriel?" Nuala shouted from the garden. "Why are you throwing books out of the window?"

By the time my mother arrived, I was lying on my stomach upon the bed, sobbing inconsolably. I couldn't stop. The tears came and came, gushing like they'd been secretly accumulating and waiting for this day to come. I felt the pillow's wetness beneath my cheek.

"What's wrong?" I heard her ask. It was as if she were speaking from the hallway. "Son what's wrong? Are you ill?" The bed sank as she sat heavily. Hands gripped my body, raised and turned me, drew me to her. I wiped my eyes and saw my sisters watching from the threshold.

"I'm sick, Mammy. I'm very, very sick."

"What are you talking about?"

"I have to tell you something."

Another burst of crushing sobs emitted. She waited till I calmed. "Tell me!"

"I'm homosexual. I'm trying to pass these exams and might get an A and I might be homosexual. It's driving me mad. I don't want to be homosexual." Another cacophony of wails ensued, and I plunged my fists into the damp pillow. "What is God doing to me? I haven't done anything bad. Why is he making me this way? I've tried and tried to cure myself, but I can't because He won't let me."

Curly white feathers spewed from one end of the pillow. My mother's face was deathly white as she seized my wrists. Caroline was crying now, and Nuala, rock still beside her, was utterly bewildered and unsure what to do.

"Leave us, and close the door behind you," Mammy said.

"The pressure's too much. I don't want to fail you again Mammy, and I don't want to be homosexual. I'm just so afraid of myself."

"Son, don't worry about your exams. You can always repeat. Let's concentrate on sorting this other thing out."

She passed her fingertips across my brow, pushing aside the damp fringe, and pulled me tightly against her breast. It was comforting to inhale her slightly pungent smell tinged with freshly chopped parsley, comforting to feel the gentle resistance of her bra against my face.

"What makes you think you're like that?"

Her question prompted more hacking sobs before I poured out my heart, telling her about Noel and the hay nest, about the handsome man on the beach, but unable to bring myself to mention Connor, Father Cornelius, or the farmer. I could never mention the farmer. I was responsible for that.

"It's a phase you're going through, Gabriel. Everyone goes through this sort of thing."

"Did you go through it?"

She was silent for a little while as she stroked my hair. "No, but then I'm not a good yardstick."

I didn't know what she meant by that, and didn't care.

"I always knew Noel's family was a through-other crowd, but I had no idea this nonsense was going on in our old pigsty. If I could get my hands on him, I'd give him a piece of my mind. I'm going down to see his mother. Yes, that's what I'll do . . . and I'm contacting the police."

Noel's family had moved to Ballynure, we didn't see them anymore, and Noel had joined the Merchant Navy and didn't come home, or so Father had learned.

I wrenched myself from her grasp. "No, don't. It's too late, and I don't want it to get out."

"I am."

I appealed next to her terror of scandal. "It'll be shaming for the family if people in Knockburn find out about this."

She stared at my face for a long moment before looking over my shoulder at the window. "You're right. After all, he was only a bit of a boy, too." She paused. "We'll ask your father and Uncle Brendan if they've ever had such feelings."

"Why involve Uncle Brendan?"

Mammy hesitated. "I'll ask John and Tommy, too."

"I don't want anyone told. It's between you and me. It's embarrassing enough without having Daddy think even less of me."

"Your father loves you, and I am going to ask him. And I'm taking you to Father McAtamney, right this very minute. Let him have a word with you."

"A priest!" My body recoiled. "I'm not going to a priest."

"You must, and you are. Father McAtamney's wise and will say masses."

"I don't want to go."

"We're going. He's old and experienced, and I'm sure he's come across such problems before. He'll know what to do to make this go away."

"Do you really think he could help?"

"Of course."

I realized all priests were not like Father Cornelius. Father McAtamney was kindly, had known me since childhood, and perhaps did have the power to set my head straight. We set off immediately for the parochial house, a sand-colored, three-story building adjacent to the chapel, where blackness projected from its upstairs front windows. The jagged branches of two monkey puzzle trees swayed and creaked in the evening breeze as we walked up the garden path to the door. His withered housemaid, her facial skin so thin, it looked translucent, showed us into the anteroom.

"He's got Mary-Kate McGuire with him, *again*," she said.

My mother and the priest's maid were early morning Mass confidants.

"That women must think she owns shares in this place. She's forever tripping here at all hours of the day and night with one imaginary ailment or another. Sure his heart's broke with her." She looked toward the study door disgustedly.

I wanted immediately to leave, because his heart would be even more broken after he heard what I had to say. The somberness of the house, its churchly aroma, and the heavy furniture added more oppressive weight to my hideous problem. Ten minutes later, Mary-Kate and Father McAtamney appeared. She clutched a ball of tissues, her eyes red and glistening, though still she managed to gawk at me as the priest escorted her to the door.

When he returned, Father McAtamney shook my mother's hand and mine. "It's not often I have the pleasure of your company," he said to me.

He looked frail, so different to my mind's eye view of him, and I realized with a start that, though I saw him in the pulpit every Sunday, I hadn't updated my childhood image of him. His face was heavily wrinkled and pasty, two thick wads of flesh gathered loosely just above his yellowed dog collar, and his shoulders stooped inside a blazer shiny from wear.

"Gabriel has a little problem, Father, and I'd like you to counsel him about it," Mammy said, after niceties had been dispensed with.

The priest ushered me across the threshold of his study and turned back to my mother, who had followed at his heels. "Eileen, you wait here."

"Pardon?"

"I'll speak to him alone."

"But I'm his mother."

"Exactly dear, and I'll call you in after Gabriel and I've had our little chat."

Cupping his hand around my elbow, he led me up the gloomy, incense-reeking room and then signaled I should sit on one of two shabby parlor chairs positioned close together in front of the unlit hearth. On the high, mahogany mantel stood an unpolished brass clock, its rectangular face flanked by two elephants pushing their tusked heads against its sides. Father McAtamney took a curly walnut pipe and tobacco pouch from his pocket and lit it. Granda Harkin's image popped into my mind.

"What's your little problem, son?"

"It's not such a little problem, Father." I let out a little laugh, as if it might somehow make the problem lighter during its telling, and peered into his seasoned eyes.

Father McAtamney changed the pipe to his other hand,

leaned over, and laid his right hand on my forearm and patted me like a child, as if letting me know he recognized my laugh for what it was, and I should just relax. He kept it there as he waited and puffed. After taking a short breath, I began my story, closing my eyes as I said the word "homosexual." I expected him to reclaim his hand and rise from the chair. He didn't stir. There was no tightened lips, dropped pipe, or cessation of puffing. He just listened without interrupting until I'd finished, whereupon his eyes lifted slowly and he looked at me.

"Son, I think it's a bit of a phase you're going through."

"Do you think so, Father?"

He puffed on his pipe, and I could hear the dry smack of his lips upon its shaft as he inhaled. "Some men go through such things."

"It seems a bit long."

"Phases can be long or short."

"What if it's not?"

Father held the pipe slightly before his lips and stared into the cold hearth. "I'm bound to say as a Catholic priest that God would still love you as one of His precious children. The Catholic Church condemns the sin, not the sinner."

"Can I still be a good Catholic?"

"If it's not a phase, provided you don't act on your impulses, there will be no sin. But, if you become promiscuous with men without compunction, then it would be a grave sin, yes. You'd be hurting yourself and, therefore, hurting God because you're made in His image." He put the pipe back in his mouth.

"I can never have sex, if I'm homosexual?"

"That is so."

"Even if I'm made in God's image and He created me a homosexual, Father?"

Father McAtamney paused, took the pipe slowly from his mouth again, and I could hear the tick of the elephant clock. The dark furrows running down each side of his mouth moved as his lips twitched in preparation to speak once more. He looked ancient now. He was so old, he'd have been retired by the diocese if there wasn't such a shortage of clerics. I wished my life could sweep by in a flash so I could be just as old and serene. I wanted to be old like him, because then the maddening urges would no longer wrack me and demand cruel satisfaction again and again and again.

"Son, the homosexual life is a difficult one. It's a hard, thorny life. If He has planned that this isn't a phase, then I will say this to you. If you're not promiscuous, if you meet and settle down in a monogamous relationship with a man, then the Catholic Church will not condone the relationship." He paused. "But, it will not condemn it, either."

I wanted no unnatural relationship with a man. "So you think it's a phase, then?"

He looked into my eyes for a moment. "That's what I think."

Part of the enormous burden was lifted off my shoulders because he'd said it was definitely a phase. I waited for some more words, but he remained silent. He stared into the black hearth for a few moments, the pipe now stilled between his lips, and he rose stiffly. As before, he cupped my elbow and asked me how my exams were going as he led me out to my mother, who immediately gave him five pounds for the saying of a Mass.

"Well, did he sort you out?" she asked, after she'd climbed into the car and closed the door.

"He says it's a phase."

"What did I tell you?" She laughed. "I'm not so slow. You were in with him for a long time. What else did he say?"

"He said the Catholic Church would neither condone nor condemn me if I ended up in a committed relationship with a man . . . should it not be a phase."

"*What?* You mean living together like man and wife and sharing a double bed?"

Her slackened jaws told me the image was too much for her to bear. She couldn't even bear the idea of watching men and women lying together on a bed on TV shows. Nor could she bear the idea of Caroline having sex, although she'd adapt eventually, because society and the Church ratified that kind of sexual act. If I were homosexual, I'd never be ratified.

"What on earth is he talking about?" she said. "He's a priest. He should have told you it's plain sinful and just left it at that."

Now, *she* was priest. I didn't reply, looked straight ahead, and the monkey puzzle trees and dark windows reappeared as she reversed in little kangaroo hops out the driveway.

"It's definitely a phase, Gabriel."

"It has to be a phase . . . because I can't bear to have these thoughts for the rest of my life."

"It's a phase, and we're driving straight to see Dr. Thompson this minute." The car engine stalled in the middle of the road. "That priest won't get any more fivers from me if he starts saying things like that. What would the neighbors say if it turns out you're that way? I wouldn't know where to look." She didn't even bless herself as we drove past the chapel. "You know, I was searching my memory as he kept me waiting. I was trying to think if I've ever met any of those sort of people. And you know what, Gabriel? There was a man who worked in my office before I got married, and I'm sure he was one of them. Gabriel, you should have seen him." Mammy chuckled. "He was so showy and shrill and all flying hands. He wore three rings on the one hand, too. Can you believe it? *Three.* The office girls laughed behind his back. He talked like this . . ." she slowed the car and waved her free hand in a grotesquely exaggerated fashion, "and such shrillness. No, son. No, you're definitely not that sort. Definitely not."

"I'm definitely not. As Father McAtamney says, 'it's a phase.' "

"It's a phase. Why, I've forgotten. Sure, you've been going out with that lovely wee Protestant girl for some time now. Think about that one. That means everything's fine. Homosexuals aren't interested in girls."

Protestantism wasn't even as evil as homosexuality.

"It's high time I met this Fiona, because I'm sure she's a lovely girl." We pulled into the clinic's car park and, as she reversed into the bay, she bumped into the wire fence boundary and caused it to bulge. She didn't notice, and turned off the engine. "I mean, if you decide she's the one, sure we'll always get her to convert."

Dr. Thompson, a family practitioner who had known me since childhood, sat at his desk with his legs apart on the claret-red swivel chair. I sat opposite him. He'd taken my temperature and blood pressure, and I couldn't understand what the heck my vitals had to do with the problem. I peered discreetly at how his pants bunched around his crotch and wondered why I was attracted to that manly sight, and not the sight of a woman's thigh disappearing above the hem of her skirt. Often, I'd observed men checking out pretty women in the street, I'd observed my own father staring also, and I could sense but not understand the savage desires behind their civilized smiles. All I saw was a pretty woman.

"When you imagine scenes with men, Gabriel, are you active or passive?" His pants folds rearranged as he leaned toward me slightly.

"How do you mean?"

His face began to pink. "When you are doing things in your mind with men, are you playing the role of the man or the woman?"

I blushed. Our conversation was surreal. "I don't imagine doing things like that." In all honesty, the idea revolted me.

"Imagine it now," he said. "Are you active or passive . . . hypothetically?"

I was a man, so I had to be active because that was the nature of a man. Men acted, and women lay back and received. That's what nature intended. "I would never allow a man to do things like that to me."

Dr. Thompson smiled broadly. "You're no homosexual. It's definitely a phase that you'll pass out of very shortly." He swiveled round to his desk and began scribbling. "You're under pressure about your exams, so I'm prescribing some Valium. It'll calm you, but I'm only putting you on it for thirty days, because it can be addictive." He tore out the prescription and handed it to me.

"Don't think about doing these things with men and it'll be gone before you know it."

"Well?" my mother said, before I had time to plant my arse in the car seat.

"He's put me on Valium. It's a phase I'll grow out of."

"I knew it. I just knew it."

"Look, I don't want Daddy to be told about this."

"I think I'll tell him."

"I don't think you need to tell him if it's a phase."

"Hmm."

"At least wait until my last exam's over, because I can't take any more of this."

That night, James and Caroline came sheepishly into my room wearing their funeral faces.

"Gabriel, you're not a queer," James said. "Look at the way you beat that chap up in your class because he wrote a pile of stuff about you on the blackboard."

"Don't use that terrible word," said Caroline. "I don't know any homosexuals but they're human beings, too."

She came over and put an arm around my neck. Caroline wasn't a person who touched. She'd never put her arm around me before. She withdrew it, pushed her thick hair behind her ears, and looked at me intently. I'd never seen such intensity in my sister's eyes. Her face was drawn taut, and she looked almost maternal, certainly older than her sixteen years, and I could easily envision how she'd look as a mother in ten or twelve years.

"Gabriel, no matter what happens, even if you turn out to be homosexual in the end—"

"I'm *not* going to be, Caroline."

"Still, I want you to know you're my brother, and I love you no matter what the future may bring."

"I won't be." I turned to James. "I'm not dying, either, so both of you can get rid of those long faces."

They laughed.

"I just want you to know I love you because you're my brother," Caroline said again.

"I'll always be friends with you, too," James said.

James' personality was a developing image of Father's: rough and ready, able to talk about everything superficial to anybody, but unable to communicate deeper emotions with delicacy. It was no wonder Father related better to him.

"Not a word about this to Nuala," I said. "She doesn't even know about the facts of life."

"She's already asked me about homosexuals," said Caroline. "I told her it's about boys being friendly with boys all the time, and that they don't care for girls so much. She couldn't understand why you're one, because you've got Fiona, so I said it's very complicated and she'll be told more about it when she's older."

A hard lump formed at the back of my throat. "This is temporary, and she'll never have to be told because I'll have grown out of it by then."

CHAPTER THIRTY-ONE

I COMPLETED MY FINAL ECONOMICS paper and, at least with regard to academic affairs, God was firmly on my side because I knew every topic examined. I didn't ask for extra writing paper, either. The pills took effect quickly, and a wonderful feeling of inner calm took root, my passion to masturbate dissipated, and I didn't feel guilty around Fiona anymore about what I'd done. The incident had happened and was now best forgotten. My only concern was that the medication would end in about twenty days and the desires and fears would return like vengeful beasts because they'd been suppressed.

To my surprise, Mammy didn't bring the subject up with Father. I assumed she'd thought about the doctor's explanation and was now satisfied, or was perhaps waiting in hopes the medication might kill the phase. The matter was still on her mind though, because I sometimes caught her in a reverie, her eyes unseeing, as if searching inwardly for culpability or reasons.

She was now Fiona's greatest advocate, and there were no more subdued grumbling or dark looks when I needed to borrow the car to take my girlfriend to dances or other places. Mammy rescheduled some of her own outings, even ordered Father to use one of his dirty work vans if his plans to use the car conflicted with mine. Most astonishing of all, she persuaded him to let me borrow the car and take it across the border to Dublin, when Fiona suggested Pani, his girlfriend, and I go there to spend a weekend with a friend of hers.

Amanda was a second-year law student whom I'd met once before. Ostensibly, our visit was arranged so I could talk to her at length about law school life, but was really an excuse for Fiona and me to spend a last weekend together because she was leaving for England the following week. Fiona's confidence was amazing: she was leaving to sort out boarding for her horses and participate in a couple of gymkhanas, even though the exam results weren't out and she didn't know if she'd met the university's requirements yet.

I fretted about the sleeping arrangements at Amanda's because it was our first time away together. I needn't have worried. The flat was enormous, overlooked Saint Stephen's Green, and Amanda showed Pani and me into a bedroom with twin beds, great French doors, and a little balcony. I could tell Pani was a little put out, though he didn't let on. He'd probably assumed because they were Protestants, they'd be more easygoing about sex and he'd get an opportunity to sleep with Ruth. The bedroom walls were plastered with family photographs, many of young men and women clasping trophies as they sat mounted or stood beside horses festooned in rosettes. A Delft wash bowl and pitcher stood on a sideboard, next to a pathetic geranium so desperate for sunlight, it stretched precariously toward the French doors.

"These Prods have a lot of money to have a second home in such a swanky part of Dublin," said Pani. He walked about the room and peered at the photographs. "Look at this. It's Fiona and Amanda on their nags. Jesus, Gabriel, they're standing beside the fucking home secretary or the secretary of state or whoever the hell he is." He turned to me, his mouth open wider than a hick's visiting a museum.

"So what?"

Curiosity got the better of me, however. As soon as Pani went out to inspect the balcony, I went over to look and was immediately riveted. The secretary of state for Northern Ireland, in a black-and-white houndstooth jacket, one hand on the horse's forelock, was indeed smilingly sandwiched between the girls. It was an unintentional study of casual power and privileged breeding, and I couldn't take my eyes off it for ages because it cut me to the quick. The photograph made me keenly aware of how different our cultures really were, how Fiona took for granted what was extraordinary to me, how even her dumb horse had greater access to the ears of government than people of my religion ever had.

That evening, we dined at Jury's Hotel, in its plush restaurant, which was à la carte and expensive. Pani's gills blanched as he examined the menu, his eyes scouring for the dish of the day, which was always cheapest, and I feared he'd make a gauche comment about prices. He didn't, though he skipped all vegetables and dessert and declined to have wine, concocting an excuse he was pacing himself. Afterward, we visited a pub near Trinity College and drank Guinness while listening to traditional music, which Fiona loved and I'd thought she'd find parochial. Pani made up for his lack of wine during dinner, sank two pints for every one of mine, and we got back to Amanda's flat around one o'clock where, within half an hour, the others retired. Fiona and I cuddled on the sofa as we listened to Holst whose music she clearly knew, because she named each planet as it arrived.

"I'm so glad we came to Dublin." She pecked at my crown with her fingers like a wren eats crumbs. "Next week, I'll be in England, and I won't see you very much until you come over, and I wondered . . ." Fiona stopped talking and the pecking ceased as she tossed back her head and gazed at the ceiling.

"Wondered what?"

"Oh, I'm tipsy and talking too much."

I don't know if it was the wine or the fact she was leaving soon, but her English accent seemed more dulcet than usual. My own sounded so harsh in comparison, so inferior, and I pondered if it would stick out badly when I was over in Britain, or whether the English and Welsh would even understand me. "Tell me, because I'm tipsy, too. That makes us even."

"It's not maybe so much a wondering . . . I feel we're really good together, don't you?"

"Yes."

"I feel committed to you and believe we'll make a go of our

relationship once we're over there . . . even though we'll be at different universities."

"I believe so, too."

"I'm glad, because I was worried about that. So many of my school friends promised their boyfriends they'd stay together, but almost as soon as they got over there, well, it was curtains."

"The onus might be more on you to make it work. I might fail, and then you'll have to come over to Ulster to see me when you're not busy."

"You won't, Gabriel. I just know you won't fail."

"Fiona, when I look about this flat, I'm reminded how very different we are." I blew softly into her hair. "Your family is so Ulster establishment. Your mother's a hoot and your father's courteous in the main, but it's all so different to what I'm used to."

Fiona drew back her face and looked at me. "Has Father been talking again?"

"No."

"Backgrounds don't matter. You know that."

"I saw the photograph of you and Amanda with the secretary of state. You mix in very different circles to me."

"I've even met the Prince of Wales too, if you must know. Look, Father's Ulster Unionist. There's no denying he's Establishment, hopes every year to be on the Queen's birthday list for a knighthood, but what's that really got to do with us? Nothing, that's what, Gabriel. I don't care about things like that, and I was brought up with it. You've never known it, so doesn't one cancel the other and make us even?" She laughed at her logic.

"Your father doesn't approve and is secretly terrified about our relationship."

"We'll be over in England and, frankly, I don't care about his terror."

"Even so."

"We'll be away, so let's not dwell on the negative."

She wrapped her arms around the back of my neck, pulled my face to hers, and kissed me. We kissed again, and again, and I began fondling her breasts. She emitted a long sigh, something she never did, and drew me even tighter, as if she desired us to merge.

"Remember you tried to get much closer to me once," she said.

"Yes."

"And I pushed you away and said we should wait until I was sure we were committed." There was a short pause, filled only by the sound of a ticking grandfather clock in the hallway. "Well, I'm utterly committed now, and I'm not just saying it because I'm leaving."

Fiona had her own bedroom, and my wavering erection collapsed at the implication of these words. This was a Fiona I didn't know. Guinness and her impending departure had made her careless. I stopped fondling as her fingers traveled to my belt buckle, paused momentarily, and passed down to my crotch where they rested upon it in velvety touch. She started to press, ever so discreetly, and next thing her fingers opened and closed like a cat's claws, testing for my erection. Wasting no further seconds, I whisked my inert hand off her breast and sat up instantly.

"What's the matter?"

"It's very late and I just got an unexpected rush of tipsiness." I faked a yawn. "We'd better control ourselves."

Fiona's cheeks reddened as she reached out to grab the arm of the sofa and eased herself up. I'd reacted artlessly, but had had to do it.

"Fiona, this is just alcohol and the fact we're away from home making us behave like this. I'm really committed as well, but I have to work through my pathetic Catholic guilt about doing something like this outside marriage." I looked into her eyes intently. "Let's make a promise not to make love until we're across the water, and absolutely sure our relationship will last. What do you say?"

"You're right, Gabriel. It is the alcohol. That's an excellent idea, and I promise."

"I do, too." I rose after giving her a final kiss. "Good night, then."

Father had asked me to return home by five o'clock on Sunday afternoon because he required the car. Within a minute of entering the kitchen, my mother came out of the living room and filled the kettle with water, but set it down again. She gazed out the window and sighed hard.

"Where is everyone?" I said.

"James is at football, and the others are watching TV." She took hold of the kettle again but still made no effort to put it on the stove. Finally, she abandoned it and sat at the table.

"What's the matter?"

"Gabriel, I talked to your father about . . . well, about this whole business."

"*What?*"

"I wasn't going to, and then I saw something in the paper and I had to know. He was reading that disgusting Sunday newspaper of his and I happened to notice a headline about a homosexual actor in London who was arrested by the police. So I asked him what had happened to the poor actor. I thought I was being ever so cunning about how I was bringing up the subject. Do you know what your daddy said? He said, 'The fruit was caught with another man.' Cross my heart, that's what he said." She made an exaggerated sign of the cross over her heart. "Yes, 'fruit' is what he said. So I asked . . . and Gabriel, my voice was shaking now, because he'd called the man a fruit and I didn't even think he'd know that's what they're called . . . so, anyway, I asked if he'd ever thought about men in that way when he was your age. Well, Jesus, I thought he was going to bite the head off me. He put down the paper and looked at me as if I needed to be committed. His face turned the color of the hallway rug, and he said he had 'no such thoughts.' That finished me. I clean panicked, and out it all came."

By now, I'd backed up against the sink and was gripping its edge. "Now I see why you were so keen I went to Dublin with Fiona. You'd planned this all along. You'd planned to ask him as soon as you got me away."

"It's done, and can't be undone." Her eyes were misty. "I wanted to respect your wishes, but this whole thing's been rubbing against my mind like a rasp. Your daddy blames Martin. He says he's a fruit. He says he can't do a man's work and acts womanly, and that he's corrupted you."

"That's a load of shite and you know it."

"Oh, it's all so confusing. What have I done to deserve such a cross? It would be better if God took me away this very minute." She sniveled to evoke sympathy, but I ignored her. "It makes sense what your father says. Martin always had to have the latest clothes . . . and now he's at that fashion institute in England. Sure, that's no place for a man. It's *him* that's put this notion in your head."

"It's got nothing to do with him. You shouldn't have told Daddy. You had to blab, instead of leaving things be."

"Don't dare talk to me like that. I'm trying to sort you out."

"I don't need you to sort me out, because I'm doing it myself. You're trying to help yourself, that's what you're doing. You're only concerned about what the neighbors will say if they find out about my phase. Well, you can stop worrying because I'm clearing off to England. I'll be gone, and then you'll not have to worry about the fucking neighbors."

"Stop swearing. You're a selfish article, and you're breaking my heart."

"I'll be away and that'll fix it."

"You're going to hell if we don't get you cured."

I turned away from her to gather myself. "I can't wait to get away from you and your damned preaching, Mammy. That's another thing you're scared of. Dying and not getting into heaven. Well, I don't think you have to worry. You've been tripping to Mass ever since I can remember, and a place has been reserved for you long ago. And don't worry, because God won't blame you for what I might be. No, I'll be far happier in London, because then I won't have you ramming fucking religion down my throat. Do you want to know something, Mammy? It's only the ignorant and peasants who need religion. It's true. People that are educated knows it's all a crock of organized shite."

"Oh, I'll be so glad to see your heels, too. I'll be so glad to see the back of you." Mammy rose from the chair, pushed me away from the sink, and seized the kettle. She banged it down on the stove. "Just clear off, you heathen. You're damned. Sweet Jesus, to think I once thought you'd be a priest."

"Uncle Brendan's educated and saw through the Church. I'll bet *he* saw how it tries to control people, just like I do. I'll bet that's why he left and just isn't saying so."

"Shut your mouth and clear out of my sight, because you're just like him, you heathen fruit. You don't listen when people are trying to help you. I took you in and this is my thanks. You've become a heathen—"

"What did you say?"

"What's all the damned racket about?" Father said. He came through the hallway door adjusting his tie. The smell of his after-shave permeated the kitchen.

Nuala advanced from the living room. "Caroline and I can't hear our ears."

She was dressed in the red tartan skirt that James and I had given her last Christmas. *I took you in and this is my thanks.* It complemented her dark coloring and, even though she was only ten, her calves were already graceful. *I took you in and this is my thanks.* Nuala looked cute in the skirt, just as I knew she would. James hadn't wanted to buy it because it was red tartan, which meant it was Protestant in his eyes. *I took you in.* He'd wanted to buy green tartan, but I knew green didn't suit Nuala's coloring. She loved that skirt and would have worn it every day if Mammy allowed her. *I took you in and this is my thanks.*

"Did you have a good time with Fiona in Dublin?" Nuala asked. She laughed. Her laughter was innocent, just like mine should have been when I was her age.

"I should be back by eleven," said Father. "Gabriel, did you fill the car with petrol?"

Nuala was innocent, and her tartan skirt was beautiful. *I took you in and this is my thanks.* I knew my sister's tastes.

"Gabriel, did you fill the car up?"

"What?" I lifted my eyes off the big silver pin on Nuala's skirt and looked at him. My hands trembled. I turned to my mother. "What do you mean, Mammy?"

"Did you fill the car with petrol?"

"Yes." I did not take my eyes off Mammy. "What do you mean?"

Her eyes recoiled from mine, she burst into tears, and rushed into the hallway.

"What's going on?" Father said. "Have you been upsetting your mother? I'm late and I must go. Stop upsetting her. I'll be back by eleven."

"What wrong with Mammy?" Nuala asked.

Father slammed the door.

"She's upset and I need to talk to her." I tried to swallow, but couldn't because my throat was restricted. "Make tea. We'll be out in a minute." I swept down the hall in a few strides and entered her bedroom without knocking. She was sitting on the edge of the bed, drying her eyes.

"What, Mammy, what is this?"

"I was angry. I didn't know what I was saying. It's this whole phase thing."

"You said, you took me in."

"I'm so confused. I haven't been sleeping well. I . . . Gabriel . . . son . . ." She lifted her hands, and they remained suspended in the air for a moment before plunging to her lap. She started weeping again. "God, what have I done? What have I done? What have I done?" Her eyes lifted to mine. "Gabriel, Uncle Brendan's your father."

An enormous jolt rocked me. My ears rang, and the bedroom walls seemed to move far away as a hazy grayness gathered before my eyes. It grew darker and thicker and seemed to merge with the ringing. Next thing I knew, I was lying on the floor, and she was bent over me slapping my cheeks. I don't know how I managed, but I dragged myself up and sat on the bed. She ran out, returning a few moments later with a glass of water in a rinsing glass caked with old toothpaste that she gave to me. The water was revolting. It was warm and tasted of copper piping.

"I'm adopted?"

"Yes," she said, and sat heavily on her wicker chair.

"I can't believe it."

It felt like I'd just had an accident and my body was in shock and could feel no pain or sensation. I just sat still and numb as she told me how Uncle Brendan had helped Granda on the farm before he went off to the seminary and how, during that period, he'd met a girl at a dance and went out with her.

"It was against your granda's will, as you already know. He was livid because he'd been pushing him to be a priest. He used to say 'all decent families have a priest and the Harkins aren't going to be any different.' Brendan was his last hope, until he got the girl into trouble."

"I'm a bastard." I'd never pondered the true meaning of that word. It was ubiquitous, the first word to roll off boys' tongues at school when they hurled insults. Now, it sounded so harsh and clinical.

"Don't *say* such a thing, Gabriel." She came to me and laid her hands on my shoulders.

"My father is my uncle, and my uncle is my father. And you? What are you to me?"

She opened her mouth to reply, and her eyes mirrored the lash I'd administered. I didn't care. I didn't care because of her years of concealment and lying. She could have told me the truth when I'd asked about him so many times.

"Who are you to me?"

The hideous reality swept through me again, and I shrugged her hands off my shoulders, rose impetuously, and crossed to the window, where I stared out vacuously. The grayness started again. Lowering my head, I buried my face in my hands, and remained utterly inert until the wooziness passed.

"I'm nothing but a sick disgrace. I was a disgrace even before I was born." I took my hands away from my face impetuously. "I'm sick and a disgrace."

Suddenly, her hands were on my shoulders. She turned me around. "I'm your mother, that's who. My tongue was too quick. I shouldn't have said what I said. I've done wrong, but I'm still your mother. Nothing can change that. Nothing, you hear. It's love and a lifetime of experiences that make us mother and son, not just an act of intercourse and a birthing."

"If that's so, why did you compare me to Brendan a few minutes ago?"

Her lips trembled for a moment before she drew them tight and withdrew her hands. I had silenced her. I had silenced her and was immediately sorry. I didn't want her silent and defeated. I needed her to go on, just like she'd always done in the face of adversity. I needed her to tell me again I was hers, but she was vanquished.

"Where's my real mother?" I willed her to hold me even though I'd just lashed her again.

"Your mother," she said. "She's dead. You were born prematurely by Caesarean section and the operation went wrong. The anaesthetic went to her brain. They didn't know until it was too late. Your . . . your mother wasn't a local girl, and she wouldn't marry Brendan. She said it was a big mistake and that she wasn't going to make it any bigger by marrying a man she didn't truly love. She planned from the start to give you up for adoption, and your father and I had been married a year and . . . ." Her eyes were riveted on my face. "Gabriel, don't think for one moment you weren't wanted. I wanted you." The fight was back in her eyes. I hadn't rendered her vanquished. "I wanted you from the first moment I set eyes on you."

"I can't believe this."

"It was all planned as soon as the family found out she wanted to give you up. Brendan wouldn't hear of you being adopted by strangers. He put down his foot, so your granda suggested Daddy and I adopt you because we were married." She laughed mirthlessly. "The neighbors were already wondering why I wasn't yet pregnant. You know how they expect a woman to get pregnant within a year or so of marrying around here, otherwise the gossip starts up there's something wrong, that the wife's barren. So your granda said I should start wearing maternity clothes and nobody would bat an eyelid. He said that way, the whole thing would be resolved because nobody would ever find out, and Brendan's disgrace would be safely concealed within the family. The neighbors would be none the wiser." She paused and reached for my upper arms, though hesitantly now. "Gabriel, it took me a little while to agree to that. And I'll be honest and say, I didn't want to do it at the beginning. But then I thought about the baby . . . I thought about you, Gabriel, and how you had a right to a good Catholic upbringing, and to be brought up by family. Your father was all for it, too."

"Granda asked you to do this?"

"I told you, your granda was a very determined man, and thought only to save the Harkin name. He ruled the roost. Everyone did his bidding. And for all his praying and holiness, he went to his grave never forgiving Brendan for what he'd done. That's why Brendan didn't come home for years, even for his father's funeral. Your granda was full of useless Harkin pride, and Brendan was bitter. They never made up."

"I'm responsible for all this bad blood. I'm responsible for the disgrace." Scenes from my childhood and youth flashed before me. Now, I understood why Granny had been crying when I sometimes visited, and why she'd compared me to him so often. Now, I understood why there'd been evasiveness when I'd asked about the circumstances of Uncle Brendan's leaving, and why Mammy had been so furious that night when she'd caught me eavesdropping at the door. "I'm a disgrace."

"Gabriel, I'm your real mother and I want you to understand something. You're no disgrace. You're my son. You're beautiful. What I said earlier, about your being a heathen fruit, that was said in frustration." She touched my cheeks. "You were part of me from the moment I saw your cheeky little face in the pram. And you had the plumpest little hands, which you kept making into little fists like a boxer." Mammy laughed, but her eyes were focused inwardly. "I loved you from that moment. It was as if I'd carried you . . . and I felt no different when I had Caroline." She gripped my arms very tightly again. "I say that, truthfully." Her gaze was now in the present, and she regarded me without flinching. "Everyone agreed the whole thing was to be forgotten and never discussed, because you had become your daddy's and mine. When anyone official needed a birth certificate and could see you were adopted, your father and I would explain the inconsistencies to them and state you didn't know and weren't to be told. You weren't to be told unless you found out." Mammy paused. "And now it's me, your protector, who's let it out. I feared Caroline might do it, but it was me."

"Caroline?"

"She discovered the birth certificates two years ago and brought yours to me and demanded an explanation. You know how she is, Gabriel. At first, she was very sad and cried, but then she saw the right thing had been done and agreed not to say a word."

My sister knew about me. My knees trembled so uncontrollably, I thought they'd give way. I couldn't stop the trembling.

"Your daddy doesn't even know Caroline found out."

Caroline knew. I needed to be alone. "I'm going to my room."

"I've made a terrible mistake. Can you forgive my sharp tongue? Gabriel, believe me, when I say you're as much my child as your brother and sisters."

"This is about who I am. I had a right to know." My voice shook. "Caroline's known for two years."

I went to my room and threw myself on the bed, my mind full of a thousand rushing thoughts. Granny Harkin was my grandmother still. But what were Granny Neeson and Aunt Peggy to me now? I thought about what Caroline had said and done on the night I'd gone crazy and she'd learned about my phase. She'd embraced me, and I'd found that odd at the time. Caroline had known then. That's why she'd done it. Did James and Nuala know, also? Had she told them and sworn them to secrecy?

I felt hopeless, adrift, but I was no stranger to that. It was just for another reason now. And why had Granda taken me riding in his horse and cart if I was to blame for the estrangement between Brendan and him? He'd known about me. I thought about those rides within the bright colors of the sunny countryside, and about the countless times I'd sneaked into the storeroom and touched and smelled his molding Sunday suit. Had he loved me out of guilt? Had he loved me because he was too proud to apologize, because I was of Brendan and, therefore, the only way an old man could still show his love? I would never know. My past was a vast lie. Nothing had been what it was. I was adopted, and no matter what Mammy had said about her love for me, the simple fact was, I was not of her blood. The bonds of love between a mother and offspring, bonds unquestioned because they form inside the womb, had had to be formed externally between her and me. And Father? The bonds between him and I had never developed, and now I knew it was because I wasn't his natural son. Now I saw why he preferred James, and why he hadn't protected or loved me like he had him. I was different. I meant obligation. He kept me at a distance because I was not of him.

The light waned as night crept into the room. I went to the window and stood for ages watching the dusk methodically paint the clouds to oblivion. My dead climbing tree darkened, and its jutting limbs grew ominously foreign, seemed even in death to mock my lifetime of ignorance until the night merged both it and the outline of the old pigsty into nothingness. I continued to stare at the nothingness until a knock on my door brought me back to the present. My mother entered.

"Are you all right, Gabriel?" Her hands were clasped. "You've been alone a long time. Come to the living room. James is home . . . I've told him and Nuala."

I didn't feel like talking or listening, but I knew she needed me to go out, and I also knew I'd have to do it soon, anyway. The meeting, for that's what it was in effect, was indescribable. The best way to express how I felt was the walls, sofa, armchairs, even the ornamental birds I'd always loved, seemed transmuted in relation to me. There were no proper or comforting words that could be said. It was apparent Nuala and James hadn't known. I could see Nuala had been crying. She never cried. She spoke first, albeit hesitantly, and that trait was out of character, too.

"Gabriel, this makes no difference, just like your not liking girls as much as boys doesn't make a difference."

Everyone agreed. The platitudes commenced, just as they always do in arduous situations: how it didn't matter one single bit; how we were still brothers and sisters and nothing would change; how we always stuck together through thick and thin, and this would be no different. My mother started to sob again. Caroline and Nuala turned to comfort her while James and I watched. After she'd finished, a stream of collective memories and family jokes ensued. It was like a grotesque wake, I the living corpse.

"You always were different," said James. He chuckled. "Remember how you ran away when Ciaran came to fetch you for the football match and Daddy wanted to send me in your place?"

I remembered that Saturday as if it were yesterday. I'd run off to the pigsty and tried to read the dirty magazines Noel had shown me. It hurt, because it showed even then I really was different. I was immeasurably different.

More joking reminiscences ensued about how independent I'd always been, and as each was articulated came a stinging reminder of how I'd never been the person I'd thought I was. I'd never been a real son or sibling. My mind wouldn't stop flicking through the past. It examined scenes I hadn't thought of for years: my parents laughing about something funny I'd done or said; their concern when I told them I felt responsible for Henry's drowning; family conversations around the supper table about local scandals and neighbors; their fury when I'd failed my first exams at Saint Malachy's, and subsequent pats on the back about later successes; Father hugging me after his release by the British army. It was as if I was compelled to scrutinize, resort, and revalidate each memory in the light of this new knowledge. And through every experience, during every moment, my parents had known. Their collusive knowing that I wasn't their flesh and blood. My head throbbed with the cold realization.

Suddenly, Nuala bounded over, wrapped her arms tightly around my neck, and kissed me fully on the lips. We never kissed on the lips. It was always on the cheek. I heard the hideous strangled gasps before I realized they were coming from me.

"I'm sorry. I don't know what to do. It's not the same. You don't know how I feel because you just can't know. None of you can know. I'm adopted. Things are changed forever."

"Stop saying this, Gabriel," Nuala said. "You're hurting me when you say these things. You're still my brother, and that can't change."

"Son, we're still a family. Nuala's right. Things have changed, but it's still the same," Mammy said, her voice very shrill. "We're all feeling awkward, but that'll pass, and we'll go on as before."

"Mammy's right, Gabriel," said James. "It's new and awkward for all of us, but tomorrow's another day." He looked over at Caroline, who was nodding vigorously.

"Only one thing has changed, and that thing is knowledge," my mother said. "The actual circumstances have always been the same. They've been the same since you were born, and the only thing that's changed is your knowledge. Everything else remains just as it was. Your relationships with your father and me haven't changed. Your relationships with your brothers and sisters aren't made any different because of what you've learned today. Those things remain the same, and the passage of time will help you see that. Time heals wounds, Gabriel."

I waited alone in the living room until Father came home. As his car drew into the driveway, I went to the kitchen and sat at the table. It was one o'clock. I'd banked up years of grudges for such a time as this, but instead I was tense. Earlier, Mammy had offered to tell him that I knew all about my past. I'd agreed, initially. I'd agreed because he knew about my phase, which made me cringe. I didn't know if I could even look at him. I wasn't his son, and now I was also a homosexual in his eyes. However, throughout the evening, I rethought the situation and became convinced I had to tell him. I was no longer a child. I was an adult, going away soon, and had to behave like one now.

"What are you doing up so late?" he asked.

I could see he was surprised to see me. He opened the fridge door, took out a bottle of milk, and raised it to his lips. I watched his throat muscles rise and fall behind skin irritated and flaky from shaving. His habit of drinking straight from the bottle had always disgusted me. Tonight, I watched uncaring.

I forced myself to keep my eyes on his face. "I know about myself."

He stopped drinking, and held the bottle a fraction from his lips. "What are you on about?"

"I know why you've always preferred James to me." My voice trembled. A surge of electricity passed through my body. "I know why now."

He looked at me as if I'd gone crazy. "It's late, and I'm tired."

"I'm not your son. I'm Uncle Brendan's."

"Luksee . . . who . . . who told you?" He set the bottle down hard on the counter.

"Mammy."

"She did?"

"You've always wanted me to be just like you, and I could never be. I tried and tried, but I could never be like you. It all makes sense now."

"How come she told you tonight?" He sat at the table. I couldn't remember when we'd last sat across the table, just he and I alone.

"It spilled out."

"How are you taking it?"

"I've got a lot of thinking to do."

"I knew it would come out one day. I always told your mother it would, but she kept telling me to shut up."

He regarded his big, oil-stained hands for a moment. I felt my skin tingle. Was he now thinking about my homosexual phase? I felt the shame flash in my cheeks.

"It makes no difference. You know that, don't you?"

"I don't know anything, anymore. I'm so confused about myself. Granny always said I was more like Uncle Brendan. I liked the things he liked, and I didn't like lorries and—"

"Brendan played with machinery when he was younger. He was always on our neighbor's tractor. I don't think that explains our differences at all."

I said nothing.

"Fathers and sons don't always like the same things." He cleared his throat. "Let's get one thing straight, Gabriel. You've brought this up before, but I've never preferred James over you, or any of the rest of them, for that matter."

"Well, I felt you did. When I was younger, you always picked on me. You always made me do all the work about the house."

He laughed. "That was because you were the eldest. It's how I was reared. That's how your granda treated me, and I did the very same."

"I tried to do well in my studies to make up for it, but it was never enough. You never viewed my successes as being equal to James'."

Father regarded his hands again. "I'm not educated. What do I know about books? I know about football and tinkering with machines because I've always been around them. I was never one for the books. You know that, son."

He paused and lifted his eyes. Mine wanted to flee. Somewhere, deep within him, the unarticulated homosexual abomination occupied a part of his brain.

"I've always been proud of you," he said. "You were the scholar in the family. You're like Brendan in that way. I was very proud of you for that, just as I'm very proud of James when he does well at his activities. Luksee, it was a great day for me when you made it into grammar school."

I remembered his pride, and how he'd boasted to our neighbors. Somehow, I'd overlooked that.

"I made no difference, and if I did, I wasn't aware of it," he said.

"I've always felt I was a failure in your eyes. And now I know I am because I'm going through this ridiculous . . ." As with Father McAtamney, I couldn't bring myself to utter "homosexual." It was hard to talk about something like that to a man who'd never thought of such things. He called them "fruits." I back-pedaled fast to try to put him on the defensive again. "I resented you. I didn't even want to travel alone in the car with you. I didn't want to talk to you."

"There were times when I knew you were acting strange. I chalked it down to you being more sensitive, or it being puberty or whatever." He was silent for a moment, as if he were reflecting on those occasions. "Maybe I should have given all of you more attention, but it wasn't in my nature. I was never one to hug or say things. I was reared that it was womanly, that men don't go in for that." His eyes swept from me to focus on a cupboard latch. "It never crossed my mind." He paused again. "And don't think I'm disappointed in you because of this homosexual bussiness, either."

My heart leaped.

"I'm rough and ready and have never had a phase like you're going through. Your mother tells me some boys go through that, so that's all there is to it, as far as I'm concerned. I won't start lying and pretending I understand it, because I don't. But then, there are lots of things I don't understand. All I'll say to you is, you're adopted and that can't be changed. You're adopted, but you're mine as much as Caroline and the rest are mine. But this other business is a phase, and that *can* be changed according to your mother. We'll get that fixed."

My head pained with the thrust and retreat of thoughts: I was adopted, he wasn't my father, no pieces of his blood were in mine, and I loved and resented him. Only I could bridge these disagreeable circumstances. Right now, I just felt grateful he didn't think less of me, or judge me, because of a homosexual phase he couldn't understand.

CHAPTER THIRTY-TWO

As I'd feared, the poisonous lusts returned with a vengeance soon after the effects of the medication ended. Once again, I resorted to trusty masturbation. I felt anxious about these feelings still, though not to the same degree. As it had that other time with Uncle Brendan, unburdening had helped. Or perhaps it was due to the stirring of acceptance.

In late August, the exam results posted and, having met the requirements of London University, I would go there to read law. It transpired Fiona had been right to be confident, because she got accepted by Cambridge, her horses were now stabled near the university, and she returned to Ulster for a week to celebrate with me. Before she went back, she and I renewed our promise to spend as much time together as our studies and circumstances would permit. We also vowed nothing would come between us. I meant the vow, though I still didn't tell her about the horrid lusts, or my new family circumstances. One could wait, and the other I was determined to conquer and she'd never need to know.

Uncle Brendan attempted to talk to me on the phone about my birth and adoption, but I wouldn't be drawn, and told him bluntly I didn't want to discuss it. He'd been a priest, and as such, charged with a duty to be truthful at all times. I felt betrayed. I'd exposed my soul to him by the grave in the meadow, and he'd had the opportunity to expose his that day as well. Thereafter, he'd also had an opportunity at Granny's, when he'd asked me if I wanted to talk about Father Cornelius again, and I'd asked him to tell me about the girlfriend he'd had before he went off to the priesthood. Now everything was out, he wanted the whole thing aired and put to bed. He offered to come over, and I wouldn't hear of that, either. After he tried to insist, I reminded him in a steely voice that he hadn't wanted to see his family for years after he'd fled to the missions, and more specifically, during his nervous breakdown. I knew it was a slap in the face, but I also knew his soul-exposing could wait until I was ready, just like I'd had to wait.

On an impulse one sunny afternoon, I said to my mother that I wanted to visit the cemetery and see my dead birth mother's grave. She said she'd also come to help me find it. Nuala wanted to come as well, but my mother forbade her. After a search, we located the grave in the shadow of an ostentatious granite monument, which stated in its inscription that interred inside was the body of a man who'd emigrated to New Orleans in 1814. We knelt on the black granite coping of the woman's grave at right angles to each other, the sharp edge digging uncomfortably below my kneecaps. Directly beneath her name, etched in tarnished gold, were the names, birth and death dates of two older people who'd passed in their seventies within six months of each other. The man's name had been Gabriel. I looked over at my mother who was whispering prayers, and she nodded twice, her eyes shining with tears that I'd also expected to shed.

After blessing herself, she rose, and I could see where the coping edge had bitten into her tender flesh.

"I'll leave you be for a while," she said.

I nodded as I stared at the marks on her legs.

"I'll be waiting back in the car for you, son."

I watched her recede, saw her pause to look back at me as she reached the paved narrow roadway, and then she started toward the car park. It felt so peculiar being alone looking down at the white, marble-chipped grave of a woman who'd taken her last breath giving me my first. After a minute, I rose, picking up the bunch of bright pink roses I'd brought, and placed them in the middle of her snowy bed. I approached the headstone, where I was compelled to trace the first letter of her name. The coldness of the polished granite stirred something within, and I felt incredibly sad. It wasn't the sadness of losing a loved one, rather it was the sadness of never knowing if she'd have come back to claim me had she lived.

"I'm sorry I never knew you," I heard myself murmur into the quietness. I lingered a few moments longer, regarding the pristine bed of chips and the pink roses, before turning away.

On the drive home, Mammy was unusually quiet.

"I'm not feeling strange or anything," I said, after a few minutes. "Time heals wounds, Mammy."

She reached over and squeezed my upper arm for an instant.

Toward the end of the summer, she came into my bedroom one afternoon while I was packing and asked if I was still in my "phase." She tried to appear casual, but I'd seen how the corners of her lips quivered before she'd asked. You know a person's gestures when you've been living with them all your life. I told her it had gone away, that I was cured. Relief spread across her face like a rising sunrise over the Knockburn hills.

During my final week, I began taking solitary walks. I went to places I hadn't visited for years. I walked underneath the arch of the bridge, where I stood and gazed at the cheerful, brown water gurgling over stones as the passing vehicles snored overhead. I walked to the crumbling pigsty, where I noticed the old beam had collapsed and the dimness in the hayloft was still alive with ghosts. I walked to the meadow and stood by old Rory's grave and took in the marching swath of fir trees. I even walked the grounds of my old primary school, its rows of windows boarded up now and the yard overgrown. In the old stuck-in-the-muck jail corner, where I'd never been banished, where I'd raced into, tagged, and set Caroline and so many of the other girls free, I pressed myself tightly against the wall and inhaled its dampness as I gazed up at the wheeling, coal black crows. A new life was beginning. I was leaving for a new beginning.

ACKNOWLEDGMENTS

In the course of writing and bringing a novel to publication there are many who enter an author's orbit, so I'd like to thank the members of my writers group, the Rebel Writers of Bucks County, especially Jeanne Denault and Marie Lamba for their diligent reading and suggestions, the Bucks County Writers Workshop, and Joy Stocke and Ben Cake at the Writers Room of Bucks County. Thanks also to Jim Levine and Melynda Bissmeyer of Levine Greenberg Literary Agency, Joan Schweighardt, Faye Rapoport, Gray Cutler, Andy Heidel, Dan Jurow, and to Hope Matthiessen, Lane Jantzen, Shiela Phelan, Kari Stuart, Meg Parsont, Kipton Davis, Donna M. Rivera, and Aron Epstein at my publisher.

READING GUIDE AND
DISCUSSION QUESTIONS

1. How does Gabriel's relationship with his mother develop throughout the course of the novel? How representative of your view of an Irish Catholic mother is Mrs. Harkin? Do you think Gabriel's parents are constrained in any manner by their religion? Do you consider Mr. and Mrs. Harkin's marriage to be a happy one?

2. *He would get no more love from me. He was Daddy to me no longer. The word "Father" was a better way to address him. Used in England but not so much in Ireland, at least not in Knockburn, it was ideally remote. I was removed from him, and it was just the perfect word. I resolved to think of him only as Father in my mind from now on.* Gabriel's relationship with his father becomes increasingly strained as the novel progresses. Discuss instances where the two are portrayed as being close and those where they are distant. To what degree are Gabriel and his father responsible for the deterioration of their relationship? Do you think Mr. Harkin treated Gabriel differently than any of the rest of his children? Would you say Gabriel's attitude toward his father is typical of a young boy's growth to manhood?

3. To what extent, if any, did being bullied as a child affect Gabriel's personality? Have you had to deal with bullying at any time in your life? As the story proceeds, Gabriel and Fergal's boyhood relationship changes from one of friendship to rivalry and finally estrangement. Why does Gabriel allow this to happen? Compare his experience of childhood friendship to that of your own.

4. Gabriel's appearance at his first dance is a romantic affair in that it takes place in an old Fortress set within a park of ancient sycamores. What are your feelings about how the women position themselves in the room and their behavior during the dance? What does this system say about Irish society, if anything? How does it correspond to American society of the same period?

5. The novel takes place during a phase of the Irish conflict known as "the Troubles." How convincing is the author's depiction of the state of Northern Ireland politics? While the conflict there is larger than mere differences in religion, to the extent that religion plays a role, do you feel the author is evenhanded in his treatment of Catholicism and Protestantism, or does he appear sympathetic to one at the expense of the other? Do you agree with the IRA man's view that Irish families like the Harkin's are in the same position as that of the dispossessed families in Steinbeck's *The Grapes of Wrath*? Regarding Gabriel's parents, whom do you feel is the more political, and why? Do you consider Gabriel to be a real Irishman, or do you agree with Mr. Harkin's assessment of his son?

6. Discuss Gabriel's reaction to his mother's shocking news and the means by which the author conveys it to the reader. In light of the revelation, examine Gabriel's relationship with his siblings before and after. Do you think Mrs. Harkin would take back the revelation if she had an opportunity to do so? How would you have dealt with this situation?

For more questions, please visit www.soncalledgabriel.com